T0153258

A NOVEL

INVISIBLE WORLD

STUART ARCHER COHEN

FOUR WINDS
— PRESS —

SAN FRANCISCO

INVISIBLE WORLD

Copyright © 2014 by Stuart Archer Cohen

All rights reserved. No part of this book may be reproduced in any manner what-soever without written permission from the Publisher, except in the case of brief quotations embedded in critical articles and reviews, and certain other noncom-mercial uses permitted by copyright law.

Four Winds Press
San Francisco, CA

Library of Congress Data is available.

ISBN: 978-1-940423-04-3

9 8 7 6 5 4 3 2 1

Cover design by Domini Dragoone

Printed in Canada by Friesens
Distributed by Publishers Group West

INVISIBLE WORLD

TO MY PARENTS,
AND TO PEOPLE WHO HELP TRAVELERS

Acknowledgments

Writing a book is like a fifty-five-hour Mexican bus ride without a bathroom. How could I not thank the following people?

Mariah Coe, whose insight and encouragement were invaluable in the early drafts, when to nearly all others *Invisible World* seemed like a ludicrous and futile gesture.

Martin Vilches and family, Xu Xingfang and Ding Wen, Li Jianying and especially Xiao Lu; they opened up new worlds for me.

I thank Steve Gorman, who introduced me to the world of antique textiles. Laurie Adelson and Arthur Tracht of Millma, Nobuko Kajitani of the Metropolitan Museum and James Blackmon of the James Blackmon Gallery were generous with conversation and information. The Textile Museum in Washington, D.C., is a precious resource and everyone should send them large donations.

Ray Lincoln, you are one in eighty, one in a million. You're an angel and I'll never stop thanking you.

Kristin Kiser's light but sure editorial guidance enabled me to keep focused long after I was ready to throw this thing against the wall. I was lucky to have her excellent help.

Dana Isaacson, thanks for helping make *Invisible World* better by making it slightly more . . . invisible.

Also thanks to David Perk, who'd rather read a manuscript with a cup of coffee in his hand than go out and play, and to Jed Cohen for providing useful editorial approaches. Maintain current levels of fabulosity at all times.

And to my wonderful Suzy, who astounds me with her ability to read the same paragraph over and over and over again. As if I needed another reason to love you!

INVISIBLE WORLD

THE POSTCARD FROM
INNER MONGOLIA

In the darkness, dazed and ringing with sleep, he heard the employee of the single night that incessantly circled the world speak his name without emotion. "I have a call for Andrew Mann from Montevideo, Uruguay . . ." The Spanish accent, an oily pronunciation of the word *Uruguay* that left him unsure of what she'd said. The small countries of West Africa palpated through his mind.

"From where?"

"Montevideo, Uruguay. Hold the line, please."

He kept trying to associate it. He'd never been to Uruguay, and he didn't know anyone who had.

"Andrew?" A man's voice coursed through, American, but with no regional markings. "I'm sorry to call you at this absurd hour but this was my best chance to get to a phone. What is it there? It must be three in the morning . . . "

"It's . . . Hold on . . ." Rolling over, the cool green arms of the clock floating in the darkness. "Either two or three . . . I don't know. I think you have the wrong Andrew Mann. You want the attorney. He's under A. Mann."

The voice cut in confidently. "I woke him up already. You're the one. You don't know me. My name is Jeffrey Holt." A vague familiarity to the name. It sounded like the label in the back of a shirt. "We have a mutual friend: Clayton Smith."

Andy dug his supporting elbow deeper into the mattress, trying to hoist himself out of sleep. He hadn't seen Clayton in six years. "That's funny. I got a fax from him today. I hadn't heard from him before that since he sent me a piece of cardboard for the . . . uh . . . "

"The solstice. I was on his mailing list also."

"Yeah, solstice. Hey..." He sat up in bed and changed the receiver to his other ear. "Where is... Utugayo?"

"Uruguay." He pronounced it like the operator. "It's a small country between Argentina and Brazil. When did you get a fax?"

"Today. About... Twelve hours ago."

No immediate reply came, then: "That's interesting. What did it say?"

Andy didn't answer, trying to shake off the watery feeling of the last sixty seconds. "What did you say your name was?"

"Jeffrey Holt, I'm an old friend of Clayton's also. You received a fax."

"Yeah, from Hong Kong. He's been living there the past—"

"Yes, I know. I live there also. What did he say?"

"Well..." He dragged the message back into his mind more clearly. Nothing about it seemed worth hiding. "He said he's going to Inner Mongolia and he's having a going-away party on Thursday and he wants me to come. It's typical Clayton." He brightened his voice as much as he could to change the subject. "How is Clayton, anyway?"

The voice came back moderate and calm. "He's dead. He poisoned himself."

An immense quiet bounced across the world from South America to Illinois, maintained by an armada of telecommunications machines and earth stations consecrated to carrying that long moment of definitive shocked soundlessness. "I'm... Well... I'm sorry to, uh..."

"You don't have to say anything."

"Thanks. I just..." This was the part where he should have been knocked off his feet, but lying in the warm bed he had no place to fall and instead everything suddenly disappeared: no bed, no telephone, only the incomprehensible news and in its wake a feeling of off-kilter novelty. Clayton would write about something like this in his letters: "Andyman, they tracked me to America, suicide calling person-to-person at 3 A.M. Hello? Hello?" A vision of Clayton pale and bent on a floor, vomit coming out of the side of his mouth, his cheek and nose pressed against fissured linoleum tile. He sat up. "Don't hang up,

Jeffrey. I'm . . . Give me a minute." The image frightened him. He needed to send some words out to get rid of it. "Yeah, I'm kind of . . . Well, we grew up together. We were sort of"—the term sounded quaint and outdated—"best friends."

A tolerant inflection. "I understand."

"It's just a surprise, that's all."

The problem of speech cropped up again but this time Holt filled it for him. "I understand how you feel. We're all upset. Most people can be replaced. Clayton can't be." The sympathetic words had a remoteness unrelated to the distance of the call. They came from a strange world of expendable and inexpendable relationships, where Clayton Smith already existed as someone in the past, suddenly finite. Soon people would be telling stories about him: the funny things he did, the wild things. The fullness of his life would take on the two-dimensionality of a fable twisted to have a beginning, an end, and a moral.

"Andrew, are you still there?"

"I'm still here."

"There's something else. Clayton seems to have planned his funeral. It's supposed to take place in Hong Kong on Thursday."

Andy winced as he thought again of the fax he'd received. "His going-away party."

"I suppose so. At any rate, he wanted you to be there. I talked to Chang: he's handling everything . . . "

"Who's Chang?"

"Louis Chang. He's a friend."

"Yeah, I think Clayton mentioned him once."

"Good. Well, Chang said Clayton left a sort of will. He wanted all his closest friends at the funeral; they'll read the will there. Can you make it?"

Andy realized something and he laughed. "Goddamn it. This is typical Clayton! He's probably faking this whole thing. I'm not believing shit till I see a body!"

The other voice responded carefully, with a softness it had lacked before. "You're right, Andrew: this is typical Clayton. He loved a good drama and he loved to make things a bit difficult for his friends. But unfortunately for us this is the last time. I'm sorry."

Andy couldn't answer. Clayton had sent him letters from all over the world, but Andy had rarely bothered to write back. Now the finality of not having anyone to write to seemed an unnecessarily harsh punishment for his laziness. "The funeral's Thursday?"

"Yes. Do you have a pencil and paper? My flight leaves in fifteen minutes."

"Hold on." He turned on the light, stumbled to his dresser to grab an envelope. "Okay."

"The service is Thursday at six o'clock in the reception room of the London Gardens Hotel. I know it's short notice."

He tried to picture the reception room of an unknown hotel, but his father's plumbing office came back to him with its aroma of dust and its upcoming schedule of tax audits and jobs to be bid. "You know, Jeffrey . . . it's impossible. I'm really tied up this whole week."

"Yes . . ." A silence. "I suppose the time to devote to a friend is when he's alive. At this point it's basically ceremonial. I was on my way to Shanghai on Sunday anyway, so it's easy for me. Silvia will be there, if you know Silvia. And there's Chang, of course. Why don't you think about it? Clayton would have liked you to be there."

The strange names tripped past him like accusations; he didn't want to admit that he knew none of them. Andy had barely left his own state. Now Clayton's death included him briefly in a secret society whose network extended into the mythical provinces that Clayton had inhabited. He hoped that Holt didn't know how long it had been since he'd actually talked to their mutual friend. "Thursday?"

"Thursday at six o'clock, at the London Gardens. You lose a day flying west so you'll need to leave by Tuesday."

"That's tomorrow."

"So it is."

The idea of Clayton's going-away party kept mixing with a flower-heaped casket, ceding to the muddy obstruction of the coming week: three bids to figure and a jumble of ailing earth-moving machines. His father's business had fallen into another crisis at the end of the month, and for the first time Andy wasn't sure they would pull out of it. "I'd really like to, Jeffrey, but realistically, it's impossible. I'm totally tied up with business. I have three jobs to estimate and we're being audited. I'm trying to help my father out."

"I understand." Holt's stiffness sounded intentional to Andy, but the whole conversation had sounded like that. "Let me give you some numbers in Hong Kong you can call. It's Chang. If you change your mind he'll make all the arrangements. All you have to do is appear." The voice dictated numbers and their provenances, offering a final word of condolence that evaporated with a faint clack into the fuzzy sound of distance.

"Wait a minute . . . Hello?" He wanted to spread out the news, to keep it from fossilizing into the past, but his last communiqué escaped unheeded into space, leaving a toneless wash of electricity in his ear. He surrendered the phone and lay back against the headboard of his bed.

He should have expected this to happen, the way one always expects extravagant people to make some gesture that can never be topped. Clayton had always pursued his own erratic schedule of abrupt departures, and he'd always expected Andy to make the jump with him, no matter how impossible. Only twelve hours ago at the office he had received the latest summons and been filled again with the familiar despair.

I'm finally going on the Big Trip, Andy. Inner Mongolia.

Clayton had been writing to him about Inner Mongolia for over three years now, ranting so vividly about grasslands and Genghis Khan that Andy, whose closest encounters with grasslands were the corned-over prairies of Illinois and Wisconsin, had begun to imagine his own Mongolia. People rode horses and carried long swords. They had wild spirits that blew like gusts across a vast openness. The rest was vague, but Andy had been planning, in a fantastic and improbable way, to make the trip with him.

He threw the covers aside with a heavy breath, then went into the kitchen and opened his briefcase, sorting quickly past legal pads and graph paper to find the faint gray missive that had come in that day. The message had been scribbled in Clayton's careless hand, the few lines of script wiggling across the page as if they'd been cast onto

STUART   COHEN

paper by a fly fisherman, touching each other then veering away, dropping off suddenly at their ends. He flattened it out and read it again:

ANDYMAN!

Clayton had been calling him that, and a half dozen other nicknames in the twenty-five years they'd known each other, including Mr. Mann, when they'd worked together as cook and dishwasher at Burger Universe, and ranging to Tiresias, The Blind Seer, for his attempts at predicting the winners of football games.

ANDY MAN!

> *The Empire is settled. I'm finally going on the Big Trip, Andy. Inner Mongolia.*
> *I want you to come to the going-away party in three days. Thursday. I have a present for you.*
> *I love you, Andy. Don't ever forget that. We're still fugitives.*
>
> *Your eternal/temporary friend,*
Clayton

He read it again, adrift in the ambiguous declaration *"The Empire is settled,"* and the last promise, *"I have a present for you."* He felt a fog coming on and he went and opened the freezer, staring absently into the wintry space then closing it after a while to fill himself a glass of water.

"*We're still fugitives.*" "They're coming, Andy, let's head for the tree fort!" Under the evergreen bush in the yard: "Okay! I think we lost 'em. Shhh...No! Let's get outta here!" Always the good guys, always too smart to get caught. Later, Clayton had ferreted out the secret back entrance to the racetrack, then the bus lines that would take them into the city and the rattling string of empty boxcars that would drop them off again near home. Inevitably, he'd chosen a destination out of Andy's reach, appearing on the front porch with a gym bag of clothing. "Tiresias, we're going to Hollywood. I've got a buddy on Sunset Boulevard who needs a couple of bartenders. Sunset Boulevard, Blind One. Hollywood."

"Clayton, I'm in college, remember? Somebody's got to be respectable so they can keep saving your sorry butt!" Andy had contented himself with promises of a summer reunion, watched his future in California drive away into the early evening traffic, knowing, in his Blind Seer way, that it was a future he would never catch up with.

A tide of useless regret filled the room, suffocating him with the weight of every letter that he'd never replied to. Clayton had posted him a dozen solstice notices, each one a carefully worked pastiche of paper and cardboard, and what had Andy ever sent him in return? A brief letter typed out on a computer? A tally sheet of the season's football bets to prove that he could still pick them?

But what did he owe Clayton, anyway? He'd barely seen him since the departure to the West Coast some fifteen years ago, except for one sleepless three-day stopover when Clayton had made a rare visit to the United States. "Andyman, let's go to the Liberty Grill and see who shows up." Bacon and eggs in the small hours with cab drivers and policemen, nighthawks whose overheard conversations Clayton had savored as the testimonies of that most exotic of destinations: Home, a lost land where at four in the morning every short-order waitress spoke infallible sentences of comfort and truth. He'd seemed out of place in America on that visit, filled with a hundred faraway locations and tales of people so brilliant and foreign they would evaporate in the stolid atmosphere of the Midwest. He had become one of them. At the Liberty he'd been telling Andy about Shanghai and suddenly burst into a phrase of Chinese whose bizarre intonations, coming from a T-shirted white man, had drawn the attention of the whole café. The night had finished with him translating Chinese insults for everyone's entertainment. He'd relished the effect so much that Andy suspected that he'd devoted his whole life to achieving it. "Okay, Clayton," he said out loud. "Where did it get you?"

The annoyance he heard in his voice bolstered him for a minute. Realistically, Clayton had ceased being part of his life long ago. He leafed through a sports magazine, trying to lose himself in the profile of the latest killer lineman, then flipped it away with a sigh and pulled Clayton's last message close to him again . . . . *the Big Trip, Andy. Inner Mongolia.*

Inner Mongolia. He could see it now on the world map that created a rectangle of blue imagination on his kitchen wall. It pertained to China, slung out along the fringe of the Gobi desert around a crescent of capitalized letters: NEI MONGOL. Above it floated Mongolia proper, and nearby the words ALTAI MOUNTAINS, XINJIANG UIGHUR and serrations denoting the Great Wall. He had another drawing inside his head, though, where the boundaries of Inner Mongolia were contiguous with Clayton's Hong Kong and his Paris and a score of other fabulous places he had written him long, funny correspondence from. He didn't need a passport to travel in those territories, nor the burden of a suitcase or schedule. It was an open country, the last open country in the world and the most remote, with tickets postmarked in Arabic and Chinese and languages Andy didn't know the names of. He kept the sheaf of letters and postcards in a folder marked CLAYTON. He never looked at it. He never threw it away.

It waited for him now at the back of the metal filing cabinet, overstuffed and out of order with the neat alphabet of utility bills and bank statements. Prying it open he spotted the blue plastic cover of the passport he had gotten in a short-lived burst of determination seven years ago. The young man in the small black-and-white photo looked formidable and ready, but the pages in which he should have stamped his exploits remained blank. Andy put it back, then gently freed the entire folder and brought it into the kitchen.

Clayton had sent him an enormous quantity of correspondence over the years, continuing to furnish bulletins of his adventures even though Andy's own letter writing had gradually decayed to sporadic dispatches that had completely lost sync with the letters from overseas. In the past few years Andy's part had degenerated to the constant feeling of owing Clayton a letter, and with the arrival of each new signal from Asia, the disturbing awareness of something that couldn't be disposed of by post. For years the apprehension had been contained neatly in the CLAYTON file, but it swept out now brutal and implacable, advertised by a papery riptide of dead handwriting. The oldest ones started in the back. He pulled out the furthermost, postmarked Los Angeles fifteen years ago, addressed to "Tiresias" at his parents' old house on Evergreen. The street number and the postal code dissolved into a wash of vast pine trees and the secret needled coolness beneath their boughs, replaced after a moment by Clayton's grandiose salutation:

BLIND ONE!

I can make you a star!
*   I can make you a whiskey sour!*
*   All is jewelry here: clothes, cars, cigarettes and wives. The goal is you die completely accessorized!*

The letter went on to describe his shabby apartment and the hip-sounding neighbors, sprayed out in a tone of naive excitement. Clayton had tagged it at the end with an invitation, the constant postscript of the last decade:

Dearth of Seers seen here sincere, Tiresias. Is Burger Underworld so very very gripping? I've got a piece of floor with your name on it, Andyman.

Burger Underworld. Clayton's term for the fast-food restaurant where they had worked together still retained some sting. It had started as a part-time job during college while he'd plowed through airless monochrome texts on macroeconomics with the idea that he might work in international trade or finance. Instead he'd risen in the ranks to become manager and had coasted along for four years with the dull hope of a promotion. At last, in one of the few decisive acts of his life, he had quit in sympathy with an unjustly discharged employee. Clayton was the first person he'd called, waking him up at eleven in the morning to receive a vote of wild approval that immediately displaced the remorse that had gathered over his head. "I can come out to California now!" Andy had told him, but Clayton answered that he was leaving the following week on his first big trip to the Orient, and Andy's savings didn't extend across the Pacific. The Blind Seer gathered his capital and invested it in his vision of the future, an all-or-nothing bet that the home team would beat the point spread in the upcoming football game. He watched the game-losing fumble replayed in slow motion from six crucifying angles, attended by the knowing analysis of the commentators, who salted the crushing moment with jokes.

Clayton had laughed. "You blew it on the Bears? Why didn't you just bet it on the *Hindenburg* coming back for one more transatlantic flight?"

"Thanks, Clayton."

"It's not a big deal. Get two jobs and meet me in a couple of months in, um, Bangkok, then we'll go up to northern Thailand and check out the Hill tribes." They'd agreed on it. Clayton had promised to keep him informed of all his movements so that they could coordinate a reunion, speaking with a certainty that propelled Andy past the football debacle and into an introductory seminar of the Clean Rite Home Products Company, a mixture of direct marketing and personality cult, in which the ultimate prize was a Thunderbird automobile painted "millionaire green" and a percentage of the gross of an army of salesmen.

He'd borrowed money from his father and bought an inventory of the products, making lists of potential clients drawn from his friends and relatives. He attempted to weave a spell with his pitch, complete with stock assurances of sincerity that had been bulleted in the training manual with "Be sure to maintain eye contact . . ." The products cost more because of the quality ingredients that went into them, quality that would save money in the long run. Even if it cost a little more, didn't quality just plain make sense? He never noticed the indulgent looks of his clients, only that the sales came in. After two weeks he reinvested his money in a larger inventory, managing to recruit the fry cook at Burger Universe as the first foot soldier of his cleaning goods empire. He came away from a company seminar with a handful of motivational tapes that he played every morning as he shaved. His sales increased. He recruited another salesperson and bought more inventory. Things were beginning to come together.

Andy opened an envelope of faint green handmade paper, subtracting the note card with the artfully ragged edges. A red thread curled along the surface, an embedded spiral like a river. It dated from thirteen years ago, Tokyo:

ATOMIC MAN!

Hey! I'm an English teacher! Never realized what a great authority figure I cut. My motto: OBEY or PAY! All TREMBLE before my MIGHTINESS!

Can capital letters alone express my OMNIPOTENCE¿¡¿¡¿¡

Learning to make paper, putting together weird constructions. No reason, just that I like it. I made this card.

He'd given an address in Tokyo where Andy could write and solidify their travel plans, and Andy remembered now that he'd waited two weeks to answer, then put it off again until he finally rationalized that the letter wouldn't arrive in time anyway. He had never thought that Clayton, who always seemed so blithely absorbed in his own adventure, might have been disappointed, but now, examining the wiry lines of outdated script, he could imagine Clayton visiting the vacant mailbox each morning, wondering what had happened to his friend. Why hadn't he written him then? He'd had the money to travel, but somehow . . . Clean Rite had been going so well. The Thunderbird had loomed closer, shining. Clayton finally called him on the telephone after two months, sounding disappointed when Andy told him he couldn't meet him in Bangkok, passing it by and describing for fifty seconds the glories of his life in Tokyo, and his new career as a paper artist. He mentioned the expense of the call and said good-bye, the final disconnection sending a wave of relief through Andy.

The letters after that spanned five years in Tokyo, all of them in unusual envelopes of artesanal paper, some delicate and pale, others striking and robust, thick with newsprint and string, bits of foil or felt. As Andy examined each record of Clayton's Tokyo life he realized that the paper itself usually reflected something of the contents. Pink flower petals floated to the pulp surface of a letter telling about a romantic glass elevator ride to a rooftop restaurant, while the envelope containing his description of the Koenji bohemian life had been artfully pasted together from comic strips. Andy remembered tugging that one open with the simple laughing thought, *Typical Clayton*, never thinking that perhaps a lot of what was typical about Clayton might have been expressed only in an idiom of unspoken symbols and acts.

He went through the Tokyo correspondence, blanching at the appearance of his least favorite nickname, Mr. Clean, and noting that it gradually had fallen out of use. The first solstice notice arrived, a splendid assemblage of orange and gray blue that celebrated the longest day of the year. A collage of lurid personalities and situations followed: a girlfriend named Saito . . . a showing at an underground art gallery, complete with a clipping in Japanese on which he had scribbled "When can I expect you?" Jeffrey Holt's name appeared for the first time, referred to as a fellow English teacher, and Andy matched it with the carefully modulated sympathy he'd heard over the telephone. Phrases that began "You asked me" or "You said that you" reanimated the forgotten particles of his life in a strange third person. "Sorry about Jennifer. I know how that feels." Jennifer, the smart one who had drifted painfully away. "Cheers on passing your Black Belt test. When I'm rich and famous I'll hire you as my bodyguard."

Karate. He and Clayton had enrolled at the same time after going to see a martial arts double feature at a drive-in; two early teens styling themselves as superheros. Clayton had lasted only a few weeks. He didn't have the patience for the endless repetition of a single movement that, over the course of years, ingrained itself at a level deeper than consciousness. For Andy, who naturally sought routine, it became a place to forget about the world and its reversals. It remained the only thing he had stayed with the last two decades and the only thing he kept progressing in. For all his training, Andy had never hit anyone outside the training hall, and an angry old woman could still push him around over the telephone. Like everything else, it translated into twenty years of kicking and punching at the air.

For a while Andy had anticipated Clayton becoming the famous artist he'd promised. An envelope contained large black-and-white photographs of an exhibition of his creations in a Tokyo gallery a year after the first one. The sculptures stood waist high, constructed of handmade paper of different thicknesses, inscribed with words like *Gone* or *Water* or Japanese characters. Some of them looked like animals, or had newspaper pasted onto them. Another clipping accompanied the photos, with a picture of Clayton in his constant black T-shirt, looking the cool American. After that, a picture of what appeared to be a gateway in a massive stone wall, but made of gold and situated among well-dressed people in some kind of large public space. Clayton's latest creation, evidently: in the letter he detailed the party at the opening, and the surprising prices that people would pay for what he now referred to as his Work. "I'm going to fly you over to do nightlife, Tiresias," was scribbled at its lower edge.

The wait for Clayton to make good on his offer had extended into infinity. Something had happened, and Clayton had evaporated. A year of nothingness elapsed between communications, the year when Andy had missed Clayton more than at any other time. Clean Rite had disintegrated in a national scandal that left Andy with a storeroom full of products now considered unpatriotic, purchased with a debt cosigned by his father. Sitting in his kitchen at five in the morning Andy felt again the anguished helplessness of the collapse, unrelieved by Clayton's distant successes and their promises of escape. Clayton! Typical! What was the difference between death and absence, anyway? That now he wouldn't be getting any letters? That instead of a visit every ten years he would have no visitor at all?

Andy glanced up at the clock again, the hour hand sweeping away his annoyance into the gray dustbin of early morning. "Where were you, Clayton?" he said out loud, repeating the question he'd asked at the Liberty Grill long ago, seeing Clayton glance down at the table, toying with the hoop in his ear. "Here and there . . . ," he answered again in the stillness of the kitchen, looking up with that flash of sad bravado. "Surfing the emptiness." Andy had let it pass at that, respecting Clayton's privacy in a tacit agreement they'd had to keep things easy. He tried to exhale his sadness in a long sigh, but he couldn't get rid of it. He looked down again at the file. The last letter from Tokyo came out of its black envelope with a soft rasp. In silver writing on ebony paper the eerie phrase: ". . . thinking about going on a trip. . . ."

The blank year followed, collapsed in the file to a quarter-inch of space, as if it hadn't happened at all. The dispatches that resumed a year later jumped around, mostly in blue airmail envelopes, their postmarks rendered differently according to the country of origin.

Some put the months first, others the time of day or the year. It led to impossible dates—the twentieth month of 1987, or the ninetieth day of July—fantastic dates on which unreal events occurred in places whose only parameters were marked by the unruly descriptions Clayton cast off in his disconnected writing style.

Hong Kong:

Year of the Dragon, Big Guy, it's here roaring and breathing fireworks and neon up and down Wanchai and nobody knows where to start. Strings of crackers make sparky radio static— can't quite get the message. Speaking Uighur! Speaking Siamese! Need secret weapon: aka Tiresias Blind Seer to aid in interpretation.

Lhasa, Tibet:

Ommmmm . . . Ommmmmm . . . Ommmman, Oh Man, Andyman!

I'm tripping! Ten-day trek to a monastery even the Cultural Revolution forgot. First foreigner to show up. "Sorry, American Express not accepted here." Rolls of yellow silk, intense cold, yak milk tea, saffron robes, and prayer wheels spun by octogenarians and ten-year-old monks. Big Decision: stay fifty years and learn to levitate or go back to Lhasa and levitate via CAAC (China Air Always Crashes) to the oh-so-worldly world. I escaped purity with a scrap of sandalwood covered with Tibetan prayers, maybe they'll help me. I'm keeping it close to my heart, like you. Heading back south of the Yangtze. Visit me in the Kong, you heap of moss!

Shanghai:

On top of all that, I'm here with the mysterious Miss Q., who's certainly going to cut my throat one of these nights and sell my passport on the black market. Check it: another C. Smith, my reincarnation as an international terrorist/drug trafficker—I hope he has my address book so he can keep sending you letters. She's a shark, she's a killer, it's only a question of

whether she waits until the money runs out before she dumps
me. We both know it. Poison, poison, poison! Yahooo!
  "Oh, hello honey. You look splendid! Why don't you take
off your clothes!"

Letters bore datelines of Borneo and New Delhi, a few from
Europe. One talked about how much he'd enjoyed his brief visit to
Illinois, and how strange it seemed to him now. They always ended
with an invitation "When are you coming?" or "There's this great
place in China we can hit." Over the years he seemed to have finally
given up on Andy replying. The postmarks began to contain more
space between them, stamped onto hotel stationery whose contents
spoke of friends named Chang or Silvia or the recurring Jeffrey Holt.
Occasionally he mentioned his work, noting that it had become
garbage, literally, that he had displayed it somewhere or that he was
deeply into "process," though Andy never defined that term with certainty. The subject of Inner Mongolia appeared with a long factual
recounting of its history, and with it the first references to "The
Empire." Andy remembered the guarded admiration he'd maintained
for Clayton during those times; the simple miracle of living in Hong
Kong still classified him as a success, especially compared with his
own life, which he didn't even consider worth writing back about.
Reading through the letters now, though, he could see that the effervescence had waned. No matter how prosaic, they always ended with
that invitation, the last one, near the end of the letters, proffered with
the exhausted phrase, "Andy; come see me, and bring a little piece of
home with you in your suitcase."
    One postcard remained, the last entry in the file, sent two months
ago. It showed an empty dining room with a sole attendant standing
at attention and looking across the picture plane. Andy deduced that
two parallel walls of the dining room must have been mirrored
because the dining room and the attendant repeated themselves in
smaller and smaller versions into the interior distance of the picture.
Small gold Chinese characters paced across the bottom of the card,
followed by their English equivalent: "Inner Mongolia Hotel."

Andy,

> *The Empire is within my grasp.*

Clayton

He looked at the front of the postcard again, the endless recession of vacant dining rooms and the disinterested stance of the waitress. What empire? He put the card down and sat back in his chair. A single definitive thought spread through his mind, like a judgment about his entire life: he would never know the answer to that question.

He was still thinking about Inner Mongolia when his father called.

"Good morning, son." His father habitually woke at five in the morning, and by seven he was bursting to talk with someone, usually Andy. Andy's methodical administration had kept the business from splitting apart under the pressure of his father's more anarchic business style, and in his father's mind they were the perfect team. "We've got a big day ahead, Andy, a really big one. I've got a plan." He initiated a blustery speech about giving a troublesome worker hell, then described with the air of a master chess player a way to outsmart a contractor who was trying to get them to do extra work. The conversations served as a morning pep talk for his father, venting the anxiety he felt for the business, and Andy had always participated in them semiconsciously. "Sure, Dad. Yeah, Dad." This morning they sounded far away, spoken with the outdated slang of forty years ago. He was thinking about Inner Mongolia, and his father's words rang foreign and trivial from that distance. Pipes and lavatories collided with the undotted *i*'s and imprecise cursives that ran off the page without finishing their sentences. Fragments of imagined Shanghai jittered in among housing complexes called Indian Ridge or River Bend, while he was thinking about Inner Mongolia, the possibilities of a used back hoe while he was dreaming of the earthy wastes of Inner Mongolia, a contract, a blueprint, the frightening pile of debt, and meanwhile he kept thinking about Inner Mongolia, the vast secret golden space that hung inside him vivid and stunning as sudden death, *Inner Mongolia.*

"Dad."

"Huh?"

"I got a phone call last night." And he told him how things are at three in the morning, as if his father had not already received that phone call years ago, or many of them, disguised as other news but speaking the same intimations of uncontrollable change and collapse. The old man stayed silent, knowing the uselessness of words in front of iron events. Andy told him about the funeral in two days and its unreachable location. He didn't mention the roll call of mysterious friends coming briefly to life, or his own buried aspirations. He didn't have the words, nor could he describe it to his father without it seeming like an accusation.

He heard his father exhale.

"I'm sorry, son. I always liked Clayton." The line went quiet a moment. "Do you want to take the day off?"

"No. What else am I going to do. It's how it is, whether I'm here or at the office. I might as well be doing something. Besides, realistically, I've seen the guy once in ten years."

"Sometimes that doesn't matter," his father said. "It's a part of your life. Sometimes it means more than you think it does."

"Thanks, Dad. I'll come in though. We've got a lot to do."

He shook some of it off with a shower. The familiar scenery of the drive to work canceled out the intriguing assortment of names that had briefly lent a partylike atmosphere to his image of the funeral. Passing the playground he realized he'd already forgotten them all, except for Jeffrey Holt, who had woken him up. If Clayton had left him something in his will it could just as easily be sent to Illinois. He would fire off a fax offering to pay the shipping. It was probably one of his paper sculptures. What a spooky night! It was fitting to think about a friend when he died, though. It enabled one to put a label on the drawer and close it. Maybe it had been closed a long time ago anyway.

The worn assemblage of office furniture greeted him with silent homilies about the stolidness of life. He went directly into his office and closed the door. A list of plumbing fixtures lay in front of him where he had left it the night before, and he began checking off with a red pen the ones that needed restocking. He leaned back after one page. It wasn't a bad life, Andy decided; it just didn't seem to have a beginning or an end. It felt temporary, a vacation life that he would one day leave to assume the job and circle of friends intended for him. Looking at his office, though, he saw a frightening permanence. Yellow work orders fluttered motionlessly in front of him, a mosaic of toilet installations and brute labor reduced to scrawls of violet ink. Blueprints crowded the cheap knickknacks sent by supply houses and clients: the golf caddie cigarette lighter, the Model-T desk organizer whose crank could be turned to sharpen pencils. On the wall a hysterically voluptuous blonde posed in a sandbox among an array of pipe wrenches and threading machines, naked except for a canvas tool belt. Beside her hung a picture of a mountain with an inspirational aphorism, sent by a bank. The silly words of Clayton's impossible invitation crawled before his eyes again, bringing with them the map in his room, its mythical names and unknown ranges so foreign to the geography of pipe lengths and pinups depicted on his walls. He had his mountain range and his colorful natives in traditional dress, all made of paper. He had his own Inner Mongolia.

His father knocked on his door, then entered with a sheepish look, as if he'd killed Clayton himself. He started up off the track from the beginning, shrugging his shoulders a few times uncomfortably and raising his eyebrows to throw a philosophical air over his speech, though it came out looking more like uncertainty.

"Andy, I'm really glad you're here helping me . . . In this world, there's some things . . . There's choices about what you do and don't do and . . . I want you to know . . ." He had gotten partly through it when they heard the outside door opening and Francis trading phrases with a deliveryman. Seconds later she bellowed: "Andy, you wanna sign for this?"

The courier held out a cardboard envelope that was striped to give the impression of speed, ripping with far-off urgency and a litter of Chinese symbols. Andy recognized immediately the familiar handwriting bursting out of each neat rectangle that had been allotted for it, the rebellious signature exploding across the entire form. No return address and for a date the inexplicable rendering of that very day, an hour ago, defying all notions of distance and sanity, as if the message had come from very close, just out of his peripheral vision. An hour ago?

Andy signed for it and walked slowly toward his office, his head buzzing with the strangeness. An hour ago? His father had gone, and he went in and closed the door behind him. A foreign gas seemed to have filled his veins; he felt he might float out the window, or disappear. His life didn't play like this. This was Clayton's life, not his. He examined the date again, as if it might change back to yesterday's, but it remained today, only an hour ago. He tore open the envelope with the apprehension that it connected him to a living Clayton, and that it might fade away into ether at any moment, taking his friend with him.

The first item came in the dark blue cardboard folder of the East Sea Travel Agency. A plane ticket. The flight would leave Chicago that night and make a stop in San Francisco, then continue on to Hong Kong. In the green block for Name of Passenger crouched the thick black type that spelled A. Mann. It refuted the complete impossibility of the trip, an antimatter to the dictates of bids and audits. Andy stared at it like a thing not real, the first mythic object he'd ever encountered, and totally unprepared for its power. He put it softly on his desk and removed the second envelope from the courier packet. The glossy magazine paper bore a lone oriental horseman amid the city that Andy recognized as Hong Kong. Somehow Clayton had inserted him riding through a street cluttered with neon, staring through the high-rises as if at the empty distant plain that occupied the back of the envelope. The letter inside seemed thick, but when Andy unfolded it the first sheet blossomed blank and wordless in front of his face. The second repeated that perfect white surface, and the third, the fourth also, explaining it all with this long phrase of emptiness, the unspeakable message about the spaces between everything that could be said or done or rationalized. At the bottom of the last sheet, in big letters sopped in black ink, Clayton had written his last invitation.

I'VE ALWAYS BEEN YOUR WILD CARD

it said. Below, the final imperative:

PLAY ME.

THE EMPIRE
OF CLOTH

I n the long-distance telephone cabin at Carrasco International Airport, near the city of Montevideo, Jeffrey Holt realized that someone had scratched the telephone number of another dead friend into the linoleum shelf. His scalp started to tingle, then his memory came to the rescue: Alejandro's register had ended 46 not 64. The eerie rush dissipated as quickly as it had come on. He could hear the round laughing tones of Alejandro's voice congratulating him as if he was a child, joking again: "How good! Jeffrey! How good! Always triumphing with the numbers."

Holt shook off the memory, closing the address book where he'd written the number of Clayton's friend in America. He always thought about Alejandro when he went to Buenos Aires, so it shouldn't surprise him that he would come back so strongly now, while the disequilibrium of Clayton's stunning exit kept wavering in and out of the stolid details of taxis and check-in lines like a heat mirage. He pushed back the sleeve of his jacket: the obligatory call to the States had eaten up his free time. His call to Claudio would have to be made in Buenos Aires.

Holt felt the carry-on bag nudging against his feet as he shifted his weight. It was his special bag, whose lattice of scratches and abrasions delineated on its black leather body a now unfathomable history of airports and taxis. The bag had traveled around the world with him, acquiring with the years the mute but reassuring personality of familiar objects. It held the pima cotton shirts he ordered in Hong Kong, and beneath them the monogrammed leather shaving kit that Silvia had gotten him for his last birthday. And it held, secreted within the lining that he had learned to sew with a nearly machinelike regularity, the deliriously rare and fragile Paracas manta that he was smuggling out of South America.

He tucked his belongings together and strode out into the summery airport, briskly moving into the security clearance with a dry smile. He submitted his bag to the guard, unzipping it for him in a courteous gesture of confidence. The guard glanced inside, then moved on to Holt's portfolio. Holt probably could have carried the textile on his arm with the same result; few people in the world could even recognize a Paracas manta, let alone imagine its value. The two-thousand-year-old textile could be sold for half of the price of a house, and now the only real risk, getting it out of its native Peru, already lay behind him. Even though Lima still waited among the dozen airports between him and Hong Kong, he would only be in transit there, traceless and Customs-less.

The flight attendant greeted him and directed him to his seat. She had straight dark hair that fell far down her tall shoulders, queenly and soft, with blue eyes. He always noticed the attractive women on airplanes. Sometimes he would develop short-lived crushes on them, entertaining fantasies of talking with them, of showing them his favorite places in Shanghai or Buenos Aires, and then they would evaporate at the next airport or walk away, to be replaced by other women, like cards in a magic trick.

He eased his bag carefully into the overhead rack, protecting the frail textile as if it were a tissue-thin sheet of gold leaf. One didn't find a piece like this twice in a lifetime. His agent in Lima had told him about it, and the mere rumor of a complete Paracas manta had sufficed to send him through the coastal desert to Ica to track it down. Paracas materials remained a mysterious anomaly in the world of antique textiles. Most now in existence had been discovered in a single burial ground in the 1920s, without any signs of a culture that was complex enough to create them. Some people claimed they came from a more sophisticated highland culture, but no cities of such a people had ever been found. Paracas textiles seemed to exist apart from anything else, the still-resonant idea of beauty from a world that could only be imagined. The more eccentric theorists claimed they had been inspired by extraterrestrials, and they made elaborate proofs relating them to gene splicing or spacecraft landing strips.

So it was with a certain comforting skepticism that he'd trodden the usual path from someone's office to someone's little cinder block home, drinking a beer while they waited for the grave robber to answer his summons. As so many other times, he'd watched a scattered assortment of textile fragments come out, each piece accompanied by the faint putrid odor of corpses.

The grave robber had excused them: "They haven't been washed yet."

"It's fine," Holt had answered, not looking up from a badly burned funerary wrapping. A few decrepit belts, a tunic faded to browns and yellows except for one little wedge that, protected by a fold, still retained its vivid reds and blues. A motley representation of styles spanning a thousand years, obviously taken from different graves, and none of them Paracas. Just things they'd had lying around the house. As usual, they waited to see if he'd bite at the lesser pieces, spinning make-believe provenances as he examined them with his jeweler's loupe. He almost always knew more about them than they did, because he knew the whole coast: the pre-Columbian trade routes and the Inca military campaigns, the implications of paired warp threads, or slit tapestry that was sewn shut or left open. He laughed at their false identifications as if at the punch line of a joke. "Nazca? How interesting! It's almost identical to a Chimu piece I bought last year!" Holt didn't worry about taking liberties with the grave robbers. He had robbed more than one grave himself.

In those early days he had been more into the adventure of smuggling than the profits of it. He had bought his way into their confidence by paying the highest prices and keeping his mouth shut. His suppliers were the cagey peasants who had schooled themselves in the habits of the dead. As a favor they had let him accompany them on their night missions into the cool, silent obscurity of the ancient cemeteries, probing with iron rods into the sand for the inaudible clink of metal against ceramic. From the surface the grave sites looked like every other part of the desert, marked only by a few piles of boulders or bits of cloth that had drifted to the top, but beneath the

STUART COHEN

soil, in their dark burial urns, crouched the mummified citizens of the forgotten town, waiting in the finery bestowed on them by their tearful family and companions. Holt himself had helped dig up the clay caskets and break them open, had stripped the corpses of their shrouds and bindings and had even found, on one Inca notable, a Nazca textile that had been robbed five hundred years before. So the *huaqueros* had heard of Holt, and they found him to be true. After a half hour another man had come in with a brown bag and unceremoniously unfolded from it one of the most astonishing textiles Holt had ever seen.

Holt had stared at it, then examined it with the loupe, then stared at it again, sipping his bottle of beer. He'd had to calm himself. Somehow, from a grave that had escaped seventy years of profanations, the inexplicable tissue of an alien life had been hoisted up to the light. It spilled out across the gray plaster floor to half the size of a bedsheet, its field of deep crimson exquisitely embroidered with the strange feathered warriors and trophy heads whose meaning had been lost two millennia ago. Only the blurred outline of the mummy's body, like a faint coffee stain in one corner, belied its age. It had completed a two-thousand-year journey to end up before him, radiant with a mysterious energy that took him away into the still realm of blowing sands and the shriek of seagulls dead for twenty centuries. Silently immersed in the colors, distant from the expectant vendors and the shoddy fluorescent light above him, Holt could see the tawny desert woven into the azure depths of a day that had run its course among a succession of days so numerous and identical that they became like seconds on a watch. The deep carmine field, still supernaturally alive and modern across the silent tide of the centuries, seemed to overwhelm the little room and the Ica outside and even Holt's own short and hectic life. It superseded the dictatorship of material objects, like the chart of a hidden world that Holt could intuit but never enter. It enslaved him.

"*Señores Pasajeros . . .*" The usual speech about emergency exits and seat backs and tray tables. He looked at the emergency exits and imagined the chaos of a water landing, wondering if he'd really make it the three rows to the door before the plane sank. The crash scenario made its appearance on every flight. Crossing water he pictured himself scrambling over his seat mates to the emergency exit. Over land he tried to picture a complete calm as he plunged to his death, right up to the moment when the seats broke loose from the floor at impact and the abrupt disintegration of the overhead luggage racks. Getting on an airplane had all the extremes of love and annihilation, something that he knew could be the same thing.

The plane began to rumble down the strip, then jumped up and glided into the air, leaving the ground with a last bump, like a kick in the ass. He glanced at his newspaper, then out the window. Far below, the sea glimmered a soft periwinkle blue, hazy and mottled with the suede outflow of the Río Plata. On the far side the pale green trapezoids of fields were stitched down by a road or a fissure of stream, like the rivulets that divide the hemispheres of a skull. Holt heard the click of a lighter from the seat across the aisle; a man frowned into a cigarette. Holt glanced up at the ceiling, confirming that they were sitting in a no-smoking row, then back at the offender. He looked near forty, thinning blond hair and a silk flower-print shirt that Holt recognized as Chinese, probably twelve-weight *habutai*. The Chinese had flooded the world with the stuff. In South America it still had one more season, could just barely carry off the casual Latin drug-dealer look, especially with the help of that gold chain looped across the open slit of chest. Holt knew that an unseen cross hung on it, comparing in his mind the idea of Christian meekness with the act of lighting up in a no-smoking zone. The man stared ahead with a crowning arrogance, as if by ignoring everyone else he could create his own private smoking area.

Holt didn't care about the cigarette: he himself smoked a bit. It gave him a feeling of being at home no matter where he went, the fragrance of the tobacco surrounding him like a favorite overcoat. The man's arrogance bothered him, though: the idea that he could flaunt the rules and get away with it. That was the kind of thing Clayton used to do all the time. Traveling with Clayton always bore as its price the constant requests to put out cigarettes and get in line, to turn down the volume. Clayton's offenses ranged between trying to slide past the regulations to complete flaunting of authority, and to make it worse, sometimes he would argue about it, turning it into a general assault on the bureaucratic mentality and loading the most penetrating insults on the person whose job it was to enforce the rules. They were slaves. They were easily replaceable cogs in the corporate machine. In China he'd gone so far that he'd been arrested, and after spending four days getting him out of jail Holt had scourged him so deeply that they didn't speak again for a year. Now, on the way to his funeral, it occurred to Holt that what had gotten Clayton was the inevitability of the rules: starting with smoking and wearing seat belts and graduating to the laws of gravity, of getting old, of needing money for retirement.

Holt looked at the man loosing the cloud of smoke, then at the empty seat next to him, and suddenly he had the intense desire to start a cigarette. He took one out and tapped the man across from him, asking him for a light. The man snapped out a yellow and blue cone of butane, his far-off demeanor changing to a more open one, relieved to have a coconspirator. Holt drew some flame in and thanked him, settling back, then glancing over at him with a shrug. The man raised his eyebrows in return.

"You're North American?" he asked him in Spanish.

"Yes. And you?"

"Peruvian."

"From Lima?"

"Yes. Do you know Lima?"

Holt recognized the warm accent of the Peruvian coast in the man's words, and it made him smile. He quickly placed him among the rich suburbs of La Molina or Miraflores, could see him playing tennis at the exclusive Regattas club. Holt used Lima as a collection point for his pre-Columbian material. "I know it well. I've spent much time there."

"You don't say! How good! And from what part of the United States do you come?"

"Maryland. On the East Coast." Holt had had this conversation so many times that it sometimes gave him a feeling of unreality, as if he was reliving an experience from several years before. After this would come "And at what do you work?" In airplane conversations everyone always had the secret desire to tell the story of their life. Not a real life, of course, but a lie of a life, an above-the-clouds version without embarrassing moments and defeats. These exchanges always had a cutoff point that eliminated any possibilities of annoyance or betrayal. Stories were traded, little fairy tales with heroes who happened to be sitting right next to you, self-enclosed morality plays with dollops of pain and fear that could always be counted on to have a happy ending, with the triumphant protagonist jetting off to another destination, or home again. Jeffrey had liked many of the people he'd met on his many flights, but for all the business cards he'd accumulated and the addresses he'd been given he had never made a friend on an airplane.

The man next to him had gone back to his private smoking section. He looked aloof and formidable again, as if they'd never had a conversation. A soft pinging sound came over the speakers and another speech began, "*Damas y Caballeros por favor . . .* " and then again the long service poem, in Spanish, about belts of security and cigarettes to be extinguished. The temperature in Buenos Aires, they were informed, was forty-two degrees centigrade, which sent a groan through the Argentines who were now terminating their vacations at the beach. Multiply by nine, divide by five, add thirty-two: the temperature would be exactly one hundred seven and six-tenths of a degree for his ninety-minute traverse of Buenos Aires. "Forty-two!" Holt said to the man across from him.

"It's infernal," he answered back. That started their conversation again. The man also needed to transfer from Aeroparque to Ezeiza to catch the Lloyd flight. The question as to whether they would share a taxi hung unasked as the plane came down to earth again. Holt didn't care about the money, and he could imagine getting stuck waiting for the other man's baggage. He mentioned the tight connection time and the Peruvian nodded. "What luck that I only have hand luggage." Holt concurred, and they entered into the gradation of relationship that Holt thought of as *Aliados del Camino*: Allies of the Road. It fell between friendship and acquaintance, its temporary nature allowing for intimacies and confessions that couldn't be broached with someone who would know those private things forever. Trust came

STUART   COHEN

easily, and loyalty, at least for the hours or days until the appearance of the mutual destination and its farcical exchange of addresses. Holt had no time for more friends, but there was always room for another ally.

Despite the cautionary announcements of the flight crew that passengers should remain in their seats, the metallic sprinkle of unsnapping safety belts started as soon as the plane began to slow on the runway. Holt disdained the illusion that time could be saved by unhooking a safety belt twenty seconds early; he always felt a certain superiority when he waited calmly for the plane to empty out. This time he stood up with the rest of them, glancing at his fellow traveler as they both pulled down their carry-ons. They were facing a hot, nervous commute, and the penalty for failure would be an unknown delay. If Holt missed even one of his flights it would destroy the entire carefully worked itinerary, perhaps making him miss the funeral entirely.

They descended the metal stairs to the runway. The heat staked its claim immediately, inescapable and angry, every breeze blowing over them like the exhaust of a gigantic engine. He and the Peruvian strode wordlessly toward the air-conditioned terminal. By the time they reached it Holt could feel a sticky dew all over his torso.

The Peruvian knew Aeroparque well, and he led them straight to a line of yellow and black vehicles at the taxi stand, glancing continually behind him and to the sides. The dispatcher asked where they were going, then opened the door of an older model Japanese car. Holt began to get in, but the Peruvian touched his arm, then poked his face into the passenger-side window. "Do you have air-conditioning?"

The driver tossed his head up in a quick nod, dismissing the idea of air-conditioning and men weak enough to need it. "I have windows."

"Better the Falcon," the Peruvian said, tugging at Jeffrey's arm toward a Ford Falcon two cars back. A quick word, then he motioned Holt inside. The dispatcher's shrill whistle followed them into the cab. He hurried over, his white plastic identity card jiggling on his lapel, but as he opened his mouth to speak the Peruvian cut him off. "Maestro, I know: the rules prohibit this. But I have a condition of the brain that prohibits me from being in extreme heat. I can have a stroke. Please, my friend and I are in a hurry. Give this to the other driver as a consolation for his extra wait." The green and white origami of a crumpled American bill changed hands, its persuasive shape cutting them loose from the curb and sending them out into traffic.

Holt turned to his companion and smiled: "*Muy mosca.*" Very fly: a strictly Lima term and the highest compliment to be had there. In the City of the Viceroys one had to be rapid, to have fast reflexes and the ability to spring out of reach in an instant. All taxi fares had to be negotiated; even the simple task of parking a car involved deciding which street urchin to pay protection to. Holt had seen currency devalued by 100 percent in an afternoon, which was immaterial if one happened to be in the bank when the latest revolutionary splinter group set off a bomb. Yes, in Lima one had to be very, very fly.

The Peruvian turned to him, impersonating perfectly the operatic toss of the head with which the first cab driver had dismissed his question about the air-conditioning: "*Porteños!*" He put his hand out. "Andreas Otero Benavides."

Benavides, like the main boulevard of Miraflores. "Jeffrey Holt."

The cab had already begun to cool off as they moved along a channel of the Río Plata past the river football stadium. "Are you going to Lima today?" Andreas asked him.

"No. I'm going to Hong Kong."

"You don't say! By Lima?"

Holt rolled his eyes. "It's a flight out of a nightmare." He named the cities like a pianist running scales: Buenos Aires, Santa Cruz, La Paz, Guayaquil, Lima, Panama, Mexico, Los Angeles, Anchorage, Seoul, and, twenty-eight hours later, Hong Kong.

Andreas loosed the appropriate puffs of air and eyebrow raises. "What a disaster! And you couldn't get a better flight?"

"I had a better one: Santiago–Shanghai, without stops. I had to change it."

"It must have been very urgent to switch to such a terrible flight . . . "

He hadn't meant to get into this. "It's the funeral of a friend."

Andreas seemed surprised, but not embarrassed. "I'm sorry."

"It's fine. That's life."

"Yes, that's life."

That brought the silence down. The air conditioner expelled its constant breeze, rustling papers in the front seat like wind among autumn foliage. The whole conversation rang stupidly in his mind: I'm sorry, That's life. A way to turn something painful and unreasonable into a social convention, to try and make it smaller. Clayton would have added his own remark to the "I'm sorry," "That's life" exchange. No, he'd say, that's Death: it gets in your face, doesn't it? It's the hammer. An expression he'd picked up in Germany: it's the hammer.

Settling back into the taxi, he looked at the world simmering beyond the fresh cell of the automobile. Andreas had been right about the air-conditioning. Holt wondered if his ally knew the unpleasant history attached to these cars. Alejandro had warned him during the junta of "President" Galtieri that Falcons were the preferred car of the paramilitary police, and he described being followed one afternoon by an olive green Ford that kept pace with him for three blocks, cruising through intersections at walking speed, three men inside staring out at him from behind ferocious black Ray Bans. He'd laughed at how he'd outsmarted them, losing them outside a shopping gallery, then poured himself a glass of red wine that he'd gulped down rather too quickly. Not long after that he'd disappeared. The big Falcon had swooped down. Holt had agonized with Alejandro's wife and the rest of the family, complained to the American embassy, which had brushed him off. He'd made the useless rounds of police stations and hospitals with Alejandro's brother, hoping the presence of a foreigner would somehow separate Alejandro's case from all the others who were vanishing. He finally flew away from his helplessness to the more solvable problems of his growing enterprise in Hong Kong. He'd kept hoping that Alejandro had made it to Chile, but then Chile went under too, and Brazil, Bolivia: the whole southern half of the continent turned over to dictatorships, a confederation of dark and ruthless states with secret agreements to help each other exterminate the enemies of Order.

Maybe France. Holt kept waiting for a letter from Paris or Madrid, holding on to the picture in his mind of Alejandro sitting wistfully in a European café while he waited for his exile to end, but over the years the finality of that exile began to make itself felt. Little by little the worry turned to horror, made worse by the void of details that led to endless imaginings of Alejandro's abduction and murder, the dreams of him returning to tell jokes and complain about politics. Sometimes in Buenos Aires Jeffrey would go visit Alejandro's mother, but they never had anything new to say to each other; they would only exchange a few words and sit in sadness among the exhausted harmonics of the past. The last time, Alejandro's brother had said: "Jeffrey, maybe it's better if we meet outside the house next time you come to Buenos Aires." That had been four years ago, and now he always seemed to end up in Ford Falcons, the preferred car of the Buenos Aires *taxistas* because they had air-conditioning and they just kept going, year after year through their rounds of the city, from Florida Street to La Boca, past Escuela Militar to touch base at the airport, immune to their cargo of kisses, smoke, and nervousness, Aeroparque to Ezeiza, always empty at the next destination.

Holt pushed his hair back and sighed. Now Clayton had disappeared. He wished Clayton was riding in this taxi now, like the time in Tokyo when Holt had finally admitted to him that the English school he'd founded wouldn't last another three weeks. Clayton had listened carefully to all the numbers that so bored him, finally saying, "How long have you known this, Jeff?"

"I've known it for six weeks. I kept hoping it would change . . . You know how that is."

He'd feared Clayton would be flip, or criticize him for hiding it, but instead he'd seemed as sad as Holt himself, letting the whirring of the bus intercede as he considered his answer. "Business is a game . . . But it's a game that's only fun when you're winning. What you've got to remember is that you're bigger than the game. And me personally"—Holt still remembered the embarrassed smile, above the chest and shoulders still hale and athletic—"you're my friend. I love you as a success. I love you as a failure. It's the same to me."

Holt wanted to continue that conversation now, to ask Clayton, how could you kill yourself the first try? Couldn't you have botched the first attempt like everybody else does? Why couldn't you wait a few more days until I got to Hong Kong? He could imagine sitting with him at the Dragon Inn talking things over. "Jeff, I'm having some problems . . ." He thought about the last hours and the possibility of whether Clayton had tried to call him in Montevideo. He probably didn't have the number, but he could have called the office, couldn't he? Holt wondered whether Clayton had committed suicide during office hours and started trying the arithmetic of time zones and Chang's phone call the same way he had converted centigrade to Fahrenheit. Instead he found himself picturing Clayton's end, when sleep started coming, and feeling now the urgency of calling the hospital and asking for an ambulance, the dreary pull of sleep, only minutes left and suddenly in a world with such an infinity of minutes they could be divided into excruciatingly small and precious bits: the moments when he would still be awake enough to call the hospital finally draining to being able to manage a turn of the head, a finger movement, a breath, a lazy thought.

How could he have mistaken the measurement of life as being months and years when finally one minute contained everything? He had known Clayton was going under, but he could never allocate the time to look more deeply because the next business detail or upcoming flight had engaged him in an endless round of puzzle solving. Holt's life was like a house whose foundations were posted on four continents, and only by the focus of his intellect and his discipline could he keep such an improbable structure up. A house like that had no room for anarchy. The terrible thought pronounced itself, an accusation slicing across his mind with a pain so sharp that it had cut him all the way through before he noticed it: Clayton's friendship had no longer fit into his schedule.

He felt himself flushing with an embarrassment made even more intense because he experienced it alone, in front of the judgmental eyes of a few dead or far-off people who already knew and could never be reasoned with. He turned to his window to try to get back into the external world, and he saw the familiar lawns of the picnic grounds on the outskirts of the city, somewhere he had visited long ago with

Alejandro when they had prepared a giant barbecue for all of Alejandro's boyhood friends. Grief piled upon grief, wracking him in the taxi with two men who shared his anonymous trajectory through a universe of missed opportunities pervaded by the smell of vinyl and the faint cologne of strangers.

Christ, he was losing it in a taxicab. He could feel it taking him away, and he breathed deeply to try and stave it off, but it didn't work and a convulsion escaped. He never cried, and now in a taxi with two strangers the ancient cloak came over him with its deep, warm familiarity, so suddenly that some small part of him was amazed.

He felt the scant weight of a hand on his shoulder. "It's hard. I know."

Jeffrey said nothing, afraid that if he tried his voice it wouldn't work right. The soft words of the Peruvian came from beside him. "You are thinking about your friend?"

Holt shook his head, waving his hand in the air at the ranks of the missing in his life. "All of them."

Andreas looked past Holt to the urban scenery, examining it as if it were a distant mountain range. "Ah, hombre. This is the problem with getting older; our social circle is comprised of more and more dead people."

Andreas's sympathy broke down the last of his reserve, and he bent his head down, taking off his glasses and clapping the rest of the world out with his open hand.

When he looked up again Andreas was watching him with concern. He heard a burst of static from the radio and then the driver muttering his code number and the word "*Aeropuerto.*" He offered his ally a shrug and a pallid smile. "And... Andreas,... what were you doing in Montevideo?"

The Peruvian answered abstractly, as if giving his reasons little importance. "I was there for a conference. And you?"

"I had some business there." Holt explained that he had a company that represented buyers. He helped American and European companies manufacture clothing in South America and China, and that—

"Oh, so you work in clothing?"

"Yes." Holt didn't mention the dealings in antique textiles that still accounted for a part of his income: Peru had certain restrictions against the export of antique and pre-Columbian cloth. The automatic vocabulary of his occupation calmed him again. It made him credible without his having to do anything. He had offices in Buenos Aires, Lima, Los Angeles, and Hong Kong.

"That's not a business. That's an empire!"

Holt waved the idea away with a smile. "They're small offices: not exactly an empire. Now I'm trying to consolidate it." He began to explain the upcoming meeting in Shanghai and the complex arrangement he was trying to work out with Villarino and the Chinese factories—

"I noticed your shoes. They're very fine. Suede, no?"

"Yes. I picked them up in Firenze."

"Firenze. I went to Firenze with my wife once. How good!" He reached over and touched the lapel of Holt's checked sports jacket. "It's silk?"

"It's a blend of silk and linen."

"Firenze?"

"I have a tailor in Hong Kong—"

Andreas cut him off. "So interesting, your business. And where is your home?"

"Hong Kong. But I travel a lot. Almost eight months of the year."

Andreas appraised him. He seemed to be impressed. "And where is your office in Lima?"

"In San Isidro."

"I know San Isidro quite well. What is the exact address?"

Holt could feel the little patch of eczema on his elbow start to itch. He pushed his glasses up on the bridge of his nose. Andreas's questions had a strange rigidity to them that put him a bit on guard. He used the Lima office as a collection point for textiles he brought out of Peru. "It's near the Camino Real, on Libertadores. Libertadores 174." The address came to mind because one of his favorite Lima restaurants was on Libertadores. He wondered if Andreas could tell that he was lying.

"Libertadores. Libertadores." He kept looking at him with an intensity that made him uneasy. "You must be a very intelligent man to maintain such a business."

"And what do you do, Andreas?"

He put his palm print on the space between them. "Afterward I'll explain it. Look, we're already here!"

The porters opened the door, fading away when Holt got out carrying his own bag. He could see Andreas peering through the rear window before he put his feet on the pavement. Their flight left in forty-five minutes, maybe enough time to call Villarino and get a fax out to Mr. Chen. They strode together into Ezeiza's tremendous lobby, tethered to each other by their mutual flight path, Holt feeling a bit uncomfortable because of his display of feelings during the drive over. They found the Lloyd counter and took their place in line behind families with caravans of baggage. Tall European-looking Argentines waited among the angular features of the mestizo Limeños. The Bolivians stood out because of their shortness and the high content of altiplano Indian in their faces. Everyone had the mixture of boredom and excitement found at check-in lines: the routine wait enlivened by the knowledge that soon their bodies would be fired miles into the air and come down to earth in an entirely different country.

Andreas touched him on the shoulder, motioned toward one of the Bolivians who was having trouble checking his baggage in. Holt noticed a flash of annoyance from the attendant as the man disputed something. "Ha!" Andreas kept his green eyes on Holt's as he laughed. "I think he feels lost without his little llama!"

Holt frowned noncommittally, and Andreas grunted and moved his bag one foot closer in the line. "I was supposed to fly first class, but they lost my reservation!"

"Perhaps you should insist."

"It's fine, hombre." Again, the eyes that seemed only inches from his face. "After all, we're living in a democracy! No?" He laughed and patted Holt's shoulder, holding his gaze for an uncomfortable moment longer until Holt smiled, then turning to the front again.

Andreas checked in, then waited as Holt handed his ticket to the woman behind the counter. "I'll seat you with your friend?"

He could sense Andreas's short muscular presence next to him. "Please do," Holt answered. A minute tingling, like static electricity, buzzed on his elbow.

She glanced down at his black garment bag. "Do you have any luggage to check in?"

Holt kept his eyes on her face. "No."

She stared dubiously at the worn black bag, plastered with tags in Chinese and Spanish. Holt knew already that his carry-on, hastily packed and bloated with the manta, might slightly exceed the international limits. "Señor, the regulations prohibit bags with dimensions of more than one-hundred-sixty centimeters aboard the airplane."

"I understand completely, Miss. And I have measured this bag a hundred times." He tried a smile. "It's close, but it just fits."

She glared at him, then wordlessly took out a tape measure from the drawer and began to unroll it. Andreas pushed in front of Holt. Holt could smell the slight citrus fragrance of his cologne. "Señorita, please: the señor has a very tight connection in Lima. It's almost as if he has to jump from one plane to the other in midair!" A beam of amusement played across her face, but she bent down to the bag anyway. In five seconds she had measured it out to 180.

Holt had a fall back. "If it's packed very full perhaps it's a little more, but—"

"Señor, I'm sorry but you must check it in."

Holt was trying to come up with a new proposal when Andreas leaned toward her. "Miss, are you telling me that in the city of Carlos Gardel, where the tango was born, a man must be penalized for packing an extra shirt?" He put his hand over his heart and recited a line of Gardel's famous tango: *Mi Buenos Aires querido, cuando . . . " My beloved Buenos Aires, when will I see you again!* He opened his hands, saying less pleasantly, "Evidently, when I have less luggage!" He speared her with his razor smile again, imploring her with a sincerity so real it seemed physical. "Señorita, as a favor . . ." She looked back at Holt, who closed ranks with a wan admission of guilt. She puffed her lips. "Fine."

Andreas imitated Holt's slight American accent as they walked away: "If it is full perhaps it's a little more." He gave a thin, almost wheezing laugh. "You're half *mosca* yourself, Señor Holt."

"A little, but I can't sing tangos like you."

"Oh, never will you convince me of that, my friend. Perhaps later you will get your opportunity to try."

Holt considered it, then remembered Villarino. "Excuse me, Andreas. I have to make a call. We'll see each other inside." Holt reached for his address book as he made his way to the telephone office. The plan had been for him to fly with Villarino to Shanghai and hold his hand the whole way. In Shanghai, everything would be signed and the disparate offices and enterprises Holt had been relentlessly maintaining for the past decade would be fused into one single giant company that would have as its undisputed head of state Holt himself. After a year of negotiating, it still felt tenuous, Villarino making sounds about backing out every time he read an adverse news report about China. "I saw a report on television, Jeffrey. They say that the central government is losing control." Holt reassuring him: television is always sensationalist, Claudio. That's their business. Yes, the Beijing government has some challenges to overcome, but the military establishment is already very involved with the free economy, so they have a mutual interest . . . Telling him the politics, then trying to steer the conversation back to the minuscule labor costs of China. No, a change in flight plans didn't strengthen his arguments. It admitted the possibility of unforseen problems.

He laid an American dollar on the counter. "Miss, I have no change. Could I make a local call, please."

"Cabin six." The rhythmic buzzing of the telephone.

"Textiles Santa Fe, *buen día*."

"*Buen día*. This is Mr. Holt calling. Is Mr. Villarino there?"

A trace of professional contrition: "Oh, Mr. Holt! I'm sorry. Mr. Villarino went to lunch early. Is there some message?"

Holt felt the muscles in his arms clenching. This kind of news didn't go well on a little pink message pad. "No. No. I'll try later."

He looked at his watch. He had a little more than twenty-six minutes. He grabbed a piece of stationery from his portfolio and inscribed a message to Mr. Chen, asking him if he could move the meeting back a few days. "This goes to Beijing." A young man behind the counter took the fax, staring with amazement at the Chinese characters Holt had written in neat files. Holt filled out the request form and waited as the man went over to the machine and looked through a book for the necessary dialing code. "Zero zero one dash eight six," Holt told him. Twenty-two minutes left. He felt a tightness in his chest and took a deep breath. He watched the attendant's fingers slowly punch in the numbers.

"Circuits are busy, sir."

Holt looked at the small dial of his watch. "It's after midnight there."

The man dialed again, then raised his eyebrows apologetically. "Busy. Better we try again in five minutes." Holt considered leaving it with him with the necessary money, but then he knew he'd spend the rest of the trip wondering if it had been sent.

He stepped out of the office and for no reason he stopped walking. His eyes lodged on the departure board, its menu of destinations clicking and changing from Rome to Madrid to Asunción to Miami. He heard the sound of a guitar, painful and crystalline, and the high twisted voice of long-dead Blind Auggie Sampson singing "Every Place to Go." "*I've got every place to go, but not a reason in the world to be there . . .*"

"I think Blind Auggie would have been really into airports, you know that?" Clayton speaking from the nineteenth-century Kirman in Holt's living room, playing an old scratched vinyl disk he'd somehow found in a Hong Kong record store, playing it five times over Holt's protests until he'd finally gotten it.

"It's rather like that Afghani tribal piece," Holt had said, referring to another carpet a few feet away from them. "They have the same unevenness. A certain primitive—"

"It's fucking *inescapable*! That's what I like about Blind Auggie! Mind if I torch up one of your blueboys?" Shifting his position on the rug, taking a cigarette out of the blue packet of Gauloise. "Yeah, except instead of trying to flag a ride with a Lucky hanging out of your mouth you're looking up at the Big Board in Buenos Aires or one of those other funky Latin places you go to, smoking a Gauloise, trying to figure out what the hell gate you're supposed to be running for. Because you've just got. . . *Every Place to Go*. It's another way of saying that you're surfing the Emptiness."

Later, the train station in Hong Kong, when he'd seen him off to go look for that absurd map that had become his only hope. Clayton had already spent the small fortune he'd made with his paper sculptures, had only his craziness left to ride on and some nonsense about Inner Mongolia. "Hey, just think of this as a diplomatic fact-finding expedition by a man without a country." Mounting the train, then suddenly rushing back to Holt, serious, pausing to formulate his thoughts, then saying only with intense feeling, "Good-bye!" Then gone, like a thousand gones; they always left that little vacuum of space.

Twenty-one minutes. Holt shook his head and walked toward the escalator that would take him up to Security with its conveyor belts and X-ray machine and the long white corridor to Lima, or Hong Kong, or a dozen other destinations telescoped together like pages in a book. He was glad he'd faxed his itinerary to Silvia the day before; it would be a relief to see her at the airport. His thoughts cramped down to seat numbers and overhead racks as he entered the tight plastic tube of the airplane. The jet had a worn quality to it made worse by the heat, which had overwhelmed the capacity of the cooling system. He clambered sideways down the passage, apologizing as he bumped a middle-aged Argentine in the face with his carry-on, giving up on forgiveness when the man didn't try to conceal his annoyance. *Fuck him*, Holt thought.

When he reached his seat he found that Andreas had taken it. "Is it all right?" Andreas asked, looking up at him. Across the aisle Andreas's empty seat waited next to a Bolivian *cholita* in her bowler hat and seven layers of petticoats, a costume straight out of the nineteenth century. She looked utterly out of place with the little felt headpiece pinned to the top of her braids and the ancient Indian face. The woman at her side had the same face but modern clothes, obviously her traveling companion. They both watched him as he sat down, smiling at him. The Indian woman gathered the dense layers of her skirts more closely to her, but the heavy fabric still brushed gently against Holt's pants. A coffee-colored *pollera*, made of industrial cloth instead of the rustic *bayeta* of the old days. A hand-embroidered lace blouse. Not bad embroidery, for South America. Mostly satin stitch, a few knot-stitched flower buds. The *cholita* noticed him staring at her blouse and shifted nervously under his appraisal. She'd probably done it herself. "Very pretty, your blouse." The *cholita* dabbed her face with a handkerchief and smiled shyly at him. "Thank you, señor." Then, "What heat!"

Seat backs, tray tables, the eternal putting-out of cigarettes. Liftoff.

"Jeffrey"—Andreas leaned across the aisle and touched him on the arm—"how did you begin doing business in Lima?"

"Oh . . ." Holt hesitated, his first trip to Peru coming back to him. His textile career had started in the lobby of a cheap hotel in Trujillo, where he'd befriended Alejandro. The Argentine had taken him along to a room in the back of a restaurant, and there he'd seen his first few fragments, struggling with his imperfect Spanish to understand what Alejandro was arguing about. The dealer, a grave robber who himself had the sharp features and tight skin of a mummy, was insisting that a certain piece came from a Moche site.

Alejandro had dismissed it with a click of his tongue and a grimace. "There's no way, Slim! It's Inca Provincial. It has the eight-pointed star. Look. Even he knows!"

Alejandro handed the scrap to him. The *huaquero* had sewn it to a piece of paper as a primitive conservation method, and most of it had faded to brown and yellow. Looking back, it had been a mediocre little scrap, scorched brown by its contact with long-ago rotted skin, but at the time it had seemed queer and luminescent, still ringing with the weird death-mystery of the grave it had been torn from. As Holt looked down at the frail piece of cloth he'd felt a strange current in his forehead, as if the fragment held an electrical charge. Alejandro had let him buy it, and he'd left the room that night with the little star and a sudden consuming eagerness to learn the difference between Inca Provincial and Moche, of tapestry weaves and warp-faced patterning and all the other mysterious intricacies of pre-Columbian textiles. Now Holt felt the usual sadness when he thought about the Inca star: a few years later he'd sold that piece for a few dollars.

He pushed away the memory, as he did whenever that question was asked, instead giving Andreas one of his half-true stories. "Oh . . . I started like most people in this business: I bought a few sweaters when I returned from a vacation. That was more or less eight years ago."

"Eight years. Tell me: who do you do business with? I have some friends in textiles. Perhaps we know some of the same people."

Holt raised his arm to rub his elbow on the seat back. He heard the flight attendant offering drinks several rows behind them. He only did a smattering of clothing business in Peru now, and none in the last few years. His glasses felt loose and he reached for the frames to steady them. "Oh, I've worked with Chaltex. With Lenceria Eximco. A bit with Textiles Amazonas for—"

"For cotton, of course. Everyone knows Amazonas." Andreas tilted his head back. "I have a good friend in Exportation at Amazonas. Who do you know there?"

Holt was really batting now, and he didn't understand why. He remembered someone he'd met at a different company. "I've worked with Patricio Alvarez. This was some years ago. I don't know if he's still—"

"Patricio Alvarez . . ." Andreas frowned down the aisle, nodding his head slowly.

"And you, Andreas? Do you work in clothing?"

"No. I work in information systems."

"With computers?"

Andreas's answer seemed slightly abstracted. "Yes. With computers."

Holt felt the pressure of the beverage trolley on his shoulder and leaned back to let it stop between them. When it moved on Andreas had opened up a copy of *La Prensa* he'd picked up at the airport. He snorted, finding it impossible to contain his disgust with Argentine politics.

"The labor union wants another raise, or they will slow down production. It's sabotage." His annoyance rattled the paper. "One cannot do business like that. Even you cannot do business like that, no?" Holt glanced over, but he could only see the advertisements for automobiles on the back page. Andreas thrust the newsprint at him: "You notice the leader is wearing a suit. The worker's hero. What do you think his name is?"

"Juan Perón?"

Andreas smiled at the joke. "No. Bernstein." He leaned across the aisle, his voice lower. "Bernstein, eh?"

Holt met his gaze, unwilling to explore the significance that Andreas attached to the name. "I don't know him."

"It was better when Galtieri was president."

Holt felt something cold shoot upward in his stomach. He started to turn back into his seat, but something kept him from sitting back quietly. He kept his voice even and remote. "Galtieri wasn't a true president. He was a dictator."

Andreas kept a slight grin on his face. His eyes, the color of martini olives submerged in vodka, never left Holt's face. "That is all a matter of spelling, hombre." His became more conciliatory. "What I mean is, they didn't have the problem of these supposed champions of the common man manipulating the simple workers for their own power. Now, there's no control. Look at this newspaper. It's all strikes, criminals in the street..." He leaned across the aisle again and spoke softly. "Here in Latin America, we need the firm hand. Without it, everything falls apart."

Holt had heard that argument a dozen times before, always expressed in the same reasonable and philosophical tone of voice, a tone that automatically excused the torture and murder that resulted from the application of that firm hand. Holt had always accepted it and let it pass. Now, recklessly, he answered him. "Andreas, I have a good friend who disappeared during the dictatorship. He didn't need a firm hand."

Andreas looked at him without expression, his eyes holding Holt's like a vise, then he raised his eyebrows sympathetically. "I'm sorry, amigo. I can understand why you're upset"—a catlike amusement at his mouth—"you have friends disappearing on all sides." His voice took on a broad comprehension. "Ay, hombre... it's difficult to accept some things, but... Maybe your friend was a troublemaker."

Holt stared at the fabric of the seat in front of him as Andreas's sympathetic burlesque reverberated with his memories of a joking Alejandro. He glanced at the *cholita* next to him, who suddenly looked down at her tray. An older Argentine man in the row ahead had craned his head around. Andreas seemed to challenge him with his look of sympathy, as if to rip it away would expose something so ugly and violent that he had to go along with the appearance. Holt became intensely aware of the physicality of him: the potent build and the flattened nose. Alejandro's presence suddenly returned, outraged at the dictatorship and at his own death, his eyes fixed inflexibly on Holt, who struggled to keep himself from shaking as he answered: "The only problem my friend had was that he couldn't accept the lies of the dictatorship. The lies of Galtieri. Galtieri and the people who supported—"

Andreas cut him off with a smile. "Politics: it's always dirty, no?" He cocked his head, then reached into his pocket. "Cigarette?"

The cart came down the aisle again, this time with tiny containers covered with foil. Chicken or beef? Holt's anger decayed into a sense of bitter nausea as the dozens of devastating replies he should have given Andreas played through his mind. He picked at his meal with his elbows splayed out like a praying mantis, trying to calm himself within the field of the malevolent presence across the aisle. Andreas returned to *La Prensa*, reading silently except for once, when he laughed out loud.

They banked, dropping toward the jungle that surrounded the city of Santa Cruz. At the landing the pilot seemed to simply give up on the flight and let the airplane drop the last five or ten feet of altitude of its own volition. They bounced a few times, swerving discomfortingly on the runway at 150 miles an hour as the flaps roared up and two hundred passengers lost their identities to a stripping wave of fear, then took them back again with a quick genuflection. He shuffled into the transit area.

Yellow signs hung from the ceiling, the clear black letters for IMMIGRATION and EXIT written out on them in both Spanish and English. Beside it, in international symbols: a suitcase, a stick figure man walking or fleeing in the direction of an arrow, the signs for dollars, pounds, pesos. Holt stopped beneath the sign, staring up at it as he grasped for the cause of its queer familiarity. "It's the *Gateway of the Ancient Garden*" and in a sudden wash of memory he remembered the symbols above Clayton's final dazzling project, the one at the big show in Tokyo, before the whole catastrophe with Misiko had blasted him out of Japan and into the round of wandering that led ultimately to Hong Kong.

STUART COHEN

By that time things had begun to happen for Clayton by themselves, driven by the momentum of gallery owners and an art world that hungered for good-looking Westerners. They'd marketed him as some sort of outlaw, a label that had suited him well because he refused to participate in the courtly norms of Japanese social exchange. He'd quickly earned a reputation for unpredictable bluntness. Strangely, it worked in his favor, because when people realized that he simply wanted to know about them, and that he in turn would reveal anything about himself that they might ask, they felt invited in to a privileged intimacy, and would arrange meetings, gallery dates, publicity, and anything else that might speed him to the top. They loved a noble savage, and Clayton never disappointed them.

What made him perfect, though, was the uncanny and delicate beauty of his sculptures. As startling as he could be in person, his work, rooted in ancient Japanese techniques of paper making, fit well into the collections of wealthy patrons or corporations that wanted something at the same time traditional and avant-garde. Holt had watched him make the transformation from bad English teacher to bad boy artist, his work developing in five years from stationery and envelopes to wall-size installations with dozens of textures and colors. One of them had been a map of the world with all the countries mixed up in time: Imperial Rome abutting Napoleon's France, Kublai Khan's Mongol empire with trade routes marked out to New York like airline flight paths. The flat pieces of paper grew more colorful, then began to solidify into objects, as if he wanted to re-create the world in paper. He'd made a telephone, with its conversation written on itself and on the table it sat on, a conversation about the doings of home interrupted by a jagged tear that revealed the telephone, the table, the conversation itself as paper.

Jeffrey had taken slides of his work and showed them to galleries, acting as an unpaid agent until Clayton had progressed far enough to attract someone more integrated in Tokyo art circles. He made sure Clayton arrived at appointments on time and reinterpreted his ruder comments to put them in a less offensive light. Later, when the flatterers and sycophants began to compete for Clayton's energy, Jeffrey had kept a distant but watchful eye on Clayton's relationships, dispersing the most parasitic ones with his succinct and brutal analyses of people's motives and methods. Clayton never tuned in to those things: he preferred to ride a wave of sensation and excitement without looking down. His pieces began to sell nearly as fast as he could produce them, and his agent raised the prices on them. He began to appear in magazines, and to get inquiries from overseas galleries about his work. All of this happening in the space of five years lent it a miraculous feeling, as if things were unfolding naturally and effortlessly, and that they would always continue like that.

When he'd been invited into the Tokyo Biennial they had gone out and celebrated. The owner of the gallery handling Clayton's work had used his influence to get Clayton an entire room at the show, an unheard-of privilege for such a young artist. Clayton had filled it with artwork, then set it apart from the rest of the show with a high scroll of wall covered with gold leaf that glowed mysteriously in the dim lighting. He'd textured it to look like massive cut stones, and punctured it with a giant post and lintel doorway of pink cast paper textured with tiny splinters of mint green. Above it he'd put one of those international signs with a stick figure man and women driven by an arrow, like a shorthand Adam and Eve being chased out of Eden. In Japanese: GATEWAY OF THE ANCIENT GARDEN. A massive, gorgeous piece, constructed entirely of paper. "If I had a dollar for every picture that got snapped in front of that wall I could retire right now!" Clayton had said. Finally, he did get that much money for it, and he did retire, exiting out his own doorway to someplace he had never revealed to Holt no matter how many times Holt had asked him. Holt sighed. He was dead now. He was dead now and he would be dead tomorrow. He was permanently dead. It's the hammer.

A twenty-minute layover. Just time to call Claudio Villarino and tell him that he would have to wait for him in Shanghai. Something unexpected and tragic had happened, but the deal was still on, of course. He could send the fax to Mr. Chen. He was about to go to the telephone office when he heard his name over the loudspeakers, summoning him to the Lloyd's counter.

"I'm Jeffrey Holt."

His scuffed black suit bag was sitting on the floor like a dog that had been picked up by the pound. A squat Indian baggage handler guarded it while the woman in an airline uniform spoke to him from above a blue and white printed scarf. Rayon, at best. Industrial. "I'm sorry, Mr. Holt, but you will have to check your bag in. It is beyond the regulation size."

Holt didn't change his expression. "It fit very well into the compartment. Why did you take it out?"

The woman looked embarrassed, then hardened her voice. "You knew when you checked it in at Buenos Aires—"

"What importance does it have? It was already there!"

He could sense the baggage handler tensing up. The woman said without a trace of apology: "I'm sorry. It is beyond the regulation size. You must check it in or ship it apart as freight."

"What's happening, amigo?" Andreas stood next to him, a look of concern in his lizard-flesh eyes. Turning to the attendant. "What's happening, *chica*?"

"The señor's baggage—"

"*Por favor, Señorita,* the man has missing persons . . . "

Holt kept his body facing the woman, turning to look sidelong at his ally of the road. The Peruvian's mouth was tensed on the edge of what almost seemed to be a grin. Holt spoke slowly, "Don't worry about it, Andreas. It's fine." To the attendant: "Check it in!"

Holt kept thinking about the fragile Paracas textile as he headed for the bathroom. How many times had he retrieved a suitcase at the baggage claim and found it soaked with someone's exploded shampoo or the leaky plumbing from the lavatory? How often did bags simply disappear, or turn up days later torn with gashes and black rubber tread marks, as if they'd been taken out to the highway and run over a few times? He cursed Andreas silently, and a tremor of rage passed through him. *The señor has missing persons!* Who was Andreas, anyway, besides a stinking fascist sympathizer?

As if summoned by his question, the familiar eyes waited for him in the bathroom mirror. Holt felt his body go rigid, but he forced a semblance of cordiality to his face. "Andreas. How is it?"

Andreas smiled thinly. "Fine. What a pity about your luggage. I tried to help but . . ." He shrugged, his mouth still wearing its ironic twist.

Holt swallowed. "Don't worry. It has nothing valuable in it." He hesitated as the incongruous mandate of winnowing out Andreas's identity in some kind of cosmic repression machinery swelled up in his head. Why was he making small talk? He should be telling him to go to hell! Andreas finished washing his hands and turned away for a paper towel to dry them. He gave off a strange energy: he seemed to ignore Holt at the same time that he was reading his shadow in the glossy surface of the towel dispenser.

It struck Holt then, the oddness of them taking his bag from the overhead compartment to check it in. Andreas's arrival at the Lloyd counter had been a bit too timely, his answers about his occupation a bit too vague. He had been attending "a conference." He worked in "information systems." Holt now found that he didn't want to use the urinal with Andreas there: facing the wall and undoing his pants had the unpleasant overtones of a prisoner stripping for a search, and that aspect of it began to reverberate wickedly through the bathroom. He stepped to the sink and turned on the water, hoping Andreas would leave, but the Peruvian instead took out a comb and began running it through his thin blond hair. Had he washed his hands long enough? Was he washing them too long? He could feel his system accelerating into the primal fight or flee syndrome, brought on not by an animal or an attacker, but by the insubstantial obligation to a murdered friend. Go to hell, Andreas! You and your fascist friends and their vicious, ignorant agendas! He reached for the towel dispenser and jerked the rough china blue leaf that dangled from it, but it got caught and he ended up with only a small corner. The next piece ripped diagonally, the next straight up. Before he knew it he had torn the towel to shreds.

"*Tranquilo*, hombre," Andreas said, pausing at the door to look full into his face before walking out. "It's only paper."

Alone again, Holt let out a burst of tense air. This was an artificial crisis. The flying was getting to him, and the sudden departure with all those loose ends dangling. He loosed a stream of dark urine into the toilet, as if letting out a poisonous distillation of all the reckless emotions of the day. As he left he looked at the little shard of Uruguayan time still clinging to his wrist. Five o'clock in the hot summer streets of Montevideo, so it had to be three o'clock here at thirteen thousand feet. Crazed time: it couldn't make up its mind where it was, or what season it was, yet it was always supposed to be a final authority, everyone's boss. Too late now to call Villarino; it clicked off one tiny stroke against him.

Andreas happened to look up at him as he passed his seat, so he had no choice but to give him a cordial *"Qué tal"* and a dry smile before continuing on to an empty seat near the back. He didn't like the obviousness of changing seats, but the burden of keeping up appearances was beginning to overwhelm him. Who was Andreas, anyway? He'd been abominably stupid to talk politics with him, especially when he was carrying the most valuable single textile he'd ever found.

The plane lifted off, and he unfolded a Santa Cruz newspaper he'd found beside him. He paged to the business section and idly surveyed the world prices of cacao, bananas, coffee, tin. Crime came next, with its lively schedule of murders and robberies resulting from the flood of fortune seekers and coca paste.

The soft ringing of the intercom interrupted the grandiose pronouncements of the editorials as the city of La Paz boiled up out of its gorge below him. Strange city of witches and skyscrapers, even the social order was upside down: Holt's wealthy friends lived at the bottom, in the greenery and the warmer oxygen-rich air. At the top, darkened by the biting sun and the frost, lived the peasants, who had migrated from the countryside to the twentieth century, building their own metropolis as a giant village, with tiny potato patches and the occasional llama chewing at the weeds. Men in business suits brushed past *cholitas* in petticoats and bowler hats. Along with them mixed the pure Indians from the remote villages, still in the hand-woven costumes that had changed little since the sixteenth century. They looked dazed, like mummy bundles that had revivified and found their way to the Witches' Market in La Paz to seek an explanation. Here in La Paz he'd found Doña Luisa, and made the leap from being a textile collector to one who bought and sold them for profit.

That had happened in the days when Bolivian textiles were sought only by a few foreign graduate students who had drifted to La Paz to write their theses. The good pieces could still be turned up and bought for a few dollars, making their way out of the country legally as "handicrafts." Holt himself was just starting out: manufacturing a few thousand sweaters in Uruguay, collecting textiles in the Andes while he waited for the production to be finished. The name Doña Luisa had drifted back to him several times over his three visits to Bolivia, recurring with the faint persistence of a raindrop: "Doña Luisa" amid a stream of conversation in Aymara, or, in reference to a particularly rare example that Holt was seeking, only "the Doña . . ." and then a mask of silence. One day he set out to find her, starting out at a store that sold confetti in the Witches' Market and bouncing from there to a disparate succession of dim little shops and storerooms, each one with some version of a Bolivian man or woman not knowing exactly where Doña Luisa was but nevertheless sending him along to someone who might know, *pues*. Two days later he ended up at the same confetti shop with the same man, who this time led him to an ancient back door on a quiet alley, turning the colonial iron latch that had rusted into the heavy wood planks. They passed up a flight of stairs and into the tiny apartment of Doña Luisa. The Doña had answered the door, the residue of a *cholita* whose tiny body inhabited her voluminous petticoats like the fragile skeleton of a bird within its plumage. Her iron-colored hair ushered out from beneath a blue bowler, seeming to continue in the gray cataracts that clouded her eyes. She bid him enter in a neutral, quavering voice, listening as he explained that he had come to see the museum. She sighed, pulling an old brass key out of a jar and shuffling over to a nine-foot-high door with an antique padlock on it.

Amid the smell of naphthalene and dust was heaped the largest single collection of antique Bolivian weavings that Holt had ever seen. For nearly a hundred years, since the day when her mother had left the altiplano to marry a rich merchant Indian in La Paz, the stock of weavings had been piling up in the room, brought by merchants and pilgrims, officials on village business and immigrants coming to start a new life in the city. All of them had heard about the crazy woman who, out of homesickness for her old life or some prescient appreciation of their true worth, bought the old and despised "Indian rags" for the suspect purpose of merely having them. Her daughter, instilled with the same respect, had continued to collect them. What she had now constituted the graveyard of a disappearing culture.

Over the centuries each village had developed its own style, an identity woven out of diamonds and stripes and symbols that had become obscure across the millennia. One pattern denoted a tribal shaman, another a woman in mourning, a festival garment, the dance of the quinoa harvest, the ceremony where the cloth was laid out under the sky as a table for the great Earth Mother to take her offerings of cane alcohol and coca leaves. Each one had been woven by a single woman as a statement of her skill and her love for her husband or child, each one a proclamation of the singular value of the tiny village they hailed from, recognizable to all: the village of Macha, the village of Pocoate, of Sica-Sica, of Tarabuco, Pampa Yampara, Tinkipaya, Patabamba, and a hundred others. Now the weavings had been abandoned, the evidence of people and rites that had been forgotten, many the last surviving example of their kind, or the one in the best condition. They were made of alpaca or vicuña or cotton, sometimes decorated with embroidery of imported silk. Among them were buried dozens of pre-Columbian pieces: hats, loincloths, burial shrouds and tunics, many with the telltale body burns and corpse smell that testified to their authenticity.

Holt looked for hours, then spent three days examining and cataloging, listening to Luisa's quavering provenances for each piece and going to bed each night with the whirl of vegetal-dyed colors filling his closed eyes. Doña Luisa had tried to sell them to the government for a museum, but the government had valued them less than the rats that had begun to eat holes in them, or the thieves who had found their way to the trove while she had been at the market and had knocked her down as they escaped with two sacks of the textiles.

They negotiated for four days, never with any certainty that any transaction would take place. Her son came as her agent, prodding her past the agonizing moments when she realized with full force that the sale of the textiles constituted the end of her life and the final subsidence of her mother's spirit. She wouldn't sell them! But no, Mama, the son pleaded, look at the rats and the robbers. At last she extracted a promise from Holt that they be preserved together in the United States, that far-off and vaguely imagined country of automobiles and mansions. Holt agreed to it, and to a price that far exceeded his own resources. Acutely aware that it could collapse at any time, Holt had called the one person he knew who would immediately wire him a large, unsecured loan without questions or demanding a percentage, who would do it based simply on the bond of friendship: Clayton Smith.

The success that followed would never be as crystalline or intense as that single amazing find. He had organized and curated shows at the Smithsonian and in Europe, followed by a coffee table book of photographs printed in New York. By the time he had sold off the majority of the collection two years later he had a reputation and a global array of contacts and clients, along with capital to expand his manufacturers' agent business. Somewhere along the way a strange thing had happened: he had become Jeffrey Holt.

They bumped down onto the runway and Holt strolled through the Transit area, looking idly at the alpaca sweaters in the handicrafts kiosks. He waited until the end to board, relieved to see that Andreas's seat remained empty. Maybe he was stopping in La Paz. He continued on to an empty row near the back, thinking he had it to himself until at the last minute a woman entered from the rear stairway and pushed an overnight bag into the luggage compartment. A smile of acknowledgment drifted across her face, then she put a purse on the seat between them and sat down. The agitated patterns of Bolivian textile set into her leather purse attracted Holt's eye. Charazani, with the unmistakable interlocking scrollwork they called "puma claw." Running along the six-inch length of scroll Holt noted a stripe of *lloque* that indicated that this fragment had been cut from what had been a very fine ceremonial piece. Holt felt a sliver of anguish at imagining the weaving that had been cut to shreds to make bags for tourists. He focused in on the band of *lloque*, stifling an impulse to pick up the purse and examine it with his loupe. A price tag still clung to the handle.

It looked incongruous beside the woman, whose tailored outfit made it seem that she'd just walked out of a department store. She had pulled her wavy black and gray hair elegantly to the sides, her angular Mediterranean face lightly dusted with expertly brushed-on colors that infused it with youth and health. She seemed in her early forties, wearing like perfume an experienced sensuality that took over the space between them, awakening in him an almost oppressive curiosity. He tried to think of a way to start a conversation, then finally gave up and made a show of opening up his airplane book and ignoring her. Holt hated this restless feeling. He would never admit that a certain phantasmal loneliness chased him around the world, like an implacable operative with a gray trench coat and a briefcase, maintaining a dead silence and a watery stare at all the empty hotel rooms and solitary restaurant meals. The Loneliness came and went as it pleased, it had no interest in antique textiles or in the profit margins afforded by overseas manufacturing. It was a hunter, a detective always closing in on the shameful recess of longing that Holt tried to cover up with his interests and distractions.

Once again the army of tray tables was marshaled into its upright and locked position. The engines heated up, the stewardess went through her pantomime of safety and oxygen masks with a dull smile, moving her arms like a marionette. He looked out the window as they threw the pavement away beneath them, then he looked down at the opening of a story by Borges: "*Sentí lo que sentimos...*" *I felt what we always feel when someone dies: the anxiety, already useless, that it would have cost us nothing to have been a little more good...* He closed it up. The woman had leaned back and shut her eyes, leaving Holt alone with his uneasiness about the Paracas weaving that had now drifted slightly out of his grasp. It mixed with the whole tone of the encounter with Andreas and the pestering recurrence in his thoughts of Clayton and Alejandro. Stupid flight!

The woman had come awake now, was flitting through the airline magazine.

He spoke to her in Spanish: "*Tu bolsa está muy bonita. Tiene una historia muy interesante.*"

Turning her head without losing her place in the magazine: "I'm sorry, I don't speak Spanish."

"Oh! I'm sorry! I assumed you were Argentine." Holt hadn't

spoken English in several weeks, so his transparent attempts to strike up an acquaintance felt doubly awkward. "I was commenting that your bag has a very interesting history."

"It does?"

He tried not to sound pedantic. "That piece of fabric is from Charazani. It's Callawaya. They're a rather unusual tribe: they have a reputation as witches and healers. During the Inca Empire they were the court physicians. They even used primitive forms of penicillin."

She lifted her gaze from the bit of fabric. "I bought it at the airport. I needed something for my daughter at the last minute." Her features softened a little bit. "Thank you. She'll enjoy that story."

"Do you mind if I look at it?" He checked the *lloque* and held it up close to her. "Do you see that black stripe? It's the exact same color as the field behind it, but you can still see it." She looked at his finger and assented. "You can see it because it's spun backward. That's called *lloque*"—giving it his best glottal stop Quechua pronunciation. "It has the power to repel evil spirits. At least . . . evil Bolivian spirits."

She looked up from the cloth at him, amused for the first time. "Do you work for a museum?" Her accent sounded East Coast, suburban.

"No. I do a small business with antique textiles."

"You're kidding!" It sparked a long conversation. Stephanie Campana worked as an interior decorator on Long Island, so she shared Holt's interest in antique textiles, although principally, and here Holt cringed, as "accent pieces." When the cart came by she took a red wine. "Why don't you join me?" Then, handing him a plastic cup with wine in it, "Where are you going?"

"Today? Hong Kong."

"I think Hong Kong is the most *wonderful* city. What are you doing there?"

Holt didn't want to go into the funeral episode again, especially after it had turned so ugly with Andreas. "I live there."

"Oh!"

"At least, as much as I live anywhere." He told her about his business as a manufacturer's agent, his "little empire" dispersed among the continents and his plans to consolidate it.

She asked him what kinds of textiles he liked, and he began his litany, even though he knew she wouldn't understand it. "Chinese textiles, particularly early Qing embroideries. Bolivian: the more austere the better . . . "

"I like kilims."

"Kilims are certainly beautiful. I prefer them to pile rugs myself. Pre-Columbian textiles are an endless source of fascination."

"Are those the ones from graves?"

"They are."

"Is that . . . well, legal?"

Holt lowered his eyelids as he smiled, playing the smuggler. "Perhaps it's not *entirely* legal. Archaeologists have their own ideas about how those things should be managed." He pushed off his suede wing tips under the seat, letting his feet breath. "I'll tell you something: when you see a truly magnificent piece, a masterwork by a master weaver of fifteen or twenty centuries ago, when you're holding it in your hands, the rest . . . It doesn't matter. That kind of piece is a country unto itself. It has its own laws. Especially"—he didn't want to say it, but it was too good a story—"if that country is called Paracas."

She suddenly grimaced and waved her hand in the air at cigarette smoke from the seat behind them. "I'm sorry. You were saying? About Paracas: what do you mean?"

"Paracas are one of the rarest of all pre-Columbian textiles. Extremely old, extremely beautiful. Extremely strange. They're one of the great enigmas of the textile world." He had hooked her now, in the only way that he knew how. Without knowing it, he had embarked on his sales pitch for that piece.

"What do you mean? How are they strange?"

"Paracas material is about twenty-two-hundred years old. It dates from a very specific time period. The Paracas style appeared suddenly on the historical horizon, with extremely sophisticated weaving and dyeing techniques, and then they were gone. And the strange thing about them is that nobody really knows where they came from. They've found the cemeteries." He described the eerie terrain of the Paracas Peninsula, the character of the land and the methods of finding tombs. "But they've never found the people who produced them. No cities or trade centers. Just some very simple shacks. Nothing but pottery."

"Just pottery?"

"Just pottery."

"But with similar designs as the weavings."

"Yes."

Stephanie kept staring at him with the same expression of puzzlement, then, "What do they look like?"

Holt tried to explain about the colors and the embroidery, then shrugged. "You really must see it. How often do you get to Hong Kong? Next time you're there, call me and I'll show you one."

"You have one?"

"I do."

Stephanie stared at him, then spoke again in a low voice. "How did you get it?"

"I bought it in Peru." He described the corpse smell and the conversation with the *huaqeros*, then the moment when they had brought in the Paracas manta.

"Well, how did you"—she lowered her voice again—"how did you get it out?"

He told her the various ways that people transported textiles, speaking in general terms: big lots could be shipped out with sweaters or handicrafts, as long as the right official had been tipped. One could secure smaller pieces inside one's pant leg. Another favorite was to open the lining of a windbreaker and sew the piece into it, then sew the lining back and wear it through Customs. He didn't mention his carry-on bag. "The risk isn't actually so great. It isn't like drugs. The only place you might get into any real trouble is the country of origin. For example, you wouldn't want to get caught with an ancient Chinese piece in China, or a pre-Columbian piece in Peru. Anywhere else they would tell you what a bad person you are and confiscate it." He drained the last of his wine, then dismissed the officials with a tone that bordered on loathing. "They have no idea what they're looking at anyway."

"Interesting." She waved her hand at the smoke again, this time more violently. "I'm sorry. Tobacco smoke really bothers me."

"Maybe we could ask the person to stop."

"I should probably just move to a different seat."

"Don't be silly." He looked to his right, where an older man was sleeping. He smiled at her. "Hold on." He stood up in the aisle and turned to the row in back of him.

"Andreas!"

Sitting in the middle seat, directly behind where Holt and Stephanie had bent their heads to converse about textiles, the blond man looked up, raising his eyebrows as if surprised. Holt felt his head snap back very slightly as Andreas greeted him in English. "*Señor* Holt! I did not realize it is you! Is there a problem with my smoking?" The perfect English, the needle-sharp approximation of a smile beneath the intimate eyes. "*Señor* Holt . . . "

"Andreas." It came out weakly. "My friend has problems with . . . "

"Of course, the cigarette!" He stubbed it out in the ashtray, then waved his hands in the air, saying like an order: "Continue. Please, continue."

"Do you two know each other?" Stephanie asked.

The Peruvian's explanation seemed woven out of magnanimousness and refinement. "What happens is that Mr. Holt and I are on the same voyage. We met in Uruguay this morning." He stood up in the aisle, looking past Holt to the woman. "My name is Andreas Otero Benavides."

Her hand extended elegantly from the cuff of her jacket. "Stephanie Campana."

Andreas took her hand in his upturned palm, bending into a slight bow. "*Encantado*"—Holt saw him look down at the gold band on her hand, something he hadn't noticed—"*Mrs.* Campana." He turned to Holt, as if expecting him to say something, but it only gave rise to an unwieldy quiet. Holt had been trying the past few seconds to properly place his hands: first on the seat back, then in his pockets, then again leaning on the seat back.

Stephanie thrust her words into the gap. "Are you going to Hong Kong also, Andreas?"

"No, *Señora* Campana. My home is in Lima."

"Oh! And what kind of work do you do there?"

Andreas answered with a trace of sadness, intent on the woman's face. "Lamentably, I work in a field that is much depreciated now."

"That's too bad. May I ask what you do?"

"I work for the government."

Her receptive expression remained as she waited for further explanation, then she said, "Oh! Well! Everyone likes to criticize the government, no matter what country you live in."

"Yes, *Señora*. Exactly. The government is only ourselves made big. We do not like the necessity of controlling ourselves, so of course we do not like the necessity of the government controlling us, even though we need it."

She nodded her head. "I never thought of it like that."

Andreas no longer smiled as he turned to Holt, his face only twelve inches away in the constricted interior of the cabin. "And what do you think, Mr. Holt?"

Holt deflected his gaze to the porthole, where the blue ocean had come into sight. Stephanie stared at him as he replied with an exhausted non sequitur: "There is no perfect virtue, Andreas. Not in a government nor in an individual. There is no perfect virtue."

The pinging came over the intercom: *"Damas y Caballeros,"* then in heavily accented English, "We are beginning our descent to Jorge Chavez International Airport in Lima, Peru." They took their respective seats again, but the conversation with Stephanie didn't resume. They exchanged comments uncomfortably, then settled in to wait. Holt turned over a thousand possible lies in his mind, proffered bribes. Was the transit lounge considered International ground or Peruvian? After all, one didn't pass through Immigration. That fellow at the embassy . . . it was Newman . . . No, it was Newlin . . . What can Andreas do anyway: he's just a civil servant. A miserable little bureaucrat! Besides, he didn't speak English well enough to understand what he'd been saying: it was always easier to converse than eavesdrop. No, I don't need a Customs form, thank you: I'm in transit. That's it! He should have said it louder, so that Andreas would hear it: I'm only in transit. *Tránsito, tránsito, tránsito!*

Without it seeming to happen, they had landed and were taxiing past the military air base that adjoined Jorge Chavez. Camouflage-painted transport planes and bombers stood out against the cement landscape. When they stood up to go Andreas took his bag down from the rack and ignited a warm smile. "A great pleasure to meet you, Mrs. Campana." He turned to Holt and put his hand on his shoulder, his bared teeth only inches away. "*Nos vemos*, Señor Holt." *We'll see each other.* The most casual good-bye, but had he given a slight nod as he said it?

"Of course, Andreas. It's been a great pleasure."

He last spotted Andreas with the crowd heading toward Immigration as the airport people shepherded him to the transit lounge. He turned to Stephanie, who walked a few steps behind him. "I'll tell you an interesting story about that fellow on the next leg. We're going to need some entertainment: There's always a delay in Guayaquil."

They were changing from Lloyd to Aero Peru, and for security reasons all the transit passengers had to claim their bags again. Holt took advantage of the good fortune to tear off the claim check, converting it once more to carry-on. By the time he and Stephanie had settled in the transit area he had begun to calm down enough to lament the fact that she was already married. He wondered why she hadn't mentioned it. Maybe she was in the middle of a divorce. "Jeffrey, could you watch my bags for just a minute?"

He watched her go toward the ladies' room, then gazed around the lobby for a telephone. Perhaps he could call Villarino at home. He didn't see any. He was running through his itinerary again when he felt someone tap him on the shoulder.

"Jeffrey."

Holt's body went rigid for a moment, then he forced himself to stand up. "Andreas!" He tried to ignore the airport security guard next to them, forcing his expression into something he hoped would be appealing. "Are you continuing your trip?"

"No, amigo. I wanted to give you my address in Lima for when you return. We can take a Pisco Sour together."

"Please! Of course!"

Andreas gave him a handwritten piece of paper with his name and an address in Miraflores. "And do you have a card for me?"

Jeffrey began to search through his pockets, trying to look intent on finding the nonexistent card. "Unfortunately"—the head wagging embarrassment—"it appears that . . . I'm sorry but I believe that I was so hurried to leave that I left my cards in Montevideo. Let me write it for you." He found a piece of paper and printed out his name and Libertadores 153, handing it to Andreas with a sociable grin.

The compact man scanned the paper, looking up again with a hard face. "Before you told me Libertadores 174."

Holt's insides constricted but he warmed into a smile. He could feel the moisture bursting out along the sides of his ribs. "Andreas, it has been a long flight, but I'm sure that I didn't forget the address of my office. Libertadores 153. I'll call you when I return. We can go to dinner." Naming the two great seafood rivals of the ruling classes: "La Costa Verde or La Rosa Nautica: you choose."

Andreas turned to the man at his side. "Take his bag." To Holt again: "Give me your passport."

The policeman reached for his bag, but Holt held on to it.

"Andreas!"

Andreas spoke to the guard again. "Take it!"

He felt the bag ripped out of his hands, then Andreas's thin voice came toward him again. "Do you have something to hide, Señor Holt? I only asked to see your passport."

"I want to see some identification first."

"Let's not play, Señor Holt, unless you want to pass the next few days here enjoying hospitality that is not included in the tourism guides. Do you need the firm hand?" He softened his voice. "I only want to ask you a few questions, and then you can get back on your airplane and go to the funeral of your friend in Hong Kong. And of course, your very important business reunion. But hombre"—with a look of regret—"if you don't cooperate we can stay here very much time."

Holt surrendered his passport like an entry ticket, trying to measure which level of official hell he'd been admitted to. He hadn't even been able to tell Stephanie to call the embassy, and she might not think to do it on her own. Holt cursed himself. He was going to lose the textile, he was going to miss the funeral . . . all because he'd needed to impress a woman. A married woman. How pathetic! How stupid to want to attract her, how stupid to try to befriend Andreas in the first place, with that fake bond, the stupid false idea that somehow they had a bond because they both knew Lima, the stupid false idea that he had a bond with anyone, based on anything! Stupid Clayton, with his stupid suicide! He wasn't even supposed to be on this flight! And now, because of his own big mouth his entire future depended on the benevolence of a fascist! And in the middle of it all, escorted down the corridor amid the stares of other passengers thinking "drug trafficker" or "What did he do?" the head-shaking Clayton from out of nowhere, dead and laughing, assuring him in his German accent that Das ist der *fucking* hammer!

Holt knew they were headed for the Little Room, a locale he'd visited several times before in various countries. It could take on many identities; in Yunnan it had been a corner of the train station, in Argentina it had been a broom closet in the police station, where they'd taken him suddenly and absurdly to ask him what exactly he'd wanted to know about his missing friend that they hadn't told him already. The Little Room at the Lima airport shared the qualities of every other Little Room he'd been in: somewhere off to the side, out of the way, with only the bare furnishings necessary for stripping down the resistance of whoever's unlucky turn had come. A chair, a table . . . This one had a two-way mirror in the wall for observation. The fundamental sense of isolation and helplessness came on as soon as the door shut behind him, and in that respect the Little Room could have been anywhere.

Encounters with the law in Peru always took place in a series of descending circles, and each level down became more expensive and more dangerous. The time to buy your way out was at the site of the transgression, before it became official. At the station, the price went up, because papers had to be filed, charges falsified, and then appropriately resolved with seals, signatures, and fines. With the first night in jail, well, Señor, the solution was no longer so easy. One had already become a prisoner, assumed guilty until proven innocent, which meant lawyers had to be retained, judges placated, and if suddenly a kilo of cocaine was discovered in one's baggage . . . Holt could feel the corridor closing up behind him: the succession of doors, the commands to sit and to take off his shoes had already begun to assume the herky-jerky pace of a nightmare.

"Empty your pockets."

He emptied his pockets on to the desk as the guard began pulling his belongings from the carry-on bag. Holt saw him going through the clothing piece by piece, carefully running the seams through his fingers and feeling them, then unpacking the toiletries, emptying his can of shaving cream into the wastebasket. Andreas examined his passport, addressing him without looking up from it. "Where are you coming from?"

"Montevideo."

"Where are you going?"

He tried to be casual. In these situations it was always better to seem to offer more information than necessary, to try and keep imposing a veneer of normalcy on the situation and hope that it took hold. "I told you, Andreas: Hong Kong."

"Your passport shows that you came to Peru on January fourth and continued on to Montevideo on January ninth." The Peruvian looked up at him for the first time. "Why?"

"I was doing some business. Then I went down to Ica for a couple of days to relax."

"What business?"

"Clothing."

"With who?"

"Not with anyone specific. I was looking into cotton prices, then—"

"Whose prices?"

"Textiles Amazonas, then I went to Ica to relax for a few days."

"Why did you come here? Why didn't you send a fax and ask the price?"

"It was on the way and I wanted—"

"Who did you deal with at Amazonas?"

"I spoke with"—Holt waved his hand, as if it would pull the words out. He was faltering—"only with one of the clerks there. It was only to gather information."

"We talked about Amazonas before. You said it had been several years. Why didn't you mention that you had seen them on this visit?"

"Because I only talked with a clerk."

The guard picked up Holt's shoe and began to examine it. He produced a small sharpened bar and began to pry off the heel.

"What other things did you do in Lima?"

Holt considered it. "I had dinner with friends. I gambled at the casino. Unfortunately losing forty-six dollars." He smiled up his captor. "I had an ice cream at Four D's . . . "

Andreas suddenly broke character, becoming for a moment the friendly Limeño Holt had met on the plane. "Ah! My daughter is enchanted by Four D's."

Holt took it as a good sign. "There is no better coconut sherbet."

"Tell me about Ica. Where did you stay?"

The tone seemed slightly less hostile. With a short breath, "I stayed at the Mossone—"

"How did you get there?"

"I rented—"

"From who?"

"It was . . . a place in Miraflores, near the Cesar."

"Why did you go there?"

"As I said, I wanted to relax for a few—"

"You are telling me that a man like you, a man with an empire, such as you, would vacation in a country as humble as Peru?"

Some mysterious mechanism of self-preservation induced in Holt a wave of patriotism for Peru that made his words more convincing. "Peru is a very beautiful country, Andreas. I've vacationed here many times."

"Who did you talk to there?"

Holt thought of the *huaqeros*, then tried to shut them out of his mind. "I didn't talk with anyone. I was—"

"With no one? Not with some other traveler"—he raised his eyebrows—"or perhaps some little prostitute? Eh?" The guard had bent the covers of Holt's address book backward and was looking into the binding.

"No, Andreas. There was no prostitute." He decided to try a different gambit. "Look, Andreas, is this about Galtieri? We don't have the same politics. Fine. We disagree. I'm sorry if I offended you. Peru is a very different country from Argentina, with different necessities and different—"

"Galtieri created order, and order is good for business. As a businessman you have no right to criticize him."

"You're right, Andreas. He was trying to create a better climate . . . "

Andreas looked at his watch. "Already almost eight o'clock. I'm sorry about the delay, Jeffrey. You're flight leaves very soon and still I have so many things to ask you." He turned to the guard. "Give me the razor."

A feeling of unreality came over Holt as the guard took out an old-fashioned straight razor and handed it to Andreas. I'm innocent, Holt kept thinking. Even if I'm guilty, I'm profoundly, deeply innocent. Andreas opened the door and scanned the hallway, then came back in. He looked at Holt as if he'd never seen him before in his life. "Take off your clothes."

"I want to talk to Bill Newlin, at the American embassy."

"Take them off!" The guard had unholstered his pistol and was pointing it at Holt's groin. Wordlessly, Holt began to loosen his tie.

"The jacket first!"

He slipped out of the jacket, and Andreas felt it loosely with one hand, without looking away from Holt. "Feels like . . . silk and linen, no? Hmm . . ." He held it up in front of him and examined the label. "Ah . . . Made for Mister Jeffrey Holt by Richards of Hong Kong . . . How fine!" He shot Holt a nod of appreciation, then continued examining each article of clothing until Holt stood in his boxer shorts. Andreas appraised him. "Silk underwear. Very pretty." Andreas tapped the razor against his hand. "Take them off."

Holt slowly pulled off the boxer shorts, then stood with his thighs close together.

"Now you tell me, Jeffrey: do we need to make a cavity search?"

"For what?"

"Coconut sherbet! What else?" The guard laughed, and Andreas's face seemed to reflect a distant mirth. "*Muy mosca*, Señor Holt. I give you credit for your resistance. But I can assure you that this is only the first chapter of a very long and difficult book. Let me help you remember that you have already made your confession."

"To what?"

"On the airplane. To trafficking in textiles." He raised his voice to a shout, pointing the blade at Holt's eyes. "In the national patrimony of my country!"

The phony rage gave the situation an even weirder and more dangerous feeling. "Look, Andreas: it's embarrassing, but the truth is that I was trying to impress the woman. I wanted—"

"Shut up! All I want from you is answers. Do you think yourself so agile? Why did you come to Peru?"

"I told—"

"Enough!" He lifted the razor and waved it gently. "Now we continue on to chapter two." He glared at Holt, waiting for an answer Holt couldn't bring himself to give, then he picked up Holt's jacket. He held the razor to the lining and jerked it through the caramel-colored cloth. A quiet zipping sound followed the steel, then Andreas peered at it, grasped the two sides and ripped it open. He examined it with great calmness, as if he just carefully created something rather than destroyed it. He cut the sleeves open, then regarded the jacket with a puzzled grimace. He spoke to the policeman, who by now had revised the other clothing thoroughly. "Nothing?"

"Nothing."

Andreas nodded thoughtfully, then told the guard to go wait outside.

He put the razor down, sitting on the edge of the desk in front of the naked Holt. "Excuse me, Jeffrey. I'm afraid we have made a very serious mistake. If you like, I can get you an application to fill out for the replacement of your jacket. I'm very sorry."

"Don't worry about it, Andreas. It's not important . . . "

"But it's custom-made."

"It was an accident."

"That's true, it was. Anyone in my position, trying to do his work well . . . "

"Don't think any further, Andreas."

"I'm sorry. Here, take your underwear."

Holt dressed as Andreas handed each article of clothing to him. He managed to straighten out the nails in his shoes and get the heels to stay on, albeit crookedly. When he was all dressed Andreas began clumsily folding his clothing to put it back in the bag.

"It's fine, Andreas. I'll put it back."

"No, I'll do it. I think you can still make your flight. Let me . . ." He picked up one of Holt's pima cotton shirts. "*Carajo!* There's a thread hanging!" He shot Holt a look of alarm, picked up the razor again. "Don't worry, my grandfather was a tailor." He opened up the razor and bent to his task. "You know," he said as he concentrated on the shirt, "you must always care for that one thread, because when one is loose . . . the whole thing can"—with a sudden lurch he sliced past the shirt and buried it in Holt's black bag. The wedge of shining steel moved across it effortlessly, leaving in its wake a furrow of bright, bloody crimson. Andreas looked up at Holt and gave him what seemed to be his first genuine smile—"unravel."

He opened the bag and quickly slit open the seam that Holt had sewn the week before. In ten seconds he was pulling the weaving out. "Sit down, Señor Holt."

Holt obeyed. It would be useless to claim that the textile had been planted, or that he had bought it as a tourist curio and hadn't known its value. A sickening feeling overwhelmed him as Andreas unfolded it and held it up, a sorrow against which he had even less defense than the fear he'd felt five minutes before. The razor had rent the gorgeous field in a single long gash, through which Holt could see a fluorescent-lit sliver of the Little Room on the other side. The cloth sagged around the cut, the wound destroying forever the mystical integrity of the embroidered warriors and their miraculous defeat of time.

Andreas began his speech. "You are trafficking in pre-Columbian textiles. This is a violation of the Laws of National Patrimony of Peru and must be punished by a fine and the appropriate time served in prison, both to be determined by judicial proceedings of the government of the Republic of Peru—"

"Andreas . . . "

"Do you have anything you want to say before I call in the guard?"

"What is it, Andreas? What do you want?"

Andreas stopped speaking and waited for him to go on, which Holt took as an opening for an offer. "Andreas, I just want to get back on that airplane and get out of here and never come back."

"Of course you do, Jeffrey. Of course." Now he took on the tone of the philosophical Latin gentleman again, grand with comprehension: "But the inconvenient part is that you have broken the law. No . . . that's a lie." He grinned. "The inconvenient part is that you were caught." He took out a cigarette, once more snapping his lighter, stopping for a moment to consider the shiny cylinder. He seemed genuinely perplexed. "And such a moral man as you, Jeffrey. With your missing persons and your funerals. So ready to take the side of the poor and the oppressed. But you know the reality, Jeffrey? You and I, we eat at the same restaurants, we both like tango." Incredibly, Andreas recited the chorus of *Rouge:* "Aplicado con pincel, tu cariño y tu lealtad, una mentira más en tu burla del amor . . ." *Brushed on, your affection and your loyalty, another lie in your mockery of love . . .* Holt sat and listened to his captor's strange pronouncement. Andreas took a plastic bag from a drawer and buried the manta in it. Holt knew it would be repaired and sold, one more addition to the market. "You lose the textile, Jeffrey. You lacked discipline. But I'm giving you another opportunity. I don't know why. Perhaps . . . we all need to do something to feel that we are not so bad." He stood up and crossed the few steps to the door. He reached into his pocket and threw Holt's passport onto the desk. He held up both hands, palms upturned, like the statue of a saint, then spoke with a hint of laughter rounding out his voice.

"Go! Go to your friend's funeral! Go and unify your empire of cloth."

THE RESONANCE
OF ABSENT THINGS

It floated there as he'd been promised, like a sign marking the approach of a city he'd heard about his whole life but had never visited. The city was his name, ANDREW MANN, printed on a white placard among the mosaic of strangers in Hong Kong airport.

His eyes moved to the face above the sign. A Chinese face, like almost all the others, rounded from the man's slight plumpness, stylish gold-wire glasses matching the business suit and burgundy tie that continued below it. It seemed composed and patient, engaged in the abstract task of searching for a man at an airport. The face out of Clayton's letter—"after a tour of the Warring States with Chang." Jeffrey Holt, over the telephone: "Chang will be handling everything." When Andy had called him the accent had sounded vaguely British, locating the details of arrival swiftly and methodically, the same way it had extended welcome. Andy stopped and gazed at the man who had been slowly materializing for six years. He had almost reached the final step of making Chang real.

"You must be Louis."

He put his hand out. "I am. Louis Chang. And you are Mr. Mann."

Andy surveyed his person. "I think we can assume that."

"Is this your first time in Hong Kong, Andrew?"

"It is." Andy hesitated for a moment, then smiled at him. "To be honest with you, this is my first time in a foreign country."

The small man raised his eyebrows almost imperceptibly, then hurried to speak. "Don't worry. I have taken care of everything. You will be my guest. My wife has already prepared a room for you at our flat. Or, if you would be more comfortable at a hotel . . . "

"No, no... I'm looking forward to it. Clayton"—the name weighed things down for a moment—"uh, Clayton mentioned you many times in his letters, so it's great to finally meet you."

"And he often spoke about you."

It surprised Andy. His true relationship with Clayton still felt like a dubious artifact that he was trying to smuggle into Hong Kong. Chang led him to a line of people that fed steadily into a belt of arriving and departing taxis. He moved with the same careful economy with which he spoke, efficiently predicting the movements of the crowd so that no step seemed hasty or out of place. "The government has plans to build a new airport..." he narrated, but Andy couldn't help letting his mind wander to the unsettling fact that almost everyone around him was Chinese, dressed just like in America, but somehow it had become springtime, with the early morning sun reaching down and polishing everything into a dreamy skewed vision. Morning? No, the clock amazingly said half-past two in the afternoon, and he felt for the first time in his life the odd mixture of weariness and electric excitement that comes from dropping into another world. A brief supernatural feeling of power, then a wave of exhaustion, then simply the dumb sensation of taxis, people, asphalt, and time all painted together in runny watercolors. Chang's words mixing in: "You can recuperate a bit at my flat. We have four hours until the funeral."

The door of the cab opened by itself, as if an unseen attendant were ushering him in. He had come for a funeral, not a party, but he couldn't shake that gala feeling, or the sense that Clayton would be there himself, ready to pop out of the coffin like a showgirl out of a cake. The sound of the engine reaching upward toward the next gear change, and on its heels a recollection of riding in the car he and Clayton had bought together, a rusted-out Mustang hot rod that they'd kept running for less than a week before blowing out the engine. On the highway shoulder, Clayton looking over from the driver's seat after the spectacular explosion and smoking halt. "You know," he said, "I've always wanted to do that!"

Chang was tour guiding about the British and the Opium War, Hong Kong history that Andy put his mind to as they floated through the city on an elevated highway. They laced magically among clusters of identical apartment buildings that formed ranks and broke them again as the dispatcher spat out destinations in staticy Chinese. They slowed down amid a close welter of neon characters. "This is Kowloon," Chang said, whatever that meant, then they pushed into the exhaust-rich air of the subharbor tunnel. The taxi driver put a moistened handkerchief over his nose and mouth.

"What do you do for a living, Louis?"

"I work for a publishing company." He reached into his suit and extracted a business card: Cathay Press Ltd. Louis Chang, Acquisitions and Serial Rights, Manager. Unreadable Chinese symbols occupied the back of the card. "We are the largest publisher of English-language books in the Orient." His tone came out somewhere between a boast and feeling shameful about boasting. "These days we are acquiring many Western books and marketing them in China. I spend a lot of time on the Mainland."

"What's that like?"

Chang smiled. "Complicated."

"How is it complicated?"

Chang's voice carefully dissected the subject. "All business is complicated, but in most places one can assume that both parties are motivated by the desire for profit. In China, business is much more involved."

"You mean because they've been Communist so long they're not motivated by profit?"

"Quite the opposite. They all want profit. But the question is, who will make the profit? Will it be the trading company or the man you're negotiating with? Or his son-in-law? And where does the money go? To the Bank of China? Perhaps they want part of it in a foreign bank in Hong Kong under someone else's name. Perhaps they want a percentage in dollars. Cash." He put it in so smoothly that Andy didn't immediately understand his meaning. "So you see, sometimes they are not so interested in distributing a book according to the most efficient way, but rather in the way that best suits their other interests."

Andy had read enough magazines to make a reply. "Is that a holdover from the Communist system?"

"Partially. But it is also part of Chinese culture. All business depends on *guanxi.*"

"*Guanxi?*" He pronounced his first Chinese word, but even though he tried to imitate it exactly the syllables sounded different in an inexplicable way.

"Relations. Many times the priority is to help your family or to return a favor to a friend, not to do things most efficiently. And of course, the government is involved with everything on some level, so that adds yet another layer."

The wonder overtook Andy that he was driving through a tunnel under Hong Kong harbor talking business with this elegant Chinese man who'd picked him up at the airport. He felt as if he were reading one of Clayton's letters. He pulled his mind back: he should say something now. "You must be quite the tightrope walker."

"I beg your pardon?"

For the first time Andy sensed his own American accent, which sounded rough and cowboylike next to Chang's delicately proffered syllables. "You must be a good tightrope walker."

Chang's expression turned inward as he puzzled out the idiom, then broke into an embarrassed smile. "Oh, yes. Tight ropes. Like an acrobat."

"Yeah, in the circus."

"Yes, of course. I walk on many tight ropes." His lips rounded slightly. "Walking tight ropes . . . I'll have to remember that expression. Yes. It's a good skill to have in China."

"It's a good skill to have anywhere."

Chang's face rounded as he smiled, and he kept looking at him. "I am glad that you came, Andrew."

Andy could feel Chang's sincerity and that it came from a history far beyond the forty-five minutes they had spent together since the airport. A sadness came over him, and with it the desire to tell Chang exactly how odd he felt to be in Hong Kong on the strength of a connection so faint it barely felt real. "You know, Louis, I'm really having trouble figuring this out."

Chang's words came out carefully. "A suicide is always difficult to understand. I've known other people who committed suicide. It's always a surprise, and it's quite disturbing. We tell ourselves we know someone, and finally we find out that perhaps they had profound problems that they never told us about. We're a bit insulted, to speak honestly. In his last act, our friend insults us."

Andy recognized the truth of his words.

"But that is only part of what is so disturbing," Chang continued. "On the philosophical level, which is at the same time one of the most essential levels, it makes us question all our ideas about knowing a person, and about how well we know anyone. And after that, we have to start wondering about our ability to know anything. We construct a fabric out of the world, and this type of thing tears it to pieces." Chang seemed to come back to the cab and the immediate circumstances. "Perhaps I'm going a bit far."

"No, not at all."

"It's excessive to say that Clayton insults us. It's disloyal to his memory."

"I don't think he would say that, Louis. I think he'd agree with you."

They emerged from the tunnel into the city again, negotiating a knot of underpasses until they were at street level again, among a mix of small shops and large modern stores and hotels.

"I think it was very important to Clayton that you come. In his letter... the one that he left me... he urged me to contact you because he had something he wanted you to have. I told Jeffrey Holt to convince you."

"Clayton convinced me. He sent me a ticket."

"He sent you an airplane ticket?"

"Yes. You didn't know?"

"It's just that"—the Chinese man frowned and then turned to Andy with an awkward smile—"Clayton had no money."

Chang cut the bag of sour plums open with his shell-handled knife and plucked one out. Hmm... Not as sour as the brand he usually bought, but he could feel the sweet acid running in his mouth like an electric field. The hot ceramic cup brought the smell of jasmine to his face and he sipped it and sat back, staring down at the towers of Hong

Kong rising around him. He had arranged everything exactly as Clayton had requested; certainly the most exacting ghost would invite him to take a moment of peace before the funeral. Besides, Clayton's sort of supernatural was the mischievous Monkey King of the Beijing Opera: he'd orchestrated this tumult in the heavenly court, then departed on his journey to the West to retrieve the sacred sutras. Chang took out a packet of Double Happiness cigarettes and lit one up, watching its spirit curl toward the open window. The only people who couldn't appreciate the joke were Clayton's parents.

A shiver descended along with the image of the two annihilated people he'd retrieved at the airport yesterday. Destroyed by much more than the distance of the flight, they'd been excruciatingly appreciative of Chang's small hospitality, as if courtesy was the only thing left to hold on to. Clayton had seldom mentioned them, only that he'd left home after high school; Chang could barely imagine what inquisition their consciences were making into this matter, but it had sucked all expression out of their faces except for abject humility and shock. For reasons that Chang didn't speculate on they had not seen their son in many years, and now they were hoping someone could make him appear again, if only as a phantasm.

In the hotel coffee shop he had outlined for them the circumstances of their son's suicide. The mother questioned him in a calm voice while the father listened quietly. She appeared to be a businesslike woman. She'd begun with the funerary details, but they had dispensed with those in less than two minutes. The burnt-over silence, then the mother's faint query: who had found him? Silvia, he'd told them, but of course that necessitated the identification of Silvia as a friend of Clayton's for the past several years, one of the circle of friends. Clayton had invited her for breakfast the day before, and she had walked into the unlocked door. The letters had all been arranged. He'd been sitting on the couch. A half-full bottle of cognac had been next to the pills, and he'd spilled a glass of it on— "Okay, okay," the father had interrupted softly, raising his hand. "I'm sorry . . . ," and in the pause Chang thought of Silvia's phone call to Singapore, the stunning announcement of death and his inclusion into its bureaucracy: Clayton had named him to execute the preparations he'd made for his funeral. "I flew back to Hong Kong immediately, of course," he explained to the parents, and then he described how Clayton had already arranged for his own cremation and the reception at the London Gardens Hotel. Chang hesitated at the matter of the final messages Clayton had left in sealed envelopes, fearing the absence of one for them would wound them even more. He was relieved when Clayton's mother took out a canvas portfolio. "He sent us something. We got it three days ago. We don't know what it is. Could we show it to you?"

She extracted a red and white courier envelope. "We couldn't read it. It has this strange writing on it. It's not Chinese, and no one we asked knew what it was. It's a collage of some sort." She pulled it out of the oversize envelope and showed it to Chang, who recognized it immediately. Strange words twisted on the page as if they'd been confined there against their will, writhing upward like smoke, a rare dying language that Chang had seen only a few times in his life. "This is Mongolian." It seemed to be a page from a dictionary, because some of the words rang out in boldface, untranslatable explanations of incomprehensible terms. Bonded near the corner shone a piece of gold leaf, and Chang's eyes went immediately to the characters that Clayton had impressed into it. "This is Chinese." He looked at the old couple sadly for a moment as he braced himself to translate it for them. "It says 'I love you.'"

They'd gone back to the hotel room after that, their unanswerable questions for the moment unaskable. It was the father who had broken down, horribly, painfully, leaving the mother to lead him away with the final request to meet with him in a few days. Even now, looking back at it a day later, the sobbing old man disturbed Chang more than anything else. Of all Clayton's shortcomings, only this ultimate and irrevocable failure of filial piety remained, for Chang, unforgivable.

He heard Andy stirring in his room. He'd known that Clayton's friend wouldn't be able to sleep. Even with the body safely nestled in the sheets the mind kept on roving like a sentinel exiled to an outpost of its own time zone. Something scraped across the floor and Chang heard long slow inhalations, some sort of breathing exercise, from its sound. How strange to meet this Andrew after so many years of hearing about him from Clayton. Clayton had talked about him often, although usually more in a symbolic way than a descriptive one. Always with that American way of talking: "The guy's a rock, Chang. You know: warrior-monk type. Benevolent. Not a deserter. He could be a True King, if he ever got the chance." For Clayton everything was a symbol, even his friends, and it seemed like at the end it had become quite difficult to distinguish which part was more real, the person or what they represented. They had discussed those things many times: which had a higher form of reality, the physical presence of something or its idea.

Clayton materialized for a moment, at once excited and removed. "Okay, Chang, it's like this: you're sitting in a hotel room in Shanghai and you're writing a letter to someone in, say, the Kong." Hanging on a cigarette for a moment, then: "And while you're writing that letter, you're visualizing perfectly the person you're writing to. Right? You're seeing them at the Blue Heaven eating dim sum, maybe you're seeing yourself there too. Okay, now . . . What's more real at that moment: your hotel room, or the Kong?"

"My hotel room is more real. The other is just a thought."

"C'mon Chang. Don't tell me one of those philosophers you studied at Oxford didn't spend a few hundred pages dispensing with that bullshit. We both know the hotel room's just thought also." Affecting an English accent, like an indignant professor, "'Chang, Chang! Must I endlessly cover old ground with you?'" Confidently: "It's a bigger world, Chang. Whoever you're writing to still exists even though you can't see them, just like the dead exist even though you can't call them up on the telephone. You'll understand this after I'm dead."

In a queer moment of recognition, Clayton's demonstration overwhelmed Chang. But you're still dead, you fool, he thought. He could see Clayton shaking his head from side to side as he answered, teasing him like a small child. "And I see you're still talking to me, aren't you?" Slamming an imaginary gavel down: "Boom! Case closed. Bring on the next one!" The sound of the missing voice somehow became the cigarette smoke fleeing toward the rising towers outside. Clayton, Chang thought, did you have to go so far to win this argument?

Andy emerged from his room with a towel draped around his neck. "I couldn't sleep. I guess I'm . . . jet-lagged."

"Yes," Chang agreed, "I can never sleep also. Do you need anything for your bath?"

"No. I'm okay. Your wife is a gem, Louis. Uh . . . through here?"

Chang showed him to the bathroom and demonstrated the idiosyncrasies of the plumbing. When he returned to the window his meditational tobacco had given up its last rope of smoke. Soon it would be time for the funeral, and the strange giveaway that Clayton had arranged. His long letter had been explicit: he had left everything at his studio, among the piles of cardboard and garbage, neatly arranged so as to inconvenience his friends as little as possible. A rare consideration. He'd left Jeffrey Holt his collection of textiles, and to Chang his assortment of books in dead or dying languages: Tibetan, Mongolian, an astonishing Manchu manuscript that belonged in a museum. His parents would receive a packet of letters and journals, and the one piece of paper art that remained from the Tokyo days, when he'd still made things beautiful. Clayton had told him that he'd come across it in a private collection in Hong Kong and had to trade a rather unusual old silk sari for it. Silvia would receive a sealed envelope, as would Andrew.

As to his late artwork, Clayton had been clear that all of it should be destroyed. Perhaps that had been his most considerate act, since it relieved anyone of the obligation to keep a piece out of sentiment. Chang had seen it over the years, constructions of cardboard and baling wire, relentlessly ugly, as if beauty were a compromise. Silvia had offered to clean out the studio but had returned the key to Chang with that anguish inscribed in her South American features. It had been too much for her. Even having Mr. Liu there hadn't helped.

Mr. Liu . . . It was odd to see Mr. Liu turn up, but he had no choice but to be grateful to him. It seemed one always ended up being grateful to Mr. Liu. By chance he'd happened to be in Hong Kong when Clayton had died, and his *guanxi* had smoothed out the paperwork that could have delayed things for weeks. Clayton's timetable had been very specific, an odd footnote for a man who'd always joked that he'd be late for his own funeral. At least Mr. Liu had been able to save him that embarrassment.

Andrew came out of the bathroom in a T-shirt and navy blue dress pants. He was dressing for the funeral now. He stood by the window, feeling comfortable enough to say nothing. Chang noticed his body; muscular in a stocky way, tightly knit together but without the beauty of a bodybuilder or a professional athlete. Thick at the waist and the chest, vaguely bearlike, a common face and body with no trace of nobility or character. He seemed in his early thirties, a few gray hairs creeping in at the temples around a boyish-looking face and blue-gray eyes. He looked like someone who would be in the background of an American beer commercial, downing his favorite brand in front of a televised football match. Coming into Hong Kong with his cheap athletic bag that said CHICAGO BEARS, he struck one as a sort of respectful younger brother, well mannered in a simple way, and properly deferential.

He declined tea but he took a sour plum, saying after biting into it: "This *is* a sour plum, isn't it!" It took him a moment to absorb the new taste, then, "Louis . . . did you have any idea that Clayton was going to . . . uh . . . take his own life."

Chang sipped his tea as he considered his reply. "Looking back, one can see the inevitability of it, but we live in a continuum, and it is difficult to conceive of it changing." A period of silence came down, then Chang went on. "It went badly for him for a long time."

"What do you mean it went badly?"

"No money. No moving forward. He had no hopes, or else, the most outlandish sort of hopes. It was like that for so long that we all began to assume it was normal for him."

"I thought he was doing well for a while. With his art thing."

"He was quite successful in Tokyo, or so Jeffrey has told me. I met him only when he came to Hong Kong, about seven years ago, and by then that period of his life had ended."

"Couldn't he have done the same thing here?"

"He could have, but he didn't. He began to work with . . . garbage, really. No one here would buy artwork like that. I think he might have sold it in Tokyo, where he had a name, but he was a poor organizer. Sculptures must be carefully packed and contacts must be maintained. I believe he wanted Jeffrey to help him, but Jeffrey had already started traveling with his business."

Andy considered it, remembering the handmade envelopes and the pictures from Tokyo. Near the end, the incomprehensible explanation that he was "into process . . . " "Would it be possible for me to see his artwork?"

Chang looked up at him, weighing the backlog of tasks that awaited him at his office against his duty as Clayton's friend and executor. "Yes. It's possible. We can go to his studio tomorrow morning. Silvia was going to clean it out, but it appears . . . Well, I'll have to arrange it. As far as I know everything is still there."

"I'd like to go." Then, after a brief pause, "Hey, I have another question for you: Um . . . if I told you the Empire had been settled, what would that mean?"

"It would mean that you were a student of Mencius. As Clayton was." Chang saw that the explanation didn't register. "Mencius was a Chinese philosopher. Have you heard of Confucius? Mencius was his follower. He lived during the Warring States period, more than two thousand years ago. At that time China was divided into many small states. To settle the Empire was to bring them together and to rule them all justly. To do this, one had to be a True King, that is to say, benevolent and fair. To settle the Empire was the most glorious thing." Chang almost laughed. "Why did you think of that?"

The American looked away, out the window. "Oh . . . "

A buzzer erupted.

"That's Jeffrey," Chang said, and he pressed the entrance button without checking to see who it was. Chang went to the door and opened it, letting in the sound of footsteps that approached in a perfectly measured rhythm from below, scuffling slightly on the stony surface. He announced himself with a sigh, then materialized, a thin man in a white dress shirt and tweedy brown pants, carrying his funeral suit in a plastic dry cleaner's bag over his shoulder. Wisps of wavy blond hair cradled a growing forehead, and Andy guessed that his athletic days were behind him. At first Andy found it hard to match the Olympian personality on the telephone to the man in front of him, but the long angular face radiated a keenness that made up for his unprepossessing physical presence. Holt glanced quickly at Chang, then immediately scrutinized Andy, seeming to send his intelligence out as an abstract force that could silently gather information on its own and report back to him. He greeted Chang exhaustedly, then extended his hand toward Andy. "Jeffrey Holt."

"Hi. I'm Andy Mann. We met on the telephone."

Holt's eyebrows went up. "You made it," he said, his voice feline and cultured, like an actor's. "Outstanding! I'd given up on you!"

"I changed my mind at the last minute."

"That's wonderful! Is this your first time in Hong Kong?"

"Yes."

Chang broke in. "How was your flight from Montevideo?"

A tiny quake seemed to go through him at the question, then he answered with a businesslike neutrality. "Uneventful." To Andy: "You know; the milk run from South America: Montevideo, Buenos Aires, Santa Cruz, La Paz, Guayaquil, Panama City . . . I wouldn't waste your time recounting them all. Twenty-eight hours. I got in this morning."

The telephone rang and Chang went to get it.

"Clayton talked about you a lot in his letters. You've been living in Hong Kong quite a while, haven't you?"

"Yes. Some time. I was in Tokyo before that. That's where I met Clayton."

"I know. He told me about that."

A strange expression flew across Holt's face, one that seemed equal parts guilt and fear. It surprised Andy, and he backed away from it. "He told me you two were friends, I mean. I think he had a lot of respect for you, and a lot of affection."

"Clayton can't be replaced," Holt said rather abstractly. His glance fell across Andy's shoes. "Good god, man! Chang, bring us some brown shoe polish!" Back to Andy. "It's short notice for everyone." Holding up the glossy envelope that contained his suit. "That's why one should always cultivate a relationship with one's dry cleaner. God first, dry cleaner second. Or perhaps it's the other way around."

Chang came back into the room. "Clayton's parents say they can find the London Gardens on their own."

"What about Silvia?"

"I have not heard from her." He looked at his watch. "We should leave here in fifteen minutes. Jeffrey, do you mind dressing in Andy's room?"

He raised his eyebrows. "No, I suppose not. Not at all."

Chang pointed down at Andy's shoes before he turned to go out of the room. "Brown . . ."

"*Miracle Mets!*" Holt picked up the book that Andy had brought along to read on the airplane and leafed through the photograph section. "Baseball's last great shining moment, as I recall."

"You know the Mets?"

"By osmosis. My father is a big Mets fan."

"Mine too! I'm like you: I'm sort of a Mets fan by associat—"

"Outstanding! Met-dom has extended its domain even to the shores of Victoria Harbor." Holt took out his black dress pants and moved slightly behind the closet door. Andy could sense Holt's physical shyness as the faint sliding sound of cloth took over the room for a minute.

"So Jeffrey, . . . uh, Jeff . . ."

"Jeffrey."

"Thanks. Jeffrey . . . what is it you do for a living?"

"I'm what one would call a manufacturer's agent. I have a small company. When people want to produce something in the Orient or in South America, I make sure that it all gets done right and gets shipped out on time. I broker the occasional wool transaction. I dabble in textiles a bit. How about you? You're in construction aren't you?"

Andy faltered slightly, his role call of failures sagging like contraband that he wished he could hide from Clayton's sophisticated friends. "Yeah, my Dad and I run a small plumbing company. My father needs the help." He shrugged. "It's not the most exciting thing in the world but—"

"It's a living. I understand. You mentioned that you had three bids to do and an audit. How did you get away?"

"Well, I just left. I guess . . . We've all got our little routines based on what looks important from *here*." He held his palm up close to his eyes. "Then . . . boom! Something bigger puts them in perspective. It's only a couple of days. Also, when I got the ticket I couldn't turn him down."

Holt stopped dressing. "What do you mean?"

"He sent me a ticket. By courier. I think it was just before he . . . uh . . . "

"He killed himself, yes." Holt cocked his head, then added, "That was a bit macabre of him."

Andy responded to the flip tone without smiling. "Maybe he had reasons of his own for doing it."

Holt waited a moment before he went on. "It's just odd, that's all. If he bought it at the spur of the moment, which was probable, it must have cost him more than two thousand dollars. That's not pocket change for anyone, even less so Clayton. Lord knows he was down on his luck at the end." Holt stepped from behind the door, now buttoning a white dress shirt over his slight paunch. Andy noticed the initials *JH* monogrammed in maroon on the pocket. Holt lingered over the last button, as if lost in its pearly surface, then his hand flew up a few inches from his waist and fell back down, the first tentative gesture Andy had seen him make. He seemed to be talking to himself. "Well . . . I could have done more!" Looking up at Andy. "It's as you said: One gets into one's routine. You think people are more or less happy, that they're doing whatever it is they really want to do."

Andy instinctively tried to relieve the man's anguish. "Chang said that you helped Clayton a lot in Tokyo."

He sighed. "I did what I could. Nothing that you or any other friend wouldn't do."

"How'd you two meet, anyway?

"At the Tokyo airport, believe it or not. We'd both just arrived. We shared a taxi into town, stayed at the same guest house. This must have been, oh"—he laughed slightly—"a good thirteen years ago. We were both a lot younger." Holt seemed to remember something, and the trace of nostalgia that had come into his voice disappeared. "Yes. I did help him with his art career."

"What was that all about, anyway. I got the postcards but I never really got a firm grip on it. He was some sort of artist, wasn't—?"

"He was a sculptor, actually. He made things out of paper. You knew that already. Beautiful things. He was very talented, very original. He worked extremely hard for five years, a bit more perhaps. It was the 1980s and market forces were right. Even given his talent and everything else, it was something of a fluke. He ended up making a lot of money in a short time. He had one piece, a sort of massive gateway. He called it the *Gateway to the Ancient Garden*."

"What garden was he talking about?"

"I don't know. Chinese garden, garden of earthly delights. That was a long time ago. He sold it to a corporation for . . . a hundred, a hundred fifty thousand."

"Then he left?"

"Then he left."

"Why?"

Holt reached over and scratched his elbow as he considered it. "It's not completely clear. A woman situation. That sort of thing. Very cliché. I thought it was temporary, but—"

"Hello!" Chang walked in with the tin of brown polish and underhanded it to Andy. "Ten minutes, then we must go."

Holt continued after he left, wrapping a strip of gray and black stripes around his upturned collar. "You told me that the two of you grew up together in the States."

"Yeah. He lived a couple of streets away. We did a lot of things together; went through high school, chased girls, that sort of thing." Andy felt frustrated by his own petty summary of what had seemed at the time like audacious explorations of a rich, fresh world. "It's sort of hard—"

"I understand. We all have people we grew up with." Holt slipped on the black jacket, then surveyed the completed image in the mirror. He pulled his silvery tie a quarter inch to the side, then spoke without turning around. "Well then, I have to call Buenos Aires, so I'll leave you to dress in peace."

Something cloudy about Holt, about the relentless punctuality of his manner and the perfectly composed sentences. He was all presentation: the exact kind of person that Clayton would despise. Strangely, the most likable parts of him were the little gaps: the hiding behind the door and the little gesture of remorse that had slipped out.

Andy took a piece of tissue and began smearing the brown wax over scuff marks on his shoes. At least Holt had caught it before he made an ass of himself in front of all Clayton's friends. But this jacket! He stood in front of the mirror that a minute before had held Holt's elegant persona. He'd bought it for someone's wedding; now he could see his shoulders bulging out the sides. Wrinkled tie, top button that couldn't be coerced into its hole even with a near-lethal tightening of the collar . . . Great. I get to be Clayton's rube friend from America.

Entranced with the smell of varnish, the reception room of the London Gardens preserved the smug ghosts of a thousand colonial overlords drinking gin and tonics and complaining about the locals. Wrought wood enclosed the walls, imported from Britain in the days when style was still ponderous and organic, the best way to flaunt it. Now it had fallen out of sorts with the electric city that Hong Kong had become. Andy found it a strange place for Clayton to choose, but Chang had explained in the car that Clayton had noted in extreme detail the precise chain of events that were to be set off by his death.

The very few floral arrangements highlighted their own scarcity, some with English placards, others with white banners inscribed with Chinese characters. One particularly large and flamboyant one dominated the room: a waterfall of orchids and glossy blossoms so spectacular that Andy had trouble believing they were real. Andy approached it as Chang arranged the contents of two large boxes they had brought in with them. The inscription was in Chinese. Holt came up beside him.

"This one's pretty impressive."

Holt eyed it carefully, seeming to be thinking of something. "It certainly is."

"Who's it from?"

"This arrangement?" He pointed to each character. "'With great condolence: Liu Da Lung.'" Turning to Andy. "Liu Da Lung. Mr. Liu. He's from Shanghai. I think you would find him interesting. He's one of the new Chinese millionaires. He started in Shanghai selling leather, and he started to make some money at it, so he moved to Hong Kong and bought himself a Hong Kong passport, then he went back to Shanghai and started to invest in joint ventures there as a foreigner. He made some more money and he went to Bolivia and bought himself a passport there."

"How do you *buy* a passport?"

"Oh, you know . . . You invest a certain amount of money in the country, and they issue you citizenship. Chang here has a house in Vancouver."

"It's not necessary to divulge my secret life, Jeffrey," Chang said without turning around. "If we're going to begin discussing private arrangements I'm sure you yourself can provide a vast amount of subject matter."

"Thank you, Chang. I try so hard to make my life look more interesting than it really is. You must do this when there's an attractive single woman around."

"That's what friends are for, Jeffrey."

Holt looked at Andy and shrugged a smile over at him. He reached out and fingered the largest flower in the arrangement, a spiky red rosette with dangerous-looking teeth. "I didn't know Mr. Liu was such a great friend of Clayton's."

Chang answered him. "Silvia called him for help before I returned from Singapore. You should be nice to him. Without his *guanxi* I think Clayton would still be at the coroner's right now."

"Mr. Liu does have impressive *guanxi*."

"I think Silvia did the right thing."

"She always does," Holt answered him. "I'll have to thank him."

Chang orated wistfully without looking up from the box: "'A man who is out to make a name for himself will be able to give away a state of a thousand chariots, but reluctance would be written all over his face if he had to give away a basketful of rice and a bowlful of soup when no such purpose was served.'"

"Very naughty, Chang. But not completely inaccurate. Is that the Big *C*?"

"Not the Big *C*, Jeffrey. The Big *M*." Facing Andy: "Mencius," then returning to his task.

Andy timidly entered the conversation. "Jeffrey, how do you know Mr. Liu?"

"Mr. Liu and I have some business dealings. Leather jackets, that sort of thing. I've known him some time."

Chang had taken what looked to Andy like a coat from the box and was tacking it to the wall. Holt made for it as if drawn by a string. "Interesting." He leaned closer, lodging his eyes some eight inches from the surface of the fabric and scowling. He seemed to disappear into it. Andy watched with surprise. He didn't see what Holt was looking at. The piece was a jacket of stiff black material, waist length, shiny in a greasy-looking way. Blue and silver swallows swooped across the black fabric in a frenzy of wing beats, winding down the sleeves and across the chest in a chaotic flutter of embroidery. A border of blue geometric shapes in a thicker cloth fell diagonally across the chest and ran down the right side of the jacket, closed by buckles made of braided cord.

"Is that silk?" Andy asked him.

Holt answered dreamily, not breaking his gaze. "Silk . . . satin weave. Looks like . . ." He turned it over, finding a hole in the rough cotton lining to inspect the back side of the shell fabric. "No. It's a single-sided *duan*. That means satin. It appears to be . . . damn, I don't have my loupe. It appears to be"— now Andy also leaned close to the garment—"six over, one under. Nice embroidery, good even chain stitch. And over here"—he moved his face over to the border—"a decent-looking brocade, don't you think? Weft patterned, one two three four . . . no, there's a light blue: six-color weft-patterned brocade. Very nice."

"What is it?"

Holt looked at him for the first time, cheerfully explaining, "It's a Chinese opera costume. This is the kind of jacket that might be worn by a martial character, a *wu shu* practitioner. It's a stock character in Chinese Opera. This piece probably dates from, oh . . . late Qing, early Republic, by the looks of it."

"How can you tell how old it is?"

"Design, first of all. Then I look at how the fabric has aged. With familiarity one can make certain deductions from the quality of the work or the fading of the dyes, and then, some of it is just . . . feel. I could be wrong." Projecting his voice across the room: "Whose is this, Chang?'

"Clayton's"

"Wait a minute. What are you doing?" Holt stepped over to where

Chang had just erected another piece of clothing, this one a shining dress of nicotine-yellow satin. A poppy plant had been embroidered onto the front, its brown and gold blossoms reaching gracefully up from the bottom to the top, ending in a single delicate bud that bent over on its stalk so gracefully that Andy could imagine its weight, and even the feel of the tiny bristles had been embroidered in pale yellow. The collar, sleeves, and lower border of the dress had been stiffened with brocade, which was in turn broken by finely stitched volutes and piping. Even Andy, knowing nothing, could see the value of the piece. Holt stood two feet from it staring fixedly.

"This is part of Clayton's funeral preparations," Chang said. "He planned the details very carefully. He left me a diagram so that everything would be in place."

"What is it?" Andy asked Holt.

"It's called a *qi pao*. Early Republic. Teens or twenties." The words came out slowly, muttered in a curatorial undertone. He seemed distracted, but by something more than the beauty of the piece. "Very Shanghai, between the wars. Still a lot of Qing dynasty in it, that brocade . . . Lots of brocade."

"What do you mean?"

He faced Andy with what seemed initially like annoyance, but quickly settled into an abstracted little dissertation. "This is an adaptation of the Manchu dress. It became popular after the Qing fell. Manchu robes had wide borders here"—he motioned along the chest and the bottom hem—"and here. That's what this brocade is about. As the years went by this band got narrower. It finally developed into the kind of dresses you see restaurant hostesses wearing. What's this?" Holt reached into the box and unfolded something made of pearl-gray silk. He held it up, his puzzled and awestruck stare freezing into what seemed to Andy almost an expression of distaste, as if he had uncovered something atrociously out of place. The jacket was very short, barely reaching to the navel, although the arms were fully cut and appropriate to a man. Round medallions had been woven on in a darker, shark-skin gray, forming a pattern with a long-necked bird and two Chinese symbols.

"God . . . I've only seen one of these in my life." He shook his head, then glanced over to Chang, who watched him without comment. "It's a lute-shaped traveling jacket," he told Andy. "Qing dynasty. It's cut for riding, see? That's why it's so short. This could be a hundred? Two hundred years old?" He stepped back and looked at it, running his hand through his hair. "Expensive piece. Where did Clayton get this?"

Chang paused in what he was doing and looked at Holt. Andy couldn't tell if he heard something cold in his voice or if he simply lacked the Western intonations that would denote question or supposition. "I don't know, Jeffrey. I thought you would." Then he added, "This is yours now. He left these three pieces to you."

Chang took the garment from Holt and went back to setting things up. It was like a curtain that ended the act. Holt wavered speechlessly for a minute, looking at the textiles already hanging on the wall then went out of the room without a word. Andy busied himself setting up chairs and picking up bits of paper or string that had fallen out of the two cartons Chang had brought in. He came across a cardboard box out of place between two flower arrangements. Smudged and dented, it was the kind of box he might find in his father's warehouse filled with copper fittings. "I think housekeeping missed this, Louis." Inside was a heavy gray powder, speckled with what appeared at first to be bits of whitish wood. "It's . . . "

"I know."

Andy folded the corrugated flaps inside and put it back, wiping away with his palm the slight film of gray dust from the immaculate rosewood table.

He was out on the balcony staring down at Hong Kong when he heard Chang greet someone. A feminine voice answered, too softly for him to distinguish any words but arresting in its low moaning quality, as if it had been frozen into a deep and permanent grief. He followed it into the room like a fragrance, stopping at the edge of the room when he caught sight of the woman, thin and fragile in a black dress, who had just disengaged from hugging Chang. Her dark hair hung straight and glossy over her shoulders, framing an elegant jawline and large wet eyes caught between her dark brows and the verdigris crescents that Andy could discern beneath her makeup. As she spoke with Chang the traces of greeting and regret shifted indistinctly across her cheeks and mouth, interrupted by a minute stutter of surprise as she glanced over his shoulder at the textiles. She motioned to them, and Chang said something, then she took a deep breath and seemed on the verge of some greater emotion. Her eyes caught Andy's at that moment, and he looked away, embarrassed to have been watching her.

Chang motioned him over. "Andy, this is Silvia."

She glanced into Andy's face, then at the floor, and at him again with an expression of amusement that might have seemed polished if not for its uncertainty. "Andy. I'm glad to finally meet you." He reached out to shake her hand, but to his surprise she bent forward and kissed him lightly on the cheek. "Clayton told me a lot about you."

"Oh . . ." The impostor feeling came back, multiplied by what he thought must be an obvious lie. "He told me about you, too." Silvia . . . Clayton's postcards and letters fluttered past, revealing nothing distinct except her name in Clayton's eccentric handwriting. For some reason he'd expected her to be older; the flawless skin that rounded the fine small bones of her eyes put her in her midtwenties, conspicuously younger than Clayton's set of friends. She seemed to have a Mexican accent, but he'd never met anyone like her from Mexico before. Horribly, he thought he saw her look briefly at his unbuttoned collar.

He lurched into a conversation. She worked for Jeffrey Holt, she told him, and she came from South America—Montevideo, to be exact, the place Holt had called him from at three in the morning so long ago. Five years in Hong Kong had yielded her an efficiency apartment in Western and the ability to speak Mandarin, "But very badly!" Andy skipped quickly through his own uninteresting biography, and they discussed Clayton; how they knew him and how grand he had been. She kept peering at the old Chinese clothes as they talked, and finally they both ended up gazing at them when the conversation ran down. "You know," Andy said, "in death all of a sudden everything's, you know, symbolic. We live so carelessly, and then . . . you find a key chain and your heart breaks."

He'd said the wrong thing. Her eyes began to brew, and he could

S T U A R T   C O H E N

only watch and feel stupid in his tight suit. Holt came over and touched her arm, calming her with talk about a mutual acquaintance and an order that had been successfully completed.

Andy saw him look over her shoulder at a tall middle-aged Chinese man who had come into the room. He wore a black suit and a gray silk tie as glossy and smooth as if it were the surfacing back of an undersea creature. His finger was armored by a thick gold ring crusted with diamonds. Despite his perfect clothing, something crude clung to him. Andy could feel Holt sending his intelligence out again to interpret something. Other people began to drift in, some Chinese, most foreigners. Three men came in wearing blue jeans and button-down shirts, an uninspired stab at dressing up. One had a beard and an earring, the others had the unhealthy look of night owls. They talked softly in an accent Andy identified as English. "Here comes the filth," Holt muttered in Andy's ear.

"They don't seem so bad."

"FILTH. It's an acronym: Failed In London, Try Hong Kong."

"Clayton had a lot of friends," Silvia clarified. "Not all of them were the most healthy people."

"Andy?"

He turned to face an older woman who seemed vaguely familiar. "It's me. Elaine Smith. Clayton's mother."

He recognized her then, beneath the startling cosmetics that age had applied to her face. Strange to see her sandy hair bleached white, and her skin pulled loose and wrinkled. The Clayton's mom who had served them spaghetti so long ago reappeared for a moment and then went away forever, leaving in her place this older woman who now could not resist reaching out and touching his cheek, as if he were a small boy.

"Andy. I'm so glad to see you."

"I'm glad to see you too, Mrs. Smith. And . . . Mr. Smith." Andy had to keep from blanching when he turned to Clayton's father. His handshake felt weak and palsied, accompanied by a greeting that came out in a whisper too slight to be heard. Andy remembered him taciturn and uncompromising, demanding that Clayton mow the lawn or clean up his room *this minute!* or appearing on Andy's porch to exact Clayton's immediate return. Now the lenses of his glasses magnified two blackened galaxies of exhaustion, and it seemed to Andy profoundly unfair that the years had levied such an overwhelming tax on him. "How's Florida?" he asked him emptily.

Mrs. Smith handled it gracefully, answering him as if it really mattered. "Lovely. We're in Boca, you know. We don't miss the Illinois weather one bit."

He explained, with a pride that surprised him, that he was working with his father now, and then instantly regretted the electrifying effect of pain it had on Mr. Smith.

"Your father is very fortunate," Clayton's mother said. "Very fortunate."

By now Holt and Silvia had drifted away, and they passed the next few seconds in agonizing silence. Clayton's mother took in a breath, then looked at him for a moment. The two of them were looking at him. At last she got her question out, her voice fragile and queerly innocent: "Andy, what happened?"

He struggled before the single question that, as their son's best friend for so many years, he should have been able to answer. The shame filled his chest and his throat. "I don't know, Mrs. Smith. I don't know."

Chang asked everyone to take their seats. Andy would have liked to sit by Silvia but instead placed himself next to Clayton's mother, thinking it might help them to have someone from home nearby in this room of strangers. The weird energy of misplaced death began to come on, coupled with the disjointed fatigue of the change in time zones.

"I thank everyone for coming," Chang began. "The first thing I should say is that Clayton cared very much for you all. He wanted all of you to be here, and he viewed this as his last opportunity to communicate with you. I think . . . I think we are all trying to understand Clayton's actions and his hopes, and I think each of us feels the burden of not trying hard enough to understand the things that troubled him so deeply." Chang went on with his speech about Clayton. The parents began to cry again, as did Silvia. She was interesting, Silvia. Talking to her was like swimming in a lake: all those warm spots and cool spots.

Chang began to go over his own relationship with Clayton, and to retell various anecdotes. Sitting in the chair, though, in the warm air and the sounds muffled by carpet, the exhaustion Andy had been ducking began to find him. He began to feel his mind sliding toward the details of the funeral: the strange old clothes and the odd unnameable tension that made everything feel a little bit out of tune. Objects and ideas began to glide away on their own tracks: Silvia and Holt toward their unknown destinations, the parents into their barely conceivable grief. All sliding in a roundabout of flowers and glowing silk, spirals of carved wood and hair styles . . . the leaden voice of Chang . . . "Clayton's life has stopped, like a watch, and with it the time in our lives that he measured." A few sobs floated up on a tang of varnish and flowers. Clayton, excited as they rolled through their neighborhood in a Rock Island Line boxcar. "Come on, Andyman, let's just stay on and see where it goes!" Finally jumping off together at sunset somewhere distant and mysterious. Darkened cows, an opalescent horizon: Iowa.

Andy felt his chin snapping down toward his chest, and he jerked it up again. Jesus, he was falling asleep at Clayton's funeral! How would that look to all these people? Andy once more got the strange intimation that Clayton was watching all this and laughing at them, or else grading his own production like a movie critic. Chang began to speak in Chinese, a weird touch that struck Andy with its outlandish sound. Clayton's eulogy, in Chinese. The marvel of it washed over him, then dissipated, and he swiveled his head around to stay awake. Holt's much despised FILTH seemed genuinely upset, their eyes glossed by tears that seemed present but invisible. The tall Chinese man listened intently to Chang, unreadable and out of place. At every glance Jeffrey Holt radiated a different emotion: a sharp anguish replaced by an even sharper anxiety, or staring at the clothing on the wall, a withdrawn calculating that manifested itself only in a slight tensing of his lower eyelids. Next to him Silvia's profile radiated its refined sadness in a way that seemed strangely effortless. Was she Jeffrey Holt's girlfriend?

He glanced sidelong at Clayton's parents. His mother shook softly, as if her chair were vibrating, while the father seemed to have collapsed inward to some remote island of numbness from which he watched the proceedings. Andy wasn't sure whether it would help, but he put his arm around Clayton's mother and squeezed her shoulders. At this she burst into a loud sobbing that drew the veiled gazes of everyone who could look without being obvious about it. It gave Andy a criminal feeling, but he couldn't let go now, so he bore with it, forgetting the false shame and falling himself near to the point of tears, mourning Clayton and his own unlived life at the same time, mourning the death that waited so steadily for his father's struggling business and his father himself, and would finally catch up with him, life lived or unlived, stupidly squandered. Whatever one could say about Clayton: he hadn't squandered his life on television and sporting events. He could hear Clayton lecturing him again. "It's all second-hand, Tiresias! You let those big corporations ram their bullshit stories into your head so they can get your money. Oh, and shall we play football this autumn afternoon? No, I've got a better idea! Let's *watch* football. Let's *watch* a bunch of strangers cripple themselves and get some fake emotion out of it! Yeah!" Clayton, in his face again. "I've got a plan, though, Andyman: Meet me in the Kong, then we'll head for Inner Mongolia. No roads, nothing. Wind and silence, Andyman. You'll finally be able to hear yourself think."

Without knowing it, he gave in to sleep, waking up only when he heard the shuffling of chairs as people stood up to leave. Clayton's mother acknowledged him with a wordless squeeze of his arm and then moved from the room with her head down, holding tightly to Mr. Smith. Andy saw Chang hurry after them. He shook his head and stood up, straying nervously among his new acquaintances until his uncertainty nailed him to a spot by the doorway. To his surprise, the tall Chinese man in the black suit placed himself before him. "My name is Liu Da Lung."

Andy felt the dry warmth of the palm in his. "Nice to meet you, Mr."—he wasn't sure which was the last name or if it was all one name. "Mr. Da Lung. It was, uh, nice of you to send those flowers."

Mr. Liu went on smiling at him. "Sorry. English very no good. My English . . . not good."

"The flowers"—pointing to the grandiose arrangement—"very beautiful."

He understood and nodded reverently. "Clayton . . . my . . . friend." They stood looking at each other, a stalemated agreement of amiability. The Chinese man reached inside his coat and pulled out a small gold box covered with red leather. Inside sat a thin nest of business cards, their words bent into the golden reflection inside the lid. He grasped one with both hands, bowing slightly as he presented it, the English letters facing Andy: Shanghai Textile Industrial Import Export Company, Liu Da Lung, Director. "You friend Clayton. You . . . me . . . "—pointing at Andy's chest, then at his own—"friends." He tapped Chang, who was passing and solicited his help in Chinese. Chang explained while the tall man beamed at him. "Mr. Liu says he is very happy to meet a friend of Clayton's from America. He liked Clayton very much. He says he must return to China tomorrow, but if you ever go to Shanghai, please call him and he will receive you there." Mr. Liu kept his grin focused on Andy as Chang finished, then shook hands again after Andy accepted his offer with the proper ceremoniousness. Still smiling, he held up his hand and accompanied the motion with a wistful cocking of the eyebrows. Regretfully, he had to go.

After a while only a small group remained.

Chang lifted a parcel of notebooks and letters, carefully tied with a silk sash, its orderly knot contrasting with the chaos of pages beneath it. "Mr. and Mrs. Smith. He wanted you to have these." Mrs. Smith took it from him. "And this . . ." He uncovered a large Lucite box, as tall as Andy's thigh. Andy had never seen one of Clayton's Tokyo paper sculptures before, although he remembered the pictures he'd been sent. This piece started as a sort of pyramid, but as it narrowed toward its point it began to lose its solidity. Its walls, which at their base had the texture of masonry, began to lose their substantiality, first changing from stone to a papery white, then disintegrating into pieces as thin and irregular as flakes of rust, held together by an unseen armature. The eye followed the shape to its top, which flared outward again, as if it would repeat the pyramid in reverse, but instead evaporated into nothing, as if the top half of the pyramid, invisible, extended out into the room. The fragility of it astonished

Andy. He had never imagined Clayton as a meticulous craftsman. The elderly couple accepted the object with a nod as Chang continued.

"Jeffrey, he left you those textiles, and also this." He extended a bronze-colored object toward him that Andy at first identified as a small kite, and then, as Holt stood up and closed his fingers on it, as an irregularly shaped envelope. It fastened at its center in a kaleidoscope of folds that Andy couldn't fathom. Neither could Holt, evidently: it seemed to spirit him out of the room to some address in the past, leaving his fingers absently worrying the unusual clasp as he looked down into his lap.

"Silvia, he left you this envelope." She reached for the small rectangle of cobalt blue, imparting a faint flutter to the thing as she took hold of it. Andy thought he could see flecks of silver embedded in it, like lapis lazuli, or the evening sky. She hid it away in her purse.

"Andrew. Clayton wanted you to have this." The packet slid into his hands with the sensation of crisp dry paper. It had a rough texture, like chips of wood laid on top of one another. It reminded him of a bowl of mints: pink and pastel green, with small flecks of gold pressed on. Not exceptionally heavy, but substantial. A bulge hinted at objects inside. In the corner of the envelope Clayton had scrawled the tiny letters: "Open in Private." When Andy looked up the others were staring at him. "I'll open it later," he said to Silvia's expectant gaze.

"I should add," Chang continued, "that he left me his collection of books in dead or dying languages, and a Manchu safe passage that dates from the conquest of the late Ming."

Andy examined his packet as he listened. Something small and rectangular, and something slightly larger that felt like paper, perhaps a half-inch thick. Definitely other papers inside.

"As to all the sculptures in his studio, he had this to say." Chang read from an ordinary piece of paper. "'They started as garbage and that's what they are. Take them into the street next Monday and let the sanitation department haul them off. Sorry about the inconvenience.'"

The last sentence's casual apology dropped into finality, certified by Chang's sudden relaxation. "That's all." They traded glances, then put together a collection of sighs. No one left their chair nor offered a fresh subject. At last Andy gathered the courage to speak. "Hey," he said, "anybody interested in grabbing some chow?"

Something deeply satisfying about opening an envelope with a sharp knife: the perfect edge it leaves always gets the contents off to a good start. After hours of waiting, Andy had finally escaped to the solitude of his room in Chang's apartment. He felt the blood rushing in his head the same way as when he'd opened Clayton's first envelope, the one he now realized had gained a day crossing the twenty-fourth time zone, just as he'd lost one coming to Hong Kong. He felt his stomach tightening as he drew the knife blade across the top crease.

The money attracted his attention first. Two thick stacks of Hong Kong dollars in denominations of a thousand. At a rate of seven to one each bill was worth over a hundred American. Andy didn't need to count it to know that it was a lot. He examined the bills, holding one up to the lamp to see the ghostly lion roaring in its watermark. It didn't say "In God We Trust" or "E Pluribus Unum," the promises of Unity and Faith, but only "The Hong Kong and Shanghai Banking Corporation Promises to pay to the bearer on demand at its Offices here ONE THOUSAND DOLLARS. By order of the Board of Directors." Only the every-man-for-himself inscription of "God and My Right" in French lent a classical touch to the red and green bank notes. He'd never seen a large amount of cash, let alone a large amount of foreign cash. Thumbing through the two piles of money he counted a hundred thousand dollars, Hong Kong, then did the arithmatic of currency exchange for the first time in his life. Fourteen thousand United States dollars. As Jeffrey Holt might point out, that wasn't pocket change.

He propped the envelope open and shook out a small plastic box held shut with a rubber band. A stack of Chinese business cards lay inside, still aromatic with the iron smell of ink. Rows of cryptic blue symbols had been set onto the little rectangle, punctuated by a few roman numbers that might have indicated a street address or a room number. Cheap printing on cheap stock. Turning it over, he saw the astonishing transcription:

INVISIBLE WORLD TRADING COMPANY
ANDY MANN, President

Andy stared at the paper, trying to understand it. At the bottom, in smaller print: "467 Dong Ting Street, Shanghai." He turned the card over again and stared at the impossible Chinese, then at his own name again, president of a sham company bequeathed to him by a dead man.

INVISIBLE WORLD TRADING COMPANY

He put it aside to check the other contents of the envelope. The East Sea Travel Agency appeared again, cloaking its offers in dark blue cardboard and the carbon paper grid of code numbers and destinations. The itinerary had been printed out on their letterhead and stapled to the ticket. Hong Kong–Shanghai. One way. It would leave in two days. Andy looked at the Chinese characters under the company name. One looked like a telephone, one looked like a fish: magic runes that would transport him to Shanghai if he chose to use them.

Clayton's letter still waited inside for him. It had been scribed on the back of a photocopy of a strange document Andy couldn't read, although he noted a large official-looking seal that had blurred badly. Clayton's writing seemed more chaotic than usual, and Andy wondered how far he'd been into the bottle of cognac when he'd written it.

DEAR ANDY,

If you're reading this now you must be in the Kong, or in Shanghai or some hotel room in the hotel universe. Maybe it's the first time you're reading this, maybe the twentieth. You choose the room.

Hope the little get-together turned out well. You know how hard it is to throw a good party: all that music and atmosphere to arrange. Last chance to make a good impression. I didn't want this one to be a bust.

Sorry about any inconvenience. I kept trying to find the best time to take off but it's hard to juggle everybody's schedule.

I can hear you, Andyman! You're thinking aloud again. What's it all about, Clayton! You drag my ass away from Super

Bowl Sunday all the way to the Kong, then you give me a pile of HKD's and a one-way ticket to Shanghai and meanwhile you know I'm scheduled to fly back to the States in two days.

Okay, sorry. The round-trip back to the States was only a trick. Knew you'd never come here on a one-way. Yes, true, kick my ass, Karate-man . . . I deserve all.

First off: don't say anything about this to anyone. Trust is a funny thing: its nature is that sometimes you get burned. Otherwise it's not trust, it's science, coercion. (Chang and I worked that out one night.) Actually, Chang is true, but tell him the minimum. He's too close to the others: and besides, I've dumped enough on him over the years. You're on your own. Be secret as space.

Explan: I have some stuff for you. Seeing as you're my oldest friend I wanted to give you something really spectacular. Unfortunately, for reasons you'll understand when you get it, I can't just give it to you. No chance to bring it back to the Kong. That's your job. It's up to you now to settle the Empire.

So you're going to China. Chang can get you a visa in two hours. Awesome travel agent guanxi. East Sea can do anything. Change the HKD's to USD's. Carry lots of cash: it speaks Chinese fluently. Bring a few travchecks just in case you do something really stupid.

I wanted to tell you something, something about the resonance of absent things. So I will. See you at the border of the Invisible World.

You're a True King. That's why I love you

Always,
Clayton

The signature ended with a wild flourish, its tail dropping off the edge of the page so surely that it seemed to continue into the room. That phrase again: settle the Empire. What the hell did that mean? Andy looked at the two neat piles of bank notes and the stack of business cards, then read the letter again. Typical Clayton: it gave all the interesting details but none of the essential ones. Now he wanted to send him to Shanghai with an address and a stack of fake business cards. Yes, I'm Andrew Mann, of Invisible World Trading Company. *What does your company do, Mr. Mann?* Hey, that's funny; I have no fucking idea!

Obviously, there would only be one way to find out. The implications of flying to Shanghai instead of back to the United States crowded into Andy's mind. He imagined his father again and the wincing encouragement he'd mumbled when Andy had told him he wanted to go to the funeral. He'd looked so old then.

He lay down and turned off the lights, but despite his dozing at the funeral and the dinner afterward, he found himself wide awake now. He tried doing his karate forms in his head, choosing two of the longest and most difficult ones and reviewing every motion, but he couldn't concentrate. The two mysteries kept spinning through his mind: the worldly one of how Clayton had gotten the money and the ephemeral one posed by the string of vague metaphysical phrases Clayton kept throwing at him like buckeyes. True King. Settle the Empire. See you at the border of the Invisible World.

He and Chang would have a lot to talk about in the morning.

"Like this," Chang was saying. He poured a bit of tea into his cup and washed his spoon and his chopsticks in it, then dumped it into a metal tray in front of them. "It's custom." Andy followed his example, then sat back and watched as his host selected dishes from the carts that passed by. At eight in the morning, the restaurant was roaring like a football stadium.

Andy made short work of the first few delicate offerings, then refilled his teacup. "Louis, where did you say Clayton's studio is?"

"Tsim Sha Tsui. We will have to cross over to Kowloon. It is about one hour from here, if we take the Star Ferry.

"You know, Louis," Andy began slowly, "Clayton gave away some very valuable textiles and things, didn't he? Uh . . . where do you think the money came from?"

Chang absorbed himself in cutting up a long noodle with his spoon and putting it into his mouth, then stabbed a soft steamed dumpling with the end of a chopstick. "You should try these. They are made of shrimp."

"Thank you." He tried another tack. "You know, Louis, I was talking to Jeffrey—"

"Yes, and Jeffrey was talking about money." Chang's interruption sounded almost testy, but his voice settled as he continued. "I'm not sure where he got it."

"Did he have a job?"

He answered him looking straight ahead. "No. Sometimes he would work as a bartender in some of the bars in Lan Kwai Fong, but not very often."

"What's Lan Kwai Fong?"

"I'm sorry. It's a nightclub area where many foreigners go.

"In the last few years Clayton spent more time there. I . . . I didn't like some of his friends. They drank quite a lot. I think some of them used drugs." He shook his head. Andy could see that it cost him to reveal more. "I didn't like it for Clayton. I didn't trust the things he was becoming involved in."

Considering the pattern and Chang's tremulous tone of voice, Andy knew what he wanted him to ask. "Was he selling drugs to earn money?"

Chang looked quickly around the table in case someone might be listening. "Perhaps. Perhaps he was. On a small level, I think possibly." He added in a metallic tone, "It was my fault. I should have found a way to stop him."

"We're all half-asleep, Louis. Like you said; it's a continuum. Every day flows into the next, and one day you're still flowing and somebody else isn't." He thought about the trip to California he'd never made, and the series of departures that followed. "You know, if you could have stopped him, he wouldn't have been Clayton."

They crossed the harbor on the Star Ferry, leaning on the railing and looking at the glorious crystal city of Hong Kong at its high-water mark. A tide of reckless ambition and commercial genius had built the city, a needle eye through which the copious wealth of Asia made its way to the West, winnowing out sapphires and emeralds and leaving them lying along the Fragrant Harbor from which it had taken its name. The towers climbed the steep green mountain like a crowd of onlookers at an amphitheater, peering into distant China to see what would happen next.

"Are you worried about the Chinese taking over?"

"Everyone is worried. Don't forget that many people came here to flee from the Chinese." He sighed. "We are just like coins being passed from one hand to the other." Chang talked about the Chinese idea of dynastic succession, where each dynasty came in strong and virtuous, then gradually decayed into weakness and corruption, finally falling to the next dynasty, which followed the same course. A virtuous dynasty had some sort of divine authority to rule. A dynasty that failed to follow the celestial order would lose it. "One could say that the British have lost the mandate of heaven. And soon, so will the Communists."

Andy only partially followed Chang's dissertation; his mind kept buzzing with the rush of the previous day and the fantastic sights in front of him. Extraordinary buildings loomed over the harbor, while below them a myriad of little boats scurried like water beetles among the slow mysterious hulks of giant freighters. Next he was following Chang through the lavender tunnels of the MTR station, the electronic ticket dispensers and the Babel of coins they requested. They got off and Chang led him through a maze of wrought iron that left them on the sidewalks. He looked into the stores as they hurried past: one sold nothing but dried fish fins, and next to it, a cubicle whose walls were covered with strange greasy disks that Chang identified for him as pressed duck. The facade of the next was festooned with clusters of skinny sausages, bright and red as firecrackers, then, two doors down an apothecary offered for sale a bundle of desiccated bats crucified on slivers of bamboo.

The little shops gave way to an overwhelming presence of giant trucks that clogged the narrow streets in a growling ritual of loading and unloading. The weather had turned colder that morning, and Chang flowed down the street in a long wool overcoat that incorporated the wind. His black-haired figure, so gracefully unlike anyone Andy had met, pulled him into a magazine life again. Passing through the street it all felt glamorous somehow, even though he knew it couldn't have been more prosaic to anyone else in Hong Kong. The simple act of being accompanied by Chang gave him a feeling of importance. And hadn't Mr. Liu, the millionaire, invited him to have lunch with him next time he came to Shanghai?

Chang directed them down a dead-end alley crowded with fire escapes and garbage cans. He turned toward a metal door and pushed a key into the grimy lock. Andy heard something scuffling in a corner of the dim stairwell. It put him on edge.

"Hong Kong has a rather severe rat problem."

They began to climb upward, large gray doors concealing the contents of each floor.

"Cheerful place."

The Chinese man's slight huffing rested faintly against the scraping of their feet on the tiled steps. "He rented this studio when he first arrived in Hong Kong. He always kept it, even when he had to borrow money to meet his expenses."

Andy didn't need to ask whom he'd borrowed the money from. When they came to the fifth floor Chang opened one of three doors and led him inside.

Andy remembered his childhood, when they'd cut up the gigantic cardboard crates that appliances arrived in and fitted them together. The maze of darkened spaces formed a second house within their own familiar house, and inside of them they would play the game of describing the landscape outside. It could be any landscape, filled with dinosaurs or candy trees. It looked like Clayton had been playing the same game. A sea of cartons offered up its turbulence of corners and edges, some cut cleanly with a razor, others folded, or ripped sloppily to reveal the bones of corrugation within. Newspapers collected in the spaces, crumpled and jittery, or stacked in unruly piles that had fallen over and dominoed across the floor. Against the walls leaned shattered freight pallets, scuffed gray or black by dirty sidewalks. Paint cans, a lopsided couch too weary to complain. They filled the room so completely that Andy had to follow an irregular network of narrow paths to move around.

At first the materials lurched together unrecognizably, but as he looked Andy began to make out individual pieces among the constructions. They came to his hip or they loomed over him like robots, saying "use no hooks" or "molded plastic flowers." Pictures from advertisements had been pasted on a few, their enticing photos bubbled with excess glue. One had been splattered with pale green paint, another with drips of red. He couldn't tell which were completed and which were still in "process," but the intentional ugliness forestalled any comment he might make. He thought of the piece Clayton had given to his parents, so finely crafted and delicate that it seemed like an optical illusion, then surveyed again the cartons rising from the floor around him. He walked over to one that seemed to be cut into a prism of some sort, with folds that in turn opened out into other prisms. Baling wire ran through a crudely cut hole and looped back, pulling itself into a rude knot. On a table, near a hot plate, a tiny sculpture had been made with a packet of Dubuffet cigarettes, the costly golden box cut and folded at the corners so that it looked like a hand, holding on its outstretched palm a piece of plastic burlap.

"I don't understand it either," Chang said across the room. He slouched on a counter, his black coat falling around him.

"They're, um"—it seemed inappropriate to say anything bad about a dead friend's sculptures—"interesting."

"They don't please the eye. He stopped trying to please the eye. Would you like some tea?" Chang put an aluminum pot on a hot plate and reached into the cupboard. "I never understood them. He would invite me here to show me something, and he would tell a beautiful story. This one, for example." He strode between the boxes and pointed to the one cut into prisms. "He told me about walking through Central, which is the part of Hong Kong where the biggest and most modern buildings are concentrated." And Chang could see Clayton again, pausing midway between pouring the tea to explain it: "Okay, Chang: Bank of China Building: right? Got it? China blows a zillion bucks to build their first building that says something other than Communism is Hell. Gorgeous building, symbol of the New China, all that shit. At the same time, some bureaucrat on floor forty-four is experiencing total despair in his cubicle; Capitalism is Hell, too. But down in the lobby, some young couple's meeting to go to a love hotel in Wanchai . . . and then there's some tourist doing the Star Ferry looking at it and thinking about those incredible skyscrapers. It's all that, all at once, and much more than that. That's the Invisible World, Chang. That's the real world. The building itself . . . The building is just a marker."

"And this," Chang explained as he gently touched the brown cardboard with the polished black toe of his shoe, "this was what he referred to. And I would stare at these pieces of cardboard and wire and I just never knew what to say to him at those times. I wanted to see it. But I couldn't see it. I heard his beautiful stories, but all I could see in front of me were packing boxes and wire."

"Hold on a second. You said something about, uh, an invisible world."

"Invisible World . . ." Chang let the words drift out across the jumble of cardboard as he rooted around in the cabinet. "What kind of tea do you prefer? Clayton has *bo lei*, a Yunnan red, jasmine . . . a rather excellent green."

"What's *bo lei*?"

"It's a very woody tea, a bit like mushrooms. Very strong."

"Let's have that."

Chang threw a palmful of the black shreds into the pot and continued. "You know that Clayton would go off on one concept or another. For example, he began to practice *tai chi chuan*, and gave himself completely to its study. Then he left it, and became quite knowledgeable about the Five Elements of Chinese philosophy and Chinese medicine. After that it was Taoism, and emptiness. Travel was his great metaphor for the Tao. At least, until he ran out of money."

Andy began to marvel at the unreconciled pieces of his memory falling into place here on the other side of the world, but Chang went on, pulling him back.

"When he ran out, he began to study Confucianism, especially the works of Mencius. I read classical Chinese at Oxford, so we had quite a lot to discuss. He had a rather unorthodox view of it. As one would expect."

"So, what was the Invisible World? Was it like, some kind of business thing?"

Chang laughed. "Business? Why do you think of business?"

"I don't know . . . "

"It was a metaphor, that's all. As I just explained." The Chinese man narrowed his eyes for a moment, then he reached into the cabinet and pulled down a coffee cup. Strangely, it was an intrinsically American coffee cup, grayish white, with two green pinstripes running around the top, the kind of cup that might be found at a truck stop. It looked out of place in Hong Kong, but Andy reasoned that they probably manufactured them here anyway. Chang pushed aside the piles of magazines and newspapers on the counter and placed the cup in the midst of them.

"When you look at this cup, what do you see?"

"Is this a trick question?"

Chang's lips turned up almost imperceptibly. "This is a trick object."

Something eerie about the cup. "Um . . . a green stripe."

Chang sailed into the story with a renewed energy: "Clayton told me once about something that happened to him at the Hong Kong airport." Clayton had returned from Paris that day, and after three months in the City of Light he was madly impassioned about an incident that had happened before he'd even left home. "I'm at the Kong port, right?" he'd said to Chang. "Crossroads of the world and everything mapped out on the big departure board: one flight's going to Moscow, one's going to Calcutta. Shanghai, Rome, New York, Port Moresby and you know, for most people, these places are just imaginary, you know? So what we're really looking at with that departure board is a map of an invisible world."

Chang, of course, letting him rant on, knowing that he was still setting up his story. "So I'm sitting in the cafeteria waiting to go to London, because, as you remember, that was the first available flight when I got to the airport, and I'm writing in my journal and then this old guy walks up to my table and asks if he can sit down. American guy, very regular-looking. Now, there's all sorts of empty tables around, but he comes up to mine. I say sure, and he sits down with his coffee.

"Now, I'm trying to finish this particular journal bit before my flight leaves and I'm trying to be disciplined. But meanwhile, I can't help thinking about this codger across from me. 'Who is this guy? What's he doing in the Kong? Maybe he's lonely and wants to talk.' I should say like, 'Old guy, what's the deal?' But I also want to finish what I'm doing.

"So as I'm debating this, he suddenly finishes his coffee, clunks it down on the table and walks away. No good-bye, no have-a-good-trip. Nothing. And I look over at his cup, and it's just . . . resonating. Resonating, with his stories that I'd never hear, the possibilities of who he was or where he might have been going. And the sense of all those things was just . . . so much stronger than the cup itself."

"He used the word *resonated*?"

"I remember that word clearly. Resonated, like the string of an instrument."

"A coffee cup?"

"Yes. More appropriately, if I could explain it for him, the empty space surrounding the coffee cup."

They were both staring at the cup that reigned over its place on the counter.

"Let me see that."

Chang handed it to him and he turned it over. On the bottom, in forest green, the words ASTORIA W. VA. had been printed into the ceramic.

"Is something the matter?"

He kept staring at the crudely stamped legend beneath the thin layer of glass. "He stole this from the Liberty Grill." He laughed, collecting momentarily the fragments of nights they had spent in front of cups like this one. He looked up. "It's a café in our hometown." Shaking his head. "That's a trip." He placed it on the counter, and Chang filled it with tea, handing it back to him. "*Bo lei.*"

They went back to tea and silence, breathing the cardboard air of the studio, Andy drinking the musty *bo lei* from the familiar cup.

"I can't answer for that other stuff, Louis. I'm not a philosopher. What I still don't get is, if he was out of money, why didn't he go back to making beautiful things again? That piece he gave his parents was gorgeous. He didn't have to end up"—waving his arm at the studio—"with this."

"I asked him that also."

Clayton at the noodle shop in Kowloon six months ago, looking down into his bowl. "That kind of beauty doesn't interest me anymore. It's superficial."

"People enjoy it, Clayton. It means something to them."

"Right. Some Tokyo executive sees a painting of a forest and he thinks it's beautiful, so he buys it and puts it on his wall and the next day he goes to work and arranges for a forest in Alaska to be cut down for pulp. He puts more value on a sculpture of a sunset than a real one. It's just cultural bullshit. Fake values, fake transcendence. It's boring."

"But people buy them."

Wincing slightly, then pointedly: "So what? People buy opium too. 'Art is the opiate of the intellectual.' You can quote me on that." Haughtily, his eyes hardening, as his voice becomes emphatic. "I'm working on something a lot bigger than that, Chang. And a lot more interesting. You're going to like it." Barely audible: "I'm settling the Empire."

Andy listened to Chang's relation of his friend's conversations. Holding the dark brown tea, Andy visualized Clayton drinking from the same cup. Not the gaunt, desperate Clayton, but the old one, from college. Chang went on. Clayton had compared himself to Gaugin for a while, but the years had worn the romantic exile myth down. He'd occasionally get a piece in a gallery, or in one of the collective shows of "new artists," whom Clayton ridiculed mercilessly as provincial and derivative. The last few years he'd tell people that he showed "around town" or "by appointment in my studio." When the sculptures would start piling up in his studio he'd take them down to the alley to be hauled away. "The last time," Chang went on, each word delicately grasped and manipulated like a peanut between two chopsticks. "Last week, before I went to Singapore. That was the last time that I saw him. It was like this; so full that we could barely move. And I asked him about it." Chang fell silent, his features made leaden by the remembrance. He took a fresh breath to continue. "And he said he was simply tired of carrying them downstairs, so tired of throwing them away. And he smiled a bit, as if he were embarrassed. And looking back"—the words strangely flat, trying to conform to an untranslatable inflection of grief—"I knew what he meant."

They both quieted. Andy wandered to the far end of the room, then spoke to Chang across the clutter.

"I just don't buy it. All the hocus-pocus in the world won't buy you a plane ticket. He had an apartment and a studio. He traveled all over China and he gave away some stuff that, if I'm not mistaken, was pretty valuable. Where'd the money come from?"

Chang had also left the mood behind and returned to his usual solicitous and careful tone. "I would explain that problem as follows: Clayton acquired most of those things when he still had money from Tokyo, and he probably bought them very cheaply, just by luck."

"But Jeffrey looked pretty surprised when he saw that old clothing. Wouldn't Clayton have shown them to him if he'd gotten them years ago?"

Chang demurred before he answered. "Jeffrey and Clayton weren't so very close in the last few years, to speak honestly." With a trace of irritation. "I think Jeffrey saw Clayton as a silly eccentric. And I think Clayton knew that."

Andy continued past the remark. "But he still went to China. You said at dinner that he'd been in and out of China several times in the past year. You said he'd been there a couple of months ago. He must have had some money."

"China is very inexpensive to travel in. Even with only several hundred dollars one can stay for a long time, if one wants to make the sacrifices."

"Yeah, but why is he borrowing money with one hand and buying me plane tickets with the other?"

Chang put his finger to his lips as he thought about it. "Perhaps he still had a small reserve left that he kept until the end."

Andy felt he was getting nowhere. Given the facts, Chang's logic was perfect. It was already noon, and the flight to Shanghai left that night. He had no visa and no clues. "Louis, I think I should tell you something; Clayton left me a pretty large sum of money. More than you could scrape together tending bar or selling a few joints." He saw Chang cringe at the mention of the drugs. It occurred to him that Chang would never ask him how much, so he volunteered it. "A hundred thousand dollars."

Chang didn't react. "Hong Kong?"

"Yeah. I told you because I can't understand where it came from, and I can't understand what he's up to. He also gave me a one-way ticket to Shanghai."

"Why?"

"I don't know."

"Didn't he leave a note?"

"Well, he did. He wants me to go."

Chang waited for Andy to finish, then, subtly, he stopped expecting an answer and fell silent in a deeper way, putting his hand to his chin. Andy sensed the man's intelligence calmly identifying every possibility for the elusive answer, then Chang returned his gaze and continued without the slightest trace of self-consciousness or theatricality: "'Only when the cold season comes is the point brought home that the pine and the cypress are the last to lose their leaves.'"

Andy considered it. "Is that the, uh, 'Big *M*?'"

"No, that is Confucius." He lifted his hand, wiping it across a field of words. "Don't tell me anything," he said. "This is between you and Clayton. But please remember one thing: Clayton named me as his executor. You can depend on me for any kind of help. Any kind."

Letting go an insubstantial thanks, Andy fell silent. Chang took up for him. "When does your flight leave for Shanghai?"

"Tonight."

"You will need a visa." Looking at his watch. "It is after twelve." Shaking his head. "It's impossible."

Andy's pained look sent him on another round of consideration. He squinted, speaking slowly and tentatively. "I'm thinking. I have a friend at the Chinese consulate. Perhaps he can help." He suddenly stood up, brisk and decisive. "Wait a moment while I telephone my friend."

Andy could feel it then, the sense of hidden things slowly coming together. People were talking to other people, calling in favors, treading on the network of friendship and history that extended from the studio to a hundred distant offices and rooms. Clayton's *guanxi* was starting to work.

THE WILD CARD

~

xcuse me!" Andy smiled apologetically and stepped to the side, directly onto someone's foot. "Oh, I'm sorry!" He backed up again, then felt something heavy bump into his leg. A man between the traces of a wooden coal cart loosed an annoyed complaint and jerked his heavy burden into motion again. Andy moved a few paces and then stopped amid the welter of lunch stands that surrounded him with their mighty black pans of bubbling oil and their braces of grilled sparrows. Bewildered and entranced by the Shanghai that had suddenly ignited all around him, Andy felt as if he were tumbling head over heels down the crowded side street. In an hour and a half he had managed to travel less than a hundred yards from his hotel. Not that he'd wasted the time. He had already navigated, rather masterly, in his opinion, the complex task of buying and eating a dumpling, and had analyzed the quality of the plumbing fixtures for sale in the Bei Gong Ceramic Factory No. 2 store. He had examined the rivets on the garbage cans and stared intently at a manhole lid and, in a triumph of deduction based on his study of a score of shop signs, he had puzzled out that a telephone character followed by a box with some lines around it meant "company." Actually, the situation was relatively under control.

"Dong Ting Street," he told the driver knowingly. He tried again, repeating it slowly, "Do-ong Ti-ing," then in a singsong, then with a laugh, then tentatively, emphatically, desperately until the mystified cabby, having failed to understand his pronunciation a dozen times running, reached out and took the card from his hand. He scrutinized the Chinese side, then turned it over to examine the English, motioning Andy into the cab. He seemed the Shanghai equivalent of the

Chicago hack: a youngish, slightly unhealthy-looking man in a short leather jacket and a woolen cap. After Andy shut the door the driver turned around to face him.

"Okay," he said, then: "Hello. How are you?"

"I'm fine. How are you?"

The driver burst into a large show of teeth. "Okay! Okay!" he said happily. He turned and inaugurated their journey with a long horn blast that made an old woman in front of the car jump six inches to the side. They commenced down the clogged little lane, passed on all sides by bicycles and pedestrians and the occasional overloaded hand-cart being tugged along by its agonized human ox. The cars attempted uselessly to assert their primacy with horns that shrieked loudly and constantly in the frustrated traffic. Andy sat back and relaxed into the belligerent clamor.

In this unexpected Shanghai he could almost believe that Clayton would be waiting for him there, at Dong Ting Street, finally ready to take the long trip together that they'd been talking about for so many years. He had no idea whether anyone would be there when he arrived. Maybe an entire staff waited for him, and an office with his name on the door. They would be surprised to see him when he walked in: the long-awaited boss they'd never met. Maybe there would be a young and pretty secretary. Ah, Mr. Mann. It's good to meet you at last. Two secretaries, and a middle-aged bookkeeper with his own small office. And what would they trade in? What did an Invisible World company trade in? "Yes, Mr. Mann, our boatload of rubber in Singapore is ready to depart for Germany. Could you authorize this document please?" "Mr. Mann," the secretary now, "the Japanese have accepted our price for the raw silk. I've drafted a reply for you to sign." Banquets at the best restaurants... "I'd like to propose a toast to Mr...." The name dissolved into the expectant look of his driver, who had pulled over and flicked the sign up on the meter. After a half hour of shortcuts and traffic jams, they had reached a small quiet street.

Andy began to reach into his pocket, then had another idea.

"Will you wait for me here?" he asked. The man stared at him blankly, so he pointed at himself—"I"—and the street—"go. You"—at the driver, then down at the ground—"wait." He emphasized each indication with raised eyebrows. They went through it twice and the driver replied, "Okay. Okay." Andy counted out half the fare and gave it to him. "Now wait! Please?"

A sensation of quiet resounded among the rows of low, tight row houses, a smoky calm lined with weary brick tenements. Mattresses splayed out over tables and chairs on the sidewalk, their ticking emerging from holes to greet the uncertain rays of the winter sun. He glanced back at the cab, then followed the ascending numbers, which had been inscribed on each building.

It wasn't there! He backtracked and examined every doorway and little shop, then proceeded again toward where it should be. Nothing! Two old men had halted their conversation to watch him bob in place on the sidewalk. He walked a bit farther to the end of the street and halted. He looked back toward the corner. Far away down the block, the cab was still waiting for him.

"Look" he said, pointing to the card's little chicken tracks as he leaned into the taxi's open window. "It's not there." The driver examined the card again, finally double-parked, and got out. Andy followed him toward the spot where his address had smoothly disappeared, relieved that the driver seemed as puzzled as he was. The driver squinted at the numbers on the building, then approached the old men who had now turned their attention completely to the new entertainment. The proffering of the card and a pointing in the direction of the missing office. Offering of cigarettes, circumspection, laughter.

The address turned out to be down an alley, actually the back entrance to an office building on the next street. The driver hesitated, unsure whether to go with Andy or not, so Andy motioned him onward. They passed through an unlit corridor to the lobby, a dismal gray chamber whose tinny fluorescent light implied an economy so miserly that it subtly diminished everything it fell on. The cab driver pressed the elevator button and after a minute he motioned toward the stairs. They climbed four flights through the grimy alley light of the stairwell, then emerged into a long hallway. Old-fashioned doors repeated themselves in a mosaic of dark wood and glazed translucent windows, numbered in the stolid typefaces of sixty years ago. The offices nearest the stairs had lights on inside, but they quickly gave way to unlit gray rectangles that looked vacant and dead. The two men paced slowly to the dimmest end of the corridor, then stopped. A business card covered the lower corner of the window, and Andy bent down to look at it. It was written in Chinese, but he recognized something about it and he pulled it off the door and turned it around.

INVISIBLE WORLD TRADING COMPANY
Clayton Smith, Director

An eerie sensation shivered through him. He still had the vague thought that inside the secretaries and the business deals were waiting for him, now maintaining a supernatural stillness. Or Clayton himself, with his feet propped up on a desk. The cold metal of the knob rotated a fraction of an inch in his hand and then stopped. The driver looked at him expectantly.

"This is my office," he started to explain, halted not only by the impossible language but by the ludicrousness of his story. "I'm supposed to come here to meet someone, or . . . to get something"—the driver listening with an amused smile, as if despite everything, he understood what Andy was saying. "I don't know!" Andy finally admitted. His companion nodded and tried the door himself. He bent down and looked in the keyhole, then lay flat on the ground and peeked through the crack below the door. The driver stood up again, shaking his head. Andy pointed to the name on his business card and then to himself, trying to make the man understand with a gesture the entire complex and unbelievable relationship between himself and the locked door in front of them.

The alternatives traded off in his head. He could try to find the superintendent and get him to open the door. "You see, I really do have a right." That would be an easy sell, especially with his extensive grasp of Chinese. He could come back the next day and see if his imaginary office staff had arrived, a possibility whose odds didn't encourage him. He could put a note under the door and wait for instructions. If Clayton really wanted him in that office he would have given him a key, wouldn't he? Unless, in his typical bozo style, he'd just forgotten.

The driver had made his own assessment of the situation. He looked at Andy and shrugged, then without further delay he bunched up his body and slammed his shoulder against the wooden door. The enormous wood-rattling bang rocketed down the corridor, and before Andy could stop him the man stepped back and threw himself at it again, making an even louder explosion than the first time.

"What the fuck are you doing!" Andy hurriedly pulled him into an alcove, afraid someone would come out of the offices to investigate. Far down the hallway an unseen door clicked open and, after ten long seconds, closed again. The driver laughed silently in an expression of glee that pulled Andy along with it. He raised his palm to hold the driver in place, then cautiously crept out in front of the door, sideways to it, gazing intently at the black metal plate beneath the knob. He swung his back leg around, cocking it as he went and driving it straight out like a battering ram. The door snapped with a tremendous wrenching of wood, bursting the lock works out of the jamb and flying open to smash against the inside wall. They rushed inside and closed the door behind them. "Okay! Okay!" the driver whispered approvingly, thumbs up for the surprise victory over the door.

Andy turned around to face the office. The scanty impression he'd gained as the door flew open bore out immediately. The office was a single vacant room, lit with one window that looked out on another building. The bare blue walls absorbed the tired afternoon light, answering each other without the interruption of furniture or decoration. Only a small wire wastebasket in the corner kept the room from being completely empty. Inside it a large sealed envelope had been deposited, a message dressed up like garbage. Plain manila, bearing the scribbled code ANDYMAN. He clenched it in his fist and made a quick search of the room, scouting around the heat pipes and the radiator. He knew he'd never be back. They heard a shout in the hallway, then voices. They gave each other a brief glance, then without another word the driver flung himself through the entryway. Andy leapt after him and they made for the stairway, running down it as the laughter burst out of them like bubbles from a diver. Flight after flight, jumping onto the landings and spinning around the twisting balustrade, their feet scraping and pounding through the old building.

Andy's palms blew open the back door with a hollow boom, then they were running down the alley and into the street, yelling their greetings at the two old men as they rushed past to the waiting taxi.

The driver launched them into motion like a pinball being put into play. Andy was craning in his seat to look for pursuers as they pulled away, he and the driver both panting from the run and shaking with the ridiculous pleasure of it. He hadn't done this since he and Clayton had beat it from the freight yard cops all that time ago. Schoolboy fugitives out of breath behind an oil tank. Andy laughed softly, then took one last reflexive glance back as they rounded the corner.

It took a minute before he felt calm enough to study the hidden contents of the envelope with his fingers. Something cushioned and something made of paper. Only the name ANDYMAN on the cover. He stopped before he opened it. Shanghai was soaring past all around them, its automobiles and storefronts only a waterfall of ideograms for something more elusive, something that could be hinted at in the envelope but never contained. He had entered a different Shanghai now, the one he'd seen when he'd read Clayton's letters and closed his eyes, the Shanghai that bordered on Inner Mongolia.

He held the envelope all the way back to his hotel room, and finally, when the moment had gone as far as it could before it changed into something else, he opened it.

There were so many hotel rooms and so many airports. So many taxis parading urbanscapes across their windshields. Explanations given to strangers, time zones borrowed and compressed; Holt, returning again after more visits than he could remember, found himself in a fugitive Shanghai. The night city formed and dissipated in a maze of places that kept seeming familiar, then melting away again in the smoky air. Dozing in the cab on the long ride in, opening his eyes to a giant slab of modern hotel, thinking, "I'm at the waterfront," but then, "No, that's Guangzhou, this is Beijing," then the blurt of a horn, lolling his head to catch the characters for "above sea" on a storefront and realizing finally that he was only dreaming of Shanghai, of a Shanghai of long ago, with Clayton sitting beside him checking on the cabdriver to watch out for detours. Clayton could fight a crooked cabdriver to the last *jiao*, and he knew all the insults. "Clayton, make sure he takes us to the right Yangtze Hotel. He'll try to take us to the faraway one, then claim we told him to."

He didn't know which hotel they had stopped at until the man in the snowy uniform opened his car door. Clayton had slipped out before him; the sodium vapor lights of the carport soaked the taxi in a bright dead luminescence that could only belong to the present.

Holt liked this place, the feeling of vast space framed by walls of carefully matched white marble. The music of a grand piano washed through the sea of polished stone, enveloping the little islands of pastry carts or potted palms, each one manned by a vaselike young Chinese woman in a slit skirt or a bellhop at attention in paper white. The concierge turned his lips up in a sign of respectful welcome, recognizing Holt from all the other times and greeting him by name. His slick black hair matched the smooth formality of his tuxedo. He spoke English with a French accent.

"Good evening, Mr. Holt." Looking at a computer screen. "We did not expect you until tomorrow."

They went through the motions of not having a room, a ritual Holt attended with the proper facade of worry and helplessness, then they offered him one of the better rooms at the same price. He thanked them profusely. It completed the latest of the long list of returned favors: Holt had brought in a shortwave radio for the concierge in the days before electronics had been available in Shanghai, enabling Voice of America to poison his mind. A little risk, a little cheap patriotism.

The bellhop ushered him out to the top floor and led him to his room, sliding a plastic rectangle into the electric lock. The suite impressed even Holt, who had tired of suites. The cream-colored carpet rolled from the foyer into a large sitting room with two armchairs and a couch clustered around a glass coffee table. A massive panel of glass formed the outer wall: Holt could walk up to it and see the void of the city thirty-four stories below his feet, only a few centimeters from his nose. A splendid tapestry hung over a beige writing table, drawing Holt toward its ropy textures of wool and silk as the bellhop brought his leather suitcases into the bedroom. The proper glassware for a dozen different cocktails waited at the bar, as well as a teapot and six kinds of loose tea leaves arranged in small ceramic canisters. A seventh canister emitted the aroma of ground espresso, a luxury that pleasantly surprised him. Silvia would like that; she never tired of complaining about the lack of good coffee in China, comparing with a pouty frown "this shit" with the spicy *café cortado* of her native Montevideo.

The bellhop opened the refrigerator to indicate the liquor and juices inside, then exited with the promise of ice. Holt moved into the bedroom, taking in approvingly the two king-size beds that sprawled over the giant space. The bathroom had been paneled in a vivid emerald marble that looked glossy enough to set in a ring, enunciated by ebony basins and a deep black whirlpool that at first glance seemed bottomless. Gold-plated faucets rang out against the stony gleam. Holt burst into a deep laugh, bouncing it off the marble and the black tub, filling himself with the ceramic reverberations. He lifted up his hands and laughed his way out of the room, chuckling over to his luggage and suddenly stopping, clutched inside by the unobtrusive little picture hanging near the corner, filling a space too small for a major artwork. Holt backed away from it, then moved closer.

A saffron-colored piece of paper hung suspended between the chrome arms. It didn't have the flatness of a regular page, rather, it had been woven of extremely fine shreds of paper, forming a damask of suggestive shapes. A dusky lilac space emerged from a frayed gap in the texture, implying a third dimension that extended inward from the frame. Holt suddenly felt the blood begin to rush in his ears, making physical the queerness that came on. He looked closely. No. A different name, one of the tens of millions of Li's in China. Not C. Smith. Not by a long shot. It didn't have Clayton's finish. Clayton's pieces had always had an immaculate finish that didn't match with anything else he did. A good piece, though. Nice to see that someone was imitating him. Certainly Clayton's colors, right down to the gold leaf under the lilac that lent it that peculiar iridescence. And that interlace . . . it was actually a little textile . . .

Again the memory of the Paracas weaving came roiling up, and he reviewed with vicious clarity the acquisition and stupefying damage of the irreplaceable manta. A Paracas manta! Turning it up had been an impossibility, and now because of some silly chitchat he had lost it forever; not only lost it, but seen it degraded by an idiot. He would never find anything like it again, except in his imagination, where he would find it often, real and unreal, like the elusive culture that had created it. It couldn't be replaced.

The door chime sounded and Holt received the bucket of ice, tipping the bellhop, then opening a tiny bottle of Scotch. He drank it next to the big window, his mind soaring out into the dark gulf studded by the burning bits of light. The grid of streets crossed and recrossed, permanently snarled by a traffic they had never been intended for. He counted six large buildings under construction in the half of the world he could see, a city booming into something it couldn't understand, if anyone ever could understand the future.

Shanghai. He still loved the place for what it had been sixty years ago, and he never stopped looking for that city: corrupt, filthy, volatile, alive with possibilities of shoddy death or blighted uneven romance. Like China itself, the city had been divided and prostrated by businessmen and warlords, at once humiliated and made glamorous by the exotic faces of foreigners. The Japanese had controlled one part, the French another, the British and Americans their own quarters, and around these magnets the effervescence of an entire world had agglomerated. East Indians, White Russians, Australians; adventurers and pretend adventurers of every stripe. Like Hong Kong's FILTH, but more troubled by war and the Great Depression, grabbing what they could before China finally stood up and shook itself free.

Holt fetched Clayton's letter from his suitcase. The envelope incorporated gold leaf into its surface, and suddenly a massive gilded wall rose up from the feathery rectangle. Clayton had made these envelopes for his opening at the Tokyo Biennial long ago. Holt hadn't known he still had them.

> Dear Jeff,
>
> What a mess: I've run out of things to say and I've just started. That's the problem with paper: it's never the right length. Like friendships.

Holt winced again at the first line, then he passed it up. Very untypical of Clayton to take the cheap shot, but there it was. A lot had happened.

> Hope you liked the textiles. I guess I had a few connections I never told you about. No biggie. It was the least I could do after all the help you gave me in Tokyo. Did I ever say thanks? Thanks. I liked the way you were then, before you got so exact.
>
> Sorry I disappointed you in Tokyo. Not just the mistake with Misiko, but the whole disappearing act. I never really was an artist. That was just something I was doing, and I got as far as I could go with it. Maybe it was a stupid call, but you know, "Shun looked upon casting aside the Empire as no more than discarding a worn shoe." (Big M, book VII, chapter 35)
>
> Of course, Shun had already settled it. Only a True King can pull that one off.
>
> Finally, everything ready for the trip to Inner Mongolia. I never told you why I went back three times. A lot of things we never discussed these past few years. I'm telling you now. I've spent my whole life trying to find a map of an invisible world, and at last I found it.
>
> You know which map. It's half yours. That was the deal. Zai jian, airport man. See you in the next hotel room.
>
> > Love,
> > Clayton

"See you in the next hotel room." The eerie part came back to him with the thought of the framed paper sculpture in the bedroom. Map of an invisible world . . . very Clayton. That old bitterness that went all the way back to Tokyo. The whole thing with Misiko. The big *M* was Mencius: Holt had borrowed a copy from Chang and found the passage Clayton had quoted. In 350 B.C. China, the master was discussing ethics with a disciple.

> T'ao Ying asked, "When Shun was Emperor and Kao Yao was the judge, if the Blind Man (Shun's father) killed a man, what was to be done?"

"The only thing to do was to apprehend him."

"In that case, would Shun not try to stop it?"

"How could Shun stop it? Kao Yao had his authority from which he received the law."

"Then what would Shun have done?"

"Shun looked upon casting aside the Empire as no more than discarding a worn shoe. He would have secretly carried the old man on his back and fled to the edge of the Sea and lived there happily, never giving a thought to the Empire."

He put the letter down and stared out the window again, then stood up and went to the telephone, dialing the Lu Song Yuan Hotel and asking to speak with Silvia Benedetti. More than anything else, he just wanted to hear her accent. He imagined the small room as the telephone's advisory buzz surged back to him. He waited eight rings, then hung up.

Holt retrieved his briefcase from the bedroom and took out his company stationery, considering his business. With much effort he'd finally gotten through to Villarino, shamelessly using the sympathy angle to explain why he would have to fly to China alone. Calls to Milan to reconfirm, likewise to Mr. Zhao. In five days they would meet. Meanwhile, he had to go to Beijing to line out production for an American company making cashmere overcoats whose shipping date was getting dangerously close. Some print patterns needed to be proofed prior to making ten thousand pairs of silk boxer shorts. Then, of course, there was Mr. Gao.

That would be considerably more interesting. Mr. Gao was his main collection point for textiles that came out of the Shanghai area. He also had collection points in Suzhou and Hangzhou composed of individuals who continually looked for antiques and borrowed them at the time when Holt would be coming. That way Holt could quickly choose which ones he wanted to buy without spending weeks combing through the hearsay and rumors that indicated the possibility of something. In the early days he would run from one house to another to find the single piece that a grandmother or great aunt had hidden away, usually turning up a disappointingly commonplace bit of clothing. Now Silvia bounced back and forth between Hong Kong and China, helping organize the details of clothing production and, at the same time, making sure the antique material appeared when and where it should.

The collection network functioned like an oil well drilled into the geology of China's past, pulling up fragments of centuries and dynasties that had been trapped below the surface. The prizes were intact garments in good condition, or else a hat or a furnishing of some sort. Usually these pieces had been made for rich commoners: the imperial textiles turned up in Beijing, except that they hardly ever turned up. The Qing dynasty had hung on until the early part of the century, so their textiles constituted most of what appeared. Besides late Qing and good twentieth-century pieces, very little existed. Cloth, like people, traveled poorly through time. It rarely made it through the phase of being old clothes, thrown out with other obsolete things. He imagined them wearing out on a succession of less dignified people as they were handed down the chain of wealth from lady to servant to tavern keeper's wife. Others disappeared in fires or were hopelessly stained during bad storage. Many fell to the periodic explosions of hatred toward wealth and privilege that the ignorant vented on beautiful things: the recent round of Occupation, Liberation, and Cultural Revolution had wiped out a wealth of "feudal" artifacts. Little survived, and of that which did, few pieces met the requirements of both fineness and perfect condition. Some days he would look at dozens of the old pieces, trying to decipher the clues in weave structure or design that would enable him to place them. Court garments, furniture coverings, common clothes: after that kind of day he would see silk as he went to sleep. The grain of it would appear close to his eyes, suffused with colors, as real and close as a veil, and in the few shifting minutes before he drifted off he could finally, effortlessly, possess it all.

That was the problem with his business; the most beautiful pieces were usually the most valuable, so it broke his heart either to sell them or to keep them. He had winnowed out the best ones for his apartment in Hong Kong so that he could look at them between trips. They sat rolled in his closet or in cedar trunks, protected from moths and from that greatest of enemies, light. Light destroyed all antique pieces, stealing away the color and vitality. That was the paradox of light; it made their beauty visible, and at the same time it started the chemical reactions among the fibers and the long-ago administered dyes that would destroy them. It made some colors darker, others it faded, and some it turned yellow or brown. Conservators had a word to describe the tendency of dyes to fade, a word that Holt found mystically appropriate: *fugitive*. A dye was said to be more or less fugitive. Some of the most fragile colors, the madder and the cochineal, pained him with their desire to flee, and it seemed to make them all the more beautiful to him. For this reason his apartment remained a poorly lit cave lined with a dark mosaic of geometrics or floral designs. Delicate gardens glimmered in the silk carpets on the floor, and on the walls the woven graphs of vanished societies cast their geometric statements into space. He kept them out of the sun though because it brought the time down on the heads of these survivors, who by dint of the darkness of a grave or an old chest had evaded the centuries. It left visitors with a sense that if they could only turn on more lights something miraculous would emerge.

The telephone rang. This would be Silvia, or the front desk inquiring about details of his credit card or check-out time. He answered in Chinese.

"*Wey.*"

"Uh . . ." The puzzlement of the other speaker came over the line for two noiseless seconds, then the American voice started up again. "Hello. Do you speak English?"

"I speak a little English," Holt answered.

"Jeffrey?"

"Yes. And this is . . . ?"

"Oh, sorry. This is Andy Mann. Louis . . . uh, told me you'd be staying here."

Clayton's friend had installed himself at a hotel whose name he couldn't pronounce. He tried to describe the local landmarks. "There's a bunch of food carts about a block away. . . . It's near this really big crowded street." He finally read the address off a piece of stationery. Holt had stayed there a few times when he'd first started coming to Shanghai: water-stained wallpaper, a rug pocked with cigarette burns. Holt could feel the hotel room and the confusion of the alien city in Andy's uncertain voice.

"Then you're in Shanghai."

"Yeah, I just wanted to look around a little. I mean, as long as I'm all the way in Hong Kong."

Holt remembered how busy Andy had professed to be when he'd called him from Montevideo. Evidently the funeral provided a convenient excuse for a vacation. He knew that Andy was calling him for help of some kind, and he debated briefly with himself as Andy described his difficulties in ordering a meal and buying souvenirs. Holt often told people he was busy even when he was doing nothing because the opportunity to sit and look into a big black gulf seemed more interesting than chatting. He *was* busy, he told himself. He was busy being alone. This was a friend of Clayton's, though, after all. He looked at his watch, heard the words "and I wondered if we could get together."

"Precisely: capital has no loyalty. One just has to be a grown-up about it." Holt surveyed the wreckage of the room service tray, then pushed it a half inch toward where Andy was drinking a can of beer. "There's two more *jaodze...*"

"No thanks, I—"

"As you like. But as I was saying, the Argentines are a partial subsidiary of an Italian company that manufactures spinning and knitting machines, so a few representatives of the parent company are coming in from Milan. Basically, the Argentines supply the raw wool and the capital, the Italians supply the technical expertise, and the Chinese supply the labor and also some capital they're wrangling out of the government. We're going after the American market."

"What do you supply?"

"Me? I know everyone, for starters. I coordinate the logistics of production and export. I help with the marketing in the United States. I get the shipments out on time. What else... Quality control. Basically, I run the show."

"Sounds complicated."

"Is complicated. I've been doing a lot of hand-holding, as you might imagine. Everybody wants in on China, and everybody is frightened. The perception is that there's fortunes to be made here, but that the road is long and crooked, and littered with corpses."

"Is it?"

Holt answered with a short laugh. "I can assure you of one thing: mine won't be one of them! At any rate, next Monday everything gets signed. After that we have a big banquet and start arranging the bribes to get the new factory built."

Andy's brows wrinkled as he regarded the merchant. "How did you get started in this? Was your father in this business?" Andy asked.

"My father? God no!" The subject's novelty made Holt voluble. People didn't usually ask about his parents. "My father was a carpenter, believe it or not. One of the few carpenters with a Ph.D. in macroeconomics. He wanted out of the ivory tower. He was an excellent economist, from what I understand. Not much of a carpenter. My mother was his student. She came from a wealthy family. She hadn't signed on to be a carpenter's wife. They got a divorce."

"That's too bad. You ever been married?"

He could feel himself stiffening a bit. "I considered it once."

"Me, too, but I considered it a little too long. She got tired of waiting."

Holt passed the subject by and sat back in his chair, frowning thoughtfully. "I don't blame my mother. Father was a bit remote. I always think of him sitting in the den in his coveralls reading financial journals. He became something of an expert on arcane stock market prediction theories. He collected them the way someone might collect obscure first editions."

"Or antique textiles."

Considering it, he let out a long rich chuckle. He was starting to get a glimpse of Clayton's old friend now. Beneath his bad clothes and his jock's vocabulary of clichés, he wasn't so very stupid. He was actually rather likable, in a bland and unpretentious way.

They stopped talking for a minute as Andy looked out at the city below them, letting the previous subject ebb. He brandished a manila envelope that he'd been holding since he'd arrived. "Hey, I have something I wanted to show you. I wanted to see what you think about it."

Holt had noticed the packet under Andy's arm and had sensed from the first that it contained something that Andy wanted his opinion on. Andy opened it and pulled out a piece of cloth the size of a notebook, then unfolded it twice.

In the first instant Holt glimpsed the flash of gold against cinnamon, and in the next he realized they formed a brocade. He sensed the stiffness of the fabric as Andy opened it to the light, intuiting instantly, from the subconsciously noted indicators of age and structure, that he had encountered a piece of woven gold. Before his startled eyes something strange began to come out of the design, something he had trouble apprehending, a glowing curlicue that developed, as Andy offered the piece to him over the greasy room service plates and the soiled napkins, into a word whose unreadable language Holt recognized but couldn't believe. He took it from Andy, holding it at a distance of twelve inches, then slowly moving it closer and closer to his face as if he would consume it with his eyes.

He saw clouds, billowing golden clouds that tapered into wisps, then bunched up again to form identical clouds in a new direction, a small scrap of the heavens clutched for centuries in someone's protective hand. The clouds didn't surprise him though; he'd spotted the design in almost every temple or monastery he'd visited, draped over a Buddha's arms, or covering a pillow. No, it was the words between the clouds that stunned him. It wasn't the Chinese character for *joy* or *dragon* that one usually found. Instead, the trace of a different empire rose out of the tawny background, strange letters that twisted like a piece of string falling through space. He went to his suitcase and fumbled out a small jeweler's loupe, then put it close to the fabric. The world filled with tiny cables of brown bending in and out of each other. Together they formed the swells on the surface of an ocean, above which shining gold threads exposed their backs like dolphins flashing in the sun. It was all so unruly at this distance, so filled with motion and life. He took the loupe away.

"Where did you get this?"

"Clayton gave it to me."

"When?"

"He left it to me. What is it?"

He put the cloth up to his nose and sniffed it, taking in the dusty aroma. Old. It had that smell of the desert. "Well . . ." He kept staring at the cloth as he spoke, his mind bouncing between the host of questions. If it was real, it was Yüan, stunningly early Yüan, a period almost completely absent from collections or museums. Where could Clayton have gotten such a rare piece? And why would he give it to someone who knew nothing about it? There were those bad black-and-whites that Zhang had showed him a few years ago, of the findings in the Huang Xia tomb . . . He called himself back to the conversation. "It's a piece of brocade, of course. An extremely rare piece of brocade. In English it would be 'woven gold brocade.'"

"What's the writing on it?"

"It's Mongolian."

Andy took a few steps closer. "How old is it?"

Holt raised his eyebrows. "That depends. To know with any certainty I would have to know the provenance of the piece. 'Clayton gave it to me' isn't much to go on. I can tell you about this type of work, though. It started showing up in numbers among the Jin Tartars, but it became most popular during the Yüan dynasty . . . the Mongols."

"Genghis Khan . . . "

"Genghis Khan, Kublai Khan. You know the story: they rode down from Mongolia and took over China. When the smoke cleared they had a lot of gold on their hands. Put that together with the entire Song dynasty weaving industry, and you get this." He lifted the piece up a few inches. "Or something else. They had dozens of different types, even gauzes made of gold. Marco Polo tells about the Mongol army using woven gold for their tents. He claimed to have seen pieces of cloth that stretched for miles. Of course, Marco wasn't always the most reliable witness."

"So how old does that make it?"

He shrugged. "Hard to say. These clouds are what they called *ruyi*-shaped clouds. *Ruyi* is a fungus. It's associated with the Taoist quest for eternal life. Also it was part of a staff that became a symbol of authority. The clouds can symbolize the heavens, but the *ruyi* also means 'good luck' or 'wishes fulfilled.' What's really odd about this one is the Mongolian characters. Maybe this piece signifies wishes fulfilled connected with whatever this Mongolian word means." He looked up. "The other possibility is that it's a more recent piece from somewhere in Inner or Outer Mongolia. That explains the script, but it doesn't explain the gold. Or it could be Manchu writing, making it Qing. What did Clayton say about it?"

He saw Andy waver. "He didn't say anything about it."

Holt noted it and moved on. "If it's early Yüan, that puts it in the thirteenth century. As a guess, before 1279, when they finished off Song China. I wish I could tell you more. The feeling I get from it is that it is Yüan. That's just a feeling though. I think it must come from an excavation. The smell—"

The phone rang. "Excuse me."

Andy watched him answer the phone. "You're here! Excellent. Come right up." Listening. "Of course. Oh, and Andrew is here. Clayton's friend. Good! We'll see you in a few minutes." Hanging up, he turned to Andy. "It's Silvia." He made a tour of the room and ended in front of the bar, opening a miniature bottle of Scotch for himself and bringing another can of beer to Andy. "Let's see what Silvia thinks about it. Do you mind?"

"Of course not."

Holt collected the remains of the dinner on the tray and put it outside the door, then sat down again and cleaned the lens of his loupe with a tissue. After that they sat waiting for her to come up, both of them looking at the piece of cloth draped over the couch. Holt sounded slightly less casual than he wanted to. "Be careful when you take it out of the country. The laws aren't particularly well enforced, but you don't want to lose a piece like this." He turned slightly away from Andy, as if something out in the Shanghai below them had caught his attention. "I might be able to help you with that."

Andy's voice became slightly more neutral. "Do you have experience with that sort of thing?"

"A bit."

A short pause. "What kind of things?"

Holt continued to study the glittering night outside. "Just textiles." He looked at Andy and smiled. "I don't have the nerve for anything else."

"Ever been caught?"

Holt's expression clouded. He took his time answering. "Only once."

"What happened?"

A delicate knock at the door, and Holt sprang up to answer it. Andy heard a short kissing sound, then her voice: *"Ah, mira la habitación del Señor! Qué lujo!"*

"It's even got real espresso."

The sound of her coat sliding off. *"No te creo!"*

Holt ushered in the woman from South America. Her hair shone, parted in the middle and falling smooth and glossy across her shoulders. The blue button-down sweater and gray skirt she wore reminded Andy of a Catholic schoolgirl on her way home from classes. She strode over and planted a kiss that barely brushed his left cheek. "Welcome to Shanghai."

Holt began immediately. "Have you talked to Mr. Gao?"

She glanced over at Andy, then back at her employer. "Mr. Gao has everything ready." A little carousel of names and appointments whirled between them, then Holt brought her over to the couch.

"Look at this, Silvia."

She gave a little gasp, then bent over and swept it up, lifting it in front of her face. Her vehemence surprised Andy, even though he could only see the sudden tightening of her back. She seemed genuinely shaken up. It pleased him that he'd gotten such a strong reaction with his piece of cloth.

"Would you care to check it with the loupe? Silvia?"

She turned slowly to Holt. "It's fantastic!" she said, almost whispering. "I've never seen . . . "

"Woven gold *jin*. You'll notice that both the selvages are intact, and the hem at the bottom looks original. What does that tell you?"

She didn't answer immediately, still awash in the mood that had seized her when she first saw it. "It tells me that . . . it has been cut on one side. That it is a piece."

"Exactly. It's a piece of something bigger. Did you notice the script? It's Mongolian." He was too excited to maintain his scholarly attitude. "It's Yüan! Early Yüan!"

She looked at it closely. "The writing could be Manchu."

He answered gleefully. "It could be! Certainly. But smell it. Go ahead. Do you smell it? It *smells* Yüan!"

She tipped her head and answered ironically. "It smells Yüan." She turned to Andy. "There are always a dozen of clues, and not one is certain, but he is flying because it smells Yüan." She rolled her eyes. "*Qué sé yo!* He is the expert, no?" To Holt: "You're a madman, Jeffrey!" She put the cloth on the couch. "Where did you find it?"

Holt pointed wordlessly to Andy, who took it upon himself to pick up the gap. "Clayton gave it to me."

He noticed her blanch, then recover. "How good! It is very beautiful. Really, if Jeffrey says it is Yüan, it probably is Yüan. He is the man who knows. Did he give you others?"

Andy tried to pass over the money and the notes in his mind as he answered. "No. Just this." Clayton had told him to keep it secret; giving it to Holt had been an act of desperate curiosity. He felt bad lying to Silvia. She seemed more trustworthy than the cold-blooded Holt, with his smuggling and his machinations.

Holt and Silvia began to talk business again, and Andy went over to the brocade and began to fold it up. Silvia winced. "Oh, don't do that! You should roll it!" She rolled it up and put it into a plastic bag. Silvia asked about his plans for tomorrow.

"I'll be around during the day."

They seemed to wait for a further explanation, but he didn't offer any.

Silvia touched Holt's sleeve. "Maybe Andy would like to go to see Mr. Gao with us tomorrow."

"Oh, I'm not sure he'd find it very entertaining." In a slightly formal voice to Andy: "Mr. Gao is one of our agents. It's a lot of little pieces, usually. Nothing quite as dramatic as this one."

"No, it sounds interesting."

They arranged to meet for breakfast at the hotel, and Andy went down the opulent elevator to the marble lobby, walking out into the cold with his textile. After the opulence of Holt's suite his room felt even flatter and shabbier, but at the same time, it had taken on a new dimension. A little pang of pure happiness surged through him. *His* room in Shanghai, far away and home all at once. He regarded it with a faint nostalgia now because he would be leaving it soon. The president of the Invisible World Trading Company had an appointment in Beijing.

Holt had spoken truly: the Sofitel Shanghai did have good coffee, served in immaculate white cups on immaculate white tablecloths, their perfection punctuated by a single pink orchid on each table. The textile dealer greeted him with a handshake and a quick annoyed glance at his University of Illinois sweatshirt, then efficiently sent the waiters to and fro in Chinese. Andy drank silently as Holt studied a lengthy fax from Argentina that had come in during the night. Andy got the impression that it contained some new obstacle to his upcoming business meeting: he kept underlining and writing in the margin, preparing his reply. Silvia showed up twenty minutes late, arriving in a flurry of apologies and small kisses planted quickly on their cheeks. She ordered an espresso and they discussed the appointment with the silk factory and with Mr. Gao, but Holt kept staring down at the four-page message that was disturbing him.

"Claudio wants to renegotiate. Now that it's all set up he's trying to squeeze me.

They started in about a company in Uruguay and the Italians, intricacies that Andy let dissolve into the ambiance of the dining room. After a few minutes Holt began gathering up his papers.

"I'll take care of this. Why don't you two go change money? I'll meet you at my room in an hour." Holt said. "No, make it an hour and a half. You can run him through the Yu Yuan."

Andy realized the conversation had turned to him again. "What's the Yu Yuan?"

Holt answered. "It's a famous garden. You'll like it." He looked at Silvia. "Be careful changing money."

Silvia looked at Andy, smiling. "Don't worry. I have my body-guard."

"Is it dangerous?"

She laughed. "No. I change with my friend every time. The only danger is that he might keep a few *jiao* because he has no small money."

They headed off along the Nanjing Lu, and the energy astonished him. The packed sidewalks radiated an ebullience bordering on the explosive, as if a dozen stadium-filling events had let out at the same time. The well-dressed citizens hurried along in leather jackets and wool overcoats, looking prosperous and sophisticated and eager to seize the latest offers. Most had battened down behind sunglasses, and some of the women wore white surgical masks tied around their mouths to protect them from the cold. It gave them a slightly tragic look, as if they were too fragile to breathe the air of the Nanjing Lu, vitiated as it was by coal smoke and the striving odor of commerce. The shops were weird variations on Western shops, with ineptly arranged window displays and mannequins that had chipped noses and outdated hairstyles. A few international chain stores had ventured to open up in this section of the Nanjing Lu, their slick displays contrasting with the amateurish efforts of the national stores that had not yet escaped the Communist aesthetic. Among it all, nearly invisible, old people clad in humble brown or blue shuffled and stooped to sweep up bits of garbage. It felt like a bizarre and never-ending Christmas rush.

"It is always like this," Silvia explained. In the past few years Shanghai had opened to the West, she told him, and even in the past few months the number of foreign shops on the Nanjing Lu had registered a noticeable increase. It had become fashionable to have investments in Shanghai, and money from Hong Kong and Taiwan was pouring in. Even if it went badly the backer could brag to his friends about his joint venture in the mother country, and come to Shanghai to enjoy the extravagant hospitality of his hosts. Now the overseas Chinese owned pieces of everything from office buildings to discotheques, although from what Silvia had heard those investments had a tendency to suck in large amounts of capital, then disappear.

The multitude of people presented a constant obstacle to staying near Silvia. He sidestepped and curved away, slowing down, speeding up, angling off into the bicycle lane in the street, or to a clear space in front of him that invariably filled up with another face, another cigarette, a curious glance, and the dark taboo gleam of animal skin. She turned to him occasionally as she spoke, checking to make sure that he kept up with her. The sight of her fine jawline and long brown hair made hard and impersonal by dark glasses and the fur-collared black leather coat, sent a minute thrill through him, one he didn't trust or want. Mist emerged from her mouth as she spoke, carved by her South American accent into a visual translation of exiled sound. He wondered how she would seem in her home country, or if the simple act of being a foreigner in this place magically transformed a person into something rare. As little as she fit in among the river of Asian faces, though, she belonged among them in another way. Like the city itself, she felt at once real and more than real.

"This way." They took a side street and began to walk along a high white wall. A large round doorway led to a small courtyard, in the middle of which presided the most bizarre rock Andy had ever seen. It looked like a lump of frothy wet cement that had been thrown up in the air and frozen in place, looming nearly twenty feet high. At first he thought someone had made some kind of extravagantly bad concrete pour, but he noticed that the whole misshapen mess presided from atop a pedestal, like a work of art.

"What is this?"

"This is the Yu Yuan," she answered. "It's a famous garden."

"No, I mean, what's the deal with the rock?"

"That is a Grotesque stone."

"I can look at it and see it's a grotesque stone."

She let out a quiet little laugh. "You should be more serious, Mr. Andy. These stones only come from the bottom of a certain lake called Tai Hu. They are very expensive and this one is *very* famous. It's called the *Exquisitely Carved Jade Stone*."

Andy kept staring at the weird monolith which appeared to him neither exquisite nor jade-colored. "I don't get it."

She stepped up to the ticket booth and paid for them: "Come with me."

She grasped his arm lightly and pulled him into the remarkable quiet of the garden. He had the sensation of falling into something cramped and illogical whose entrance, once it disappeared around the corner, would be impossible to find again. A labyrinth of corridors and courtyards opened and closed in a seemingly random assortment of spaces and directions, made even more chaotic by haphazard jumbles of rock and clusters of uneven foliage. They passed through a cave and across a tiny bridge that leapt across a miniature stream, and through the rockeries and lattice screens he caught glances of other grottoes just out of reach.

From somewhere deep in his memory, the phrase "Chinese garden" fluoresced with connotations of intricacy, and again that feeling of arriving at a mythical place as Silvia's voice curled into his image of emperors and long silken robes: "What you must remember about the Chinese garden," she said in her low, burnished tones, "is that it is all the world, but ·made small. Like those few bamboos over there: you have to look at them as a grove of bamboo trees, standing in the mist, which is that white wall behind them. And these rocks here represent a . . . an *escarpment* . . . high in the mountains. So walking there we are walking past a grove of bamboo and also a high mountain, in just a few steps." She stopped, as if letting him think about it, then went on, her eyes flickering with little shapes of light and dark, like the shadow of leaves: "It is the walls that make the Chinese garden. They take this little space, and they divide it into many many little spaces, into many little views, and like so, they try to make it . . . *infinito.*"

"You know a lot about gardens."

"No. I have been to this one before, so I look very smart. Clayton knew very much. It was one of his . . . obsessions. He told me about them."

He liked the sound of her voice: it had that special depth that he'd noticed from the beginning, an almost painful gravity even when she joked. Hearing his name with her rounded *a*'s, "Ah-ndy," it sounded sophisticated and serious, rather than the childish overtones it always bore in America.

She set her elbows on a balustrade and rested her face on her hands, looking down at the water where the ghostly orange shadows of giant goldfish moved slowly up to the jade-colored surface, then disappeared again. A frail-looking bit of her wrist lay exposed between the leather sleeve of her coat and her black gloves, scored by the faint blue lines of her veins.

"How did you end up in Hong Kong, anyway, Silvia?"

Her pleasantly absent face showed she'd answered the question many times. "It's a long story, but not a very interesting one. You know that Argentina exports very much raw wool to Hong Kong and China. More or less, I was working for the Argentine wool secretariat and then they sent me to Hong Kong."

"More or less?"

Her voice stayed low but it became playful. "More or less. It is not an exciting story."

"And that's where you met Jeffrey, in Hong Kong?"

"Yes. Jeffrey came to the office one day to get help with an export he was making from Argentina to China. Perhaps four years ago. I met Clayton through Jeffrey." She turned to him, her cheek resting on one hand now, her eyes narrowed in suspicion. "And now we know why I am here. But what about you, Mr. Andy? Eh?"

He was clearing his throat, the most transparent sort of liar. "Well, Shanghai was always a place that was special to Clayton. He told me a lot about it, so, under the circumstances I felt like . . . if I didn't go see it now I probably never would."

She continued staring at him without moving her head. "Mmm. And how long will you stay here?"

"Actually, I was thinking about going up to Beijing for a few days, you know, see the Forbidden City and all that."

"More or less!" Her smile grew wider and she shook her finger at him. "I get a strange feeling about you."

He tried to conceal his immense pleasure. "What makes you say that?"

"The first thing . . . I know I am stupid to be telling you this, but maybe that is the Latin blood. The Chinese, you know, are so cold. Me, I just say it. The first thing is that you couldn't come to the funeral, but then you come. Jeffrey told me that. Next, you have that valuable textile, one that even Jeffrey has never seen before. And the last thing . . . "

"What's the last thing?"

"The last thing is that you are in Shanghai, and everything in Shanghai is a little suspicious!"

He laughed out loud and she joined him. "Silvia, I'm afraid you've been reading a few too many spy novels."

"Don't say that: spy novels are my bible!" She looked at her watch, still laughing, and stood up. "Can you find the way out of here? I am completely lost."

"You're kidding!"

She reached out and pinched his arm. "I am kidding."

They found themselves on another street, the bustle of the Nanjing Lu resuming at the next corner. "Now we'll go to change money."

Andy had heard of changing money on the black market but he had never understood it. As they continued up the Nanjing Lu she explained that there were two kinds of currency: one was the money used by the Chinese people, called *renminbi*. "The other is FEC, for 'foreign exchange certificates.' The government makes you buy it at a terrible exchange rate and then they make you use it to pay for your hotel and all the other government things. It's a very good business for them." The regular currency, the Renmin Bi, could be purchased at a much better rate from money changers in the street. "Where do the dollars go?" he asked her.

"People always need dollars. They want to get their money out of the country, or they want to buy foreign goods. Businesses need them for foreign transactions. Who wants Renmin Bi? No one outside of China. And inside China they've been hiding them under their beds for the past twenty years. They want to turn them into something more useful." She stopped walking and stared intently at a triangular corner a hundred yards away. "That's where we're changing money. Usually . . . "

He looked over to where she pointed. Several men lounged around with their hands in their pockets, their animation increasing when they spotted the two foreigners approaching.

"That guy isn't Chinese," Andy said, indicating a short man with blackened teeth and red hair. His Caucasian skin and green eyes puzzled Andy.

"He's Uighur, from Xinjiang province. Chinese Turkistan. They're white there."

Andy spotted two other white men watching them from a doorway across the street, peeking out from inside Chinese army coats.

Silvia addressed the Uighur in Chinese, and Andy could tell by his halting reply that he didn't speak the language well. He didn't use the same tone or rhythm as the Chinese people or even Silvia, but instead spit the words out with an effort that made them sound overbearing. He kept an odd half smile on his face. The other money changers crowded around, eagerly interrupting one another to offer better rates, in Chinese to Silvia and English to Andy, implying their trustworthiness with phrases like "Good for you" or "You my friend, I give you eight-five." Andy felt uncomfortable having the men so close to him. He kept backing away.

"My friend isn't here," Silvia said. She nodded at the Uighur man. "We'll change with him."

"Are you sure this is okay?"

"Don't worry. He's often here. He has seen me changing. He thinks if he gives us a good rate I'll change with him instead of the other man."

Andy accepted the explanation and followed them away from the other money changers, whose offers of better rates trailed off behind them. The Uighur man led them into a foyer lined with peeling green tiles. The sounds of the cars outside penetrated and resounded in the stony space. Andy watched the man carefully as he counted out the money, trying to count with him but losing his place among the shuffle of bills.

"You must always count their money first," Silvia said as the man handed her the stack of bills. She counted them and grimaced. "It's missing twenty kuai. Now I'll give it back to him and he'll take more out while he's pretending to put more in. It's bullshit." She said something to the man in a hard voice and gave the money back, turning to go. The man panicked. Looking at Andy, "Sorry! Sorry! Now good . . . . now good!" He stuttered something in Chinese to Silvia that stopped her.

"Sometimes they try to cheat you, and if they can't do it they change at the right rate. It's not a big thing."

They followed the man into the back of the foyer again, Andy watching his hands carefully in case he tried to pull something out of his pocket. He wasn't enjoying this adventure anymore. The man grinned at him and said something in Chinese to Silvia, who replied in a low, almost threatening voice. He started counting again, even faster than before, then lost count and started over from the beginning, straightening out bills and turning them around so that they all faced the same way with a meticulousness that impressed Andy. "Why is he doing that?" Andy asked.

He should have heard the men behind him, but a bus passed at that moment, soaking up the rustle of their clothing and their footsteps. He only suspected when he saw the money changer's eyes slide quickly past his shoulders, and then he felt the pressure behind him, and the sudden embrace that padlocked his arms tightly to his sides and sent a sudden sharp pressure into his solar plexus, like an uppercut to the body. He went limp for an immeasurably small time as his mind lost its foothold, and then the fear descended on him, with its language of animal dominance that dispensed instantly with a lifetime of admonitions to be gentle and kind. He shook his body side to side, trying to expand his arms out of the cablelike hold, but the ferocious strength of the man behind him compressed him more, the two fists clenched so tightly and painfully into the pit of his stomach that he couldn't breathe. It resembled nothing he could remember from class, only dim things from the long-ago playground. Everything had a desperate brutal feel. The money changer had grabbed Silvia's wrist with one hand and was thrusting the other into her purse, papers flying out of it as she tried to wrench herself away from him while from somewhere a third man had moved around to his front and started to reach for his waist. Andy twisted to avoid him, still unable to break the grip or the fist in his stomach that had him on the edge of a spasm. He could already feel the strength threatening to leave his body when something came back, something he had probably practiced a thousand times that now seemed utterly different from before. He looked down and saw a dirty tennis shoe near his feet, a cuff of denim slanting up to the unseen adversary behind him. He lifted his foot and he stamped as hard as he could on the top of the shoe. A shout came out near his ear, so human and communicative that he had a millisecond of confusion trying to connect it to the invisible opponent, but he shut it out and brought his foot down again, mustering even more force than the first time and scraping it down the front of the man's shin before slamming to a halt on the foot that seemed made of hard rubber.

The man was lifting his feet now, Andy could feel the grip loosening. He saw stray limbs crowding around his head and he realized he was getting hit but he couldn't feel any pain. He stomped once more on the other foot, missing all except for the big toe, then he shot his elbow straight up along his side in a fast, sharp motion, like the upswing of a piston moving precisely to the unseen jawline in back of him. He felt the soft click of bone, and as the grip evaporated he bent forward a few inches, bringing his heel up into the groin behind him with a force that nearly lifted the man off the ground. It squeezed a final high childish yelp out of him, like a stepped-on dog, and Andy lost his balance and stumbled forward a few steps.

He had the urge to turn and see if the first man had gone down, but out of the corner of his vision he saw a fist approaching him. It seemed to travel very slowly. He noticed that the thumb protruded slightly above the fingers, wondering for an instant if the man employed some obscure Chinese fist he'd never encountered. A gold ring stuck out from the middle finger. As he watched he saw his shoulder come up by itself, deflecting the blow to his forehead. The world bounced, then he brought his arm up as the punch slid away. He dropped down and threw a simple straight punch with his right hand, and as his body twisted toward his opponent the thought flashed, I'm not hitting him hard enough. I'm moving too slowly. It seemed to take a long time to cross the twelve inches of space between them, finally reaching the lowest rib, the one that floated between the skin and the unprotected bottom of the lungs. To Andy it felt like he was hitting a bag of water with a tiny crust of ice on it, elastic and brittle at the same time, and as he felt it giving way he had the sensation of hitting the softest of feather cushions. It had a wonderful peaceful quality, then in an instant the graceful loitering of time rocketed back into motion. The second man seemed to be collapsing inward, and without thinking Andy drew his right fist halfway back and flattened it into a wedge. He swept the man's arm out of the way and snapped the edge of his hand into his attacker's Adam's apple. He had meant to stop some of the force, but the impulse got confused and he hit him hard, much too hard, feeling a horrified amazement as the trachea bent inward, absorbing a force so great that he could feel the small bones of his hand bruising with the impact.

The man began to fall, his head bowed down over his chest as if he suffered some great shame. Andy watched him for a fraction of a second as he fell to his knees, then turned to Silvia. The money changer was saying something in his non-Chinese language, pointing to the bills that littered the floor, holding Silvia in front of him. Andy took a step toward them, then the Uighur heaved Silvia into him and broke for the entranceway. Andy let him go, looked Silvia over, then down at the second attacker. "Jesus Christ!"

He was writhing on the floor, clutching at his windpipe as pink foam formed at the corners of his mouth.

He bent down. "I'm sorry, I'm so sorry!" He looked up again at Silvia, who stood with her mouth slightly parted. "We've got to help him. He's going to die!" Turning back, "I'm sorry! Oh, Christ! Now look!" Pounding the floor, "Shit!"

"Andy, stop shouting. We're going to go now."

"We've got to help him. Do you know how to do one of those emergency... I mean, you use a pocketknife and a Bic pen. Emergency... shit!"

The other man had turned over on his stomach and was trying to drag himself toward the exit with a strange mixture of delicacy and clumsiness. "Andy, listen. We're going to leave here and we are going to get help. We will help him. You don't say anything. I will talk. But we have to go now so we can help him more quickly. Do you understand?"

"But your papers!" He darted at the slips of paper that had been scattered on the floor, crumpling them into his pockets. "We can't leave without your papers!"

"Andy!" She had a faint smile as she extended her hand down to him. "Come here. We're going to get help."

Outside, she produced a tissue. "You have blood all over your face." She daubed at it and told him to hold it *there*, on his forehead, and took his hand, leading him quickly away. The crowds along the sidewalk swirled around him like a breaking wave of black hair, pointing at his bloody face and shooting agitated bursts of tones at him like accusations. She steered him through the hotel lobby to the elevators, and in the quiet wood grain of the elevator he began to shake uncontrollably, suddenly finding that his legs had disappeared. He slid down to the floor of the cubicle, the soft classical music bringing on nausea.

"Silvia, I think I'm going to throw up."

"Hold it in. We're almost at my room."

The doors opened, and the identical entryways of the hotel corridor spun past, branching off to every side like the blueprint of a Chinese character, the one for confusion, then Silvia was sticking a flat piece of plastic below the knob. "We're almost there. Just a little bit more."

It swung open and he pushed past her into the dark bathroom, feeling for the toilet, then collapsing on his knees into a series of dry heaves, then the spasmodic vomiting of fear and panic into the bowl. It came out in a liquid rush that threatened to choke him, used-up violence that had to get out. When he opened his eyes the lights had come on, skating inside the clean beige surfaces of the hotel bathroom. In the mirror he could see the tears coming out of his eyes, the blood on his face caking around where the ring had cut him. He remembered the man lying there, breathing out pink foam between the spaces of his teeth, and he shuddered again.

He washed his face and scraped away the taste of sickness with a hotel toothbrush, watching the bright blood mingle with the white foam at the drain. When he looked up again the veil of carmine had begun to spread out thinly over his wet skin, coming down through his eyebrow and in front of his temple. He flushed the toilet, then wiped away the blood again with a tissue.

"Can I come in?"

"Sure."

She sucked in her breath when she saw the cut.

"I think it was his ring."

"Do you think you need ... ah ... *puntas*?" She moved her hands as if sewing.

"Stitches." He sighed. "I don't know. Maybe. No. I don't think so." He watched her looking at the jagged cut in the mirror, then their eyes met in the glass.

"It will make a very honorable scar. Wait. I have something for it." She searched through a nylon toilet kit and took out a small plastic bottle. "Alcohol." She sat him down on the closed toilet and leaned forward to clean him up, bringing to him the warm scent of her skin mingled with perfume. He winced when the alcohol burned into the ripped flesh of the cut. "Don't be a baby. You're my hero, you know that? You beat those men in five seconds. Do you study *wu shu*?"

"I'm an instructor." He felt like he might be blushing. "It's the only thing I do well."

"Oh, I don't believe it is the only thing you do well." A period of mutual silence punctuated her remark, then, "Do you have many secrets, Andy?"

"Well ..." He pondered whether to pretend some mysteriousness. "I did pay a guy fifteen bucks for the answers to my freshman chemistry exam. How about you?"

She unfolded a white handkerchief and pressed it to his head. "I don't believe you. You are a friend of Clayton, and all Clayton's friends have secrets. You could be an assassin."

"I don't think assassins throw up after they kill someone." The image of the Chinese man struggling on the floor came back to him. "Did you get help for him?"

"Here, hold this tightly to stop the bleeding." She leaned back again. "I sent someone in. I told them a man was hurt and needed help. I think they understood."

"You *think*?"

"She understood, she understood! I saw her going toward the building to look. This is not New York, you know, where they let you die because they have a lunch appointment."

They sat without speaking as Andy remembered the perfect arc of his ridge hand to the throat, a part of his mind taking the form of his master admiring the well-executed technique. Silvia went on calmly, "I think that he has a hole in his lung and a crushed trachea. In my opinion, he'll die. Emergency medicine in Shanghai moves very slowly. They have to find a telephone and call the hospital, then the ambulance gets caught in traffic. You see how the traffic is here. It's a disaster!"

Andy stared down at the tiles between his feet. For years he had nourished the fantasy of killing someone, visualizing a thousand times the knuckle blow to the temple or the hammer fist to the base of the skull. In the countless repetitions of motions and forms the invisible opponents had always disappeared at the moment of impact, not lay gasping on a dirty concrete floor amid sputum and cigarette butts, defeated human beings, like himself. "This is too weird."

"Andy." Her voice relaxed. "You saved us."

"I saved us a hundred bucks."

"Didn't you see his knife? In his other hand? He had it like this." She held the toothbrush so that it stuck out the bottom of her fist, hidden behind her wrist. "When you hit him he was trying to grab you and bring it like this." She swept it across in front of his eyes.

He looked at her. "How do you know all this?"

"I had a boyfriend who was a commando. Now come into the other room. I think you should lie down a little while."

She had taken off her coat, and her hair spilled over a burgundy silk blouse that looked like suede. He sat down on the bed, half reclining against the padded headboard. The thought floated past that they should call Jeffrey and tell him that they'd been delayed, but he didn't want to admit the existence of an outside world yet, and he let the idea drift away. Somehow he'd gained safe passage to a walled city, but he had no assurance that if he went back outside he would ever be let in again. "We still need to change money."

"Why should we change money? We should go and rob someone. You could just hit them: *paf paf!*"

He laughed at her girlish punches. "You know, Silvia, there's this thing called 'reality.' I suggest you check it out once in a while."

"You shut up! Did I tell you to lie down?"

He falsified a sheepish acquiescence and slid farther down onto the bed. Everything that had happened in the past two hours was so outlandish that he was afraid of letting his real self intrude on it.

"Move over a bit, please," she said, and sat down on the edge of the bed. "Let me see your wound." She leaned in and lifted up the bandage on his forehead. He could smell her hair and the waxy fragrance of cosmetics. They rushed into his nose and his brain, filling his world while she hovered close to him. He trained his eyes toward the rectangle of light across the room. "It looks like it stopped bleeding . . . Your cheek is swelling up." He could feel himself starting to shake from her proximity, and the thought flashed through his mind that the whole day was going like this. Her cheeks tensed into something that almost became a smile. "You're shaking. Is something wrong?"

"It's just been an intense day. That's all."

She stood up again. "Green tea or red tea?"

"Either."

She filled two cups from the metal thermos and put their lids on. When she looked back up at him her smile seemed to convey a secret humor. "And how do you like Shanghai now, Andy?"

He considered it. "I think Shanghai's a very interesting place."

His understatement amused her, and he took the opportunity to laugh off some of the tension.

"Shanghai *is* a very interesting place," she agreed. "I'm still finding out about Shanghai, but Hong Kong has begun to bore me. When you get used to the neon it is only a provincial colonial town. Did you hurt your hand?"

He had been wiggling it around, exploring the ache in the knuckle below his index finger. "No. It's okay."

She brought him the tea, and he sat up to receive it. "I made you red. It has more caffeine. To give you energy." She took a seat again by the window, looking out at the city. The quiet had a dreamy comfortable feeling, a welcome slowness after the rush of events. The clicking of the ceramic cups demarcated lengths of time that were at once random and perfectly proportioned.

It seemed an appropriate time to ask her. "So, uh, Silvia, did you know Clayton very well?"

She looked directly at him. "We were lovers for a time. Is that what you wanted to know?"

He tried to conceal his embarrassment at the way she had gone directly to what had been lurking at the margins of the question. "Well . . . that's not exactly it. I just wondered if you knew much about what he'd been up to, uh . . . lately."

She grimaced, as if wondering why he would ask her that. "He was working in a bar called the Burma Tiger. You know he was drinking very much."

"I know about that stuff. But he also went to China a few times in the past year, didn't he?"

She frowned down at her tea. "He went to China, yes."

Chang had mentioned that Silvia had found Clayton's body. Andy didn't want to dislodge that memory from wherever she had put it away. "Um . . . Mr. Liu. Those flowers he sent were pretty spectacular. Was he a good friend of Clayton's?"

"Mr. Liu? No. They liked each other, but . . . Really he is an associate of Jeffrey. I called him because"—a slight tremor seemed to be waiting at the edge of her features—"I was alone. Louis was in Singapore and . . . "

"I know. Never mind."

She went on, with effort. "You want to know why he would send such flowers. I think to show respect for Jeffrey. Mr. Liu is very much a businessman, but he is decent." He heard her sigh. "Could we talk about something else?"

"Sure. I'm sorry." He regretted bringing the whole thing up.

"What about you?" she said.

"What do you mean?"

"What about your life: what is it?"

"What is it?"

"Yes. Like me: I'm bored with Hong Kong. What about you?"

He considered the daily round of work, lunch, dinner, and television. Karate students in white suits. Blueprints with coffee rings blazoned into them. "I ask myself that all the time. What is it?" He turned his empty hand over, a manual shrug. "I work for my father. I'm trying to help him out." He could only half believe his words even as they came out. He'd been trying to help his father out for too many years for it to be simply that.

"And you teach *wu shu*."

"Yeah. That's kind of my little domain."

"And there you are the absolute ruler."

"Oh, I wouldn't say that. It's more just training people. You teach them to kick and punch, but . . . it's sort of . . . training the spirit."

"To do what?"

"Um . . . change money?" She didn't seem amused by his remark. "I don't know, exactly."

"People always like to use that word, *spirit*, but they don't say what it is."

"I don't mean like in a supernatural way. It's more like the essence of a person. What they come from and where they're going. What they'd like to be." He watched for her reaction, afraid he might bore her if he went on about it.

"See, nobody comes to class just to learn karate. It's always something deeper. Maybe a person feels powerless, or they want to correct things that were done to them when they were small. Maybe they got pushed around by their parents and they're angry. You can see it in the way they fight. You've got the brawlers; they always want to get in and hammer you. They want to dominate. That's their spirit. Then you've got the escalators. You hit them, they hit you back a little harder. You take it slow, they speed up a little. They've got to win. That's *their* spirit. You've got the victims. They have a victim self-image, so subconsciously they let you hit them. Other people are too nice."

"What do you do with them? The victims and the nice people?"

He smiled at her, narrowing his eyes. "You try to bring out their dark side."

Her amusement spilled out into the room. "Have you ever shot someone?" she asked.

He weighed the ridiculous question. "Not since my last undercover mission for the CIA. How about you: have you shot anyone this week?"

"No, but I know how to use a gun. My father bought me a pistol and he taught me how to use it. A nine millimeter. Browning."

He wasn't sure if she was joking or not. "Why did your father think you needed to know how to use a pistol?"

"My father is *militar*."

"What do you mean?"

"Forget it." Tossing her head to the side. "It's all politics." A tiny frown. "It's stupid."

Before he could pursue it she got up and went into the bathroom. Her words echoed with tile overtones. "Blood, blood, blood!"

"I'm sorry. I'll clean it up."

"Forget it!" The door closed and he heard water sounds. When she came out she cut off another attempt to apologize. "Forget it. The hero does not clean up. Besides, we have a maid." She stopped in the center of the room, putting her fingers to her temple. "This light gives me a headache." She pulled the gauze curtains closed, then narrowed the space between the second layer of heavy shades, hauling the room into twilight. The sudden dimness stripped away the daytime feeling and the sense of being located in a world of events, leaving, instead, this darkened ether where she began again, her voice stroking him with that low deep sound, like the black trees in a frozen landscape. "I like hotel rooms. Every time you turn around they are clean again, like you are not even there. You can look in the mirror, and you are just . . . someone in a hotel room."

"I never thought about it like that."

She sat down on the edge of the bed again, her hand lightly on his thigh, the expression below her dark and perfect brows so composed and decisive that he felt as if he'd been drugged. "I don't believe you, Andy. Not about the gold brocade or anything."

The moment had gone uneven and queer, something he thought Silvia had caused but that, in a last shred of reflection, he traced to every encounter with every woman. The most exotic journey of all was to the foreign country of another human being; always that question of borders and what defined them. She gave him no clues. He examined the skewed bit of room caught in the mirror, then the ceiling, returning helplessly to the delicate ferocity of the face above him. It faded off then, all of it; the furniture and the rented space, leaving only the shining netherlands circumscribed by the unsteady cartography of her eyes.

The ring of the telephone exploded into the room like a grenade, jerking both of them back. It was Holt. Mr. Gao was waiting.

Holt had that feeling again, the feeling he'd had when he'd seen Andreas walking toward him in the transit area of the Lima airport, and when Villarino's fax had arrived that morning with new demands. The ground was slipping out from underneath him. "Something's wrong."

Silvia detoured around a clutter of parked bicycles as they walked to a bigger street to look for a cab. "What do you mean?" she said across them.

"Something's not right with Gao."

"I think that also."

"There's too much missing. All the good pieces are missing. The best ones. I didn't see anything there that I can get more than six or seven hundred dollars for. They don't even pay my travel expenses. I'd need dozens like that. And did you notice the prices?"

She finished his thoughts with absolute certainty. "He has another buyer."

He spotted a taxi, but it was too far away to flag down. "It's something like that. There's a strange energy there." He waved at the taxi anyway, defying the two hundred yards of traffic, then exploded out of the futile effort. "Damn!" His voice flattened out. "Two years. Supposedly there's a relationship. He's still got my book on Qing embroideries."

"It could be that—"

Holt stomped his foot, crashing his fist downward. "He knew *nothing* when I started with him! A stupid jade dealer, that's all! A curio salesman! Damn it! This just keeps happening to me! Every time I turn around I'm getting . . ." He bent his forehead to his palm and shook it, then looked up. "When I was in Peru, on the way back . . ." He closed his eyes, waving his head from side to side.

She brightened up. "Ah! Peru! You still have not showed me the Paracas manta you told me about! I am waiting to see it!"

He allowed himself the luxury of a long sigh, then composed himself. Smugglers didn't cry. "Forget it. It's gone. Let's try up there."

"What?" She stopped walking and faced him. "Don't tell me you lost it! How? What happened?"

"Problems at the airport." He started walking again, tossed the words back over his shoulder. "Just forget it. It's in the past. I'm more concerned with Gao."

It took her a moment to catch up with him, then she kept pace for several steps. "Mr. Gao is working for himself."

He accepted her simple pronunciation. "You're right. I suppose I shouldn't be a Pollyanna about it. That's business. Should I dump him?"

"Get your book back first. Then, he can go to hell. We've got three other people in Shanghai."

"They haven't gotten so many great pieces lately either. Maybe we're reaching the end in Shanghai." The overtones of his statement rung for a moment, making him lose the flow of his thoughts. "It is a finite resource. Maybe I need to spend more time in the west: Ninxia, Gansu, Nei Mongol, that area. I can get us clearance to go to the areas still closed to foreigners. The East is getting too picked over." He imagined hotel rooms with concrete floors and unchanged pillows bearing yellowed traces of other people's hair pomade. "I hate to do the small towns again, but perhaps that's what it takes. That's probably where the really great pieces are hiding. Otherwise we're back to working Katmandu, like all the other dealers. Let's walk up to the next corner."

"How will you do the small towns and run your business?"

Precisely that question had been assuming larger and larger proportions for Holt during the past year. The complexity of his manufacturing operations had been steadily growing, as had the seriousness of the money he earned from it. Business had its own logic whose natural progression, so measurable by the figures in the bottom line, made other considerations seem nebulous. The antique textiles and their comparatively modest profits had become an increasingly inconvenient sideline, and now he felt almost as if some malevolent force were trying to drive him out of it. The problem was that of the two, he loved the textiles and their arcane revelations far more than he ever would the coming and going of funds and yardage that constituted HOLT IMPEXCO.

"I don't know. I don't know how I'll do it."

"Perhaps you don't need the textiles anymore."

"It's not that I need them . . . "

She must have picked up on his hopelessness. She squeezed his elbow with her gloved hand. "Don't worry: we will find a way. For Jeffrey Holt, there are no problems without solution."

"Sure. That's easy—"

"Remember the problem we had with quota last year, we couldn't get any? Remember how impossible it looked? And then, finally, you were selling quota to other people at two times the price."

That *had* been a rather silky maneuver. Lunch with Mr. Liu, a few phone calls . . . When the smoke cleared he had found quota and made seventeen thousand dollars. Her vote of confidence brightened him up again. "So, what's the story with the pilgrim?" he asked her.

"What story?"

"You know."

He arched his eyebrows at her, and she laughed. "He's very sweet."

"Are you blushing? Silvia? Is that you? Blushing?"

"I'm not blushing. Here's one!" She jumped out in front of a taxi that was slowing at the curb, waving at the driver as Holt opened the door for the passenger. She scooted next to him on the glossy vinyl seat. "Your hotel?" She directed the driver and turned to Holt again. "So you might go to Ninxia to look for pieces?"

"You don't get off that easy! I want to know about the strange red color on your cheeks."

She shook her head, grinning. "It's the cold, stupid."

"Please. The spectacle of Silvia in Love is a little bit too much for this tired heart."

"He's a nice guy, that's all. And he doesn't have a million complexes, like *some* persons that I know."

"Ooooh." Holt shivered in an exaggerated shimmy. "It's rather chilly in here all of a sudden."

Silvia made a small fist and punched him in the shoulder. "You are going to think you are a little penguin if you go on like this."

"He does have a certain winning naïveté, doesn't he? The wardrobe has got to go, though. I haven't seen that many artificial fibers in one place since I visited the Du Pont factory on a sixth-grade field trip."

"He's a very nice man."

"Yes, and I've seen you squash some very nice men."

"I do not squash nice men."

"Jimmy?"

She rolled her eyes. "I did not squash Jimmy. We both agreed that it would be better. It was a mutual decision."

Holt shook his index finger at her. "You are so very very bad!"

"Shut up!"

"And what was that other fellow's name? Ray? The bond trader?"

"Ray was impossible. There was no room in his Rolls-Royce for anyone besides him and his ego. If you knew him better you would have seen he was impossible. That was . . . *auto-preservation*."

"So what's the story with the pilgrim, Silvita? Ah!" He opened his mouth as he put his hand to his brow. "Don't tell me you're taking the fall!"

She was laughing now. "You shut up!"

"No. I can't believe this. This is too much!"

"Shut up!" She held her fist up to threaten him, tucking one lip under the other.

"Oh! Has he been giving you boxing lessons? That is a wild one, about the money changers. I can't wait to hear his side of that story." Holt settled down a bit. "It's interesting. When I met him he seemed utterly ordinary. I couldn't see the connection between him and Clayton. The next thing I know, he pops up in Shanghai, accompanied by this little cloud of odd events. That gold *jin;* that's a museum piece."

"It is spectacular."

"And from Clayton! That's the oddest part. Where on earth did Clayton get it? And why would he give it to Andy?"

"Maybe he got it in Inner Mongolia."

"Why do you say that?"

"He went there several times. Maybe he found it on one of his

STUART COHEN

trips. Maybe it is one of those pieces that someone keeps locked in an old box for a hundred years."

Holt considered it. "You mean seven hundred years. It looks archaeological to me. Museum material. Did you ever see that lot from the Huang Xia tomb; the one in Shanxi? They put the showiest pieces on display in the big museum at Xi'an, but they had dozens of others that got squirreled away at a provincial museum farther north. Zhang showed me some bad photographs a few years ago."

"Zhang . . . "

"From the Shanghai museum."

"Oh, Zhang."

"It's hard to see Clayton doing the grave robber thing, though. He wasn't a plunderer."

"Not like some other people."

"Gee thanks."

Silvia's mouth tightened, then she tipped her head sideways. "How much did you offer him for it?"

"I didn't."

"Why not? He doesn't even realize what he has."

Holt thought of the bone-strewn cemeteries in Peru, annihilated by *huaqueros*, and the pieces he'd bought for a few dollars from Bolivian peasants who didn't imagine that somewhere far away their great-grandmother's handiwork would command more money than they would earn in a lifetime. He felt like a hypocrite when he told her, "It's his. It's what he has left."

The moment tumbled unexpectedly into sadness, and Holt found himself oddly moved by her answer as she looked at him. "You are a good man, Jeffrey."

"Oh, I take a stab at it on occasion, like everyone else."

They had reached one of the swollen tributaries of the Nanjing Lu, and the car had come to a dead stop, reduced to honking its horn like a boat in distress. "Ah, Shanghai traffic. I keep forgetting why I love this place so much."

Holt noticed a guarded tone in Silvia's next question. "Tell me about Buenos Aires; did you see Chachy?"

Chachy was Silvia's best friend in Buenos Aires. "I was only there a couple of days. I got bogged down in Montevideo." She looked disappointed, then Holt added, "Jorge heard she's pregnant."

"Don't tell me! Fantastic!" They discussed the schedule of the pregnancy and the deservingness of Chachy to conceive. Holt had no more news of anyone and they lapsed into silence again. Silvia's slender face became smooth and expressionless as she stared ahead, then Holt could only see her long black hair as she examined the noodle shops and pedicabs that inched past outside her own window.

"I told you I'd buy you a ticket. It would be your bonus."

"And one day I will accept your offer."

Holt felt himself moving into the frigid waters of Silvia's past. He'd asked around after he'd hired her: she'd turned out to have a family in the wealthy Montevideo suburb of Pocitos, her father a retired army colonel who now owned a garage. For some reason she hated his guts. A story in there somewhere, one he didn't particularly want to know. Let her have her own life. Aside from that, they'd turned out to have a circle of mutual friends in Buenos Aires, tango people associated with one of the cantinas in San Telmo where Silvia had worked. One of the funny things about Silvia was that she always seemed homesick for South America, but she never went back.

Holt turned to his own window and lost himself again in the enigma of the woven gold *jin*. Its appearance in the face of his bad fortune upset him in ways he never would have suspected. When the jet lag woke him up last night he'd pulled out Clayton's letter and suddenly the allusions to "connections I never told you about" had taken on a fresh and disturbing relevance. Clayton had money from nowhere, and Holt's contacts were drying up. Interesting coincidence. He reached around and massaged the back of his neck. No. Clayton had been his oldest friend, hadn't he? What's more, he didn't have the guile. It made as much sense as the last part of his letter, where he babbled on about his ridiculous map. The map . . . Holt pursed his lips, for the first time troubling to imagine a piece which, if it did exist, would make the gold brocade seem like a dish towel. It appeared in his mind for a second, luminescent with the same red as the lost Paracas weaving, then subsided again. No. Among all other things, that was certainly impossible.

■   ■   ■

After two busy signals and a dead line, Andy went over the instructions once more with the switchboard operator. He'd meant to call from Hong Kong but things had gotten away from him, instead he was hurling it out now from Shanghai. According to the clock in the lobby it was 7 A.M. for his father: perfect timing for their daily pep talk.

"Hello?"

"Hi Dad, it's me!"

"Well hello, son! Are you at the airport?"

"Dad, I'm calling from Shanghai."

"Oh." His voice dipped. Andy could hear the faint enthusiasms of the morning radio show in the background, then his father's rejoinder. "Shanghai. You don't say. I thought you were going to Hong Kong."

"I went to Hong Kong, Dad. I had to come to Shanghai."

"Why?"

"Clayton wanted me too. It's kind of hard to explain."

On the other side of the world, his father tried to imagine his son in a place called Shanghai. He thought of French prostitutes and Chinese gangsters, the legendary postwar Shanghai of his teen years. "Shanghai. I always wanted to go to Shanghai. Why did Clinton send you there?"

"Clayton, Dad. Clayton. I told you, it's kind of hard to explain." He looked around the calling center, remembering Clayton's instruction to tell no one. "It's really weird. He gave me fourteen thousand dollars and a bunch of business cards that say Invisible World on them, and they have an address here in Shanghai. They have my name on them. He gave me a plane ticket, too."

"That's a lot of money."

"I noticed. I talked with his friend in Hong Kong and I can't figure out where he got the money. It's a guy named Louis Chang, a Chinese guy. Really nice. A prince. But he said Clayton was broke the last few years."

"If he was broke how'd he give you fourteen grand and send you to Shanghai?"

"I don't know, Dad. This whole thing is really weird."

"How could—"

"Wait a second, I'm not finished. I went to the address on the cards and there was nothing there, just an empty room. The only thing was this envelope with my name on it and a piece of old cloth. Really old, like seven hundred years. From the Mongols. It has gold in it."

"Is it valuable?"

"Kind of. I don't know! That's the whole thing! I don't know anything, and everybody I meet here speaks six different languages and I can't even order breakfast!"

A calm voice. "Are you all right, Andy?"

"I'm fine, Dad. It's just weird."

"You know, there's a lot of bad elements in Shanghai. It's famous for that."

Andy touched the bandage on his forehead. "That was fifty years ago, Dad. I don't think it's dangerous anymore."

"You said you didn't know what was going on."

"I don't. But I mean, I know some people here." He named Holt, describing him reassuringly as a businessman, the one who'd called from South America. "There's this Chinese guy too, some kind of millionaire, I think. A friend of Clayton's. I met him at the funeral." He couldn't keep a slight flourish out of his voice. "He's taking me out to dinner tonight."

"It sounds very exciting, son."

"Uh, Dad. I have to go to Beijing."

"You do."

"Yeah. It's part of this thing with Clayton. He left something for me in Beijing. I don't know what it is yet."

"How long do you think that will take?"

"I don't know. I just . . . have no idea. How's it going at the office?"

"Oh." The answer had the husky tone that always infiltrated his father's lies. "It's a little tough, but we can handle it."

"What's up? How's the D–9?"

"The D–9's out for ten days, and we couldn't find one to rent. Frank even tried some outfits in Indiana. There's nothing available."

"So what are you doing on the Kovakis job?"

"Well . . ." His father seemed to be steadying his voice. "We lost it. I called up Mackey and explained the problem, but he wasn't too sympathetic." He retreated into vagueness. "You know how it is."

The phrase "we lost it" resounded in Andy's brain. They had both regarded the Kovakis job as their salvation. "Were you able to reschedule the audit?"

"No."

Neither said anything as Andy considered the implications. "How's Mom?" he asked.

"She's fine. She's in the shower right now."

Another silence, one in which Andy couldn't help remembering the devastated remains of Clayton's father at the funeral. He took a deep breath. "I'll be home tomorrow, Dad. It's seven o'clock here. I'll get the first flight in the morning."

The old man didn't answer immediately. He cleared his throat. "No, son. You go on with your trip."

"No, Dad. I already went to the funeral. That's what I said I was going to do. I can't just leave you—"

His father stopped him. "Listen to me, Andy." Andy heard a slight rustling and then the radio snapped off. He heard him return to the phone again. "Listen. Life is . . . life is mostly D–9's and people calling you up on the phone looking for money. You know what I'm saying? It isn't Chinese millionaires and a dead guy telling you to go to Peking. What I'm saying is . . ." He seemed to struggle for the words but finally reduced them to their simplest form. "I want you to go."

The short sentence overwhelmed Andy and he couldn't reply to it. At last the single and irreplaceable voice that had been beside him forever started in again. "Shanghai, eh? Wait till your mother hears about this."

"Dad. Thanks."

"Ah! It's nothing to thank me for. I'd better get rolling, son. I've got to be at the bank at nine."

"What are you going to tell them?"

His father sounded foxy again. They were back to the old pep talk. "Same old bullshit. I'll say to 'em: 'You guys wanna close me down?

Here's the keys. You'll get ten cents on the dollar.' That's one offer they've never been too eager to take me up on."

Half a world away, Andy smiled. "Thanks, Dad. I'll be home as soon as I can."

"Oh, we can handle it." His voice took on that World War II tone, the tough guys from another generation. "Just watch your ass."

"Come on! You know me: always ahead of the power curve."

His father laughed, a sound that remained with Andy after the click of the line going dead. He kept the receiver to his ear. He didn't want to lose his father. He wanted to hold on to the laugh. After a while he gave up, and it faded into the lobby of the hotel.

"Ah. Mr. Mann. I am Sen Zhi Guang. I am Mr. Liu's interpreter. It is a great pleasure to make your acquaintance."

Barely more than five feet tall, Mr. Sen gripped Andy's hand in a cool, birdlike shake, maintaining a restrained smile. Despite his thin hair and a face that looked as if it had been working far into the night for the last thirty years, his fur-trimmed leather jacket salvaged for him a youthful and stylish air. His speech had a gentle, hesitant quality, as if he was struggling not only with the language, but to conform with the rules of an extraordinary tact. "Ah, yes. Then, this way, please. Mr. Liu is waiting for us in his car outside." A large Mercedes waited at the end of his gesture, its midnight blue enamel bending the reflections of neon signs into exotic cursives across its surface. A young man in a leather jacket and a tie opened the car door for him, revealing Mr. Liu, who smiled at him from within. His eyes shifted up to the bandage but his expression never changed. "Hello, Mr. Mann!" Ridges of calf-colored leather rose and fell across the secret space of the automobile, scrunching quietly as he took his place. He heard the door latch, then the noisy contentions of the street became remote as they got under way. Mr. Liu said a few words to the driver, then turned to Andy, looking him in the eye as he spoke to him in Chinese. Mr. Sen craned around from the front seat to translate. "Mr. Liu asks you how you like Shanghai."

The faraway moaning of the engine somewhere beneath him. "Shanghai is a very interesting place," he answered.

Mr. Sen translated, and Mr. Liu again nodded in agreement and smiled. Mr. Sen continued the conversation, as if he knew instinctively what his employer would say. "And Mr. Mann, have you gone to the Yu Yuan?"

"I did go to the Yu Yuan. I liked it very much."

He stopped for a moment, framing his next question. "Have you walked along the river? That area is very famous. It is"—he smiled as if implying something mildly embarrassing—"the old Shanghai."

"No. I haven't gotten there yet. I've just been, you know, walking around, trying to order meals. Stuff like that. I had a, uh, little problem when I was changing money. That's where I got this." He pointed to the bandage.

Mr. Sen's expression stayed the same. "Oh." He chuckled, which Andy sensed indicated uneasiness rather than humor. "I am quite sorry to hear that." He relayed it to Mr. Liu, who nodded seriously and responded through Mr. Sen that there were many bad men in Shanghai. Mr. Sen meticulously phrased his next question, tagging a smile on to the end. "Mr. Mann, may I ask: what happened?"

"I was with Silvia and a couple of guys came up behind me while the guy was counting out the money. It was a setup. Things got a little out of hand." Andy recognized the signs that his American idiom was going over Mr. Sen's head, so he clarified it. "Three men. One grabbed me from behind and another started reaching in my pockets." He wasn't sure how to describe the next part, with men collapsed on the floor and the terrifying moment when the crowd had surrounded him. Mr. Sen and Mr. Liu were both looking at him intently. "They hit me, I hit them." He shrugged. "That's what makes a horse race!" He listened to himself as the cliché came marching out of his mouth.

Mr. Sen's empty smile stood in as his mind seemed to race around Andy's idiom, then he translated to Mr. Liu, waving his hands at the end to indicate a mixed-up battle.

The fact that Andy hadn't lost any money impressed Mr. Liu. He looked him in the eye, and his persuasive masculine tones swept over Andy like an anointment, borne on the crisp alcohol scent of his cologne. He motioned out the window and pushed his hands out into space, finishing by smiling and clapping him on the shoulder.

"Mr. Liu congratulates you. He says that you must be very strong to escape from three men. He says you've seen much of Shanghai in a little time. Shanghai is a big struggle. It has always been like that. At one time, China did not control Shanghai: foreigners controlled *everything*. Many bad men. After that came Liberation." The narrative smoothly passed over the four decades of Communist rule. "Now we have opening, a new China. If you want to be on the top, you must always struggle. Struggle with the rules, struggle with the government. You must cooperate with your friends."

Andy translated Mr. Sen's tactful English back to him. "*Guanxi.*"

Both of the Chinese men laughed, and Mr. Liu exclaimed something to Mr. Sen. "Mr. Liu says that perhaps you are already an *expert* on China!"

The foggy air went past outside, punctuated by colored lights and the constant look of curiosity on the faces that tried to see through the glass as the Mercedes nosed through traffic. Andy felt strange addressing Mr. Liu in English when he knew he wouldn't understand, but he spoke directly to him, imitating the protocol Mr. Liu had set. "What business do you struggle in, Mr. Liu?"

Again Mr. Sen translated. "Mr. Liu has many businesses. He has some clothes business, and also he has some . . . real estate . . . business, I think you say." He added on his own initiative, "Mr. Liu is very clever." Mr. Liu waited for Mr. Sen to cease, then put out another long paragraph of his deep-voiced speech. "Mr. Liu began only seven years ago. He had a very small office. He had no air-conditioning, so even when it was very hot, he was"—Mr. Sen imitated wiping sweat and waving an imaginary fan"—with a fan, you see?" Mr. Sen laughed. Andy felt he was hearing the recital of the company legend. "And Mr. Liu would like to know: which work do you do?"

Andy felt mildly embarrassed. "I work in a plumbing business."

Mr. Sen didn't know the word *plumbing* and Andy had to explain about pipes and toilets, then the translation passed and Mr. Liu nodded. He seemed about to reply but the driver said something, and at Mr. Liu's command the car pulled up to a large building. They passed through a double door into a marble-lined lobby, then stepped into the elevator. Framed pictures of a restaurant and a nightclub with dancing couples advertised the attractions of the penthouse. Also, strangely, women wrapped in towels. "This building belongs to Mr. Liu," Mr. Sen explained.

The elevator doors split apart, revealing a young hostess in a long red satin dress. Two angular points of hair leaned across her smooth face, like anodes that now electrified her expression as she saw Mr. Liu, the Big Boss. They greeted each other and exchanged lively pleasantries in a staccato lilting and hissing that clattered completely against what Andy imagined they were saying. He wondered how much could never be translated, a thought that was amplified by the smooth thigh lancing out from her dress as she led them past a painted screen into the restaurant. Dozens of aquariums covered one wall, their blue-green glow disturbed by the writhing of living things. It's the sea, Andy thought to himself, and then they were going down a corridor to a small private room set with a single round table. On the walls around them hung a feast of opulent silk: robes and jackets, banners and articles of clothing whose function Andy couldn't identify. Hats adorned one entire wall. Little bags of velvet or silk covered another. Some of the pieces bore the fading and stains that he would expect from something old, but in the dim light and his own ignorance, he didn't dare to guess their age. He half expected Holt to come walking in.

"Mr. Mann, are you also interested in ancient cloth?"

Jet lag again: he felt a yawn coming and he locked his mouth closed and yawned through his nose, reducing it to a slight trembling of his chin. At last: "I'm interested."

"Mr. Liu also appreciates very much the old . . . textiles. These little bags, they are all perfume bags. Many are more than two hundred years old." Each sentence seemed to have a definite stop after it, like a telegram. He lurched forward again. "Do you like the pieces here?"

"They're very nice."

Andy wasn't sure what else to say, and Mr. Liu broke the mood with a big smile and a gesture that he should take a seat at the big table. Mr. Liu took out his telephone and sat down next to him, poring over the menu.

The banquet began to accelerate. Three young, well-dressed women appeared, chatting gaily at the introductions and glancing curiously at Andy. Andy looked at them more closely as they sat down; one had a slightly cruel-looking face with a long nose and sharp, slitted eyes. It seemed like a face from an old print, a particularly Shanghai face, whatever that meant. Mr. Sen noticed Andy's puzzlement and clarified it. "They have just come to enjoy the dinner with us. Do you think, ah, that they are pretty?" He smiled, then chuckled at Andy's reply. "Good. We will eat dinner together, and then we will go to dance. Then, we can have a massage. Yes . . . is that okay?"

The thought of the massage scurried through his mind, but before he could make a decision about it tea came, then a succession of cold dishes were put on the table: small plates holding cloves of sweet pickled garlic, roasted peanuts, boiled chicken cleavered to bits and served with soy sauce and sprigs of greenery.

"You use chopsticks very well, Mr. Mann. You have been to China before?"

"Never! My father taught me," Andy told him proudly, remembering how he had taken the family out for Chinese food every Sunday of his childhood. It amazed him, sitting with Mr. Liu and his entourage in this ornate restaurant in Shanghai, that in his unsuspecting way his father, a man who had only been out of the country for a war, had prepared him for this moment.

Toasts were made: "To our foreign friends!" and then a plate of boiled shrimps appeared on the tide of warm feeling, bringing on a second toast, this time "to cooperation." Andy watched in surprise as even the most delicate of the women popped an entire shrimp into her mouth and patiently extruded bits of antennae and shell. A plate of abalone arrived, its delicate white meat perched inside the blue interior. "These come from Harbin," then the cranelike intrusion of the chopsticks. A rush of new foods began: a plate of squid, scored like a pineapple, and another of steamed crabs, broken into pieces and reassembled so that they looked intact. The story of the fight was retold by Mr. Liu, with the appropriate expressions of admiration and sympathy from the others. More toasting, more curious glances from the three women. They questioned him about America through Mr. Sen: "They would like to know . . . " "She asks you if . . . "

New and peculiar dishes were delivered, piling up among the plates and the bamboo steamers already on the table: a fatty pork roll flavored with caraway seeds, unrecognizable green vegetables, translucent white rectangles that Mr. Sen explained were made of rice paste. Even after everyone had abandoned all but the most halfhearted attempts to pick at the food, new plates kept coming, filling Andy with despair at his obligation to try to eat some of them. A whole flounder arrived, its eyes trained on the ceiling, and another plate of fried eels. At last a bowl of soup was brought, a refreshingly light broth with bits of blackened chicken and vegetables in it. Halfway through Andy discovered a caterpillar twirling lazily around with the bits of spice at the bottom of the bowl.

Mr. Liu produced a bottle of cognac. The bell-shaped glasses appeared and a respectful hush descended. They raised the glasses and Mr. Liu proposed a toast in Chinese, directing it at Andy. "To friendship and cooperation." Andy took a sip of the fiery brandy and felt it cutting like an acetylene torch through the food packed into his stomach. Yes, yes yes, he was Marco Polo at the court of the Khan. He seemed to be getting some kind of electricity going with the girl with the Shanghai face; smiles were traveling back and forth across the table. Mr. Liu offered him one of his expensive cigarettes and lit it for him, the first cigarette Andy had smoked since his teenage years. Mr. Liu was posing some sort of question, and Andy focused his fuzzy attention on him with a scowl, as if by concentrating hard enough he might understand his language.

"How many people work for your father's company?"

Andy knew from doing payroll that they numbered eighteen. But if he counted the temporary help and the other contractors that worked with them, not exactly as employees, but yes, certainly cooperatively. "Sixty or seventy, depending on how many jobs we're running." The number still sounded miserably small, but slightly more substantial than eighteen.

"Then your company is flexible?"

"Yes. We adapt to the circumstances."

Mr. Sen passed the information to his boss, and Mr. Liu nodded appreciatively, then raised his eyebrows as he replied.

"Mr. Liu asks if your company has ever thought of doing business in China."

Andy looked at Mr. Liu's attentive face. His company, doing business in China? A wave of incredulity came over him as he thought about it. Andy's mind filled for a moment with the startling new image of himself as an American contractor, running operations in Shanghai with the help of his partner, Mr. Liu. "We haven't until now. We've worked in other states before but . . . we've never really considered China, no."

The small man translated and Mr. Liu nodded his head heartily. Andy exchanged a smile with the thin-faced woman. Mr. Liu was asking him something again.

"You have many interests. Even on your first visit here you know much about China. And you use chopsticks very well. I can say, I think, that you like our Yu Yuan garden. And because you are a friend of Mr. Smith and Mr. Holt, you probably know something about old clothing."

Andy had never heard Clayton referred to as Mr. Smith before. It took him a second to figure out who Mr. Liu was referring to. "Not really."

Mr. Sen went on. "Mr. Liu is a great collector of old clothing. He always pays the best price when he buys."

Andy looked at Mr. Sen and Mr. Liu. They both smiled at him.

"Mr. Liu was quite sorry when Mr. Smith died."

To his horror, Andy felt a massive yawn taking hold of him. He clamped his mouth shut and locked his gaze on the robes as his chest filled up with air and his head tilted back. He felt like his eyes were going to pop out, and when it finally ended he gave a little grin to Mr. Sen. "Well." He didn't know what to say. He tried to adopt the proper tone of reverence. "There's no replacing Mr. Smith, is there?"

Mr. Sen relayed it to Mr. Liu, who watched him intently. "And Mr. Mann," he continued, "how long will you stay in Shanghai?"

"I'm going to Beijing tomorrow, as a matter of fact."

"Beijing! How fortunate you are!"

"Yeah, you know: check out the Forbidden City. Eat some Peking duck. China is so incredible." He found himself looking at the Shanghai woman again at the precise moment he finished his thought. "I want to see more of it."

The slightest tremor of amusement crossed Mr. Sen's mouth. "I understand. And do you know at which hotel you will stay in Beijing?"

"Not yet."

Mr. Sen nodded, glancing at Mr. Liu. "And now . . . perhaps we should dance. Okay?"

The bill was summoned and signed, and one last glass of cognac appeared in front of him. Mr. Liu made a call on his telephone. People and actions succeeded one another with a buttery lack of definition: the closing of the elevator doors again, the top floor of the hotel and a large television screen that people stood in front of as they sang. Clumsy attempts to waltz while Mr. Sen glided gallantly with the youngest girl and Mr. Liu watched it all from his seat. Andy's head snapped down from exhaustion, and he looked up and shook it off, people were smiling. He was in a sauna, then a warm shower, then a corridor, a series of doors each with the name of a different city on it. MILAN. PARIS. BANGKOK. Cities he'd never been to. NEW YORK, which hung open to reveal what looked like a hotel room, then TOKYO and STOCKHOLM, and he realized the whole world was there, just like the Yu Yuan, the entire world, and they put him in . . . was it RIO DE JANEIRO?, a television and chairs, the massage table with metal bars on the ceiling so the masseuse could balance while she walked on his back. That's what he'd heard; that they walked on your back in the Orient, and now he saw it was true, and who knew what else was true, but he was asleep before he could prove any of it, drifting wonderfully away as he thought of the Yu Yuan and Silvia, and then a burst of cool night fog and the coach of sleep was pulling up in front of what took shape as his hotel, Mr. Liu gone, the streetlights cushioned in a pillow of pink mist. Only Mr. Sen, next to him in the backseat, the splendid and archaic delicacy of Mr. Sen as he relayed Mr. Liu's apologies for being absent, then: "Mr. Liu would like you to call him if you have a need for something. If anything . . . unusual appears."

"What do you mean?"

"You are a stranger to China, Mr. Mann. And you are a friend of Mr. Smith, so Mr. Liu would like to help you."

It took him a few seconds to get past the drowsiness, then the sense of something immense and imperceptible overtook him, making him stare for a long time into the placid face of Mr. Sen, who revealed nothing.

When he reached his floor he had to pound on the desk to summon the sleeping floor attendant from the back room. She handed him a pink slip and walked him down the hall to his room. On the slip were the words "Holt Breakfast?" and a phone number.

Holt was waiting for him when he reached the restaurant. After the previous night's dinner, the white china ambiance of the Sofitel café reinstated a sense of order: the coffee cups and the silver pot of coffee were already waiting for him on the table. The pink orchids had been replaced with orange ones.

Andy could see the surprise pass over Holt's features when he first glimpsed the bandage and the uneven contours caused by the swelling. The attention embarrassed him. "Sorry I couldn't make it yesterday. I needed a little break."

"Wow," Holt said, with a suppressed smile that instead came out as a general lightening of expression. "I guess I should see the other guys."

Andy pulled his chair out and sat down. "No, maybe it's better if you don't see the other guys."

"From what Silvia says that might entail a trip to the underworld."

Andy found himself without an appropriate answer. Holt seemed to expect him to crow about it, but remembering it still made him jumpy and started the adrenaline flowing. He shouldn't have hit him that last time in the throat. "Oh, he's probably okay. Silvia's a little bit dramatic."

Holt retreated a bit from his jocularity. "Would it bother you to tell me what happened?"

Andy had heard dozens of fight stories over the years from other karate people: they always had a smug chronological order and usually ended with victory. People kicked other people's asses, they smoked them, dropped them, crumpled them, always with a crystal-clear description of the winning techniques. Mercy might be offered or refused, adversaries always seemed formidable, but they always got outsmarted in the end. Even losing fights became victories because they always defended some principle or faced impossible odds. Andy realized at last to what extent everyone had lied to him, because the stories always took the form of a series of events, leaving out the fear and the disturbing mix of sadness and elation. They probably didn't lie intentionally; they just didn't have the words to express something so big contained in such a short incident.

"No, it doesn't bother me. I can tell you about it. Basically—" A young woman appeared with the menu, and Andy closed it after a brief look. "Can you just order me some scrambled eggs and toast, please?" He waited as his companion laced the air with tones that still retained a strange American accent, then he continued. "Really, I was stupid. I never should have had my back to the door." He paused, realizing that the story actually began with the movement from one locale to another as the money changer set them up. A small part of his sympathy drained away. He began to describe the events that led up to the incident. He found himself fitting them into a linear progression, even the description of his strikes. Holt listened to it all with an interest that rivaled his attention to the origin of the Yüan brocade.

Andy became aware that the encounter and the piece of gold cloth had raised his status in a way he didn't completely trust. Before he'd been a hick from the Midwest. Now, he was the wild card.

Holt sat back. "Clayton never told me you were such a tough guy. I'd better not cross you."

"I don't know that I'm so tough. Maybe 'fucking terrified' gets the idea across better as far as yesterday's little event."

Holt gave his dry laugh. "And what happened afterward?"

He felt a slight motion in his head that he tried to keep from showing in his expression. "Silvia bandaged me up. Basically, I went back to the room and zonked out."

"Understandable."

"How'd it go with the textiles?"

Holt showed annoyance in his usual way, a slight crinkling of the mouth that now seemed a bit petty. "Not well. We think Mr. Gao is selling to another buyer."

Andy frowned. "That hurts."

"That's business. No sense in being a Pollyanna about it. The more disturbing development is with my South American partner, but I think I've got that particular tiger tamed also. How about you? I've heard that having gotten such a splendid introduction to Shanghai hospitality you're decamping for Beijing."

"Yeah. I always wanted to see Beijing."

"You've barely seen Shanghai."

"Hey." He pointed at his bandage. "I think I've seen enough." Andy could sense something more behind Holt's pleasant inquiry, so he wanted to be extra convincing. "Really, I don't have much time. I have to get back to help my dad. If I want to see Beijing . . . I mean . . . "

Holt merely watched as Andy terminated his explanation with a shrug. He let the conversation hang there for a few seconds, then his features relaxed into a friendly amusement. "Andy, you are a *very* poor liar. I'm telling you that as a friend." He tapped on his saucer, looking down on it, then raising his eyes to Andy. "What's going on? Maybe I can help."

Andy felt himself blushing at his own transparency. "If I have something I need help with you'll be the first person I'll call. Really, I just want to—"

Holt's hands went up. "Consider me convinced. I'll be at the Bejing Marriott the day after tomorrow. Let me know how you like the Forbidden City."

"Is Silvia coming too?"

If Holt denoted his interest, he spared him the embarrassment. "Silvia's going tomorrow, but actually she has a few days off."

"What's she going there for?"

"Silvia has a little business venture of her own, which is fine. She's told me about it."

"What kind of business?"

"Jewelry. Gemstones. That sort of thing. I think she said she deals with a Thai."

"Hmm." Andy struggled to decide how to approach the subject, deciding finally to hope that the conspiracy of the sexes might carry him through the awkwardness. He wanted to find out how to reach her in Beijing. "I, um . . . find her very interesting."

As much as he interrupted, Holt always seemed to give a person plenty of time to finish their sentence if it was something uncomfortable. After a long pause he answered with flawless neutrality. "That stands to reason; Silvia is a very interesting woman."

The waitress arrived like an angel. Andy picked up his fork. "Wow. Real eggs. Real toast!" He held the plate up to his face and lavished a few kisses on it. "I am dumpling-ed out."

Holt smiled. "If you haven't tried the rice porridge you don't know the true greatness of Chinese cuisine."

"Is that that glue stuff?"

"With the pickled vegetables and hundred-year eggs in it, precisely. I only eat it under duress. Chang loves it."

Andy worked away at his eggs as Holt split a croissant in half. Holt refilled his coffee for him and gave him a section of the *South China Daily News.* In that way they passed a wordless but pleasant quarter hour together. Holt folded his paper up and glanced at his watch. "It's nearly ten! I've got to get moving. Have you bought your ticket already?"

"The guy at the desk told me I should just go to the airport and get one. Is that true?"

"That works."

They both stood up. "Marriott, right?"

"Marriott."

Andy tried to seem casual. "When did you say Silvia is coming?"

"Tomorrow morning." He hesitated. "She usually stays at the Emerald Garden. Wait a minute." He copied an address from his black leather book and extended the little yellow slip to Andy. Andy thought he detected the scarcest expression of warmth in his smile. "I'm sure she'd be disappointed if you left China without saying good-bye."

Andy stood in line at the airport for nearly an hour before a man from Taiwan took his money and passport and pushed to the front of the window to buy him a ticket. He checked in and passed through a nonfunctioning Security gate into the waiting room. Video monitors were displaying a fashion show of Chinese-made clothing. It had been playing when he'd arrived, and now, two days later, they were still at it. Cool models took the runways like the tall icy Shanghai women who floated past him in the airport lounge, haughty and composed, as if they were alone in an unpeopled universe that existed to watch them pass. He found his gate and checked its correctness with a German businessman. When the plane took off he was still thinking about Silvia and the woven gold brocade.

He took out the cloth and the square piece of paper with the address on it.

> *Andy,*
> *A name: Lu Xiao Yu*
> *She's an old friend of mine in Beijing. I want you to look*
> *her up. Drop my name, give her one of the business cards, and*
> *ask for the package.*
> *You'll find her at the Beijing Opera, Dazhalan Jie.*

There was another piece of paper, handmade with a rough sage green texture. Scrawls of calligraphy descended the page, six Chinese characters that Andy had stared at so long that they'd begun to seem familiar. One repeated itself three times. He'd finally taken them to the reception desk of the hotel and showed them to the most sympathetic of the clerks there. The woman stared at it with a look of distasteful puzzlement, then showed him what each character meant. Now, as the airplane tilted upward, each little maze of brush strokes transformed itself, in a metamorphosis perceptible only by the mind, from ink on a paper surface into things that had meaning. Andy could read them himself—his first and only phrase in that language:

无
时 — *NO TIME*

无
序 — *NO ORDER*

无
限 — *NO LIMITS*

FORBIDDEN CITY

He spent the whole day feeling as if he should be somewhere else. A young man at the airport sold him a voucher and put him in a taxi to the Bei Lin Guest House, a near duplicate of the Yangtze Hotel in Shanghai but even more dilapidated. The same dark brown furniture squatted tightly around the bed, whose polyester spread bore craters formed by meteorites of burning tobacco. Low-watt bulbs gave off greasy little pools of light that died off a few feet away from their sources.

Bei Jing: Northern Capital. He'd expected something quaint and ancient, streets lined with pagodas and houses with upswept roofs, a genteel version of low, tight Shanghai. Instead he'd arrived at a city with wide modern boulevards and immense open spaces, like a huge strip mall without any stores. The famous Tiananmen Square had proved to be large and vacant, a public space so barren he couldn't believe it had been designed with human beings in mind. The guidebook attributed it to Mao. Only the immense red wall of the Forbidden City, crouched behind its massive brick gates and a few rain-coated tourists, hinted at something other than a missing past and a faceless present. The wide sidewalks and streets gave a feeling of emptiness, chilled by rain that came down incessantly a few degrees above freezing. He didn't care about the sights and he didn't think he could find them anyway. Illiterate, uncultured, and mute, he just wanted to be home.

Chinese Opera. Was that some sort of comedy thing? His shabby little tourist handbook gave only the sketchiest of accounts: "gaudy costumes," "hilarious antics." Two sentences and then on to the

Summer Palace. He wished he could turn to Silvia right now and say, What do you think? Should we grab some Peking duck before we head over there? Instead, it took him two hours of mistaken cab rides and retraced steps to make his way to the massive red brick arch of the Qianmen Gate.

Qianmen Street belonged to an older, more human-scaled city, filled, as his guidebook had predicted, with an array of restaurants serving the famous duck. The food markets and the profusion of hanging lights cheered him, and the glossy bright skins of raincoats and umbrellas shone in the glistening air like bits of confetti. According to the map, the Dazhalan Jie lay behind a three-doored gate over . . . *there*? He walked over to the entrance of the narrow lane, then stood before it, unsure of the next move. He bought a hot yam from a charcoal-filled oil drum and examined the map.

"You are lost?"

A young Chinese woman with wire-rim glasses and a puffy down coat presented herself with a slight grin. Her short hair fell around her wide pale face in little waves, a beauty parlor response to living in a country of relentlessly straight locks. Though she had spoken first she looked as if she might run away. For a moment he became acutely aware of the bandage over his eye. "You speak English."

The nervous pleasure of striking up a conversation crossed her mouth in an elusive tremor. "I very badly speak."

"No, you speak well!"

"Oh, no. Not well." She gave a small laugh. "You . . . are . . . very kind."

He liked her at once because of her plainness. He'd become exhausted with sophisticated people whom he felt he had to measure himself against. "I'm trying to find the Chinese Opera. I was told to come to Dazhalan Jie." She didn't react so he tried again. "Da! zha . . . *lan*?" Then again, "Da zha! lan!"

"It is just here! This is Dazhalan Jie. You are looking for what." She pronounced the question like a statement, and Andy realized that she had to struggle to find the correct English intonation.

"Chinese opera." He saw the blank look and leafed furiously through his guidebook for the right page. "*Jing-ju. Jingju.*"

"*Jingju!* You look for *jingju.*"

Andy confirmed it, congratulating himself on his Chinese. "I'm looking for a person, actually."

"A Chinese person?"

"Yes."

The girl seemed to agonize for a moment, then said, "I have little time. If you want, I help you." Then, "*Jingju.*"

She led him through the gate into the densely peopled street, threading among women holding bundles and cyclists who walked beside their machines. Dazhalan Jie was less than twenty feet wide. It must have been a foreign shopping area before; the facades of old colonial department stores made promises of British splendor they could no longer keep. As they walked, the young woman verified that he didn't fit into any one of the three standard categories of foreigner: student, tourist or businessman. "Why do you come to Beijing?"

They stepped out of the way of a man yoked to a two-wheeled food cart that he trundled behind him. "I guess you would say that a friend sent me. I'm looking for something."

"What are you looking for?"

Andy shrugged at his absurd predicament. "I don't know!"

Her perplexity shamed her, and she gave a pained smile. "I'm sorry. I don't . . . understand."

"This probably sounds very strange, but I don't understand either. I only know I'm supposed to look for a woman named"—he pulled out the note, reading off the name as he imagined it should sound—"'Lu Xiao Yu' at the Chinese Opera at Dazhalan Jie." He finally gave her the letter to read. She ducked into the doorway of a store so that she could unfurl the letter without getting it too wet, then read it carefully, moving her lips with each word.

"You are looking for a person, and this person has a package."

"Yes."

She stopped. Suspicion replaced her earlier expression of puzzlement . "What is in the package?"

"I don't know." He tried to think of how to explain it. "I'm doing this for a friend."

"Why he does not come himself?"

"He's dead." He struggled to alleviate the frown that was gathering at her mouth. "Yeah. Um . . . I know it's, uh, *unusual*, but he wanted me to get some things that he left in China and bring them back to America."

She nodded dubiously, and they started walking again. Two blocks down a crowded alley she pulled them over at a theater. Movie stills of heroines and armies on horseback had been tacked inside the glass cases.

"This is the Dazhalan Theater. Before they played *jingju* here. Now, I don't know. I will ask." She returned in a moment. "They no longer play *jingju* here, only in summertime. She does not know your friend. Other theater not far distance to here. We can go."

They got off Dazhalan Jie now, into smaller streets that were lined with open booths draped unceremoniously with pants, shirts, and jackets. Clients looked at themselves in hand-held mirrors, or quickly slipped on a pair of trousers while the proprietor studiously looked away.

The attendant of the second theater counseled them briefly, then went back to counting a pile of tickets. "Only films here, but he say that we can go to another not far distance from this place." Again they set out through the streets, past shops selling herbal medicines and others that resembled delicatessens, but this third theater had only films and an occasional acrobatic show.

The girl made a slight grimace, not of impatience, but of anguish, as if she were failing him. "I am very sorry. Not easy, find your friend."

"Don't apologize. I should apologize to you. What's your name?"

"Li Meiyu. My English name is Wilda."

"Wilda." It sounded as if it came from the last century. "That's a nice name. Wilda, you've been very kind. I have to thank you for your help."

"Not very helpful . . . "

"I feel bad taking up your time."

She seemed almost offended. "Don't worry my time. You are far from your home. We must find her today. Tomorrow I go to Tianjin with my classmates. One week." She responded to his alarmed look. "That man say one more place maybe have *jingju*."

They started again through the crowded labyrinth of the shopping area, past little teahouses and jewelry stores and onto the smaller streets where the shops became stalls again. He could smell urine, and see the mushy trampled remains of potato skins and cardboard underfoot. People kept staring at him as he passed; a young person would occasionally call out "Hello!" but when Andy answered they would turn to their friends and laugh.

"There!" Wilda pointed to several Chinese characters near the top of a poster. "She is here tonight."

He bought tickets for both of them, hardly able to believe that only a few hours separated them from taking the next step in Clayton's bizarre little treasure hunt. He noticed for the first time the red nose and weary look of the woman who had been wandering around in the rain on his behalf, and he felt an enormous surge of affection for her. "You know, I'd like to eat Peking duck. Would you join me?"

He wanted to lead her back to one of the large famous restaurants on Qianmen Jie, but she stopped him. "I know a good restaurant for roast duck. Not so expensive."

"Don't worry about that. It's my treat."

"No. You are far from home. Don't pay so much money for things."

She led him through the streets again, stopping at a glass window filled with rows of dark orange roasted ducks that hung by their feet. Inside, cooks in white aprons and hats moved among massive wooden chopping blocks and an ancient and blackened stove. They passed into the fragrant warmth of the restaurant she named as "The Very Great Duck."

Andy looked around. The restaurant didn't share the grandeur of its namesake. Stark white plaster caught the bluish light from humming tubes and sent it back out into the room without softening or diffusing it. A few faded photographs of the Great Wall suffered on the walls, and the tablecloths told the tale of previous meals in a vocabulary of tea stains and dried-out grains of rice.

She consulted with the waiter and chose the dishes, then took off her coat and hung it on a hook with her umbrella. The many layers of underclothes she wore gave her body a blocky look. She told him that she was studying international trade at the university, and she thanked him for a chance to practice her English. She'd originally come from a province whose name Andy didn't recognize. When she graduated she wanted to go to Shenzhen, in the South, where she felt more was possible. Andy guessed her age at twenty-two, but he didn't ask. He told her about himself. His work in the United States in construction seemed to make her think that he was a kind of real estate magnate. "You must be very rich!" He denied it, laughing. "No, Wilda. I'm not rich."

"You have a true heart," she said.

He couldn't discern exactly how she'd arrived at that conclusion, but a plate of cold sliced meat interrupted his wondering. She poured some soy sauce into a little dish for him, then grasped a piece with her chopsticks.

"I want to ask you a question, Andy."

"Okay."

"What you think your friend want you to get from him?"

"Wilda, I have absolutely no idea." He told her the whole story, starting at the letter in Hong Kong, then iterating backward to the fax, and even the remote nature of his friendship with Clayton. He minimized the part about the woven gold brocade, describing it merely as "an old piece of cloth." A cook came out to slice up their duck, and Andy paused to watch the deft wedge of metal vanishing into the brown duck and reemerging as each sliver of glistening flesh fell to the table. Wilda showed him how to wrap up the duck with scallions and plum sauce in the pancake, and the crispy skin dissolved in his mouth with an exquisite roast sweetness. A shower of hot dishes began to arrive at the table and he resumed his story. Between the straw mushrooms and the steamed fish she listened to the rest of it with an unchanging expression of interest, interrupting only to offer him food. At the end she went on eating silently. "What do you think of all that?" he asked her.

She answered by putting a water chestnut into her mouth, making him wonder if she'd understood. "It must sound pretty crazy," he prodded her.

She spoke with the straightforward authority of a bureaucrat giving information about the required paperwork. "You must find Lu Xiao Yu. If no, you pass all your life asking what is answer."

He nodded his head as he appraised her, making her shrug. "You're right."

"I do not understand why your friend make it so hard for you."

"I don't know either. He said it was something he didn't have a chance to bring back to Hong Kong, and that I'd understand when I found it. I guess . . ." The explanation about Clayton's eccentric character evaporated as he thought of Chang's admission about the drugs and the inexplicable sums of money and rare textiles. He felt a sudden uneasiness about Holt and Silvia and Mr. Liu. He was glad he hadn't told them anything. "I don't know. There's a lot of things I don't know." He remembered the gray opera ticket in his pocket. "I'm hoping that in a few hours we'll both know a little more."

They had nearly finished the meal when Andy noticed a tentative look in Wilda's face. She wanted to say something, then prefaced it by reaching over and filling his teacup. "Have you ever been to Lincoln?"

"The Lincoln Memorial, in Washington?"

"No. Lincoln"—she struggled with the word—"*Nabaska.*"

"Lincoln . . . Nebraska!"

"Yes. I'm sorry. I very bad speak English."

"No, no. I understand you. Why do you ask about Lincoln, Nebraska?"

"I had a friend in America. He came to Beijing to study."

"Oh, what did he study?"

"He study Chinese." She seemed to feel the need to clarify. "We were good friends. Not boyfriend. Only good friend. He came to my home village to meet my family one time."

Andy wondered if foreign men commonly met the families of Chinese women, and what that meant to the family, but he had to content himself with the ambiguous overtones that remained from her description. They had the feeling of hopes that hadn't been realized.

"Are you still in touch with him?"

It took her a moment to grasp the expression "in touch." "I wrote him letters, but after one year . . . no answer. I also change living place." She looked down at the plates. "Now I do not know where he is."

He wanted to ease her embarrassment. "Maybe he moved."

She took out a piece of paper, unfolding it painstakingly and asking him as if he might ridicule her: "Maybe when you go back to America, you find him for me."

He took the piece of paper, the evidence of a man named Philip Harris, at an address in Lincoln, Nebraska. The printing had been done in his hand, masculine and orderly. Andy tried to see Nebraska the way Wilda did: a distant place that, without famous landmarks to give it shape, remained an uncharted area of the imagination, like the blank spaces on the maps of early explorers. She still carried the slip of paper around with her like something dear, the dog-eared promise of a better fate. "I'll be happy to look for him." She tore a small piece of paper out of her notebook and copied the address, writing her own on the back of the little slip, linking them together by the minuscule thickness of paper and the layer of ink that spelled out their names. Andy watched the effort she made to set down the foreign alphabet. For some reason, it had become his lot to be entrusted with these missions.

When they reached the opera house a multitude of men in dull work clothes were milling around outside, factory workers who had received opera tickets as bonuses and now hoped to sell them on the street. Opera had lost much of its popularity in the past decades: when they went into the lobby Andy noticed immediately that most of the crowd had reached the latter part of their life. If he had expected an elegance reminiscent of opera premieres in the West, replete with pearls and evening dresses, the functional blues and grays of the old people buried the idea instantaneously. Only a few of the men wore suits or long overcoats in dark blue or dark gray, clustered in groups among the last fading Mao jackets of the elderly. People talked loudly in the plaster-walled anteroom, smoking and spitting, holding jars of tea. The whole room had gone fuzzy with the gray blanket of used nicotine. Wilda bought a cheaply mimeographed program for a few *jiao* and an usher showed them to their seats. "I will tell you which is Lu Xiao Yu."

The blast of strange music shattered the feeling of shabbiness. It resembled nothing he'd ever heard before: a dissonance of cymbals and drums that sounded like a closet full of kitchen utensils overtaken by an earthquake. The twanging of plucked instruments came in followed by a gruesome off-key lament of strings. A thin tormented clarinet embroidered it all. He'd never heard such music! And never before had he seen such a costume! It leapt into space, a shining mountain of satin topped by a glittering crown that raged up off the character's head like an exploding firecracker. The stiff red fabric of the gown sparkled with dense embroideries of silver and glass marshaled into intricate flowers or fretwork, casting off light at each fluid movement. At first he had difficulty imagining a person underneath the yards of material and baubles. She seemed a caricature of a Chinese woman, her face made pale with makeup and then heavily rouged around the eyes, making them deeper and wider, an effect heightened still more by the extra slant created by the heavy mascara.

She opened her mouth and burst into a tremendous atonal caterwauling that stunned Andy with its energy. She would sing for a time, then she would stop and the pounding din of the orchestra would take over for a few beats of what began to identify itself as a melody, then she would sing again. Another character appeared, this time in a long blue robe, strutting across the stage while devoting himself to the posing and preening that seemed to establish his importance. "That is Minister Li," Wilda informed him. He looked fat and overdone in his voluminous blue suit. Painted-on spirals and eye patches transformed his face into a grotesque shadow of Chinese character.

Minister Li spoke to the audience in a deep voice, a declamation clarified for the audience by strips of Chinese characters projected onto a white screen next to the stage. His voice had a wistful character to it, as if he was continually shouting into a storm and having the wind carry parts of it away. She smiled and glided over to him in small steps, then addressed him in an extreme falsetto that rose and fell between two points that, had they been poles, would not have marked north and south, but rather Modesty and Coyness, or some different scale of values that Andy could recognize but not comprehend.

Wilda explained the story to him, something about a minister and the king's daughter that quickly became lost in the welter of family relations, retainers, counselors, officials, daughters, and rank-and-file

soldiers that shared the same splendor of costume as the most important figures. The confusion wearied him, and he could feel the familiar tendrils of sleep stealing up on him. Wilda had told him that Lu
Xiao Yu would not be appearing onstage until after the intermission.
He relaxed into the darkness of the auditorium, peppered by spurts of
applause and the clicking of the instruments. The characters progressed through alien climaxes and resolutions, battered by fate and
the hammering metal and wood of the musicians. At particularly dramatic parts a character's lines might be set off by a few sharp clacks;
at other times a minister or king would come front and center and
soar up to a crescendo, holding it and modulating it, his eyes bulging
and mouth opened wide, then, after an impossible length of time,
twist it upward to end on a last powerful up note, like a whip made of
sound, and then the whole audience would explode not into cheers
but into short guttural bursts of voice, like cries of pain. A few times
he saw the audience give the same frenzied grunts for the mere movement of a sleeve or turn of the head.

He made it through to intermission, filed out with Wilda into the
lobby packed like a jewelry box with its wadding of cigarette smoke.
In the concrete bathroom the men were lined up ten deep behind each
urinal. It reminded him of the football stadium bathroom at halftime,
except instead of watching the win/lose puppet show that had become
the American metaphor, they had come to observe something far
more complex, a fanfare of beauties and gods. He could only perceive
it as sensation, a whirl of colors driven by a deep insistence, but he
sensed that somewhere beneath the costumes and the archaic plots
the archetypes of behavior were being held up for show, miniaturized
and made more than real by the stylized movements and ornate costumes. Just as the boy next door who became a quarterback meant
something to him and his friends, he knew that a similar link must
exist between the sleazy beard-stroking Minister Li and the corrupt
government ministers that Chang had told him were now all over
China. An amazing thought overwhelmed him: he could learn
Chinese. He could decode the whole vocabulary, picking up each
word and putting it in his mind the same way he'd learned to block a
punch by doing ten thousand motions. He could walk through the

garden and make sense of it, and unravel the intricacies of Beijing Opera. He could!

When he returned to the lobby he felt elated. Wilda waited for him with a cup of tea, and he questioned her about the opera. She had seen little opera herself; her generation had little interest in the slow rigid entertainment, preferring the lurid fantasies of movies and television, where the same opera stories were often acted out in naturalistic melodramas. Few young people wanted to train for the opera now: it was so very difficult, and no one could ever see your face. Now, everyone wanted to be a film star.

He asked her about the next part of the program. The second half contained two operas: *The Deception of the Empty City* and *Lady Zhaojun Crosses the Frontier*. She was about to explain the plots when the lights flashed and they trailed back inside.

A city wall and its arching gate spanned half the stage. Wilda explained: war was raging between the states of Shu and Wei. The Wei general floated across the stage in a gorgeous blue robe laden with thick swirls of gold. A long white beard hung to his waist. The Shu leader seemed more scholarly, with a mitered cap instead of a crown and a dark beard. Alas, he had been betrayed: his supporting general had neglected to bring his troops up, leaving only a skeleton force of old guards to defend the city. In a brilliant ruse, the Shu strategist threw open the gates and cavorted on the battlements with a lute and a pitcher of wine, commander of an imaginary army too mighty to be challenged. The Wei general, arriving at the paper city and suspecting an ambush, retreated forty *li*, giving time for reinforcements to arrive. The drama ended with the satisfying execution of the treasonous subordinate and, according to Wilda, the Shu leader's acceptance of responsibility for his misplaced trust, as befitted a good Confucian. "With false army, he save his city."

Andy had woken entirely now, devouring each costume and movement. The tilt of a wrist or turn of the head implied an emotion or character, intelligible to the audience in the same way that a *wu shu* master recognized the motions whirling through the air as being strikes or blocks. Wilda leaned over to him. "Your friend is star in next part. She is Wang Zhaojun." The tangle of strings and striking mallets billowed out over the rows of faces, and she appeared, adorned with a dozen glowing colors and a crown that stood a foot higher than her head, dangling tassels and furs, shooting off baubles and globes and striped antennae that wavered when she moved. Her face had been whitened and heavily rouged like all the other young women in the dramas: its individuality stripped away so that she became simply the princess, a generic woman given identity by her costume and her role. What would she look like in person? He could imagine her as slender and gorgeous as her character, moving gracefully to meet him after the production, wearing the poised expression of determination that had been painted onto her face. Andy thought he could see a difference between her movements and those of the earlier female characters, that they somehow conveyed more emotion. Indeed, when she slowly turned her face to the side and declined it to the floor, lifting up her long white sleeves to hide her sorrow, the men of the audience sent up a punctuation of earthy grunts.

She had much to be sad about. He struggled to make out the words that Wilda whispered humidly into his ear. "This western Han dynasty. Two . . . *thousand* years past." The emperor had sent her as a peace offering to marry a chieftain of the barbarians beyond the Great Wall. As she makes the long journey to the frontier, beset by the wind and cold, she remembers her family at the capital and the opulent life at court. Finally, with a last look backward, she crosses the frontier into exile.

The crowd exploded with applause, drowning out the music that they knew marked the end of the opera. It far exceeded any of the other ovations, and it made Andy proud to think that Clayton had friends in the highest strata. He suddenly became anxious that, having finally found his star, she might slip away. "I think we'd better go find her now." Wilda nodded, and they pushed across the knees of the still-applauding opera fans. He let Wilda take over now: she led them to the back of the theater, approaching each employee with a mixture of politeness and succor, until an old man stopped them at a pair of doors. Wilda spoke respectfully to him, motioning toward Andy, who the man looked over dubiously. He answered something, shaking his head, and when she insisted he loosed a burst of angry words.

Wilda turned to Andy. "He says no one can pass. Doesn't want hear why." The man looked off to the side, as if they weren't there. Without his cigarette and his defiant scowl he might have looked like a benign old grandfather. Instead, he embodied all the pettiness that Andy had seen in China; the tyranny of the ticket seller or the hotel clerk.

"Better we try outside. My other idea."

She led them outside to a narrow passage that ran along the building. "We will try this one." They walked along the dark brick. Andy heard a scurrying up ahead of them, where he could see a small pile of garbage. Why was he always ending up following people through alleys? The solution always seemed to be waiting down a long passageway that at the last moment opened into another corridor and a different space. This alley opened out into a miserable little courtyard formed by the butt ends of several buildings that squatted together around the theater. An open door poured yellow light out of the back of the theater building. As they stepped into the dreary stairwell, a voice challenged them, "Ho!"

They turned. Seated by the door an old woman in a dull brown jacket and pants was pointing at them. The appearance of a foreigner at her back-door post must have introduced a measure of novelty in her boring vigil; within half a minute she and Wilda were conversing like an old aunt and her niece. Andy heard Wilda pronounce the barely recognizable words "Hong Kong" and "Shanghai," and he saw the woman nod at him with a smile. "She says you are very strong. And very handsome." Andy returned her affectionate grin, embarrassed at the compliment. "Tell her it's only her kindness that makes me handsome." Wilda told the woman that, and it amused her. She beamed at Andy now as she spoke in an ancient English that probably hadn't been used in fifty years. "You . . . like . . . *jingju?*"

"I like it very much."

The woman laughed like the smallest of children, escaping for a moment the gray hair and lines of her old age. The infinitesimal transaction of language, called back from a long-ago education, seemed to justify at last the efforts she had made in her far-off youth, as if they'd been made for this casual moment. She started to formulate another question, then waved her hand, still smiling as she spoke to Wilda in Chinese. She offered to take a message to the one who was Lady Wang Zhaojun.

Andy took out one of his Invisible World cards, handing the blue and white ticket to the old woman.

The woman smiled and bowed, disappearing through the door.

Andy raised his eyebrows. "We'll see."

A minute later she came back, opening the door for them and flipping her fingers toward her. *"Dzo, dzo!"* she said excitedly.

They moved through the gray plaster corridor of heating pipes and bare lightbulbs, then through a pair of big metal doors and down another corridor clogged with the furnishings of a celestial kingdom: silver-colored furniture, golden teapots, tables and chairs in lurid colors, giant banners partially unfurled, gilded staffs and parti-colored maces and axes made of wood. The atmosphere of glorious make-believe framed perfectly this almost unreal appointment with the beautiful Lu Xiao Yu.

A middle-aged woman opened the door for them. Andy took her to be the dressing room attendant; she smiled quietly and motioned them in. The brick walls of the shabby dressing room had been painted white but were now dusty and bare except for a long mirror with a counter in front of it. The rest was crowded with the billowing satin costumes of empresses and concubines, or the dutiful daughters of kings. The woman who had opened the door wore shapeless trousers and a plain blue sweater. Her hair no longer had the lustrous ebony sheen of the young Chinese women but had turned more of a charcoal gray, lightened by strands of white. Andy asked Wilda if Lu Xiao Yu would be arriving soon. "This is Lu Xiao Yu."

She came over to him, her pale, unreddened lips modestly curved upward in welcome. Andy had expected Wang Zhaojun, the courtier whose beauty had secured peace for the Western Han. The appearance of the tired-looking woman before him left him off-balance, as if everything around him had changed again. He put his hand out and she took it lightly then let it go. She spoke to him in Chinese.

"I'm sorry. I don't speak Chinese."

Wilda took over for him, and the woman made an exclamation of understanding. Her voice had a mellow even tone to it, very different from the falsettos she had employed on the stage. It was hard to match the two beings together. Wilda translated for her.

"She says: 'You are friend of Clayton, yes?'"

"I am."

"She says 'Clayton is good these days.'"

Wilda translated it without imparting the rising inflection that indicated a question, putting it out as a statement of fact that located Clayton once more in the present. He imagined him somewhere in Beijing right now, the old Clayton he'd sat across from six years ago at the Liberty Grill. "When did she last see Clayton?"

The meaning of the sounds went back and forth, transformed from language to pure idea and then to language again. The opera singer hesitated. "She says, 'One month past. He very . . . happy.'"

He noticed a trace of rouge stranded at the edge of her eyebrow. He didn't know if she was telling the truth or glossing it over out of politeness. Maybe "very happy" simplified an unhealthy manic elation, or something more complex that Wilda lacked the vocabulary to properly express. And then the possibility, remote and shining, that everything stood on the verge of changing to its opposite. That Clayton had been happy, that the funeral was a sham, that the notes and the textiles all meant he was still alive. His next words issued forth even more awkwardly because he himself had lost his certainty of their truth. "I'm sorry to bring bad news. Clayton is dead."

Wilda translated, and the woman repeated the last part of her phrase, the shock appearing like an expression of concern. Wilda's translation shadowed her words.

"He die how?"

"He poisoned himself."

The woman leaned sharply back at the translation, then moved her head back and forth. Wilda said something that sounded like hissing, but in a quiet voice, and she put her hand on Lu Xiao Yu's shoulder. Lu Xiao Yu again turned to Andy. Wilda translated her slow voice.

"She do not understand. Clayton very happy. What happen to him?"

Andy took in a deep breath. "I don't know."

She nodded, observing him, then he gave her what he could: the details of when and where, all of which the woman absorbed calmly and with averted eyes. When that first level of details had been exposed she nodded her head and sighed. She stood up and wandered across the room to her mirror, where she noticed the spot of rouge and wiped it away, then dabbed the tissue across her eyes. She put on an old red sweater and came back to where Andy stood and told him something.

"She thanks you," Wilda translated.

"Tell her I'm sorry to bring her such sad news. Clayton sent me to her."

The words made their way to Lu Xiao Yu, who bowed slightly.

"Umm . . . there's one other thing. Clayton told me that she had something for me."

They took a taxi to the *hutongs* where Lu Xiao Yu lived, and even the cabdriver became lost in the maze of narrow streets. They entered a courtyard, then went up a stairway. As she put a kettle of water on she told how she had met Clayton. He'd come to her dressing room after the show with a bouquet of flowers. Maybe he had meant to be a suitor until he found out that she was an old woman.

"Oh, you're not so old!"

She waved her hand through the air at Wilda's translation. "She says: 'Not so old that she don't like hear you say it!'" They had become friends after that. She would teach Clayton about the opera. They would go to dinners after the theater. He would visit her for tea. "'Clayton have many friends in *jingju*. People like him very much.'"

She poured him a cup of green tea and presented a plate of sweet crackers from their crackling cellophane wrapper. The poverty of the place surprised him. She had one room, with a single blackened gas burner and a concrete sink that caught a steady trickle of icy water. In the corner a narrow bed held the neatly folded blankets and pads that kept her warm in the chilly atmosphere. It reminded Andy of a prison cell. Framed rolls of calligraphy hung on one wall, and also a beautiful brush drawing that rendered a pagoda on top of a mountain in washes of gray that somehow suggested color. She noticed him looking at them. All of them had been given to her, she said. Once she had had very much more: beautiful things, old things. Now . . .

The story ended there, or rather took off to be completed in his imagination. Wilda explained that during the Cultural Revolution *jingju* had been attacked as the art of feudal times, and many actors had been destroyed. Andy didn't press Lu Xiao Yu for details. He began to approach in his mind the indelicate question of the package that Clayton had told him to ask her for. He took out Clayton's note and asked Wilda to translate it for her. "She say she waiting for you to ask. Your friend have told her you will come."

The woman went over to her bed and extracted from beneath it a rectangular box wrapped in newspaper that had already begun to yellow. She put it on the table in front of Andy. He asked Wilda to tell him their date: they came from five weeks ago, which, if they hadn't been tampered with, would corroborate Lu Xiao Yu's report of when she'd last seen Clayton. Should he open it now or wait until he returned to the hotel room? The two women waited without speaking, trying not to look at the sealed package sitting on the table, then Lu Xiao Yu defused the moment by refilling the teacups with hot water. He thought of Wilda's patient accompaniment throughout the day. He owed it to her. Carefully unfastening the tape, he peeled off the newspaper and examined both sides of it. Nothing written: just newspaper, with its thousands of frantic characters racing across its surface with their outdated and now irrelevant notices. The box underneath also seemed ordinary: corrugated cardboard that had held a product he couldn't identify from the green-inked characters. It had been closed with paper strips that had been pasted over the seams. He took out his pocketknife and slit them.

He could see, beneath the message, a whirling forest of green and blue, something made of yellow cloth. He wanted to put the note to the side and go straight to the object behind it, but he forced himself to examine the sheet of flimsy paper that Clayton had left for him. He read it silently.

DEAR ANDY,

If you made it this far, you're as resourceful as I knew you always were. I hope you liked Lu Xiao Yu. My 2nd mother these

long cold stays and days zai Beijing. Hope she didn't take the
news too badly.

    I kind of like that robe. Early Qing dynasty, before Qian
Long. The emperor's chifu. Had to break a few eggs to get hold
of it, but you know the old saying: you've got to break a few
eggs to paint something in egg tempera. Anyway, don't adver-
tise the fact that you have it. It's not completely mine, techni-
cally. But hey, why get hung up on technicalities!

    Okay. You're in Beijing. I'm in Beijing, sort of. Stash the
robe someplace safe because you're going on a long trip. Farther
than Tokyo, farther than California. You're going to Inner
Mongolia. (Don't tell me you're surprised. You knew it would
turn out like this, from the first message.)

    When you're searching for the ultimate textile you have to
make a few detours. There's a place called Ulamqab, northwest
of Beijing. Go to Darhan Banner. Ride to the monastery at
Helan Qi. Look up an old monk called Rartha. A very special
man. Show him your business card. He'll give you the last
thing, the most valuable, the map of the Invisible World.

    Remember: secret as space until you get it, then confer with
Jeffrey Holt.

    This is the best part, Andy. The trip to Inner Mongolia.
Dress warmly. Settle it.

See you.
CLAYTON

    He was seeing him, all right. Without saying anything he unfolded
the yellow robe from its poor case, eliciting whispered gasps from the
two women.

    It seemed less a robe than a separate universe of pattern and color,
swirls of embroidery and gold thread rioting so chaotically over the
piece that it overwhelmed his sense of design and left him with a
momentary feeling of vertigo. A cloud or wave would assert itself,
then it would fall back into the mass of stitches and spirals that
swarmed over the creased field of the garment. Dragons made of gold
filaments coiled and uncoiled amid the torrent of threads, hissing

silently as they flexed their long white claws. He looked at the letter again, and the possibility rose up and swallowed him, the idea that this robe had belonged to an emperor. It seemed to have a glow, but one that couldn't be perceived with the senses, only intuited. Some part of Clayton, some part of an emperor, of a splendid throne and the rumor of court intrigue. He felt it and he tried to formulate the thought somehow, to crystallize it into a rule or statement, but it got away from him before he could get his mind around it. He kept looking at the robe, turning it over, looking at the lining inside the neck and the golden scales on the dragons. Was it old? Was it valuable? Was it real?

After a wordless two minutes Lu Xiao Yu offered him more tea, and Wilda let go of a sigh, and he realized the lateness of the hour and how at some point they would need to find a taxi. When he turned back to the robe it had lost its aura, converted once more into a piece of clothing.

Lu Xiao Yu said, through Wilda, "This is the coat an emperor could wear."

He agreed, then told her that Clayton had referred to her as his second mother, and that he apologized for any sadness that he brought her. It wasn't a literal translation of the note, but an accurate one. It brought her sadness back as a simple fatigued breath and glance off to the side, as if by looking away she secured a private place to grieve.

He told them the rest of what the letter said about going to Inner Mongolia. Neither of them had any idea where Helan Qi was or recognized the place names. They both agreed that they sounded Mongolian, but even Lu Xiao Yu had no idea why Clayton might want him to go there. Wilda had begun to show the day's wear, and Lu Xiao Yu looked at her and made a gentle remark that even Andy could translate.

The actress sighed and stood up. She began packing the robe away again, folding it carefully and laying it gently into the box. Giving it a last reluctant look, she put the top back on, tying it shut with a piece of twine she rescued from a drawer. She conferred with Wilda about the proper bus to take to get back to the center: it would come wandering past in fifteen minutes. Andy thanked her and put his coat on. They all ended up in front of the door, and she handed him the box. He was about to express his gratitude when something about her trans-fixed him. With minute precision she raised her hand and swept it across the room, dispersing in an instant the shabby interior. A strange force seemed to animate her now, to turn her head slowly to the side, and bring her arm up to shield her eyes with an imaginary sleeve. Her forefinger touched her thumb in an ephemeral gesture of perfect grace, and then her face swung away again with a supernatural deliberation, as if to a carefully chosen point in the heavens. An eerie falsetto came coursing out of her mouth in a succession of swooping elongations and sad birdcalls. It passed through the room like a weather front, leaving in its wake the crackling ionized atmosphere of rain.

"What is it?" Andy asked Wilda.

Wilda seemed to come a long way back to make the translation. "It is from very old opera. She says 'The Duke of Zhou cannot possess the Empire. Not with ten thousand chariots...at his hand." She looked past him, her mouth open, as she searched for the words. "To be a True King...in this time of...dis...dis-order"—skipping ahead—"I hear the cranes pass in the west." She fell silent a few seconds, then gave up. "Too difficult. English very difficult."

"What does it mean?"

Wilda kept the same even expression, explaining it only with the inability to explain. "It is *jingju*."

The opera star had given her eulogy. Maybe she had said it now because she would have no one to say it to later, or because it was fitting to have this brief funeral with Clayton's friend, the American with the cards that said "Invisible World." Andy thanked her again and she bowed again, and then they were simply facing each other. She stepped back, then spun her gaze around the room as if she were missing something, suddenly unwilling to see them go. Opening the door for them she looked exhausted and old. All traces of the beautiful Han princess Lady Zhaojun had disappeared, as if she had aged two thousand years in an evening.

The lobby of the gigantic hotel stretched two entire blocks, done in different colors of marble with details of dark oak. It formed a little island of Western culture for the well-heeled tour groups that it processed through on overpriced excursions to the Great Wall or the Summer Palace.

Having no place else to go in the miserable weather Andy had arrived an hour early, wandering into the Western-style coffee shop whose decor vaguely suggested a European drawing room of the last century. He was about to look over the menu when he saw her. Across the black and white floor tiles: the dark hair, the long back. She was talking to a small Asian man. He felt a buzz of excitement, unsure if he had the right woman; he kept staring at them until he recognized her purse. Her companion noticed and stared back at him, his focused, cold hostility making Andy look away. They seemed to be transacting some kind of business.

He finally crossed the room to her. Her back was to him, so she didn't see him until he was lurking at her side. The man with her seemed nervous. She glanced up at him, her face blank at first, then changing to an expression of pleasure. "Andy! You are early, aren't you?" She stood up and kissed him on the cheek. "How are you? Sit down, sit down, *amor*. Tran . . ." She said something in Chinese, in which Andy heard his name and the words *Hong Kong*. "Andy," she went on in English, "I present you Mr. Tran."

Her table mate favored him with a transitory tightness across the mouth that had nothing pleasant or friendly about it. The small table had been intended for two people, so he had to pull up a third chair and wedge it awkwardly between the marble surfaces.

"So, tell me: what have you been doing since you arrived in Beijing?"

"Nothing. Looking around. I went to the Chinese Opera last night. That was interesting."

"I love *jingju*." She adopted a falsetto and waved her finger in the stylized motions of the theater.

"I can see you're a fan."

The other man said something in Chinese that seemed unrelated to opera. Andy could tell that it was a second language for him. She answered him in a flurry of monosyllables.

Andy tried to be pleasant. "Where are you from, Mr. Tran?"

"He does not speak English, Andy. He's from Cambodia."

"Oh." There was a short silence. "Well, I don't want to break up your meeting."

He waited for her to object, but all she offered was a blunt smile. He pushed his chair back and stood up.

"Why don't you wait for me at the reception, Andy? We'll finish up here before very much longer."

She appeared a half hour later, clicking down the hall in a blue wool blazer and short red skirt; part schoolgirl and part provocateur. She brushed her lips across his mouth as her perfume washed over him as she bent close, ridden by a grace note of gold earrings among her black hair. She reached up to touch the bruise on his cheek with her fingertips. "It looks better," she said, doctorlike, then she grasped his shoulders and kissed him again, smiling with her narrowed eyes as she stayed close. "Don't bring out my dark side this early in the morning, Mr. Assassin!"

Andy tried to maintain his equilibrium. "I never bring out anyone's dark side before noon. How was your flight?"

She expressed her boredom with a sour nod. "We didn't crash. But I did not sleep at all last night. Look." She rubbed the slight darkness under her eyes. "Really, I am insomniac. It's terrible. And you? Can I ask if you have made contact with your secret government agent, or should I just follow the trail of bodies?"

"Don't bother; I've hid them well. What's the deal with Mr. Personality?"

"Mr. Tran?" She became bland. "We met each other last year in Yunnan province, near the frontier. He is in the gem business. I have a small business selling gemstones to some stores in Hong Kong."

"I get weird vibes from that guy."

"I have a business relationship with Mr. Tran, that's all." She looked behind her, then confided quietly. "The truth is, Mr. Tran is not a very nice man."

"What's his story?"

"Mr. Tran is a refugee. He was part of the last government, but when that government fell he had to go into hiding."

Andy hesitated, remembering an article he'd read recently about the slaughter in Cambodia. "Uh . . . wasn't the last government the Khmer Rouge?"

"It could be. I don't know his party." She sighed. "Really, I hate politics." Shrugging the feeling away: "How is it out there now?" She loosed his arm and darted toward the door, peering at the sky outside. "Still gray." He drifted along behind her. "Not so bad now. I think it has stopped raining." She turned back to him, lighting him up with her understated smile. "Have you been to the Forbidden City? You know it is very close from here."

"No, I haven't made it there yet."

She gave him a skeptical look. "For a person that came here to see the sights of Beijing you are doing a very bad job of being a tourist."

"I went to the Chinese Opera!"

"You went to *jingju* but not to the Forbidden City? Everyone goes first to the Forbidden City. You even said—"

He touched her shoulder. "Silvia. Does everything have to be a conspiracy? I wish my life were half as exciting as you make it out to be." It startled him, the way she grasped his situation so thoroughly through her spy novel logic. Luckily he seemed to have sidestepped her again.

"Let's go! It seems to be my destiny to always be your tour guide."

They walked a few blocks along the wide boulevard and then they found their walk accompanied by a long red wall. Reaching a vast open plaza that Andy recognized as Tiananmen Square again, Silvia led them through a ponderous brick gate garnished with a giant portrait of Mao.

Though Andy had grown up among the highest buildings in the world, he had never seen anything more massive or imposing than the entryway to the Forbidden City. The walls rose at least five stories, crenellated at their top and bulging thickly at their base. They had an almost supernatural feeling of impenetrability, amplified by the unreal sensation that he, Andy Mann, was actually standing in front of them. A few minutes later he was surveying the courtyard of his imagination. It was all there: the quiet white marble, the gigantic sunken patio and its gray ringing space. Mysterious galleries surrounded the square with their hypnotic succession of columns in dark lacquer red, while across from him, several hundred yards away on its high stone platform, loomed the magnificent palace building, its steep upswept roof floating in the mist.

She took hold of his arm. "Come on. We have eight hundred buildings and nine thousand rooms still to go."

They descended the steps that led into the huge courtyard. "Here the emperor had his public ceremonies," Silvia said. She went on interpreting as they gazed into each massive building: here in the Hall of Supreme Harmony the emperor presided, in this Hall of Middle Harmony he conferred with his ministers. The Palace of Heavenly Purity, the Hall of Union, the Hall of Preserving Harmony: each building's name alluded to the emperor's role of bringing celestial order to the empire, each one's failure testified to by a badly translated English sign telling when it had been built, burned, and rebuilt. Nonetheless, they all lined up perfectly, north to south, on an axis that projected their essence out the gate into Tiananmen Square and all of China, a vision of harmony that had never succeeded in permeating the unruly empire.

"So this was all for the emperor?"

"All of it. He was the Son of Heaven."

"You know, if I'd been born into this, I would think I was the Son of Heaven, too. How could you not think it?"

Silvia spoke without looking at him, leaning out over the stone balustrade into the entrancing view. "Clayton said the same thing."

The unpleasantness of the day had kept the number of tourists down, so the outsized spaces were nearly empty, their puddled marble pavement shining like wet iron. They walked on beneath galleries and into small museums. Silvia would sometimes hold his arm, then go off to look at something and come back to him again. They chatted about what they saw, and a bit about Holt and his mannerisms. "When he scratches his elbow it means he's lying." She laughed. "When he is eating a bag of dried fruit it means that his hemorrhoids are bothering him."

They discovered a small stage where opera had been presented to the nobility. The antique costumes had been set up on mannequins. He saw one with dragons on it, like the robe Clayton had given him, and he considered telling Silvia about it. Despite Clayton's admonitions of secrecy he needed an ally. He could feel the finitude of his time and the towering impossibility of finding a place that even Lu Xiao Yu and Wilda had never heard of. It was like attacking a skillful opponent; any movement left you vulnerable in some way.

Silvia led him farther into the Forbidden City. The monumental buildings and large spaces fell behind them, giving way to a more intimate maze of small courtyards and alleys. He followed her down a long red corridor, empty except for the gray vapor trapped between the walls.

"Really, I like the name Forbidden City," Silvia said. "It always makes me think of the entire idea of what is . . . *prohibido.*"

"Prohibited."

"Prohibited, yes. I always think of that. So many things, they are . . . prohibited. You build the walls around them, and no one can come inside, because if they come inside, they can do damage."

"You mean like laws?"

In the billowing fastness, her words came out like a poem, or the beginning of a confession. "But truly, one wants them to come inside." Several footfalls intervened. "Like when I told you my father was *militar.*"

She had embarked on a new course, apropos of nothing and without explanation. "I remember you telling me that."

He let the quiet sounds that came in from the distance mingle with the ether that surrounded them. Such a strange place, composed of solid walls and mist. It reminded him of the Yu Yuan.

They turned into a series of compounds that had once housed the royal family, each one with its own miniature tree or rockery for the amusement of the long-passed imperial clan. Through the windows they could see the austere furniture sitting empty and cold beside charcoal braziers that hadn't been lit in generations. Strange rectangular books wrapped in blue cloth sat in neat grids of cubbyholes in the library while elaborately carved beds waited beneath silk pillows. He couldn't help but imagine sitting in the chairs and sleeping in the bed, and amid the peculiar desolation of the place lingered a hopeless desire to be the emperor himself.

The rain had started again, barely distinguishable from the soaked air. They took cover under one of the galleries, and Andy peered into the crusted window of what he guessed had been a servant's quarters. Now it housed several buckets and paint brushes, the shabby storage room of the workers who maintained the grandeur of the palace. He could see Silvia's reflection facing him in the glass.

"Silvia?"

"Yes."

"What does it mean that your father is, uh ... *militar?*" Something pulled at her features from inside, and Andy spoke again. "You wanted me to ask. So I'm asking."

He was looking at her in profile as she continued staring into the grimy little room. Her jaw trembled slightly above the fur collar of her coat as she sighed. "My father is *militar* ... "

He waited nearly a minute for her to start again with her out-of-place story.

"Some years ago, you can remember, the Communists were getting very strong in South America. There were many ... terrorists, you understand? Robbing and kidnapping. ... So the military made a *golpe*. They took over the government. Not just Uruguay. Everywhere. Argentina, Brazil, Chile. In many places the same thing happened. They had to kill some few people. Bad people. It was necessary. It was a kind of ... war, you understand? But yes, also, some people became confused. You know, in everything there are always some mistakes."

She stopped there, and he waited. He was beginning to shiver from the cold. At last he said: "And your father was one of those people who took over."

She turned away from the window, but rather than look at Andy she gazed steadfastly toward a moon-shaped gate across the way from them. "No. He helped the people who took over. He had to protect the state. That was his job. But some very bad things happened."

"Like what?"

She kept looking toward the gate. "You can use your imagination."

He didn't know what to say. She wanted to talk and she didn't want to. He put his hand on her shoulder. "You know, you're not responsible for your father's actions."

He might have expected her to cry, but instead of looking upset she wore an almost childish expression of surprise, as if she was reliving a startling event from long ago. "You can say that. Yes. Of course, Andy. I also can say that. But many things happened. Do you understand? Many things I would like to tell you about, but they are very difficult. Maybe you even could say that I . . . I killed someone."

He stared at her in amazement, the fragile-looking bones and the shining black hair. "What do you mean?"

She started walking again and he walked beside her. They passed through the gate and out into an alley. She related it to him with an almost affectionate detachment, as if she was telling a bedtime story. "I was very young, Andy. Fifteen. I didn't know the way that things happen in those times that are so political. I had an enemy at school. One of the girls who came from the lower classes. She had a . . . *beca*. You know, where they give them money to study? And this girl . . . hated me. I don't know why. I did not do anything. But really, she hated me. She always used to call me *milico*." She took on a look of disgust: "'*Milico! milico!*' She talked about me to the other girls. I was so tired of hearing it. Maybe I could have bear it, but then there was a boy that I liked, and she talked to him with all her . . . poison . . ." With a businesslike coolness: "So that was it with the boy."

Andy waited for her to go on, then tried to help. "It would be natural for you to—"

"Fine," she interrupted, "that day came. My father asked me if I had noticed any subversive activity in the schools."

She fell silent again, looking into one of the gates they passed. "Look in there: it's another Tai Hu stone, like in Shanghai."

He glanced at it without comment, waiting for her to go on. When she didn't he prompted her. "So he asked you about subversive activity . . . "

She stopped and faced him, a fey smile drawn across her face. Her head shook slightly. "Andy! Isn't it clear?" She shrugged and started walking again. He watched her leather back receding for a few steps, too stunned to know if he should pursue her or let her alone, then he caught up with her and took her arm, afraid that anything he said would come off as trivial and obvious, realizing as they ambled wordlessly among the compounds that he no longer knew where they'd come in or where they were going and that neither did she.

At last Silvia sat them down on a bench and looked down at the pavement. "Every day I think about it, and every day it doesn't change. It is something that has no remedy." She let out a long swish of stale air. "Let's go on. I don't know why I am telling you this." She stood and took a few steps away from him, then turned around and hugged him, turning her face up toward his and pulling him down to her. He felt the pressure of her lips for a moment along with the fleshy taste of them, then the awareness of them gave way to a rippling sensation in his head. She turned her face to the side and squeezed him.

He had to tell her now, about the robe and about Clayton. It felt like the only thing he could offer her, a gesture of intimacy more significant than moral palliatives or talk of letting go of the past. "Silvia, I need your help. Clayton gave me something." And with the sound of his own plain words came the awareness and the acceptance, not like an opera or a melodrama, that all passion was forbidden passion because it involved letting someone all the way in, of letting them hurt you if they chose to. He had entered now: he couldn't turn back. He had entered the Forbidden City. The thought flew away, leaving him outside the Gate of Earthly Peace with her, getting into a taxi.

A sour look flashed across her features when she saw his room, then she tipped her head toward him ironically. "How did you come here?"

"A guy at the airport recommended it."

"He gets a commission from the hotel for sending you here."

"Oh." He'd actually begun to like the depressing little room. Sometimes it almost seemed cozy, even the musty smell that always greeted him when he opened the door. He turned on all the lights and opened the curtains, but the combination of rain-filtered gray from the alley and the putrid fulgence of the bulbs did little to illuminate the drab interior.

She seemed to notice his dismay. "Really, this is not so bad. When I was starting, all of my hotel rooms were like this."

By now he had picked up the pantomime of hotel room hospitality. "Could I offer you some tea?" She chose green, and he used the silent moments of preparation to try to get his bearings. The memory of her room in Shanghai permeated everything, along with the hurried kiss in the Forbidden City. He didn't know where to start.

"Do you know I have two names?" She put out the question in an ingenuous voice, like a child playing with dolls. Her sophistication seemed all gone now.

"What do you mean?"

"I have my Spanish name, Silvia Benedetti Jimenez, and I have my Chinese name, Qin Mei Hua. Qin is the family name, because it sounds like Jimenez. Mei Hua means 'beautiful flower.'"

"That's a good name for you."

"A friend in Hong Kong named me. I would like to give you the Chinese name Ma. Like this." She found a piece of stationery and began scribing on it. "For a family name. It is the word for 'horse.' It looks like a running horse, no? With these four strokes here?"

Andy looked at the four jittery dashes below the body of the character. "You're right!"

"The next would be . . . I don't know." She pushed the paper toward him. "I can't give you a full name without a dictionary. I'm sorry."

"That's okay: it takes a whole lifetime to make a name. That's my theory, anyway."

"Maybe it would be 'warrior' because you saved me from those robbers."

"Did you think I was saving you? I was just trying to save my own ass. Luckily we happened to be on the same side."

Her eyes shifted down, then surfaced again accompanied by a smile. "You are always so funny!" She tossed her head to the side. "What is it that you wanted to show me?"

He went to the closet and took out the box Clayton had left him. The yellow silk glimmered inside, like a box of dusty sunlight. "I'm not sure what to make of this. I think it's pretty valuable." He took it and spread it on the bed, stretching it out along its length like a sleeping person. He flattened out all the wrinkles and extended the arms to the sides, the strangely shaped cuffs reaching for the earth. She said nothing as he did this, and then the dragons and rainbow-colored clouds covered nearly all of his bed, asserting an imperial presence that even now made the whole room kneel in subjugation to it. Silvia moved closer to it and examined the part near the bottom composed of clouds, then looked at the scales in the dragon. "This is very pretty, Andy. Did you buy this?"

"No."

"How did you get it?"

"Clayton gave it to me."

Her eyes gleamed. "Clayton gave it to you! When? Don't tell me in Hong Kong!"

"No, here. At the Chinese Opera."

His admission seemed to strike her physically. She looked at him with disbelief, intoning slowly, "Andy, that is a very cruel game to play. Do you think I felt so little for Clayton that your joke does not affect me? Clayton is dead. How can he give it to you at the Chinese Opera? It doesn't have any sense!"

"He left it with a friend."

"Who?"

"With a friend of his at the Chinese Opera. About five weeks ago. A woman named Lu Xiao Yu. She plays Lady Zhaojun."

Silvia nodded slowly, her attention on the robe.

"Is it valuable?"

"What did he tell you about it?"

"He said it's from the early Qing dynasty. Before Qian Long." He pronounced it "Kwin," uncertain of how it should be spoken. "Something like that. Here, I'll show you the note."

He gave her the piece of paper to read and she submerged in it. She had a strange expression when she finished. She sat down at the edge of the chair and hunched over to stare at the floor, tapping her foot absently.

"What is it?"

She put her fingers to her head and pushed her hair away from her smooth forehead and the long black lashes of her scrunched-up eyes. She drew in a long breath, moving her head slowly side to side as she let it out. She came over to him and put her hand on his shoulder.

"What is it? Is it valuable?"

Her voice had sunk down to its low grieving registers again.

"Andy, this is very beautiful. Very beautiful. But it is not from the Qing dynasty. I think Clayton was only . . . not playing a joke, but . . . he wanted you to get into the excitement of things."

"What is it?"

"This is a Chinese Opera costume."

The back of his neck went tight, pulling his head away from her words. He moved close to the robe and looked at the blue and green threads racing across the swells of yellow silk. "Are you sure?"

"I'm sure, Andy."

"But he said it's from early Qing dynasty. Before Qian Long! Like . . . an emperor's robe or something. Even Lu Xiao Yu said it's the robe that an emperor would wear!"

She put her hands on his upper arms and looked into his face, speaking slowly and clearly. "The personage of an early Qing dynasty emperor in *jingju* would wear it. That is what she meant." She tilted her head to the side in a little gesture of regret.

He broke away from her and stood a time without having anything to say, then sat down on the small portion of the bed not covered by the robe. "Well. You never know, do you?" He kept looking at the terrain of waves and clouds that had deceived him. He couldn't believe it. He couldn't believe Clayton would pump him up with visions of an emperor and then crush him like this, especially in front of Silvia, to whom he had revealed it like some great secret.

"You are very disappointed."

"Well . . . of course."

"I'm sorry."

"It just . . . It doesn't make sense. He gets me all the way here . . . for an opera costume."

"Still, it is a very beautiful piece."

He kept looking at it, trying to see it clearly without the aura of what it purported to be. The glorious dragons glared out of its chest, every scale lined with gold, or perhaps, some metallic thread that approximated gold. Nothing of Clayton's seemed to be itself with any firmness; it kept flickering from one thing to another. This imperial robe that was an imitation of an imperial robe, that became one on the stage, that even lying here on the bed continued to be phony and sacred at the same time, sanctified somehow by the history that Clayton had attached to it. Things weren't one way or the other; they were all of them at the same time.

He lifted up the oddly curved sleeve and dropped it on the bed again. That feeling of being in a labyrinth returned, and the only thing he could know about it with certainty was that he hadn't reached the end yet. "It's been very strange, Silvia. The whole thing. I'm not sure what I should do next because it's getting very weird and he keeps asking me to go farther and farther. You can see it in the note. He wants me to go to Inner Mongolia. I mean . . . what's the story with Inner Mongolia? Why is he telling me to go there? Listen to this." He picked up the note. "'Look up an old monk called Rartha. A very special man. Show him your business card. He'll give you the last thing, the most valuable, the map of the Invisible World.' What the hell is that supposed to mean? What's he talking about 'the ultimate textile?'"

"I don't know, Andy. I think perhaps it is more of this game that Clayton is playing."

"Should I go there?"

"To Inner Mongolia?" She shrugged, her eyes turning to the robe again, then back to Andy. "I can't answer that for you. I think it will not be easy to go there. Particularly now, in winter. Do you have time?"

"How long would it take?"

"I don't know the place. Probably, with the trains and buses . . . to find out where it is . . . one week . . . more."

The urgency of hurrying back to help his father had been the secret organizer of this trip, doling out extensions in increments of a day or two. It didn't smile on the idea of another week. Andy remembered his father's voice when he'd spoken to him in Shanghai.

"It would be faster if you came with me. I'll hire you as my guide."

She laughed. "Andy, I would love to be your guide. I'm sure that nothing would be more enjoyable. But I am not very certain that I can explain to Jeffrey why I must suddenly disappear. We have that meeting next week."

"He told me about it." He sat down in the chair and read the last part of the letter again. When he'd finished, the false costume was still lying on the bed, an inexplicable fraud. He sat back. "I've come all this way."

"You can go. Of course. But if you go there, and you find another joke, how will you feel?" The sadness came back to her features again, something that couldn't be identified by any physical change of the mouth or the cheeks, but rather reflected itself in her movement, a slow liquidity as she lifted her gaze to him. "I would like to help you, Andy. Perhaps I can think of a way to arrange to go with you. I will try. Only please, why don't you tell me all of it? I can help you understand."

The fabulous robe lay on its back as if floating in a pool of water, grand and timeless. It almost took the place of Clayton's missing body, lying in state here in the room. It could wait another minute for him to admire the flat planes of her face and the delicate jaw that ended in a pointed chin. He was living Clayton's life now, he'd gone beyond his own, or else pushed his own into something else. Now, for the first time, he was the one who could answer the questions. The room took on a powerful intimacy.

"It started in Hong Kong, Silvia. No. It started before I even went to Hong Kong. I got this fax from Clayton inviting me to a going-away party. He said he was going to Inner Mongolia. That he'd settled the Empire." As he told the story she watched him, then gradually shifted her gaze off to the robe on the bed. She asked no questions, only took it in silently. "And these business cards . . ." She scrutinized them with a distant attention, as if examining a star through a telescope. "So in Shanghai I went"—putting the card down and resting her chin in her hand, staring up at him through the eaves of her hair that slanted down across her inclined forehead—"the door in. Kind of wild for a minute there. So that was how I found the woven gold thing, the one you saw in Jeffrey's hotel room. But also, he left this note with it." He fetched the note about the Chinese Opera out of its envelope and handed it to her, then handed her the calligraphy, which she regarded from within an abyss of silence. She seemed so numb that Andy translated it for her, uncertain of her grasp of Chinese characters. "'No time, no order, no limits.'" He shrugged. "Is it typical Clayton, or what?"

Something about her shoulders made him stop, the suddenly

STUART   COHEN

intensified droop or inward curve of them. He saw them shudder a little bit, and to his amazement a tiny cry of grief came from her down-turned head. "I'm sorry. I didn't mean to . . . "

"I'm always feeling the wrong thing at the bad time." She whispered between the sobs, each word torn to pieces. "When I'm supposed to feel sad I feel nothing. I'm an idiot. I'm *malcriado . . . bad!"*

Andy wasn't sure what to say, so he made the obvious comment. "You're not bad, Silvia."

She didn't remove her gaze from the floor. "You barely know me."

"I know you. It's not your fault."

She spoke into the carpet. "It doesn't matter if it is my fault. It simply is." The tears took hold of her, shaking her body and forcing her voice into a rumpled string of lumps and hollows. "It's all mixed together. It won't stay apart. I'm so bad!" She fell into another reel of sobs, and Andy lost track of his thoughts. He felt useless in front of her pain, so he just stood there with his hand between her shoulder blades, rubbing the surface of her blouse back and forth as if he were polishing a coin.

Neither of them had said anything for a long time, as if they wanted to let the energy of the room dissipate before they got on with the rest of their lives. His belongings had extended their domain to all parts of the room, and he beat them back into place. With a musty whispering of satin the robe began to retreat to its scuffed container. Silvia attended it wordlessly with her swollen eyes, following it as it gently crossed its arms and doubled itself in two, retiring to the cardboard box that had been its home.

"Don't put it in tightly."

He laid it softly in and pushed the top flaps down. He put the box on the dresser. "I'm exhausted," she sighed. "Do you mind if I lie down for a short time?"

"Of course not."

The bed squeaked as she sat down on it. "It's cold in here. Do you feel cold?"

"No, I'm okay."

"Hmm." She sprawled backward on top of the quilted spread.

"Would you like me to turn off the lamp?"

"It is so small that I can barely notice it anyway. But yes, turn it off." The sound of the light snapping twice, faintly, and its buttery yellow glow left the room. He went to the nightstand and turned off all the other lights. Only the sooty brick light from the window came in. He could see her staring at the ceiling. "This hotel room . . . all my hotels used to be like this, when I was starting. Always dark, like this." She went on dreamily. "They are so . . . funny. You take all your things out and hang them up, and it is your home. The best home in the world. Then you pack them again in your suitcase . . . and before you even can get out, it is someone else's room again. Of course, you always leave things. In one you leave your notebook, or a pair of socks under the bed. You leave your shampoo in the corner of the shower. I like to think of them all forming a trail of where I've been, except, truly, there is no trail. The maid picks up your socks and your little bag goes to the home of the woman who brings the towels. There is no trail. Only the one you keep in your head." She stopped talking and turned her face to him with a little smile. "*You, you, you.* I like the second person impersonal that you have in English. That '*you.*' It's you, it's I, it's no one."

Andy was lost now; paralyzed in his chair, holding onto his cup of tea like a lifesaver.

"Andy?"

"What?"

"Are you a believer in custom or . . . *renovación*?"

"I don't know what you mean."

"Do you think a person can change simply by wanting to change very badly, or do you think they will go on living as they have, because it is their custom?"

He considered the strange question in the light of everything she had told him about her father and her past. The interior of his office back home came to him, with its picture of a mountain and the messy array of billing slips and blueprints that even now had to be filling his desktop. "I guess I have to say I'm a believer in . . . uh, renovation, if the person has a strong enough will. I want to believe that, anyway."

"I want to believe that also."

A cart rattled by at the end of the alley outside. The hollered solicitations of the driver traveled faintly through the glass, still maintaining even in their foreign intonations the sense of a long, tiring search.

"Rags," Silvia said.

The image of the unseen ragman faded away with the clacking of his horse's hooves, and Andy found himself sitting tensely with the lukewarm teacup between his fingers.

"Andy."

"What?"

"Why don't you come close to me? You know that I want you close."

He came over to the bed and sat at its edge, and she moved over and patted the empty place, still warm with the heat of her body. He lay facing her on the narrow bed, and she raised herself up on her elbow, her eyes traveling from the small bandage on his forehead to his eyes, then down to his mouth and his round cheeks.

"You are not a pretty man, Andy. But you are a beautiful man."

The light cool feel of her fingertips surprised his skin, curving from his cheekbones down to his jaw, then gliding along the side of his neck. He looked up into her face. Her dark brown eyes looked down at him with a mix of softness and piercing intensity that startled him. He lifted his hand up to her side and touched it in a way that seemed to him extraneous and ineffectual, then he held her waist as she brushed her lips lightly along his cheeks and his forehead before touching them to his mouth. Her tongue had a hot liquidity imparted to it by the tea. He could feel its point moving slowly between his lips. Her sense of fragility had evaporated now. The body that had seemed so reedy and delicate had become substantial, and now lay on top of him with the full weight of a human being. Running his hands along the curve of her buttocks he suddenly realized that she was a woman, corporeal and alive, not an idea or an angel or a savior or a girlfriend. It could never be mapped. It could never be described.

He felt her teeth at his neck, and the frightening sensation of her soft wet mouth closing around his jugular vein made him arch his back. He heard her laugh, her fingertips coursing roughly through his hair, and he laughed also, although not sure at what. The smooth texture of her skin against his hands felt at once close and inconceivably distant.

She made a gentle sigh as he touched her breasts, and then she reached back to undo her brassiere. They came loose into his hands, and the strangeness of the moment gave way to a primal goodness that bore no argument or doubt. Tugging at their clothes, seeing the long flat curves of her stomach and hips. *This woman . . .* " then lost in the downy warmth of her belly and her torso . . . *woman . . .* the sight of her above him, coating him with her exquisite warmth, her long hair and upturned face dissolving the particularity of the moment, rendering it mythical so that he was not simply he nor she she, but every woman, living ivory in a cloisonné room, her body as weightless as her hair that swirled around and about them, a vision of ink. "Like this." She guided him, feeling his fingers against her, the fullness and the ticklish aching sensation running up her spine to her breasts, clouding her head. She looked down at him, and he looked so boyish, astounded by pleasure, this strange mix of killer and child who didn't even understand what he had. She had grasped the secret root of him, and tremors crossed his face each time she moved. She bent down and brushed her breasts along his chest, feeling the hairs caress them like a carpet of tiny fingers. It felt good, in this hotel room, this funny innocent. She could see the scarlet bruises along his ribs from the fight, though even injured they looked so much stronger than Clayton's stavey bones, and at the end the worst, when he lost interest in eating. Clayton's image came back to her, and she lost the rhythm of her body, had to change positions so that Andy wouldn't know. She carried it off well, finally putting Clayton aside to feel the brute intrusions of the man behind her. Touching herself, the urgent moment, then the violent wash of tingling sensation spreading from below, lost in pleasure and the breaking of the wave.

She woke up next to Clayton, feeling him at her back and turning drowsily to him. It felt good, like he would take care of her the way he always did, wrapping her with his familiar smell and the singular way he had of holding her so weightlessly. Soon he would be cutting up an orange for breakfast and making tea. "I always travel with my own tea. *Bo lei cha.* It's good for the heart meridian." The moment hung there only a short time, an entire universe where Clayton was alive and next to her, then something large and dark started to surface, pushing Clayton away and oppressing her with the sensation of sharpness and entanglement. The memory of what had happened expanded like a fireball, jerking her eyes open to the miserable little hotel room and the sudden rush of blood to her head. She unclenched her teeth, feeling the complaining ache of her jaw muscles and the tightness at her temples. She held still, carefully relaxing her face and opening her eyes. There was a body next to her, a living one. Her mind searched calmly for its identity, and in moments she had recollected the previous night and the impossible dilemma that accompanied it.

The solution had tried to insinuate itself to her as she'd drifted off to sleep, but it had been inconclusive, and lying in bed with Andy she'd pushed it away. It came back to her though, like a vicious but loyal pet that had been following her from the moment Andy had revealed the gold brocade in Shanghai. She carefully got out of bed, looking for her clothes in the dark. A razor of pink light coming through the curtains cut across the mound of silk and deflated socks, showing a fragment of each piece, and she put them on as quietly as she could. She had to go now, before dawn came. She felt around for the box and the letter, quietly withdrew the gold robe from where Andy had left it. A drowsy stirring from the bed. "What's up?"

"I'm going to get something and come back. It's a female thing. Don't worry." She put down the box of textiles and went over to him and kissed him, then found herself lingering there and putting her arms around him. Maybe she should simply get back into bed, cover herself up to her eyes with the opiated sheets, and say nothing at all. Maybe she didn't have to decide right now. He put his hand on her arm and squeezed it sleepily. "Okay. I'll be waiting for you." And that sealed it, closing up her coat and sending her out into the frigid night of the Northern Capital and the darkness it had accumulated.

What would Clayton say about her heart meridian now? *Severely yin deficient,* or maybe just, *It's fucked.* For a while, Clayton had talked of meridians and *chi* with the same certainty as a pious Catholic describing the resurrection of the Lord. Yin *chi,* yang *chi.* He'd informed her about the state of her energy within fifteen minutes after they'd met, at a bar in Lan Kwai Fong almost four years past. This place had been turned out in a World War I flying theme, the Allies, of course, with a giant mock-up of a Spad Vll soaring across the ceiling. A foreigner bar, filled with young travelers making the rounds of Asia, in blue jeans and grubby shirts, temporarily detached from their backpacks but still carrying them. In suits and ties were the executives, the ones who never learned Chinese and remained forever stranded between the worn-out exoticism of Hong Kong and their own sense of being somewhere a few cuts below London or Sydney or wherever they came from. They clubbed together after work to complain about the locals. A few Chinese circulated among them, elegant in their sleek business clothes, smoking "555" cigarettes and drinking Scotch. These were the Chinese who could speak English, French, and Mandarin, as well as haggle over ten cents with the street vendors in their native Cantonese: people like Chang.

Clayton had been tending bar, or rather, presiding over the bar with an attitude of disinterest so complete that it seemed unbelievable that he was actually working there. It had struck her the moment she saw him. He didn't seem attached to anyone or anything. When Holt had appeared Clayton informed the other bartender that he would be taking a break, just like that, the classic "fuck it" attitude. He wore a black T-shirt and had slicked his hair to the side in a style at once hip and archaic. She'd liked his face. He had the build of a malnourished athlete, but she didn't care so much about bodies. She'd already had her Commando, the perfect Hard Man, to whom the world was a dichotomy of victor and vanquished. He always won, and she could have married him if he hadn't fallen so stupidly in love with her. He'd gone syrupy and she'd gone to Hong Kong, to appear in that bar across from Clayton Smith who had assessed her without any particular friendliness. Holt had introduced them, then disappeared to talk to an acquaintance who had hailed him from across the room. "What do you drink?"

"Scotch on ice."

He went behind the bar to pour her the Scotch, charging her nothing, and one for himself. As he measured out the drink he began to talk. "You know, no one really likes alcohol." He put the glass in front of her. "It all tastes bad. That's the long and the short of it: it tastes bad. We spend our whole lives trying to find drinks that taste less like poison than others, or telling ourselves we really like it." He sauntered around the bar and crumpled into the stool next to her. "I mean, we're drinking a Scotch right now. Okay. But what we're really drinking is all the associations we have with Scotch: that we're sophisticated. That we're rich, or, well, at least a little rich. We're drinking the idea that we're the kind of people who really like this stuff, whoever they are."

She hadn't known what to say to this sudden onslaught. She looked at her hand curled around the glass, then she lifted it toward him, looking him right in the eye. "Cheers!"

He'd let loose a huge laugh that subsided into slit-eyed suspicion. "Hmm. Unshakable. What's her bio? Let me guess: you're a drug trafficker. Right?"

"Correct."

"You're a drug trafficker masquerading as a student of classical Chinese music. Also an expert on Ming dynasty ceramics, particularly . . . tea utensils."

"Ming *and* Qing dynasties."

"I'm sorry, Ming *and* Qing."

"Don't begin to subvalue me already. You don't even know me. I could have you killed for that." A haughty toss of her head, "Now, get me another ice cube for my drink."

He'd laughed, and slowly gotten up and gone behind the counter to the ice chest. Finding a chip of ice the size of a pea, he reached over to her glass and plopped it in like a timpani drummer hitting a key note. "Okay. You work for the Argentine wool office and you're helping Jeffrey out with his business. You got to the Kong a few months ago. Jeffrey and I have been friends for a long time, but we do occasionally talk."

"Now tell me your biography."

"My bio . . ." He looked up at the ceiling and down into his glass, then he raised his eyebrows and said with an airy sigh: "To be honest with you, I'm not a great believer in chronology. But I'll give you my bio." He paused so that she would listen more closely, dropping his voice, as if describing something mysterious and incompletely understood. "Three minutes ago I was standing at this bar and two people walked in. One was Jeffrey Holt, the other was this . . . woman, slim, about twenty-one, with long black hair. She looks kind of fragile. She looks kind of dangerous. After that I spend thirty seconds pouring a couple of drinks and then I sit down and start talking to this person from South America who is completely out of place in Hong Kong except for the fact that being out of place here is a sure indication of fitting in perfectly. And after talking with this woman for a short time she asks me for my bio and I say: 'I'm not a great believer in chronology.' Every aspect of life radiates out of this single moment in a million directions. Some of them go to China. Some go to Tokyo. America is somewhere in there, of course, and various years and places occur, but also"—he spoke as if he was letting her in on a secret—"equally important are the little moments that can't be described in capital letters or in order. So what real thing could I possibly convey with a succession of years? To say I'm this or that construction? To try and convince you I'm the kind of person who likes Scotch?" He shrugged, then laughed at having completed his circle.

"*Carajo!*" She shook her head, the amusement curling up her lips. "You are a talker!"

"I'm a talker. I admit it: I'm a talker." With a tilt of his head: "And now you have the first element of my bio."

She laughed out loud. He'd more than answered her question, but at the same time, not answered it. He didn't seem to be trying to impress her; he just seemed to relate to people like this. So unlike most men, who trundled out their curriculum vitae and their attitudes like a company looking for investors. "I must say: I'm flattered that you think I look dangerous."

"You know why I think you look dangerous?" In explanation he held up a pack of cigarettes with a single prominent Chinese symbol that looked like two identical tightrope walkers linked together. "Double Happiness."

"Because I smoke cigarettes?"

"No, because I smoke Double Happiness. Most popular brand in Hong Kong. It's lethal." His features took on the exaggerated glee of an advertisement as he broke into a little song in Chinese, then sang the same tune with English words, "Everybody Wants Double *Happiness!*"

The sight of him singing in Chinese made her laugh with amazement. She touched her fingers to her forehead, her lips still pursed from his joke. "You have lost me."

"Never mind. It's my own stupidity. Anyway." He grew suddenly winsome. "It's nice to meet you. I didn't mean to run you over. I have a habit of doing that sometimes."

After that he'd told her she looked out of balance. Her pallid complexion, the flecks of light in her corneas. "It's your heart meridian. What's after you?"

"What's after me?"

"Yeah. I can see it by looking at you. Some people come to Hong Kong for the adventure and some people just leave to get away and end up in here because it's far away from whatever it is they want to get away from."

She'd pushed out a laugh, then said, as if a little bored, "Oh? Do you read tarot cards also?"

"No. I read spirits. They're like tarot cards."

She'd felt uncomfortable, a little afraid. He seemed like some sort of freak, but he wasn't a freak. The truth was that he'd been totally accurate. She wanted to back him off a little bit. "You have an unusual way of introducing yourself."

He'd turned goofy again, smiling at her in a way that encouraged her to smile. "I know. I'm always like this. Can you imagine what my job interviews are like?"

And against her will, they'd become friends. He would call her and take her to strange marginal places in Hong Kong, parties peopled by artists and what seemed like criminals, and to visit friends who lived in slums. Up until then she had socialized almost exclusively with foreigners, but Clayton spent much of his time with Chinese people, managing a passable salad of the difficult Cantonese dialect. He took her to meet incense merchants who told her about the strange woods and resins that occupied their back rooms. She had her fortune told and acupuncture treatments for her insomnia. In Chang's glorious apartment in the Mid-levels she listened to the two friends' attenuated investigation of tea, Confucianism, and the invisible world. Visits to cheap hole-in-the-wall restaurants interspersed every outing; Clayton prided himself on his knowledge of the cuisine and taught her how to order meals. She started learning Mandarin. His past intrigued her. Holt filled in the biographical details about Japan that Clayton had deemed so unimportant, and as she came to know him she began to see a different man, one who could focus on a single vision with a tenacity and discipline that sucked the surrounding world into its sway. This was the man who had taught himself to read and write Chinese in six months, who in a few years had learned to create paper sculptures that won him success in a country that had specialized in paper making for centuries.

When the time came, she had seduced him with ease, knowing from the beginning that he wanted her and that she merely had to choose the moment. She chose China, in Guangzhou, their first night away from Hong Kong in a closet-size hotel room that looked out on the elevated expressway. She had originally specified separate rooms, just to torture him a bit, but she'd grudgingly acquiesced when the hotel only had one vacancy. A sole double bed insinuated the coming proximity from the moment they opened the door, making its obvious statement: one bed, two people. A dangerous-looking plastic fan scarred with cigarette burns gave the room its only ventilation in the steam room heat, along with the traffic noise blowing in through the window. Outside the dilapidated balconies piled on top of one another among the grubby windows with their fluorescent-lit lives. A shower to wash off the sticky train wind, the towel wrapped around her. "Should we go to dinner?" "I want to rest a few minutes." The bed's dirty cotton blanket, lying down on her back, awkwardly inhabiting the same space with him for the first time as he sprawled on his part of the bed saying something about the Pearl River. Did you know that the Chinese considered pearls the concentrated essence of the moon? A sigh, the wordless wait, then the tentative stretching of a limb across the space so that it brushed against another limb, lightly, but with a neon intensity that frightened her. Clayton almost seeming to recoil, as if afraid of the next step, and for a moment she feared it, too, feared the path that accelerated from the equilibrium of friendship, which could go on forever, to the status of lovers, which would always end, end badly, her dropping him with a few impersonal words, like a tango, and Clayton couldn't bear that so easily. He had no wife to go back to and no past to go back to either, he only had his beauty and his emptiness. She looked over at him and he was facing her, the corners of his mouth nervously pursed, she nervous, too, because at last she had something to lose, though she didn't know what, she didn't know anything except that she stroked his cheek and he reached for her and then everything got lost. No memory, no name. She grasped him like a desperate prize.

She walked up the narrow *hutong* toward the bigger street. At three in the morning the absence of taxis resounded in the empty avenue, stranding her with her ungainly box in the leaden, watery night. The rain was coming down interminably, trying to wash away the whole city, softening with each drop the pasteboard that contained the robe and the letter. She tried to shield it with her coat, but could only hug it closer to herself, as if Clayton himself lay neatly folded in the dark interior. She had it back now. Even losing the *jin*, the *chi fu* would make Mr. Liu happy. He had nearly always maintained that perfect smiling equanimity with her, except for last week, after they had searched Clayton's studio. They'd spent hours looking through his ridiculous cardboard, and all the time Clayton so freshly dead that she kept expecting him to come walking in, white and vomit-covered as when she'd found him. Mr. Liu had searched silently, looking under every box and in the ragged cushions of the couch. A burst of annoyed Mandarin: "Why don't you help me? This is your fault! Your fault!" What else could she do but shrug and smile, turning back to the window so that he couldn't see her face.

She'd hid between the exhausted covers of an address book she'd found on the sill, quietly examining the constellation of addresses in a dozen Chinese towns, some in characters and others in alphabet, and the name of a woman in Berlin, a man named Carlo in a small town in Italy, Illinois, New Delhi. In that single little book intersected histories from across the planet, the casual exchanges and the bitter longing, like a map, like the limitless number of lines that can intersect at one single infinitely small point. How many young people were living the excitement of their twenties for the rest of their lives in places they themselves might barely remember, living it forever in the outdated pages of the register? She looked up her own name, but the book listed an apartment she'd left a year ago. It hurt her a little, that he hadn't written the new one in. It fell like a mute pronouncement on what had happened in the end.

The thought of it stopped her. She looked out into the shiny void of the abandoned avenue, hoping to spot the yellow light of a taxi. Nothing, only the bleary red disk of the traffic signal and the other night lights scattered through the darkness like coins. She thought of Andy in his dreamy bed like a bather on warm beach sand, his calm voice. Why not go back? Perhaps they had a little more time left, another week or two. She could go back and explain that the robe hadn't really been Clayton's, that it belonged partly to her, or completely to Mr. Liu. Then they could softly talk and drink tea while she proposed the possible solutions. He would listen calmly, and then they would decide. She could do that. After all, it had never belonged to Clayton.

"I tell you, Andy, it is really very complicated." Once she started with the truth, though, it took on its own life. She would have to explain that it hadn't really been Mr. Liu's either, that in a sense it also should go to Jeffrey Holt, since she worked for him. Honesty would unravel it all the way back to her own embezzlement of the textiles, and then everything with Clayton. Some men would ride gallantry into the ashes, but how gallant would he be then, when he understood how she really was?

Why wasn't it there! She wanted to imagine it into existence: the glowing yellow roof light with the characters for *chu dzu* coming into sight far off down the avenue, beneath it a weary man in a down coat who would appraise her as she climbed in, calculating how much extra he would charge her on the pretense of the hour or the distance, or that she didn't have FEC or that she was carrying a box or any of a dozen other reasons for overcharging that they always settled on foreigners, somewhere on the list: Western women running away with stolen textiles must pay one hundred times the amount on the meter.

She would pay that now and not even negotiate: anything that would get her farther away from the urge to go back to the room and tell him everything, to finally try to clear the whole thing and collapse for a while. To be held and to rest.

No, that would be giving up, just when she had almost everything. Do this, *hija:* call Mr. Liu and tell him you have the robe. Don't mention the tapestry, at least, not until you have it in your hands and can negotiate the price with him. From Clayton's description that piece was much more valuable than any other piece she'd ever handled, and a lot more dangerous. People would go very far to get something like that. Perhaps she would do better to bring it to Hong Kong and hide it, or even better, get it to England. That's what Jeffrey often did because there were no antiquities laws there. They had never signed the UNESCO agreement.

What a pity she didn't have Jeffrey's help on this. He had all the connections and the knowledge. He could negotiate. Perhaps when he saw Clayton's tapestry they could patch up the damage from the robe and the other textiles, or maybe she could arrange it so that he wouldn't even find out. An extraordinary textile would go very far in soothing Jeffrey's suspicions, and Clayton would not be there to contradict her.

Finding it had been lucky. Clayton had heard of the robe from friends in Beijing, and they'd gone there together two months before to see it and hear the story. An old man killing himself with cigarettes and washing the nicotine down with a special herbal tea from the doctor. He'd been a servant to a Kuomintang officer between the time the KMT had looted the Imperial Palace and their flight to Taiwan. 1949. The Communists were at the edges of the city, and chaos had infiltrated the ranks of officers like an advance guard. In a careless moment he had rifled the trunk and deserted his master. He delivered his rationale for the betrayal with a tone of saintly patriotism: he couldn't bear to see the KMT make off with the national heritage. He had reason to believe his story would convince them: it had worked in 1949 when he'd saved himself a bullet in the head by presenting the Communists with most of the treasures. He spit into the wastebasket. He'd been lucky, he said. He had only gone to prison for five years.

So simple, she'd told Clayton. We pay the old man his three thousand dollars in cash. Mr. Liu pays us twenty thousand, and we each make eight thousand dollars. For some reason that he wouldn't reveal, Clayton had needed a lump of money. She'd gone back to Mr. Liu and persuaded him to front her the cash. The robe was very expensive and the seller wanted the money, ringing and singing, before she would let it go. Mr. Liu probed for details, bringing out a bottle of cognac that had cost seven hundred dollars at the Hong Kong Duty Free and pouring her a large glass. You are very clever to find this woman in Shanghai. We could do very much business together. But it would be safer for him to go with her to buy the robe, wouldn't it? He could pay her the commission afterward.

She'd held fast; she had a right to protect her source. She went on quickly, giving him only enough to make it seem plausible, instead luxuriating in the fabulous details of the robe, its gorgeous brocade made of peacock feathers, the perfect condition. We are friends, he'd told her, we must trust each other. But it is a very great amount of money! It is, she agreed, it is a great amount of money. She could understand if he was not comfortable with it: perhaps this was not good for him. He was a very clever businessman. He knew much more than her.

She'd known he would trust her. After all, they had a working relationship, and he'd given her half that much before to run various errands for him. He'd smiled at her: friendship first, business second. Without trust, there is no friendship and no business. And so he'd given it to her, a thick stack of hundred dollar bills that made her nervous. Twenty thousand for the robe and five for the other textiles she had gotten for him. They'd gone back to Beijing together, and for some reason, desperate as he was for the money, Clayton had suddenly become reluctant when they arrived at the old man's little apartment. Some pang of loyalty toward Holt, who really had nothing to do with it. She'd had the cash with her and she'd bought it, including him in the deal whether he wanted to or not. He'd swallowed it, but it had given him an indigestion that stayed with them the rest of the trip. By the time they reached Shanghai he had gotten so morose that she didn't even want to sleep with him anymore.

Then that morning in the hotel room, two weeks later. Shanghai, the Lu Song Yuan . . . Holt was paying. They'd looked out at all the big new buildings standing out from the red tile roofs, enjoying the moment of triumph when all the textiles were laid out, waiting for Mr. Liu to arrive, and she'd gone in to take a shower and when she'd come out his atrocious surprise: the sight of the empty bed, of no robe, no riding outfit, of no Yüan woven gold, only the memory of their colors hanging in the air like fumes, and the awful moment when Mr. Liu arrived to find not even the memory, just an empty room and twenty-five thousand of his dollars missing. It wasn't something that could be fixed with a smile.

She suggested calling the police, but Mr. Liu didn't even acknowledge her voice. She realized that along with Mr. Liu's useful network of friends there probably lurked a few enemies, and that the police, with their tendency to bring in higher levels of scrutiny, weren't an option. He sat down and pulled out his package of Dubuffet cigarettes, not even offering her one, communicating with that gesture a rage that began to frighten her. He ignored her offer of tea, staring at her in a terrifyingly steady way, the way one might stare at an object. She was relieved when he turned to the window again, waiting as he calculated the value of his relationship with her and with Holt, the insult of being cheated on a business deal. Her future was blowing back and forth inside his mind. She didn't know how long it went on. At last he'd stood up and put on his coat. You must return the money or the robe before Spring Festival. The money or the robe, she'd answered. You can be sure that I will have one of them, Mr. Liu, along with the *jin* and the other pieces. He'd shaken her hand, now back to his amiable smiling persona. I have great confidence in you, Silvia. Call me if you need anything.

She had feared that Clayton would expose everything, but luckily, he must have had a different plan. Holt had arrived blissfully ignorant of her "private arrangements." He'd analyzed the mediocre pieces she had reserved for him and calculated their worth with his mixture of obsession and detachment. "It's a little disappointing," he concluded with a sigh. "I would have expected some better pieces." She felt sorry for him in his bewilderment, and she'd made an effort to show him extra kindness. She had continued the week with him, meeting with the factories in Shanghai and Hangzhou where they oversaw production for an American company, continually fearing the single phone call to Holt that would send everything clattering to the dirt. What she really wanted to do was find Clayton and slap his stupid face, and to slap her own for letting him take advantage of her. Many bad nights, her expecting him to call her up and bargain with her for her affection. She dreaded the pathetic conversation that would result, but there was no sign of him. In a queer way, she respected him more since he'd double-crossed her, and the haunting phenomenon of missing him began to take an inexplicable place in her routine. She never had a chance to reassess everything; six weeks later he'd turned up dead, after calling her up and inviting her for breakfast. She had thought he was calling to make things right again, but instead that yellow lake of vomit and the gray body facedown in it, wearing his clothes and his hair and his apartment but no, that couldn't be him! Clayton!

The soaking wind wet her face as she pushed the memory aside for the thousandth time. The frightening possibility that Mr. Liu had had him murdered had ridden in on the shock of his death, but then the notes had been found and it had all changed to something even worse. The funeral and that horrible postcard with the reflected rooms. Instead of a note of endearment or apology, only his stupid philosophy, as if he'd never loved her at all, or comforted her, or helped her learn Chinese or anything! The one last idiotic quote: "'Mencius said: A benevolent man extends his benevolence from those he loves to those he doesn't love. A ruthless man extends his ruthlessness from those he doesn't love to those he loves.'"

The rain fell faster, soaking into the cardboard box. She'd left her gloves in the hotel room and the joints of her fingers were starting to stiffen. *Carajo!* She would have to walk up to the next traffic light, where all the restaurants were. Maybe one would be open and she could find a telephone or a taxi crossing to another part of town. The black branches reached down, and for some reason she thought of the tree-lined streets of her native Montevideo, when the late-afternoon sun strode down them like a Belle Époque dandy in a fawn-colored top hat. Fragments of sunlight through the leaves, wrought iron and the names of architects proudly engraved in turn-of-the-century masonry: "Martin Berzoni, Constructor." She'd seen that name every morning on the cornerstone of her neighbor's house. Then the generals had taken over, bringing her father his sudden success, and they'd moved to Pocitos, where everything was brand new.

Cursed rain! Cursed dead stupid Beijing night and ridiculous Chinese! The occasional driver passed by on some obscure errand; maybe she should wave one down and tell the driver that it was an emergency. She'd done that with Clayton once, that first trip together, in Shanghai, and he'd had to make up a story because she didn't speak Chinese. "What'll I tell him?"

"Tell him anything. Tell him we're going to help a friend who wants to kill himself!"

He gave her a pained look. "You're crazier than me, you know that?"

When she created little stories for people he'd go along with them, but he'd tired of it in the end, especially when she had left him in the hotel to go out with a friend, telling him she had to sign a contract with someone on Holt's behalf. That had been near the end of their first year together, and somehow he'd run into them, turned angry and inward so much that she'd had to go back to the hotel with him.

"I told you I lie. I never tried to conceal that from you. You even—"

"There's limits!"

"That's my invisible world. You have yours and I have mine." Sitting and talking, behind him a large Chinese landscape painting that promised the isolated serenity of distant misty peaks. A stone stairway wound in and out of sight, ever higher to a tiny pavilion that hung at the edge of an abyss.

His downcast look. "How do you think it makes me feel? Huh? Why don't you imagine for a moment how it feels."

Staring up at the landscape, hoping he would think she was deep in thought. She was imagining the view from the pavilion, the stone benches and the tormented juniper trees that clung to the cliffs of the faraway promontories. She just wanted to shut him up: "You know, Clayton, you're always talking about the Emptiness. Why don't you just do it?"

A drainpipe drummed a stream of frigid rainwater across the box lid, and she cursed at her carelessness, trying to brush the water away with her wet hand. She moved under an awning and scanned the block. Far away in the rain something that looked like a taxi huddled against the curb, lightless and immobile. A sleeping driver inhabited the cab, bundled up against the cold in a down jacket and hood, his mouth hanging open like a murder victim. They recognized each other and he started the engine.

The hotel lobby, with its concierge slumbering away in his chair. She always kept the key herself instead of leaving it at the desk, so she passed quickly through the lobby and into the elevator. Her room looked so clean and orderly. Everything hung so nicely in the closet, her American shampoo a neat little sentry of good grooming at the edge of the shower. Everything had been unpacked and settled in. She pulled her garment bag from the bottom of the closet and laid it flat on the crisply made bed, then she took down the assortment of silk blouses and woolen skirts she traveled with, laying each one carefully into the holder of her garment bag. The urge to call Andy again, and with it, Clayton, looking tired at the Blue Heaven. "Silvia, why don't you just listen to your spirit once in a while? I know it's in there."

"What spirit are you talking about, Clayton?" He had gotten so annoying in those days. "That is all metaphysical bullshit. What is a spirit? Do I need to take it out of my pocket when I pass through airport security? Maybe I did, and I forgot to take it back at the other side."

So much stupidity. She put her shampoo and other toiletries into a plastic bag and pushed them into a pocket of the case. She hesitated. Where would she put the robe? She took it out of its box and laid it on the bed. She would just look at it a minute, that's all; pour a cup of tea and try to organize her clothes, the rainy night, and all the mixed-up thefts and mistakes. The landscape of stiff silk rose and fell across the bed, a geography of colored clouds and snarling dragons made of peacock feathers. It was far too wide and grandiose to fit comfortably in the garment bag.

How did she get into this, anyway? She hadn't meant to steal the textiles from Holt. It had simply developed naturally, on its own, and more than anything she felt like a spectator to the whole event. It had started last year, when Holt had been out of touch for a week. He'd been at the beach in Argentina, away from telephones, and she had been in charge of collecting the textiles. An antique dealer in Hangzhou had called because he'd heard that Holt bought old clothing, and he had a piece that might interest him. At the same time Mr. Liu had called looking for Jeffrey, and the two of them had gotten together, and somehow, for convenience's sake, the textile and the money had changed hands, and Mr. Liu had said that it was much easier to deal with her than with Holt, who was always away, and it had just begun like that, innocently. After all, the new dealer had never met Holt. Why should Holt be included? And it had gone like that until Mr. Liu himself was sending her to find textiles for him, especially ones he didn't want to approach too closely, like the Yüan dynasty woven gold that they had gotten from the museum. And Mr. Liu was generous, of course: if he liked someone he helped them make money, and that was how she had met Mr. Tran, who sold gemstones for the Khmer Rouge. That was how things were: they didn't always happen as one recognizable event, but sometimes as a series of tiny occurrences that were too small to be decided on but that mounted up suddenly to a huge mound of earth that separated you from where you'd been standing before, when you were still loyal.

She went back to packing. She would have to put the textiles in a plastic bag and carry it in her hand, the twenty-thousand-dollar robe in a laundry bag that said SOILED CLOTHES. The rain had brought the winter coal smoke onto her skin and into her hair, so now—a fast shower.

She let the warm jets of water play over her. She could close her eyes in the water and get to that warm comfortable nonplace that had become home. She could feel pampered and cared for, like an embrace, and the cubicle, limitless in the obscurity behind her closed eyelids, could allow her to go to her apartment in Hong Kong or even back to

Montevideo. Her bathroom, the old-fashioned brass plumbing with white ceramic levers that said *Caliente* or *Frio* in tiny blue script. The huge old tub that she had to step up into, and beside it the shelf of gray marble that held the soap. Her father had brought back the letters of the alphabet from the United States to stick onto the walls, and they'd always stayed there, her name bouncing through the color spectrum among hearts and little pink cows. *S I L V I A*. She'd used to ride on his back like a horse when she was little, his arms like pillars. He had the biggest muscles in the world, and was always so certain of everything: who was right or wrong, who was strong or weak. Later, the other girls at school always whispering, "Her father is *militar. Milico, milico!*" The horrid girl who had rubbed mud all over her. The beach house, where they'd arrived to find that someone had painted ASESINO on the door in dripping red letters and not a single neighbor even mentioned it, as if it belonged there, like an address or a house name that said The Breakers or The Seagull. *Asesino*. Murderer.

And now she saw the same word, faint but unmistakable, on every door she lived behind, tracking her to Hong Kong the same way her father finally had that last time, when he'd found her through the wool secretariat and they'd talked on the telephone. Everything had been so superficial and casual the first minute, until he'd asked, "*Querida*, when will you return home?" and it had all surged up again and filled her mouth with the cold words, "After you're dead." Her mother bleating, accepting everything the way she always did, by pretending ignorance. "Silvita, how could you say that?" He was unforgivable, though, and he had made her unforgivable too. She could never go back, never be able to sit in the bars and cafés of her old Montevideo, with its rustling leaves and old motorcars, its nineteenth century lingering in the beautiful old buildings on the Eighteenth of July and its unmistakable aroma, too complex to ever be described, of innocence.

How stupid to let her blood start shaking over those things again! It wasn't anger now, because anger had the opposite effect: it took her away from everything, made her frigid and remote enough to issue the perfect cutting phrase. This would have been a good time to be with Clayton, because he knew this emotion and he understood. When it came over her he took care of her, stroking her hair calmly and softly, the same way the needles of warm spray rubbed her hair now, silently kissing her cheeks and her forehead until she could start crying, and relax, and know that no matter how tainted she felt he would always recognize her spirit, the one she claimed didn't exist, and that however victimized or hidden it was, it remained unsullied and incorruptible, her own.

How stupid to cry again! Here, in the shower of a hotel room in Beijing. Absurd, when she was living such a good life, an exciting international spy sort of life, to cry about someone who had stolen things from her. She'd filled her quota of crying at the funeral, now she had other things to do. She turned off the water and listened to the drain, then she toweled off and finished her packing. All questions about her destination had sloughed off with the residue of coal smoke and sweat. She was going to Inner Mongolia.

The idea of the Mongol tapestry came back to her.

Clayton had let it slip in passing one night when she'd come to his apartment for dinner out of some feeling of old obligation. Sometimes they would get together again for a few days or for a week, until she would get tired of him. Three months ago, the merciful October coolness. He'd seemed fresh again that night, and it let her go back to simpler days for a short time. They'd dissected Holt for nearly an hour, a subject they had both become mildly fixated on, when Clayton said that he knew of a Yüan dynasty woven map that Holt would kill for. She'd disputed it, saying that she'd never heard of a woven map, let alone one that old. "Is this more of your Invisible World joke?"

He'd gotten suddenly serious. "I showed you that Manchu safe passage. Do you think that was so easy to find? I found some of Jeff's best pieces for him. There's a lot of things I haven't told you about."

Slightly bored. "Of course, Clayton. You have so many unsolved mysteries."

"Fuck you."

"Go ahead!" and he'd grabbed her and pulled her pants down, she felt like laughing, then suddenly he was inside her with only the bare flesh of her behind exposed to his skin, reliving the old days of the hotel rooms of Guangzhou and Shanghai when everything had been so beautiful and wild at the same time, discussions of *chi* and Clayton's concepts and then making love crouched on the floor or standing up in the bathroom, carried along by the stolen eroticism of hotel rooms and their "who are we? who cares?" striptease. For a little while that had come back again because Clayton had mystery again, he was a little bit ahead of her, and it made her want him once more. They'd gone to China together for the last time two months ago, everything degraded to the point where she alternately cherished him as she'd used to and couldn't stand being around him. And he, almost slavish, could no longer captivate her with his Chinese slang or his knowledge of history, because now she knew all the slang and all the history, she had her own Chinese friends and business appointments, and they were the kind of people who weren't impressed by a failed artist who'd done great things a long time ago.

But sometimes, when they were away from everyone and he felt comfortable, he would make a quiet observation, the kind of magical vision he'd had when they'd met, and for a moment her universe would swell to something bigger, and she would feel the old awe she'd felt back then, and love him the same way: as desperately and imperfectly as the first time. She would want to protect him and to feel him close to her. And that might go on for an hour or a night, and then he would start droning about some Chinese philosopher, or she would have a business appointment that he didn't fit into, and she would be back to hating him, back to wanting to destroy him out of simple annoyance. This would have to be the last time; she couldn't stand it anymore. And gradually, between the cutting remarks and the lies just to get out of his sight for a few hours and the hotel rooms where they ripped the sheets off the bed, he told her about the tapestry.

"It's Yüan. The monks said it's a map of the Mongol empire that was being sent by Ogadai Khan to the pope."

"That's impossible. Describe it to me."

"It's *kesi*. Slit tapestry weave. Some embroidery. It's not strictly geographical, the way we would think of a map. It's more . . . conceptual."

"Don't start with your 'conceptual.'"

"It's more . . . accurate than a geographical map. What does a map show except who you are and what your world is? A geographical map shows a theoretical location of things from outer space. But how accurate is it, really, except that we've all accepted its conventions. You ever read the footnotes on those maps of the world where Greenland shows up as this massive—"

"What's the point, Clayton?"

He raised his voice above hers, insisting on finishing. "South America is actually seven times bigger than Greenland, even though it looks smaller—"

"And what does your map look like?"

He wouldn't answer. She'd put herself contrite. "I'm sorry, Clayton."

"This map includes time."

"Please explain to me what you mean."

He shrugged. "I mean, you're missing the whole point of what's great about this thing."

"I know, Clayton. I'm impatient and I'm shallow. You know I have trouble understanding your ideas. They're beyond me! Can you simply tell me what it looks like?"

He stayed quiet for a moment, then he answered her in a defeated voice, as if she was taking from him his last treasure. It seemed to exasperate him that she would do that. "Don't imagine a map of Asia, because it doesn't look like that at all. There's a big area done in a deep blue color, and the borders of it are outlined in gold couching. The Wall's on there. It's gold. And there's a lot of cloud done in different colors. That's the empire. It shows the Altai range, but it doesn't have the traditional ocean-mountain-cloud scheme. Then different parts of the empire are marked off with red borders, and they tell which region of the empire it is in Mongolian script and Latin. Like, at the top it says "Terra Mongolis.""

"Why Latin?"

"I told you it was a present for the pope. One of those Italian traders probably spelled it out for them."

"What else?"

"Oh, it shows I think Tibet and Siam. What I think are parts of

India, and the Uighur lands. Song China is still hanging on south of the Yangtze. There's human figures, too. They're detailed down to the eyelashes. They're practically real. They're more than real."

"What kind of condition is it in?"

He'd let a space come in before he answered. "Mint. The monks kept it out of the light. They buried it during the Cultural Revolution. They'd only put it up on special occasions." He stopped and said quietly. "It's beautiful. It's the most beautiful textile I've ever seen."

"Clayton? I think it would be very interesting to go and see this tapestry."

"You mean to see it and buy it."

"First, see it."

"It's impossible."

"Why?"

"It's just impossible. I don't think they would even show it to you." He'd changed tack suddenly. "Silvia, you're so misguided. You can't settle the Empire by—"

"Why don't we go there, Clayton? I've never been to Inner Mongolia. You and I can go. You and I." The idea thrilled her. Monasteries in Tibet were yielding a trove of good pieces, tribute and offerings from all over the Buddhist world deposited there since the ninth century. Now the American and European dealers were mining them, collaborating with textile rings in Lhasa and having them smuggled out over the Himalayas to Katmandu. Sometimes they turned up stained with yak butter and smoke, victims of the worship they had been intended for. Others turned out immaculate, hidden away in a chest or an interior room among the thousands of monastic cubicles. Tibet was no longer a secret; everyone knew about the Turkish carpet from a monastery that had recently sold for a million dollars. It had even become a sort of adventure destination for young dealers. But Inner Mongolia . . . no one went to Inner Mongolia.

Fine. Now she would go. She sat down to look at the note again. She recognized Clayton's scrawl and the loathing came back to her again. That stupid rebellion against penmanship and order. So he'd had to "break a few eggs" to get the robe. Don't worry about that now, *querido*.

She skipped down to the directions, sensing that she could easily

STUART COHEN

get bogged down in the other parts of the letter. Ulamqab, northwest of Beijing. She took out her dictionary and looked at the minute explosions of Mandarin splayed out along the railway lines and roads. It took her nearly a half hour to locate Ulamqab. She would have to take the train to Huehote, then go by bus. Clayton mentioned something about a business card, too, but she couldn't worry about it now.

The darkness waited for her, holding rain and unfriendly cold. Four-thirty. She packed the last of her belongings and woke up the concierge to pay her bill. The taxi came and she put her two bags on the seat next to her. The peasants from the countryside slept among their dirty bundles. In the Foreigners waiting room, the steady pull of grimy time and its relentless fluorescence filtered down from the distant ceiling onto the worn and tawdry furniture. An old man guarded the tunnel like a human signboard with black frame glasses, directing travelers to his right with a wordless wave of the hand, a gesture he'd made so many tens of thousands of times that he'd streamlined it to a brush stroke. A rumbling of steel, a hiss. The smell of coal smoke, soft and pleasant. On the dirty gray platform someone had scattered a deck of cards. Five of diamonds, jack of spades. She stepped on them as she boarded the train. She knew they didn't tell the future.

It arrived after the shower, little by little, as he sat marveling at his ability to attract and bed this strange and beautiful South American woman. He'd never slept with a woman with an accent before. The memories of the night, and the quiet expectancy of the future curved everything into the perfect hotel room moment. He could make himself green tea, and drink it calmly and comfortably here in China, in the ancient city of Beijing he'd heard about his whole life but never actually expected to visit. Soon he and Silvia would go together to the cold, wild place he'd been directed to so long ago. He would interview with a monk and give him the ticket that would at last open the door to his life.

He was thinking about the business cards that said "Invisible World" when he noticed the absence of the box. It puzzled him. He looked beneath the heaped-up covers at the foot of the bed, then under the writing table. Maybe she'd put it aside so it wouldn't get stepped on. No, the closet radiated an intense vacancy, not empty, but rather full of the lack of the robe. Could housekeeping have come into the room and taken it while he had his head under the shower? The maid had seemed a bit shifty, after all. He weighed the chances of the maid stealing in and going straight for the box. No. He looked in the closet again, then under the bed. Then under the heap of bedclothes that he'd heaved to the side thirty seconds before. No, still no.

Silvia had taken it. She probably wanted to store it someplace safe while they traveled north to look for the last piece Clayton had left him. She was probably packing now for the trip to Inner Mongolia. She'd known they would go together without having to exchange a word about it.

It began to arrive almost imperceptibly, lightly touching him like the first raindrop of a storm. He'd finished his third cup of tea and a package of cookies he'd bought the day before. The maid had already knocked at the door to make up the room. His mind kept throwing out reasons for her lateness, and among the traffic and business that she had to conclude had flickered the possibility, very hypothetically, that she wasn't coming back. It seemed almost comical, the kind of thing that might happen to an unfortunate movie character. He wondered if he should leave a note on the door and go out to breakfast, considering the possibilities of where to go and how to describe their location to Silvia, and then his mind circled back to it again, that ridiculous idea of her not coming back and it turned instead into annoyance at her lateness. Maybe she couldn't call because she didn't know the hotel's phone number. He picked up the receiver, looking on the little telephone menu to find the correct number for the front desk. Busy. He stepped over to the closet and opened it. The vacancy reproached him and he shut it in, going back to the telephone and spearing the buttons with his fingertip. Still busy.

He would go out to breakfast. Next door. Yes.

Dear Silvia, I waited for you for breakfast but I guess you got tied up. I'm next door (on the left side). See you soon.

Andy

He used a straight pin from the hotel's little paper sewing kit to fix it to the door.

He pushed aside the beads of the dark, underheated restaurant. The attendants sat in front of ashtrays and bowls of rice gruel. They looked annoyed. His appearance prompted a round of fierce-sounding language, and then one of the men waved him away. "No eat." He pointed to the watch that clung to his thin arm. "No eat." The others seemed to discuss the stupidity of a foreigner who would expect to eat at that hour of the morning, probably the kind of foreigner who would let someone steal away with his valuables and sit waiting in a hotel room for her like an idiot.

Andy backed away from their chorus. The front desk helped him call her hotel.

"Not here."

"What do you mean? Can you ring her room?"

A muttered unintelligibility off to the side, then the words pronounced with the cut-off harshness of Chinese syllables: "Check! Out! She . . . check! out!"

"She checked out?"

The man muttered something off to the side and then a new voice came on, still Chinese but with a crisp confident sound. "Emerald Garden Hotel. Can I help you?" Andy went through the story again, the whereabouts of his friend Silvia Benedetti, and the pause heartened him for a moment. They would probably put him through now. "I'm sorry, sir. Miss Benedetti have already check out."

"What time?"

Another pause. "I'm sorry, sir. At faw fawty-two, Miss Benedetti have check out."

"Did she leave a message?"

"I'm sorry, sir. Don't have message."

He heard himself thanking the man and he felt a hand putting the receiver down. He felt the chair behind his knees and then he sank down, surprised to find himself on the other side of the room. He felt cold all of a sudden. His legs were trembling. He thought that perhaps he should go into his room, but standing up and going there seemed like a tremendous effort, and if he ran away maybe everyone would know how stupid he had been. He pushed the sleeve of his sweater away from his watch. The texture of the knit wool at his wrist seemed very far away from his eyes. Eleven-thirty.

"Sir." The young woman at the desk smiled shyly. Her embarrassment halted her, then she began again. "Very sorry, but we must ask you pay double room. Rules of managing office."

The door to his room hung open, still bearing the note that kicked him in the stomach as he approached. "Dear Silvia, I waited for you for breakfast but I guess you got tied up . . ." He pulled it down and slowly crumpled it, drawing the curious gaze of the maid who bent over the side of the bed and hurriedly erased with a final tuck of the sheets what remained of the previous night. His ears were ringing, the same as when he'd taken a head shot at a tournament. "I'd like you to go away, please," he told the woman, then he stood by the open door and motioned outward. "Go."

The sense of being alone and far from home came on so suddenly and strongly that it almost made him sick, like he'd stuffed in a meal of foreign cities and experiences and now he needed to vomit the whole thing up again. He knew that she'd taken off, and that she'd probably go after whatever Clayton had left in Inner Mongolia. A map of some sort, a map of an Invisible World.

Where was Clayton's note, anyway? He checked through the papers on the desk: a receipt from the Yangtze Hotel, a bill for the phone call to his father, restaurant tabs added up uncertainly in Chinese. Under the bed? No. Could the maid have put it in the drawer? No, and no. Maybe he'd put it back in his other pants! Checking yesterday's pockets; that momentary relief at feeling the gentle resistance of paper among the cloth and then . . . No! Silvia's laundry bill from Shanghai, a fax of Holt's South American itinerary with a short letter in Spanish, directing him not to Inner Mongolia but to that distant moment two days ago when he'd scrabbled among the groaning men and the withered leaves of People's Money in the lobby of that building. He threw a punch, and then a dozen more, then a mix of palm strikes and ridge hands and hammer fists that flailed stupidly in the air. At last he sat down on the bed.

He remembered something that had happened a long time ago,

when the master had taught him how to fight a losing battle. He'd been an upper-level student. The class hadn't begun yet and he'd been talking to the master, who was quietly slipping pads on his hands as he discussed sparring techniques with him. Andy had been in midsentence when he perceived a blur of motion at the side of his face, then everything exploded into blue sparks. "Okay, let's spar." He couldn't believe it at first. The master had never treated him with anything other than kindness, but when Andy didn't react he'd moved in and hit him in the head again, setting the gong inside his brain into another round of vibrations. The sickening feeling of being overmatched seized him. He stepped back and covered his head. "Don't cower," the master had said, his voice completely neutral. To emphasize his point he stepped in and snapped Andy's head to the side with an open-handed strike, and Andy could feel his legs start to go limp. Andy realized that they would keep fighting until the master knocked him out, or until he started fighting back. He caught the tiny fragment of a glove approaching his face and felt the painless popping of little lights inside his skull. He backed away, keeping his guard up, and kept moving until his head cleared. Resigned and calm, far from the limitations of his personality, he went after the master.

Now he saw with crystalline perspective the entire comedy he'd been participating in. In a smooth ellipse his trajectory had taken him from his desk in his father's office to this tiny hotel room in Beijing. The appearance of the foreign money and the bits of textile fell away, and the exotic personages he'd met, like Silvia and Holt, no longer seemed either exotic or foreign. For the first time, it all felt natural. It felt natural that he would fly to Hong Kong and to Beijing, and that he would sleep with Silvia and suffer her betrayal. Life insisted on surprising and betraying; a person could only be an amateur at living it. And him, maybe always a bad amateur at that!

He laughed, big and round, as if he'd just told Clayton the whole story and Clayton had blown it all out with some silly comment and was rolling around on the floor. *Blind One! Always betting on the Hindenburg!* And at this abysmal moment, he'd never felt so content and comfortable. He'd slain the money changers. He'd kicked in the door in Shanghai and walked through it to the Beijing opera, and now he was sitting in this hotel room in China flat on his ass because of this woman. And it was all tremendously funny, and how it needed to be because when you dished out the wild card it didn't mean you won, it just meant that you'd play, shrugging off all the rules that you'd spent your whole life setting for yourself. And once you did that, you had an inexhaustible supply of wild cards, if you just knew where to look for them.

It took him a half hour to realize what he had to do. By the time he'd gotten through to Holt's hotel in Beijing, he felt a marvelous calm electricity coursing through his body.

Holt let the sounds of the lobby echo around him. He could imagine himself on the bottom of the sea, the occasional muffled loudspeaker herding together tour groups like the muffled sonar of whales. The day hadn't gone badly, starting with a breakfast with Mr. Wang, one of Holt's first business associates and still, in some senses, a friend. Lunch had been roast duck with Mr. Zhou, the factory manager and his friend from the Export Bureau, who always got them quota. Holt had called the meeting to thank him, finalizing his gratitude with a gold fountain pen. Afterward, though, after the handshakes and seeing them into the taxi, Holt had felt an unattached sadness. Somehow everything in his life seemed to have gotten grayed and flat, like a picture on a cardboard box.

Holt looked Andy over as he entered the lobby. He could sense an urgency about him, maybe something about the way he didn't pay attention to the opulence of the hotel the way he had in Shanghai, but walked straight over to him without looking to the side. Holt stood up. Without wanting to be, he was glad to see him. For the past few days an uneasiness had been rising within him. At first he had attributed it to jet lag and to the strange welter of emotions surrounding Clayton's suicide, but the evidence of Mr. Gao's double-dealing had unsettled him further. He had nothing concrete to focus on, only the implausible appearance of the Yüan textile and the nagging sensation of some secret disarray.

"Mr. Mann! How's Beijing treating you?"

Andy smiled. "Rather badly, Mr. Holt."

Holt wasn't sure he'd heard right at first; the verdict had been delivered so cheerfully. He'd suspected something when Andy insisted on meeting with him. "I'm sorry to hear that. Is it anything I can help you with?"

"Could we go to your room?" When they got there Andy spoke before he'd even sat down. "Four o'clock. Is that too early for a drink?"

"It's cocktail hour somewhere in the world. What are you drinking?"

"Oh, anything. Whiskey."

Holt opened the miniature bottles and poured them into glasses. "Do you want me to call down for ice?"

"That's okay." Holt handed him the glass and sat on the edge of the dresser. Holt liked this room: it looked down on the Forbidden City a half mile away. Andy took a sip of the brown liquid in the glass and made a face. "I hate this shit."

"It's hateable," Holt agreed amiably. "Did you get together with Silvia?"

Andy shuddered slightly, and Holt wondered if things had gone badly between them. "We got together," he said evenly. He went to the window and glanced out, then turned back to Holt. "So, did you finish all your appointments for the day?"

Holt felt an uneasiness insinuate the room. "Yes. These were more courtesy calls than business meetings. I took some associates to lunch, people who helped me. You know: eat a big meal, hand out gold pens. Not to be cynical about it. Everything's personal relationships here. It doesn't all turn so nakedly on the dollar, like in the States."

"And what are your plans?"

"As I mentioned, I have that rather important meeting in Shanghai the day after tomorrow. The Argentines and the Italians will be coming in."

"I see."

Holt noted Andy's absent reply. "What's on your mind?"

Andy looked at him with such intensity that Holt thought he could feel a note of belligerence in his voice. "We'll get to that." A slight hole in the sentence, then: "How's your new acquisition?"

It felt like a loaded question, but Holt didn't know with what. He assumed Andy was referring to his last ventures. "To be frank with you, Shanghai was disappointing. I think my suppliers are selling to someone else. There seems to be a general dearth. I might have to start going out west."

"Out west," Andy repeated, keeping his eyes on him. The spoken part stopped but the conversation continued in a long silence. He put his drink down and shifted out of the confines of the table. "Where out west?"

Holt unconsciously stepped back. The bandage near Andy's eye amplified the seldom-felt but immediately recognizable atmosphere of impending violence. He remembered Andreas taking out the razor a few days ago. "Well . . . Ninxia, Gansu, Inner Mongolia, Tibet. It's either that or get out of business. I haven't seen a good piece in six months."

Again, the slow-motion response. "You haven't."

"Only Clayton's. Is something wrong?"

Andy listened to him, then moved back to the window. He started to pick up his drink, looked at it, and put it down. He said nothing for a long time, watching Holt and then staring emptily at the computer Holt had set up on his desk. When he spoke again he seemed more relaxed. "Have you got a beer in there?"

Holt fetched one and opened it with a hiss. He felt nervous as Andy approached him, but he took it out of his hand and sat down in the armchair again. Holt resumed his seat on the dresser.

"Jeffrey. If I had a textile, a really old one . . . "

"How old?"

"Like, oh, I don't know."

Holt looked at him. "Chinese?"

"Yes. But maybe it would come from a monastery somewhere. Like in . . . Inner Mongolia. Would that be, uh, valuable?"

Holt looked at him. He sensed a deep unease in Andy. "This has something to do with Clayton, doesn't it?"

He waited for the affirmation, then walked over to his suitcase. "Andy, I want to tell you something." He pulled out the letter that Clayton had given him and read it out loud, flattening out the words so that it wouldn't sound as if he was trying to re-create Clayton's voice. He skipped the part about Tokyo and Mencius, finishing: "*'I've spent my whole life trying to find a map of an invisible world, and at last I did. You know which map. It's half yours. That was the deal.'*" He put the piece of paper on the desk and sat down on its edge.

"About three years ago Clayton came to me. He was very excited about something. He'd read about a monastery in Inner Mongolia, in western China, where there was said to be a wall hanging, done in *kesi*, which is a slit tapestry weave. According to the book, this tapestry was a map of the Mongol empire that the Khan was sending as a gift to the pope. So Clayton took off to find this piece."

"That sounds like Clayton."

"Yes, but there's a catch. His sourcebook for this information was an old pulp novel of the twenties. It also had Genghis Khan's phantom army charging over the plains to rescue the hero from bandits, that sort of thing. It was completely fictional. The author threw in the tapestry for effect. I researched the author. He also wrote a book about the Zulus, with an elaborate cannibal scene that's totally false. British guy, imperialist adventurer type. One still runs into the modern version every once in a while in the bars at Lan Kwai Fong."

"Did Clayton know that?"

"If he didn't know, it wasn't because I didn't tell him. You know how he was. Anyway, he went there and he came back claiming that he'd found the monastery, but he was very mysterious about whatever else he found there, which I suspect was nothing. As you can see from the letter, he seems to have gone back a couple more times. For what I don't know."

"Jeffrey, how much would a tapestry like that be worth?"

Holt ignored the question. "I have a friend in New York, a carpet specialist. Once someone came to him and told him he had a piece of the *Spring of Chosroes* carpet."

"What's that?"

"The *Spring of Chosroes* carpet?" Holt warmed into one of his favorite stories. "That's a carpet that belongs to all of us, Andy. Because it's never been found. Supposedly it was a giant silk carpet, sixty cubits on each side, which is about ninety feet. Persian. Probably flat weave, slit tapestry, like a kilim. It was a garden design, with streams, pathways, gates, birds, trees. All the flowers were made of different colors of precious stones woven into the fabric. It was created to remind King Chosroes of spring during wintertime. Imagine that: there must have been hundreds of colors woven into it, and thousands of individual flowers and animals." Holt could see it now: the garlands of woven greenery and a flock of peacocks spreading their tails. A footbridge crossed a stream, sheltering a pool of quaintly rendered fish, and over there a palace surrounded by flowers made of lapis lazuli. For a moment he was lost in the garden.

"What happened to it?"

"Oh. It disappeared when the Arabs invaded in the seventh century. The story is that the conquerors cut it up into pieces and divided it among themselves. No one has ever seen it." He stood up and went to the tea thermos. "So naturally, when someone came to my friend and said he had a piece of it, my friend was interested. And this is an astute man. Three generations in the carpet business. His home is . . . Well, it's beyond description. It's what you imagine a sultan's palace to be like, except it's all real. He probably has a half million dollars' worth of carpets in his living room, and not because there's such a great quantity of them." Holt remembered a kilim that had been draped over a couch, its colors so charged with caravans and sun that it made him feel he was standing in a Delacroix painting. "It's paradise." He looked up again. Andy still waited for him to continue. "So what I'm telling you is, the man has seen it and he knows. And I don't say that about a lot of people. But in this case, it was like watching a successful middle-aged executive being jerked around by an eighteen-year-old girl. He doesn't see a woman, he sees his own youth. With the carpet, I don't think my friend was looking for a textile. He was looking for a dream. I don't know. Clayton could probably describe what he was looking for better than either of us."

"So what happened?"

"Someone approached my friend. An old German man. He called him on the telephone from Germany because he couldn't enter the United States. He said his father had been one of the archaeologists who first started exploring the Middle East in the late nineteenth century. At first my friend was skeptical, because the piece is so mythic. No one had ever seen it before. The German sent him a picture, then some fiber samples. They tested out to the right time, and they matched the dyes that are indigenous to that part of the world. My friend flew to Frankfurt to look at the carpet and finalize things."

"How much did they want for the carpet?"

His laughter arched out into the room. "He'd never tell me that. At least several hundred thousand." His amusement spilled out again over the rim of the teacup. He waited for Andy to prod him, then digressed even further. "It's interesting, isn't it? People always want to hear the end of a story. Everyone wants to fall into the unknown, and the opportunities to do it get rarer and rarer the older they get. It's our best escape. A good unknown is the greatest gift you can give someone."

"So what happened?"

"One thing you have to understand is that he told me this in his apartment, preparatory to showing me his most valuable treasure. He had a side room that he'd fitted out with a separate alarm system. Mind you, he had a significant system already set up for the apartment. So he unlocked it and ushered me in and there it was on the wall." Holt stopped. The cooling system of the refrigerator abated, bringing a deeper level of noiselessness into the room.

"What—"

"It was shit!" Holt nearly shouted, pouncing on his first word. Laughing. "The colors had faded so badly that you couldn't even make out the design without examining the warp interlocks. It was so full of holes that the overwhelming impression was of the backing that he'd mounted it on."

"What about the gemstones?"

"There was one little piece of garnet still hanging on by a few threads. It was insanity." An excited undertone. "He was so proud of it! He got totally lost looking at it, like he'd eaten an ounce of hallucinogenic mushrooms. He was back in the Sassanid Empire somewhere, listening to the court musicians. And this was something with no provenance."

"I thought you said he was an expert."

"Oh, Andy, he is an expert. But that makes it even worse sometimes. That's what you don't understand yet about textiles. On one hand, it's just an organization of fibers to make them occupy space differently. But to the collector, it's much more than that. It's a postcard from someone who lived a life you can barely comprehend, and three centuries after they've died, it finally reaches you. Whose hands gathered the thousands of cochineal beetles to make this pink stripe? What husband did they make it for? Nothing is just a piece of cloth. I see lives here. I see other civilizations and other minds. That's why even when you get a piece of shit that's totally burned by time, even something that you wouldn't pick out of a garbage heap, the man who knows, the man who knows . . . can look at that and he doesn't see a rag, he sees a world. He sees that world clearly. He enters that world!" Holt's posture had frozen, only his mouth and eyes existed. "And I'll tell you something about Clayton: he saw everything like that! Everything! He could walk into a, a grocery store and the next thing you know he's lost. He looks at a barrel of dried shrimp and he sees them swimming around in the ocean, schooling up around a bag of dried seaweed. Or he might start contemplating the deeper ramifications of the label on a jar of pickles." Holt's cackling came out in a high pitch. Sitting down in an armchair, quieting a bit. "Objects were just symbols for him. They were shorthand for a bigger world. And that's why you'll never make me believe he found that wall hanging, because that would mean he succeeded in making his whole world come together. And people don't commit suicide when their world comes together: they do it when it falls apart. Clayton could have done anything with a piece like that. It's freedom. It's more money than either of us have ever seen. He could have done anything. I would have helped him. He knew that."

"How much would it be worth?"

Holt narrowed his eyes. "A piece like that . . . If it existed, and I still don't believe it exists . . ." Andy could see something else creeping into his face over the doubt, an eerie mystical cast. "You'd have to smuggle it out of the country of course, but that's not so difficult. Silvia and I could arrange that. Then . . . you would have to sell it." A dreaminess pervaded the spaces between the short sentences. "Of course...you don't just sell something that valuable openly. No...No." Matter-of-fact again, looking Andy in the eye. "That would create a major stink. Any museum in the world that tried to display it would have the Chinese government up their bunghole in a heartbeat. Making off with the national patrimony, are we? No, you'd have to auction it off at one of the major houses, pretend it just came out of someone's collection in Europe, or else tie it to a third country, like Tibet or Turkestan, so nobody's sure which country has a right to claim it in the first place." He looked past Andy's ear, imagining a different world. "But they'd want provenance, wouldn't they? Yes...And you have to be careful when you falsify something that big, it attracts too much attention. Far too much...Too many people look into those things, they're troublemakers. Because this would be a very famous piece, Andy. This would be the piece that shows up on the front page of the *New York Times* in an article about the exploding market for antique textiles. With lots of hand wringing and finger pointing, of course. And there would certainly be an interview with the Chinese cultural attaché condemning the whole thing."

"It sounds like it might make some problems."

"Oh. You have to know how to organize it, Andy. We could get some old paper, cook up a letter from somebody's great-grandfather in England, telling about the interesting curio they bought on their vacation to Tibet.... I have a friend on The Strand that plays with that sort of thing. So that gets it out of China long before 1970. You can end-run the whole UNESCO convention." Holt laughed, then settled back. "Another route would be to sell to a private collector. You get less money than an auction, but it's safer."

"How would we find one?"

Holt smiled. "Andy. I could probably find a collector right here in Asia who would buy it simply on the strength of my guarantee."

"How much is it worth?"

He shrugged his eyebrows. "Seven hundred thousand. A million. It depends on the condition. If it's beautiful...much more. The Song dynasty produced some incredible *kesi*. The Mongols overran the Song, so they used the same weavers...produced for the Khan as a gift for the pope. The Khan would want to put his best foot forward, wouldn't he? One usually does when his next step is on someone's neck." Holt loosed his deep laugh again, then drifted away as he admired the imaginary map. It would probably be embroidered also, with each country delineated by gold wefts and perhaps the thread made of spun peacock feathers. "It could be something truly truly gorgeous." Coming back into the room. "So you could add several hundred thousand on that account. More. Also, we would be talking about something of immense historical value, on the order of the Bayeux Tapestry. Three million . . . nine million."

The sums compressed the energy of the room into themselves like a black hole, going far beyond the range of the phrase "it's only money."

Holt dispelled the feeling. "But Andy, make no mistake about it. This piece doesn't exist. I don't know what Clayton's got you looking for, but I've known Clayton a long time. I know how he was. He didn't distinguish between his ideas and reality. It was all one for him. I'm positive that—"

"But you didn't know he had the textiles he gave you."

Holt recoiled a little. Andy's tone came at him with an accusatory ring, bringing up once again the unsettling drought of good pieces in Shanghai and, even queasier, the exquisite material that kept appearing through Clayton's eerie sleight of hand. "No. I'm still trying to figure that one out. Clayton had a very good eye, but he wasn't an expert. The pieces he gave me are very beautiful, especially the riding coat. That's a real prize. My guess is, he got lucky."

"Wait a second; do you really have to be an expert? Something Clayton did have was time, right? Maybe he could turn up things that you might not be able to. I mean, look at the thing he left in his office. The Mongol dynasty—"

"Yüan dynasty. Yes." The reminder of the woven gold *jin* threw Holt off a little. Everything else—the riding jacket and the other textiles—could be explained away as lucky finds. The glittering fabric with the *ruyi* clouds on it contradicted all of them. "That piece is definitely archaeological. I don't know how he got his hands on that one. That's easy in Peru; they're all over the place. But not here. Stealing that would take some major *guanxi*. A lot more than Clayton had."

"Stealing it? Are you telling me—"

"Okay, I don't mean, exactly, stealing it. I mean using *guanxi* to get it. Someone knows the director of the museum or the dig, favors get exchanged, perhaps some trades are made. The dig gets new equipment or someone donates something to the museum. It's not exactly stealing. It's . . . rearranging."

"What about Mr. Liu?"

"Mr. Liu." He stood up. "Mr. Liu! Now what makes you think of Mr. Liu?"

"Well, nothing, really. They knew each other, right? He's rich. He likes textiles. Everybody says he has a lot of *guanxi*."

For the first time Holt wondered how deep the ingenuousness really ran. "Who told you he liked textiles?"

"He did."

"Really? I didn't know you and Mr. Liu were so close. When did you talk?"

Andy didn't answer him.

"When did you talk?"

The silence had an adversarial feeling to it, and every second that Andy delayed answering escalated it. Finally he spoke in a soft tone. "Jeffrey, I think we both need to remember that I don't have to answer your questions. I've been honest with you—"

"Really? Are you sure you've been honest with me? Because I'm not so very sure. You're asking me indirect questions about textiles and values. You're mucking around with my employee and my client. You're Clayton's friend and I thought I should entertain you, but don't be sanctimonious with me, Andy, please. I told you in Shanghai you'd never make a good liar. You should have believed me."

Andy's face had always seemed transparent, incapable of concealing something for its own benefit, but to Holt it suddenly became the visage of a liar more expert than any he'd ever encountered, as prosaic as a sidewalk or a vending cart. "I am tired of all these half-truths you've been feeding me: 'Clayton gave me this in Hong Kong! Mr. Liu is just a casual friend of mine!' It's a fascinating coincidence: my textile sources start to go bad, and you, who, pardon me for saying it, know nothing at all about textiles or China, start to show up as . . . what? Mr. Liu's agent?"

"I'm not Mr. Liu's—"

"Then who's agent are you?"

Andy answered calmly. "Clayton's."

"Oh! Excuse me. I thought Clayton was dead."

"That's not what I mean. Clayton had something for me, and he sent me on this sort of . . . mission."

"I see: you're on a mission. Mr. Liu sent you to Inner Mongolia to find this imaginary tapestry that Clayton's pulling his leg about."

"No. Why don't you—"

"Well you and Mr. Liu are in for a big disappointment because I know Clayton. I know how he was!"

"Tell me about the robe."

"What robe?"

"The emperor's robe! Clayton said it was early Qing dynasty. Before . . . Quinn Lung, whatever that means. Is it yours?"

It was eluding him. As fast as he could try to put it together the new things kept coming and they simply didn't fit. "What robe?"

"The one Clayton gave me. Is it yours?"

"What do you mean?"

"Then Silvia didn't give it back to you, did she?" His voice dropped. "I didn't think she was going to." Andy returned to the window and looked out again.

Silvia's name further upset the already volatile mix of names and events. "What are you talking about? What robe are you talking about?"

"Clayton gave me a robe. He gave me the gold brocade in Shanghai—"

"Clayton is *dead*!"

"I haven't seen a body! Have you?"

"Don't be ridiculous."

"He left it in an office in Shanghai, along with a note sending me to Beijing. He left the robe with a friend of his at the Beijing opera no more than five weeks ago. I found her and I got the robe. Clayton said it was early Qing dynasty. Before Quinn Long!"

"Ch'ienlong! The *Ch'ien long* emperor!"

"Okay, Ch'ienlong. But then Silvia said it was a Chinese opera costume."

"What do you mean? When did Silvia see it?"

Andy's fury whipped out so sharply that it frightened Holt. "She fucked me to sleep and took off with it! Last night!" Even as the words came out of his mouth the anger turned into a laugh. He threw his arms up. "I'm so fucking smart! She took Clayton's note telling me where the tapestry is, too. It's somewhere in Inner Mongolia."

"She took them? While you were sleeping? That's—you must have misunderstood her! She's—"

"And she didn't tell you about them. I think that's pretty interesting."

He tried to keep up an appearance of equanimity. "Well, I've been out of my room—"

"Jeffrey, you've been out of a little more than your room. If I were you I'd think a little harder about where your textiles are going."

"Thank you for your advice, Andy, and for your assessment of my character. And perhaps while you're dispensing Zen koans you could tell me why, if you're such a straight arrow, why you've been lying to me since Day One? And lying very obviously, I might add."

His answer came slowly, something between an apology and an embarrassed expression of condolences. "I lied to you because Clayton told me not to trust you."

Holt managed a queer little smile. "He said not to trust me?"

"Do you want to see the letter?" He searched through his pockets, unexpectedly pulling out two tightly folded bundles. "Oh! These belong to your employee. You might want them for your records."

Holt took them out of his hands as he tried to absorb Clayton's warning. How could he accuse him! He, who had helped him in Tokyo and had it blow up in his face. Who'd endured the debacle with Misiko and who'd lent him money until he'd had to just say stop. Holt rolled his eyes, mustering his most dismissive tone of voice. "It so happens, Andy, if you really must know . . ." He lost what came after that. Nothing did. He started over. "This whole business with Silvia and your—your opera costume—it's all just a bit over the top."

Clayton not trust him! He clung to the two papers, unfolding them as he tried to think of a better response. One of them recorded the dry cleaning of a blouse in Shanghai. The other he recognized immediately as the fax he'd sent her from Montevideo the day before he'd left, showing his itinerary and alluding to the Paracas weaving being safely in his bag. Paper-clipped over it was a bill for twenty-five dollars from a Hong Kong office center, certifying that two sheets had been faxed back to Uruguay. A weird swimming feeling came over Holt. He lifted the computer-printed words of his itinerary. A note, written in Spanish in Silvia's even, polished hand. She had followed business etiquette admirably, a neat column of words in the upper left corner directing it to the recipient, in this case a certain Andreas Benavides, Habitación 607, Hotel Alvear, Montevideo, Uruguay:

"*Estimado Andreas, Aquí encuentras el itinerario revisado del Jeffrey Holt. Como puedes ver . . .*"

"What is it?"

Holt felt that he was gazing down at his shaking hands from far away. Like an earthquake on the little page, the trembling seemed to break down the masonry of sentences into disconnected words that he couldn't focus on long enough to hold together. "Dear Andreas, Here you will find Jeffrey Holt's revised itinerary. . . . *la manta de Paracas . . . dentro del forro . . . muy frágil.* As you can see, Holt has changed his flights . . . *muy frágil* . . . in the lining of . . . *tránsito en Lima, como hemos discutido* . . . remember that it is very fragile . . . *de Paracas* . . . in transit in Lima, as we have discussed . . . *muy frágil* . . . await your . . . Hong Kong or . . . *frágil* . . . Emerald Garden Hotel in Beijing, (86)755–6493392."

"You okay, Jeff?"

Paracas . . . His ears felt hot. "Excuse me."

He went into the bathroom. "But I can't sing tangos like you, Andreas."

"Never convince me of that, friend. Perhaps later . . . your opportunity."

"What's the story, Silvita?" With all the certainty of the master business mind: "He has another buyer . . ." Gao's smugness with the second-rate textiles, the showy bouquet: "Who's this one from?" "That's from Mr. Liu." In Shanghai, with her look of alarm and sympathy, "Don't tell me you lost it! What happened?" Phony assumptions of friendship parroted back and forth, and Silvia, with that submerged dark smile he'd always had such affection for: "You're a good man, Jeffrey." And all the while him making arrogant declarations, implying wisdom to himself with his historical explanations and his textile knowledge. "The man who knows, Andy, the man who *knows*... he doesn't see a rag, he sees the world." Impressing women on airplanes with his travel and his business and his "little empire" of facts where he spoke five, no less than *five* languages in which he could be misled and humiliated.

The falseness expanded beyond any one person or event until it began to infiltrate everything: the moments of friendship, the happy banquets, the cakes served in restaurants, the shopkeeper's smile, the grave robber's handshake, the afternoons at Alejandro's house, the leaves, the sky blue. It went beyond the counterfeit of human interaction to the whole construction of the world. A wall barely remained a wall, a tile barely a tile. All a forgery, like the relationships he had believed in and the self he had created, explained to him so clearly in an airport bathroom of mirrors and disconnected obligations to the dead and Andreas with his strip-search eyes and his mocking comfort: "*Tranquilo*, hombre, it's only paper."

Holt stared down at the blank white floor, as if Clayton had scrawled their entire history across it: Clayton in Tokyo, building Holt up to impress a woman they'd met at one of his openings: "Jeffrey is the brains behind this operation." That peculiar grace, putting his hand on his shoulder when Holt's English school had closed. "Hey! I love you as a success. I love you as a failure." Then, years later, Clayton downcast about Silvia, riding the ferry to Lantau: "Come on, Clayton. Get a grip on it." His condescension at Clayton's weird metaphysics. His trace of gloating when he'd lent him the money to look for his crazy textile. Finally every sentence he'd ever uttered had had rot in it, always corrupted by stray thoughts and hidden self-interest; the deeper motives always revealed themselves to any close look, and Clayton hadn't needed even to look closely. He could almost see him nodding his head as Andreas recited his absurd tango in Lima: *"Brushed on, your affection and your loyalty, another lie in your mockery of love . . ."*

Holt didn't know how long he stood in the bathroom. After a while he flushed the toilet for the sake of appearance and went back into the room. Andy was watching him, his boyish and unremarkable face suffused with a sympathy that Holt could still, even with all that had happened, dare to imagine was genuine.

"You okay?"

Holt went over to the closet and pulled down his coat.

"You—"

"I'm fine," he answered quietly, then he rubbed his forehead, as if trying to push away hair that no longer existed. "It's worse than I thought, that's all." Andy watched him. Only for the briefest instant had he ever seen Holt without some carefully appropriated attitude overlaying whatever true self was underneath, but now he saw it, and the man looked empty and worn.

Holt spoke as he stood in the middle of the room holding his camel overcoat. "You asked me if I'd ever been caught, and I told you once. I didn't tell you that it was five days ago, on my way to Hong Kong. I had a very rare piece. A beautiful, a very special piece. Too valuable to sell. It was . . . supernatural. Something I'd been looking for since I knew anything at all about textiles. They seized it when I was transiting Lima. Silvia set me up."

Even with all that had happened, the amazement showed in Andy's face, then he shook his head. They both stared in directions where their eyes wouldn't meet, thinking about Silvia. Finally Andy said, "I'm really sorry about that, Jeffrey."

"Oh, don't be. It's my own stupidity."

"Yeah. Well, you're not the only one who's been stupid." He turned and looked out the window again. Holt could tell that he was looking down at the rhythmic eaves of the Forbidden City. "You know, we're amateurs. You, me, even Silvia. It's like karate: there's always an opponent who's bigger and faster than you. Life's that opponent."

Holt acknowledged his words, then, "Let's get out of here."

■   ■   ■

They went out for a walk in the late afternoon rain. Beijing seemed smothered in a sopping gray rag. They crossed Tiananmen Square, Andy glancing at the heavy red walls that concealed the Forbidden City, presided over by the face of Mao. The gusts pushed the weather underneath his umbrella; it soaked into his shoes and crept up his pant legs. They didn't talk except to agree to go to Qianmen Street and look for dinner. By the time they'd gotten there the winter evening had come down and the cheerful lights of the restaurants were springing across the soaked pavement. Holt led them into a place, and a large metal pot of tea arrived. Andy could identify the faint smell of jasmine in the steam that whispered from its spout. Holt ordered, politely inquiring for Andy's preferences, then they sat back into the simple vacant pastime of watching the white-coated waiters as they went about their job. Holt took out the wooden chopsticks and separated them with a crack, then rubbed them together to smooth them out. He was facing the window, and his attention drifted through it to the distant place he contemplated things from, and though Andy hesitated to interrupt the furious sorting process he knew was taking place, he needed more from Holt than someone to order him dinner.

"You know, Jeffrey, I've been trying to be clever, and I'm really not that clever."

Holt tightened his lips a bit. "That's a good preamble."

"I know you don't owe me any explanations. It's not like you invited me."

Holt didn't answer at first, then Andy saw his face turn cool and analytical again; the examiner of textiles, picking apart the threads. "On the contrary: I did invite you. From Uruguay. Remember?"

Andy wasn't sure what tack Holt was switching to. "Well, I guess that's true."

"I was carrying out Clayton's wishes. It was my obligation."

"That's true."

"I'm not so completely untrustworthy as Clayton made me out to be, you know. I could have been better: we all could. Why don't we make an agreement; you can ask me some questions and I'll answer them, then I may have a few questions for you. At that point we can reassess where we stand."

"Okay."

"Ask me."

"What does Mr. Liu really do?"

Holt exhaled. A bitter amusement played across his features. "Mr. Liu has good connections with the Communist party. His brother-in-law was the mayor of Shanghai. In China the state owns everything, right? So let's assume that they decide to release some land to build a shopping center or a hotel. Someone has to be in charge. So if a person has the connections he can find someone in Hong Kong to develop it with him as a joint venture, and end up with a good amount of money and even a concealed ownership of some sort. Once you've got money on your side it's like anywhere else; you make more connections, and you become known as a friend of this person or that person. The restaurants get better, and you get an expensive foreign car. And then people start coming to you. And one day you're Mr. Liu."

"So what's your connection with Mr. Liu?

Holt put his teacup down and picked up his chopsticks. "He's a client."

"A client for what?"

"For textiles. Occasionally he solves problems for me. Bureaucratic problems."

"Huh . . . and where did Clayton fit in?"

"Until three days ago it never occurred to me that Clayton did fit in. Mr. Liu is my client. Silvia works for me. Clayton was friends with Silvia; perhaps the three of them went to dinner once. Silvia called Mr. Liu for help because nobody else was around who could manage things when Clayton died. Mr. Liu helped because he and I are friends." He shrugged. "That's the bullshit version, anyway. I think the whole thing is rotten."

"Did Clayton ever deal in textiles?"

"He used to pick up the occasional piece for me, but not lately." Holt snorted, but the humor had a trace of melancholy in it. "I used it as an excuse to underwrite his trip to that monastery."

A dish of pickled garlic cloves arrived, and Andy gripped one with his chopsticks and crunched into it. "Mr. Liu took me to dinner in Shanghai. He and another guy."

"A small man? About fifty? Mr. Sen. That was very hospitable of him. What did you talk about?"

"His business. How sad it was about Clayton. That sort of thing. Most of it seemed pretty casual at the time. You know, I felt like— almost like he was offering me a job."

Holt surprised Andy with a laugh. "He does that one well, doesn't he? Did he break out the cognac?"

"As a matter of fact, cognac was broken out." Andy remembered the toasts and the parting moment with Mr. Sen in the car. "It seemed like he expected me to have some sort of information about something."

"What sort of information?"

"I don't know. Like, did I like textiles, did I know much about them. It was pretty oblique."

"Mr. Liu is the master of the oblique. How did he find out what hotel you were at?"

"I don't know. I figured he asked Chang."

"Or Silvia. Just being friendly. Just a friendly, friendly guy, Mr. Liu. I've never seen him meet anyone of any conceivable usefulness without handing out a business card and inviting them to lunch."

Andy's lingering sense of importance at Mr. Liu's invitation deflated. "So about the stuff that Clayton's been giving me—"

"Describe that robe to me. What color was it?"

"It had a lot of stuff on it."

"Dragons?"

"Yes."

"Dragons, clouds, ocean. The four mountains that define the limits of the universe. It's a map of the universe. When he puts it on, he becomes the force that animates it." He could see he'd lost Andy. "What color was the base fabric?"

"Yellow."

Holt leaned in toward him. "Bright yellow? Or peach yellow?"

"Bright yellow."

"That's the emperor's color, at least with court garments, depending on other factors, of course."

"But how do we know if it was a Chinese Opera costume or not?"

Holt smiled at him. "That's the easy part, Andy. Tell me about the sleeves; were they wide? Or did they have cuffs shaped like horses' hooves?"

Andy considered it. "No, they weren't really wide. They were kind of . . . They were black. And they had this weird shape."

"Like horses' hooves."

Andy lit up. "Yeah, that's what they were. Hooves!"

"That's it then. It's Manchu. If you went to the opera you probably noticed that the emperors and ministers have costumes with wide sleeves that they can throw around. Real Manchu material has those other kinds of cuffs. The court robes always had them."

The waiter was bringing two plates of vegetables and flesh. One was brown, the other a tan color sauce.

"Who were the Manchu?"

"The Manchu were nomads from the northern forest, originally. They gradually started their own little state just north of the wall and set up a Chinese-style bureaucracy. Some generals in the Late Ming let them inside the Wall to help put down a rebellion, and they liked China so much they decided they'd stay and run things for a few hundred years. That's the Qing dynasty. They made their cuffs like hooves to remember their past."

"You mean it's real?" His voice had taken on an edge Holt hadn't heard in it before.

"It appears that way, from your description. How many claws did the dragons have? Four? Or five?"

He seemed agitated, blowing out a puff of air. "I don't know."

"Ming has four and early Qing sometimes have four. Later Qing always have five. Let's try something else: the dragons. Were they big? Imposing? Or were they small and meticulous; a little less raw visual impact in and of themselves."

Andy muttered the question to himself. "I'd say . . ." He thought a moment, then shook his head. "I don't know how to answer that. What's big? What's meticulous?"

"That would have helped us place it in early or late Qing. They had styles just as we do, but their styles lasted hundreds of years. Ours last a season." He grasped a green pepper in his chopsticks. "That's why Clayton mentioned Qian Long. He standardized all the court clothing in 1759: who could wear what on what occasion, the color, the cut, the iconography. You might say he was the ultimate fashion dictator."

Holt queried him more about the arrangement of the dragons on the garment, and about the particularities of the design: was it embroidered or tapestry woven? Finally: "That's all I can tell you about it without having it in front of me. My guess is that Clayton had it right. It's probably early Qing, with some late Ming stylistic nuances, like the big dragon. Don't take it too hard, but I think that robe might have more to do with Mr. Liu's hospitality than your sparkling personality. He probably thought you knew where it was."

"You're hurtin' me, guy."

"Just the facts, ma'am, just the facts. Clayton might have talked him into his Mongol *kesi* map, too."

It surprised Andy how Holt's mood had inexplicably lightened, as if he'd secretly found a solution to everything that had happened. "What would that be worth, the robe?"

"Good condition? It depends somewhat on the provenance. Fifty thousand. Up to a hundred fifty. This year. In five years, who knows?"

The figure struck Andy back to contemplation of his plate. Holt thought about the robe, constructing his own robe out of pieces he'd seen in books or museums. The apparition fixed itself more rigidly than a photograph, somehow rendering true everything else in the story that Andy now began to relate to him between bites, one that started with the fax and the plane ticket that had arrived by courier. He listened to the phantom other half of the events he'd experienced: the cheap business card with Andy Mann, President, and the appearance of the woven gold *jin* at the alleged office of the Invisible World Trading Company. He saw Mr. Liu as they ate dinner in a room Holt himself had dined in, imagined Silvia at her most seductive in her hotel room. "Luckily, I met this young woman on the street, and she helped me out." And with those words Holt, too, had a young woman on the street—"the Beijing opera"—where Holt heard the enthusiastic grunting of the aficionados, saw the delicate toss of the sleeves by the Lady Zhaojun. And just as Holt could imagine now the part of the story that had been so opaque to him, and see it woven into the startling existence of the gold *jin* and the Manchu robe, he could almost distinguish, against the dim, incense-darkened walls of a lamasery, the glittering map of an empire that no longer existed, or that would always exist.

Andy finished his story with the lament that Silvia had taken the note with her. "So anyway, I'm kind of on my ass."

"I'd say that's something we have in common." Holt poured him another cup of tea. "As you said: Life's a pretty big opponent. But"—thumping his hands on the table—"that's life in the Empire." The well-dressed office men of Beijing flickered past the windows in their fine gray overcoats, like moths.

"Every place is misty here." They were traversing again the vast gusty space of Tiananmen Square. "You ever notice that, Jeffrey? Shanghai was misty and this place is misty. I don't get China: it's the most concrete place I've been: you know, low-tech, people in your face, all that. It's so concrete, and then . . . everything's always disappearing into the mist."

"That's how it is here in winter. If it's not fog it's coal smoke."

They let it sit there for a minute, then Andy began again. "Do you think there's any way I can get that robe back?"

Holt considered. "I suppose you could go to the police and file a report. That might take a day or two. You'll have to tell them all the details, of course. All of them. Then they'll have to schedule some inquiries, and they'll need to find Silvia and question her. That could be a week or more. It becomes a matter of time, really. And I don't know how much law and order you're going to inspire when you tell them how you got the piece." Holt turned a dry grin on him. "Or how you lost it, for that matter. Even if they locate it, do I really think they'll give it back to you? My guess is they'll say you don't have a legitimate bill of sale." Holt felt embarrassed to add the next part. "Or they could go the other way: they'll want to know about everyone else involved in the abusive imperialist traffic of their national treasures. They love a righteous scandal, especially if it involves foreigners. With a little luck, we could end up with a full investigation."

"Which would implicate you."

The wind snapped Holt's umbrella inside out, relieving him of the necessity of answering. They had left the classical silhouette of the Qianmen Gate behind and had reached the middle of the massive plaza. Andy went on, his voice pressed into flat tones. "I kind of hate to see it end like this, Clayton's . . . plan, or whatever it is . . . was. It's not the way it should end. I sort of . . . fumbled, I guess. I'm a little out of my element, here." The conversation lapsed, then sputtered up again. "Maybe Silvia will go after it. Hell, maybe you can go with her. She might need your help selling it or something."

Holt faced Andy so that he could see his irony. "Silvia and I will certainly have a lot to discuss."

Andy had pulled his shoulders tight against the wind, and he walked fast to get out of the cold. The inadequacy of his windbreaker gave him a hunted look. "It's been an experience, I guess. I just feel like I let Clayton down, somehow. I wish I hadn't been so stupid."

"Do you still want to go to Inner Mongolia?"

"I want to go, but . . . the only thing I remember about the place is that one of them starts with an *H*. And there's a monk named Rartha that I'm supposed to give an Invisible World card to."

"Clayton never lacked a sense of the dramatic." The remark had no real meaning. Holt said it to buy time while he considered his obligations. "It would be extremely cold there. It's colder than Beijing."

"Have you been there?"

"I've been to the capital once, Huehote. I was sourcing cashmere cloth."

"Well, from what I remember of the note, this monastery's not too close to the capital."

"It would be a dry cold. A lot colder than this. Then, outside the cities, there would be a lot of wind. Most of it is outside cities."

"I'd have a hard time finding it even with Clayton's directions. I can barely get around Beijing."

"All things considered, I think you've done quite well." They turned on to the huge boulevard where the troops used to march past the all-seeing eye of the Communist Emperor Mao. It was full of traffic now. The multitude of bicycle riders protected themselves with long plastic ponchos that they draped over the handlebars like an apron. Holt answered his question before he could ask it. "It's unfortunate I have that meeting in Shanghai. I might have been able to help you somehow. If I call it off now it may never happen."

"Oh . . . it's not your responsibility. I need to get home anyway. I just wish I hadn't been so stupid." Holt saw him turn the side of his mouth down. "There's probably nothing there anyway. Like you said."

In an unexpected way, the remark bothered Holt. To hear Andy, who had faithfully followed each of Clayton's directions, accepting his own negative logic seemed to snuff out whatever remained of Clayton's life. "That might be going a bit far. I think it's unlikely. I don't think he'd go to all this trouble for nothing. He did find the robe."

"Maybe I'm wrong about the robe. Maybe it really is only an opera costume."

"You're not wrong."

The singing of the bicycle bells went on around them, like the song that led the workers home each evening. Margarine-colored taxi beacons moved from the middle of the road to the side, stopped, then out to the middle again. The electric sleet glowed pink or yellow around its host of streetlights like the most fugitive of dyes, one that could never be set. Holt felt the overbearing responsibility of the meeting in Shanghai and of the whole life he had so carefully composed out of *guanxi* and airplane tickets. At nearly forty years of age everything could be settled into place, including his youth and the aspirations he'd had, even his flawed friendship with Clayton Smith, which would finally stop its nagging and accusations. Or he could not settle it. Holt felt a giddiness coming over him. "You know, I read that book."

"Which book?"

"The pulp novel, about Mongolia. Clayton gave it to me. I read it and gave it to Chang."

"Oh. How was it?"

Holt laughed and grabbed Andy's shoulder, leaning close to his face with a leer that felt slightly hysterical even to himself. "It doesn't matter how it was. What I'm telling you is that Chang has it." Andy looked at him with an expression of mystification. Holt felt his eyes bulging as he made his immense and magical leap into thin air. "And if Chang has it . . . we have it."

INVISIBLE WORLD

It doesn't make sense that a dead man can narrate his own story, but almost everything is narrated by the dead anyway. Edison describes the late ashes of a party with his electric lights. In some poor, frightened Chinese mind Grandpa Mao goes on hammering out the difference between Capitalist Roaders and Good Communists, again and again, waking his listener up in the middle of the night in a cold sweat. All those noisy dead people, leaning on their horns and telling you what to do. Go here, go there. Even in a state of ten thousand chariots the citizens of the Invisible World vote early vote often for their incongruous agendas.

Reclining in my palace, listening to the traffic noise of Hong Kong spattering my open window. The dispatches had been drifting back to me from the outposts. From the State of Mem, a paper scroll comes in with the imperial seal raging on it in lipstick red: "Lord Clayton, the winds of rebellion stiffen the Imperial banners." The Duke of Pos comes scraping up for an audience, kowtows, arranges the sleeves of his silk robe: "Oh Son of Heaven, a famine has come upon the land." The feudal lords barely conceal their sneers, and the Minister of Finance had long since weighed in at the most inappropriate times.

The Empire was doing the greased pig thing, slipping away from me. It was settle it now or take on a permanent job peddling insurance in a bar somewhere. Looking here, looking there, in the shops selling dried fish fins and the glorious Harborview hotels where the doorman fixed me with his blackened-penny eyes. Surveying the crates on the street in the factories of Tsim Sha Tsui and the gray industrial between-building light. Hong Kong had finally boiled down to being merely Hong Kong, monolithic and businesslike, no matter how I tried to paint it.

I found the tapestry in the book, the one by Whitcomb; his *Travels Through Inner Mongolia*. English tough guy prose about horse-and-cameling it through the steppes at the turn of the century. *"Renegade Mongols . . . heeding the savage call of their ancient marauder's blood . . . I stood my ground, moving my hand toward the holster of my Webley. I feared that British arms might be my only salvation."* Adventure in the grasslands, Adventure in the desert, Adventure in Beijing, and in the middle of all that tiresome fucking Adventure, in less than a paragraph, the sacred prize that Whitcomb never thought to pistol whip with his Webley: a map of the Mongol Empire woven out of silk and gold. Supposedly a gift to the pope that never reached Italy, a kind of "top this one, buster" from the Great Khan, Son of Heaven, to the Catholic god's man on the scene, instead got stranded seven hundred years later at a monastery in the middle of nowhere, a textile beyond rare and worth more than a fortune. Even Holt, the master smuggler, would bow down before it. Even Silvia.

"It's the Empire, Chang. If I find it I can unify the Empire."

Chang with his deadpan skeptic face, always only showing 25 percent of the emotion of any other human being. "Clayton, surely others must have looked for such a valuable antiquity."

"They were ruthless men, Chang!"

"What do you mean?"

"Chang, Chang, must I hammer you with The Big *M* again? He said: 'There are cases of a ruthless man gaining possession of a state, but it has never happened that such a man gained possession of the Empire.'"

"Mencius was referring to Benevolence, Clayton. You are distorting—"

No, Chang, he's talking about settling the Empire! The real Empire!

Chang with his tea-drinking answer: a sip, a stare at the bottom like he's staring into a lake. Chang like one of those Confucian officials, always dutiful and severe, and behind that mask, supremely benevolent. At the end he gave me the extra for rent and smiled.

"Perhaps you are right, Clayton." The perfect straight man: "Mencius said, 'It is never anyone's proper destiny to die in fetters.'"

Silvia didn't return my call again, so I went over to the studio to try and put something together. The whole place was filled with garbage and I ended up sitting and drinking tea all afternoon, looking at the dozens of boxes I'd dragged up. I drafted up a letter to Andy, telling him how great things were. I kept thinking of this place of exquisite cold and perfect emptiness, someplace so far away that almost nobody went there, and at the same time, someplace inside, because I'd felt that way for so long. It just had this absolute symbolic truth: *Inner Mongolia Autonomous Region*. What could be more real than that?

I decided to go, gathering up a thousand dollars I'd wrung out of prison terms at various workplaces. On top of that a thousand Holt gave me to buy him any textiles I found. I told him that made us business partners, that if I could bring the map back half of it was his.

Still with that restrained little smile, dry as dust: "Count me in."

At least he'd stopped trying to talk me out of it, noise that shattered my spirit. He came to the station with me, pointing to photographs of embroideries and mentioning this or that detail. I said to him, "Jeffrey, I think you've seen me off on more trips than anyone I know."

He looked up from the book, hot and uncomfortable above the accordion of wrinkles in his linen suit, improvising not very well: "The journey of ten thousand *li* begins with one step."

My reply, equally lame behind an equally dopey smile: "Or one pointless gesture." He carried my bag to the tracks, as if I wouldn't be carrying it the next ten thousand *li* myself. I left him at the platform like a road sign.

Whitcomb had badly transliterated the Chinese names. There were three major systems for using the English alphabet to write Chinese words and he hadn't used any one of them, instead substituting his own totally inconsistent renderings that could only barely be hung on to a real sound. Beijing wasn't even *Peking*, but instead his own idiotic *Pay-cheen*, an allowance for which the book's editor should have been executed. Every ten minutes I wanted to go back in time and choke the daylights out of the guy, but the daylight had long since gotten away from him, and I was stuck with these ridiculous syllables and the possibility that somewhere out on the steppes endured this one truly great textile of the nomad empire.

No one in South China knew anything about Inner Mongolia, so I shelved it until I'd been rattled north to Beijing, the old Mongol southern capital. At the station peasants learned to ride the escalator, humped together in the vast Hard Seat waiting room sitting on their bundles like refugees. God over the loudspeaker prophesying in Chinese his inscrutable schedule of departures and arrivals. I spent five hours there trying to find someone who had some idea of where I thought I wanted to go. There were no tonal marks in the book and no one understood my pronunciation enough to relate it to a map. They listened curiously to the weird white guy; where did he come from? and I said *"Meiguo, Meiguo, Meiguo"* so many times I couldn't hear it anymore. *Wo zai Meiguo lai.* "I from Pretty Country come." America. No one knew. Some thought it was over here. Others thought it was over there. They dragged their dirty fingers across the map, picked their noses, spit. Hard-Seat language for "I don't know."

I finally ended up on a train. Hard Seat, of course. Go to the capital and improvise. Basically a hunch, something that feels pretty solid when your feet are dangling. Families and students had packed out all the cars to where you couldn't get through the aisles, people standing and leaning and trying to grab a two-inch sliver of seat to rest on. Heaven decided to try the carrot instead of the stick for a while, procured me a foot of horizontal vinyl among four already drunk Mongolian bureaucrats on the way back from Beijing. They plied me with clear liquor, a substance that exists all over the world, called *wodka, bai jiu, aguardiente,* moonshine; virulent and lethal in a hundred languages. One guy was cadre, kept thinking he could advance his career by proving me a spy. Maybe move up half a yuan in the pay scale. I told him I worked for the Khan; textiles. After that I bribed him with currency I'd printed up in Hong Kong: denominations of three, seven, nineteen, and ninety-seven, all prime numbers. I laid one of the ninety-sevens on him and his eyes nearly popped out. Probably hadn't seen that much money his whole life. Stick with me, buddy, and you might just get rich: Liu style. That silenced him. I had a million business cards and I wanted to give out every one of them: Invisible World Trading Company, Shanghai. I was a high roller, working for the Khan. I populated my country that way.

In the long span of daylight we'd cemented a friendship that would last a lifetime or until we got off the train, whichever came first. I woke up six hours past my destination with empty seats all around me and vacant black night carving out my reflection in the window. It looked like it lived in a different universe than the regular one we're always stuck in, a freer universe where every flaw made a person more tragic, even if it were actually a simple boring flaw, and not a godlike one. Started thinking about Misiko again, the last time I'd seen her, the whole melodrama with Jeff. In Tokyo I'd tried to settle the Empire with beauty and women, and for a while it looked like it would work. Always more women, more beauty, the fascination of a new body and also a new sculpture getting bigger and more lovely. I felt it starting to converge, the way the lines on a painting all lead back to one vanishing point. The flashes started coming, some vast unity I could almost express, then one morning I woke up with Jeffrey's girlfriend and the Empire crumbled underneath my feet, war on every border, temples burning and blood flowing deep enough to float a soda can. A good time to walk away, to find out what lies beyond the self and its little games. A very young man's move, to leave like that. It took me five years to realize I'd made a permanent decision. Then I wasn't such a young man anymore.

Trains always pull those thoughts out of me. The wheels all sound like the Rock Island Line or the Burlington Northern and with the right amount of exhaustion I can relax all the way to Illinois and imagine I'm on a freight car with Andy somewhere between Davenport and Iowa City dreaming I'm in Inner Mongolia.

Had to double back to Huehote, capital of the Autonomous Region. Something creepy had started to form, like in a comic book where magic fog begins to take on shapes and *kazaam*! it turns into a dragon or a witch. Silvia'd shot me through some bad turbulence and I hadn't fastened my safety belt beforehand. I'd been trying to settle the Empire with benevolence. Supposedly, a benevolent king could roll the Empire in the palm of his hand, but it hadn't been working too well for me.

Checked into the Inner Mongolia Hotel, a big slab of modern building that marked my whereabouts like a tombstone. I recognized it immediately as the kind of hotel room people commit suicide in. Blank white walls, traffic noise. Fluorescent lights that go through everything like some kind of horrible X ray. A little archipelago of stains on the bedspread charted out this one's spilled tea and that one's moment of passion. A fall-apart room, half prison, half nothing. I'd been surfing the emptiness for a long time and I could see the surf was definitely up. I opened the window and looked out. It was the eighth floor. I decided to go downstairs and get something to eat.

They'd stashed a lone white guy over in the corner like they were ashamed of him. Gray beard, suit and tie. He smoked a particularly acrid kind of small cigar and I have to admit that I liked the idea of him filling every place he went with his horrible blue poison. I needed some payback after getting gassed in a million little rooms. He turned out to be a cashmere merchant from Edinburgh, trying to make some new contacts. He told me the best cashmere in the world came from Inner Mongolia. I told him I had the kind of room that drives people to suicide. He looked at me a little strangely. "I had that room last trip," he said, and I knew right off he was a spirit guy. When you throw a line like that out there you find out right away who you're talking to. I've got another one I use on airplanes. Where you going? Death, same place you're going. A good conversation starter, or stopper.

He asked me what had brought me to Inner Mongolia, and I told him I was looking for a famous tapestry I'd read about, one that had been commissioned by the Ogadai Khan as a present for one of the popes, a map of the Mongol Empire.

He used his Scottish accent to tell me in a gentlemanly way how fascinating that was, and that One would Suppose that an Item of that sort would be Quite Valuable.

I just want to see it, I told him. I'm not looking to make a killing on it.

He said he hadn't imagined that I was.

I ordered us both Mongolian hot pot and they brought over a heap of stringy raw lamb meat and some sprouts, leaves, noodles. The blue alcohol flame oozed around under the little container of water like mercury. He'd been here eighteen months ago, in the dead of winter, when it had been twenty-five below and in the old city big blocks of frozen urine waited outside the public latrines to be hauled away. His wife had given him his walking papers the week before, dispensing with all the bullshit about finding herself and needing some space and just telling him "I'm bored with you," get out. I pictured a middle-aged Silvia. His story sounded a little one-sided, but no matter what brings it on, when your life gets vaporized you can only get so much mileage out of throwing the blame around. He'd decided to make a business trip. That hotel room had been waiting for him, Inner Mongolia, the dead of winter...

He trailed off into a little silence break, then I started up. Yeah, Inner Mongolia Autonomous Region: it's kind of the perfect metaphor no matter how you slice it.

He knew what I meant.

We shoveled the noodles and boiled meat into our mouths. "So where did you find your information about this tapestry? Are you a specialist in antiquities?"

"I read about it in a book. Some British guy was writing about his adventures in Mongolia in the twenties. He saw the tapestry in a monastery out in the middle of nowhere and they told him where it came from."

"What makes you think there's any truth in it?"

"What makes you think what I'm telling you now has any truth in it?"

I let that one sink in for a while. I didn't have to make any sales. After a while I said I knew it wasn't exactly like reading about it in the *Encyclopedia Britannica*. What is, you know? You kind of have to decide: do you want to live in the world according to the alleged facts, or do you want to determine the facts yourself? Some of the things in the book probably happened. Others he'd probably cooked up to make it more exciting, like any story. The man had listed a succession of places, and I'd follow them.

"Did the author's list include the Suicide Suite at the Inner Mongolia Hotel?"

"Oh," I told him, "that's only temporary. It's when they book you there every time that you've got a real problem."

He laughed and motioned a waiter over. I saw that he knew the word for beers.

I liked him a lot. Bold and rude, because he understood. I told him about Tokyo and how I'd built the big gold wall around my sculptures. I'd wanted to make them into a Chinese garden, where everything inside was a metaphor for a bigger world. I described it to him and the whole fantastic scene at the opening. That had to have been, oh, five years ago, but I kept reliving it.

Several beers had already booted us out of the Politeness Club, so he went ahead and asked me if I was so bloody successful, why did I leave?

I told him I'd just stopped believing in that stuff anymore, Beauty and the market for it and all that. I'd basically stolen my closest friend's girlfriend away chasing after it, and when I'd woken up to the reality it had just made me crazy and I'd had to get as far away as possible on this earth. I'd gone to the most god-forsaken little town I could find, where no one spoke enough English to ask me about anything and I'd somehow found a nondescript room and just gone insane with boredom. I didn't make anything and I didn't do anything. The highlight of each month was taking the bus down to a city to buy more yuan. I learned Chinese because it bent my head around. And that was how I'd first gone to Inner Mongolia. Somewhere between there and here I'd lost the Mandate of Heaven—

"The Mandate of Heaven?"

"Yeah. Heaven backs you till you fuck up too much, then you're history. Christianity, God strikes you down, right? In Confucianism, you just get left slowly twisting in the wind while the world takes everything away from you."

He nodded and thought about it a minute, then asked me what one had to do to get this Mandate of Heaven back. I told him there's two steps: Step one, find the Map. Step two, unify the Empire.

"Unify the Empire?"

"Elementary, my dear . . . what is your name, anyway?"

"Fabian."

"Fabian. Let's go back for a second. Back, *back* . . . " I did my best public TV British voice "'*far into the misty recesses of time.*' You can probably say that better than I can."

"How far back are we?"

"About twenty-five hundred years. Warring States period. China's divided into lots of little states and they're constantly . . ." I left the blank for him to fill in.

"Warring."

"Yes! There's lot's of little kings and they all have the same dream. They want to turn China into one big empire."

"With themselves as emperor, I suppose."

"That goes without saying. The question is, how do we do that? The obvious approach is you tax the commoners until they have nothing, build a big army with ten thousand chariots, and go over to Shu or Qi or Wei and say 'hi!' That's sort of the Control approach; dictators love that one. Now, enter Confucius and his pal Mencius. They're wandering from kingdom to kingdom, dispensing advice. They say the way to settle the Empire is through benevolence. Just treat your subjects well and everybody will want to be part of your state. You can roll the Empire in the palm of your hand. You know: 'When T'ang marched on the East, the Western barbarians complained, saying, "Why does he not come to us first?"' That's the Benevolence approach. Here, finish this."

"I'm half blotto as it is."

Gan bei!

Gan bei Gan bei.

We lifted up the glasses and drained them, set them down among the fallen noodles and shreds of cabbage left after the hot pots had been taken back. He tells me he doesn't see what any of this has to do with the map.

Okay, I know, it's a little vague. It's not too clear to me either, to be honest with you, but here's my feelings on it. Let's say you've got lots of little states. That's how most people live, all compartmentalized. Over here, you've got the state of Imagination. Over there, you've got Memory. And all the other states: the state of Far Away, the state of Obligation, the state of Possibility; there's a lot of them. Those are the states that make up the Invisible World. And then of course you've got the biggest, most powerful state, the one with ten thousand chariots and ruled by a merciless fucking tyrant, the state of Material World. That's the empire I want to unify. I call it the Conceptual approach."

"And you think if you find this map you'll unify the Empire?"

"Yeah."

"Maybe you should call it the Leap of Faith approach!"

"Hey, fuck you, Fabian. I didn't say I had all the answers. I'm following my spirit. Haven't you ever done that? I'm kind of surfing here, I haven't tried to conceal that. Maybe I'm wrong, and if I am, I'm the only one who takes the consequences. You want another beer?"

"Oh, why the devil not?"

I flagged the waitress, who by now wanted us to leave so she could talk to her friends without any disturbances. I pleaded to her sour face for two more beers, and she laughed at my Western smile and went for them. Fabian had lit up another one of his smoke bombs. He talked at the smoke in front of him. I suppose every man dreams of his empire, doesn't he? As shabby as it may be. Or cruel or sad or bloody ordinary. Or brilliant.

Or all of those things, Fabian, in succession. One minute it's gold, the next it's stone, and then suddenly it's only paper. But that's okay, Fabian. It really is. Because there's some places you can't measure your way to. What I'm looking for, you don't find with some orderly careful calculation.

He understood. I was glad I'd found someone I could tell it all to because otherwise it would have been just me and the eighth-floor window of the Inner Mongolia Hotel and it might have gotten messy. When we'd had the last beers I knew it was safe to go upstairs and that I would probably be okay for a while. As for him, he'd be back to Beijing by tomorrow noon. He gave me his card and shook my hand with a clear, honest affection. He told me to look him up if I ever got to Edinburgh. Oh, and do drop me a line to let me know how your endeavor turns out. I think you're going to find it.

I gave him one of my Invisible World cards and a lucky three-er and a couple of seventeens.

What's this? he asked. He was looking at the portrait of Kublai Khan I'd lifted out of a history book. The ninety-sevens had Genghis on them.

It's currency of my private country. I'm granting you citizenship.

He let out one of those startled but unshakable British Oh!'s. These are quite well done, he said. He looked up from the bills and he thanked me very deeply. He told me it was an honor to be a citizen.

Yeah, well, don't spend it all in one place.

I felt like we'd known each other a long time and that something important had happened between us. It's always like that when you're traveling. I was sorry to see him go.

I bounced around Huehote, not sure which absurd direction to head next. I kept trying to come to grips with the fact that I'd come all the way to Inner Mongolia looking for something I'd read about in a pulp novel. This one had to work because something else was coming out of the mist. Exhaustion. Every trip was starting to seem like a circle, and all those circles together formed a whirlpool that sucked the sense out of everything. I went to the university and spent a couple of hours finding someone who could tell me where the place I was looking for was. He was a professor. He wanted to know why I was going there but I played it straight and told him I wanted to see an old monastery I'd read about. He said he wasn't sure if there was a monastery around there or not. It was a very great distance. If he knew about the tapestry he didn't let on. After that I sat down and had tea.

In Inner Mongolia you always have enough time to think. You can think think think think think until you're wandering around in some Chinese garden of a labyrinth. I like to let my mind wander, but it has the habit of wandering into bars filled with sour old men, or up to the edge of some large blank space. Andy kept coming to mind, sitting in his dad's office way off in the Midwest, where we'd both started. Still the same, Andyman: unquestionably kind, unquestionably loyal, the only person in the world who could still look at Clayton Smith and see someone dazzling. I could never break him loose, always one thing or another held him—maybe that's the nature of the world, or the nature of a person reflected in the world. Last time I'd seen him he'd looked desperate and sad, or maybe beyond despair, just sad, filling the Liberty Grill with his sadness like some kind of slow music. The inability to write a letter or buy a ticket had buried him. Impossible to budge him out of Illinois then, but now I could, sitting in a restaurant after the lunch rush, the waiters throwing down new white tablecloths and setting a side table for their own meal.

I put him in Hong Kong, the old naive Andyman, trying to figure out the menus. Let's see: shall it be cubes of pig's blood or boiled fish maw? Chang was there, yeah, Chang, because Chang in his bureaucratic way was a spirit guy too, and he would look after him for me: the True King's Confucian advisor. I put them at the Blue Heaven together. Andy's asking about the strange food and the different types of tea, trying to figure out some great mystery he never thought of before, and Chang giving him the Confucian perspective on everything. Jeff, of course, another story. Jeff would measure him the way he measured everything, to see how many arm's lengths away he would have to keep him but still maintain him in orbit. But really he would know Jeff in the first twenty minutes, he'd see his messed-up spirit behind the cool, perfect special effects: businessman, smuggler, expert, fugitive. Holt, with his stupid misdirected way of settling the Empire.

I could see them together in Shanghai. Jeff would dazzle him with his textile visions, he'd open up that other universe just long enough for Andy to get a peek inside and then they'd both be hooked to each other. When Jeff does his textile routine you have no choice but to fall into that little piece of fabric and the world that's woven into it. He's good at it: it's his substitute for real human expression, something he buried a long time ago, with my help. Yeah, they'd both be hooked, together they made a whole person.

I could see them on a train, traveling Soft Seat, of course, the big recliners with grimy white tablecloths and lace curtains. Andy looking around, wondering when the son of a bitch across from him would quit smoking for five minutes. Smoke, cough, smoke, cough. He turns to Holt, "Why doesn't he just put a fucking gun to his head and save himself twenty years."

Holt doesn't even notice it, of course, though the smoke comes his way, too. The missing *chi fu* floated up the aisle of the train, then dissolved into a man selling tea and bags of dried beef. "Don't fight the cigarettes," he advises Andy. "They always win."

Andy shoots one last look of contempt at the man and settles back into his seat. "How much longer?"

Holt looked at his watch, then discounted it with a frown. "Ten hours? Twelve?" He shrugged. The exhilaration Holt had felt at his decision to go to Inner Mongolia had begun to play hide and seek with a jittery sense of futility. The faxes to Villarino and the Italians had been vague: family emergency, a few days . . . He had already worked the sympathy angle fairly hard when Clayton had died, and this second time it had felt stale even as he had written it. He didn't have time to wait for their reply, and he didn't really want to know it. Villarino had been trying to back out for a month; if they didn't meet on that day, they would probably never meet at all. Okay, Clayton, you win: I am casting aside my empire and hoping like hell that it's no more than discarding a worn shoe.

Fine; he'd made the great leap of the spirit. But what came next? He reached into his traveling bag for the long scroll of paper that had come up from the hotel's business office, courtesy of Chang. In bombastic antique prose Whitcomb made the arduous horseback journey to a far-off monastery. The sketchy description of a large tapestry:

> *The golden threads glittered and winked in the candlelight, brought to life amidst their bed of* bleu céleste *by the monks' steadfast devotions. Shivers ran down my spine as I stared at this legacy of the mighty Khans, who had proclaimed the largest empire in the history of Mankind.*

In the margin Holt had scrawled the name "*Rartha*" and "*starts with 'H,'*" the only things that Andy could remember. They had spent the night finding a map and trying to stick the erratic place-names in the book onto it. Then to Beijing station in the early morning, steering through the maze of platforms and waiting rooms. Gray filthy world, hissing and thundering. Now they talked about details: what time they would arrive in Huehote, what they would do when they got there. They kept the most important things private, each one trying to comb out for himself the nest of motives and lies.

They had begun the series of switchbacks that climbed into the Western Hills before they began to talk.

"Where do you think she is now?"

"Silvia?" Holt pursed his lips, answering with a neutrality that impressed Andy. "Huehote, or farther. I assume she's on her way to the monastery to get that piece."

"I thought you said it didn't exist."

"Perhaps Clayton told her something he never told me. People do that when they're involved."

Holt recounted the arc that Clayton and Silvia had described those several years ago. It had seemed unlikely even when it was happening, as if everyone involved was carefully suspending their disbelief. Silvia usually ended up with rich men, but Clayton had become intimate with her in some way that Holt didn't understand. They'd defied the odds for a year, then it had gone bad. He told about listening to Clayton on the ferry to Lantau Island, the agonized confusion woven into the colorful background of junks and freighters as he'd tried to immunize himself to the pain with various philosophical antidotes. "It wasn't one of the tidier splits I've seen. After that they were on again, off again. That was worse. I steered clear of the whole thing." Andy took it all in with a thoughtful silence, one that the textile dealer knew was attached to the roller coaster of the past few days.

Holt looked out the window and spotted the Great Wall lapping across the ridges, immense and fantastic, dividing the old cultivated China from the wild plains outside, like a giant garden wall. It fell behind, leaving only the charcoal-colored trees that clawed their way across the snowy surface of the mountains. "We're leaving the Middle Kingdom now," Holt said. "After this it's all barbarians."

They went on another half hour without the burden of a conversation, then Andy stretched his legs out into the aisle and arched his back. "So what do you think happened? With Mr. Liu and all."

"The gold *jin* is stolen. I'm almost positive that it comes from a museum in Shanxi. I saw a picture of it a few years ago. That's a very rare iconography from a very rare period."

They got into a long discussion of the logistics of the betrayal—a subject Holt attended with a detachment that bordered on humor. "It's all conjecture at this point, but my best guess is that Silvia's been skimming my sources for the best pieces and selling them directly to Mr. Liu. Clayton got in the middle somehow." He gave in to the downward pull of the missing textile for a moment, then he finished. "The Paracas piece was probably an independent study project. Mr. Liu doesn't buy South American material."

"But why would—"

"Because that's Silvia. She looks at every relationship as a balance of power, and she can't help trying to tip the balance in her favor. She's like a shark; she has to keep moving to breathe."

Andy absorbed Holt's diagnosis as he crumpled an empty cellophane packet of sunflower seeds and then, finding no receptacle to throw it in, put it back on the little table between them. He looked up from it to Holt. "I thought she was your friend."

Holt disclaimed it with a shrug. "So did I. It appears I was wrong, doesn't it?" Holt's nonchalance suddenly wore through to its acid edge: "But I intend to get very unwrong." He sagged back into his down coat, and a sigh propelled his next words. "That seems to be my luck with friends. I can't exclude Clayton from that either."

"You mean because of this whole thing with the textiles?"

A woman in a white smock offered them hot water from a large kettle wrapped with rags, but Holt waved her away. Andy asked him again. "Because Clayton was involved in this—"

"No. It's not that. My sense of it is that he was involved, but that he had different motives. Otherwise I wouldn't be here." He turned his gaze to the window as he added quietly: "It's not that."

"What is it?"

Holt spotted the side of the train as it followed them around the mountain. He could make out the glassy shadows of other passengers upright in their own squares of scenery, drinking tea or talking, waiting for the destination they would arrive at a few seconds after him. He envied the muted contours of their lives. Their families and networks of friends seemed far apart from the stupendous betrayal that had cut his legs out from under him.

"Oh, it's been so long that I feel idiotic to still be harboring it." He let his words subside into the rhythm of the tracks, listening to how they changed from one beat to another. "You know that Clayton had a period of great success in Tokyo. If he'd stayed he would have become famous. I'm sure of it. This was more than ten years ago, so we were all ten years younger. We were all in our twenties. So that becomes an important factor. And then the fact of being in a foreign country, and suddenly receiving all manner of attention and invitations, which could be difficult to integrate anywhere . . . The point I'm making is that it would affect anyone's judgment."

Andy knew he shouldn't say anything, that the best thing he could do was listen, like the Chinese man across from them, who had poised himself unashamedly attentive, seeming to understand everything through Holt's grievous tone of voice.

"So . . . Clayton and I were something of opposites. He was handsome, he had a good sense of humor. He had that gift of confronting people in a way that pushed things to a more profound level, so he made friends easily"—Holt smiled as he remembered an encounter between Clayton and another artist—"when he wasn't antagonizing them."

Andy nodded. "I certainly remember that!"

"As for me, I wasn't handsome, I wasn't graceful . . . "

"You have a certain charm—"

He held up his hand. "I'm not saying that I'm an ogre. But I'm not the type who has scads of women around him or people clamoring to have him as an ornament at their next party. That's what it was like for Clayton in Tokyo."

"And it went to his head."

"No. Those things never affected him. Clayton never deserted me. He always brought me along and shared his success with me, as much as one can. I can't count how many events he got me invitations to. But he was on a path of excess. He produced work at an incredible rate, and he went through women at the same speed. He wasn't so bad at first: you could at least say that they were girlfriends. Later, I might see him with three different women in the same week. And he became completely absorbed in this world of . . . sensuality, and his sculptures...and this sort of...limitless fantasy world. A lot of people's feelings got hurt." Holt stopped as the memory came back to him with a freshness he hadn't experienced in years.

"What I'm telling you is that he was out of control. At that time, I was seeing a woman named Misiko. I was doing translations at a news agency and she was working there. And—we were somewhat serious. At least, I had hopes of becoming serious." He considered it now, the interior of the train losing out to the image of the long-disappeared Misiko carrying a stack of letters across the office area, always arrayed in the sharp cut of what had then been fashionable. That had been his first impression of her: how stylish she was, with her red lipstick and gorgeous clothes. "I think she was serious also, but when she met Clayton she developed a fascination for him, because he was so unlike anyone..." Holt fell silent again, looking through the frosty pane that bore the smudges of hair grease and fin-gerprints. "People get transported by the moment. The heart's the monarch, right? They call it that in Chinese medicine. And some-times it's not a steady, wise monarch. Sometimes it's a capricious monarch." He raised his eyebrows as he considered his own words, then went on. "When it all came out Clayton couldn't come to grips with it. He fled. Misiko didn't do any better: the shame factor over-whelmed her. She quit the company without notice, which in Japan is the professional equivalent of committing suicide. She left me a long letter apologizing. She loved me, she wasn't worthy...That was the general idea. I think she went back to her hometown."

"You never had a chance to talk about it with her?"

"No." He inhaled, as if to propel his next words. "So there I was in Tokyo. It was like a neutron bomb went off in my life. You're familiar with those: they kill all the inhabitants but leave the build-ings standing. Not to be self-pitying about it but—you can imagine it: no friend, no girlfriend. I didn't even have anyone to complain to. It was just..." He held his arms out, then chuckled instead of com-pleting his sentence.

Andy listened to Holt, his eyes focused on him as if he were trying to recognize a familiar face at a great distance. "And you stayed friends with him?"

"I didn't see him for more than a year, almost two years, then he showed up at my door in Hong Kong speaking Chinese."

"So he went to China that year?"

"I would suppose so. He never admitted it. In a way, I think he wasn't anywhere that you could attach a strict geography to, and that's how he left it." Holt sat up and pulled down the pant legs that had bunched up at his thighs. "As to being friends . . . There's a lot of error in this world. It's part of the wholeness. At times like that it's a major effort not to be petty. I wanted to be friends. We both did, but that issue always came between us."

"Until now."

Andy's words surprised Holt. Finally he nodded his head. "Yes. Until now."

They descended to the plains again, decided to split a bag of dried meat and a packet of crackers Andy had bought on the platform. They washed the salt away with tea, and they stared out the window without speaking for a while. Holt took out a monograph that he'd found in Beijing. Andy couldn't read the title, but he guessed from the cheap paper and the poor gray-toned photographs that it had been printed in China. "What's that about?"

"This? It's about the influence of minority traditions on Middle Kingdom headwear."

"Sounds like a real page-turner."

Holt stared at him for a moment without saying anything. "You know, I was just thinking that I should buy our friend here a few packets of cigarettes for being such a good neighbor."

Andy held his hand up. "Please . . ."

As if on cue, the man across the aisle embarked on another fit of coughing and made a long elaborate series of liquidy throat clearings before spitting. Andy cringed and moved an inch closer to the window.

"Why does someone collect textiles, anyway?"

Holt closed the booklet. "That's two questions: why does one collect anything at all? And why, out of the universe of things that one can collect, does one choose textiles?" The merchant looked at Andy as if considering whether Andy really wanted to hear the answer, then swept the waste from their meal onto the floor and put his monograph on the table. "First of all, you have to realize that someone who collects textiles, I mean a real collector, is different from someone who merely enjoys a textile. Collecting involves an idea of completion. A collector who wants to have a good representation of nineteenth-century Bolivian material knows that it will never be whole until he comes up with a good Charazani *ahuayo*. And a dedicated collector will go looking for it. He has the pleasure of the search, and the pleasure of completion. You can get a similar effect from collecting baseball cards. Why does someone want the entire World Series champions from 1976? Is it because they love the Mets?"

"'76 was the Big Red Machine."

"Be that as it may. What we're talking about is order. Cohesion. I think that's a big part of collecting. As to 'why textiles...'" Holt shrugged. "Status is one reason. Mr. Liu collects rare textiles, so Mr. Liu is a man of refinement. Mr. Liu can pay five thousand dollars for something that most people don't understand, so Mr. Liu is rich. Mr. Liu owns something that belonged to an emperor, so Mr. Liu is a member of the ruling class. How deeply do we want to look into this?"

"What about, 'because they're beautiful'?"

"I was getting to that. In my opinion, textiles are unique among the world of beautiful things. For one thing, even though they're very design oriented, like paintings, they're also very physical and tactile. Rugs, for example, corrode differently depending on what dyes are used and how tightly spun they are."

"What do you mean by corrode?"

"Wear out, pack down. I met a rug man who told me he could run his hand over the rug and feel the different colors by how they corroded, and that if he were blind he could learn to enjoy the colors like that, by the feel of their patterns weaving in and out of one another." Holt leaned back. "And that, my friend, does not happen with a baseball card."

"My nephew might not agree with you."

"Maybe you should pick up a few pieces for him, get him on the right track. It so happens that I have a few late Qing insignia badges he might like. Let's see, I've got golden pheasant, quail, Mandarin duck."

Holt pointed at him, saying brightly, "He could collect all nine ranks of the Qing civil service!"

"I don't know, Jeffrey. You must have been a real 'different' little boy."

"The only kid on the block with an orchid collection."

"Didn't you play sports or anything?"

Holt seemed to be cheering up. "Table tennis, Andy. A game at which I'm still quite capable of giving you a ferocious drubbing."

"That's okay, I've had my ferocious drubbing for this week. Is there a food car on this train?"

"I'm sorry: did I finish? Did I say: *I'm* finished talking now? That's it; I forgot! I'm becoming senile! I must have just said, 'I'm done answering your question now, Andy. Why don't we talk about food?'"

Andy raised both hands. "Could you please finish answering my question, Mr. Holt?"

"Why of course! So, besides being beautiful—"

"Hold it. You're busted." Andy felt pleased that he finally had a valid objection to Holt's monologue, something he'd been thinking about since seeing the textiles hung up at the funeral. "Isn't beauty an acquired taste? Someone who doesn't know textiles might look at . . . that riding jacket, say, and think it's just some drab old shirt from someone's basement. Like that *Chosroes* rug that your friend bought: anyone but an expert would have had the good sense to see that it was just a rag."

Holt pounced on him. "Is it just a rag? Are you sure? Then why is a shiny piece of silk beautiful and a shiny piece of synthetic material gaudy? Why is an old carpet precious when you can buy a machine-made one at the discount store for one fiftieth the price? I'll tell you why: it's everything you don't see. The age, the time of its creation, the stories and values that are attached to it. That makes things valuable, and that's what constitutes a human consciousness, or a civilization, for that matter. Is that woven gold *jin* just a rag? If it is, you can reduce everything to the same status. After that, the only thing left is food and shelter."

Holt paused in case Andy might answer him, wetting his tongue with the hot tea before finishing. "What's magic about textiles is that they retain that dimension of all the lives that have passed through them. They were worn, they were used for making offerings, they were stepped on and washed in streams. It's there. You can feel it. And not just that. A textile is a crystallization of a culture. Of history. You can look at an imperial court garment, like the one Clayton gave you, and it goes off in a thousand directions. On one hand, it represents the history of the Qing dynasty. On another, it's one of the culminating stages in the evolution of the Manchu tribe. At the same time, it's a part of a Chinese textile tradition that goes back five thousand years. You can trace the history of its iconography, the dragons and clouds and sea and mountains, or you could trace the history of that particular emperor, how he grew up, what he did in his reign, what rituals he wore that garment for."

And then, of course, you have to include the person looking at it: the events that brought them to that spot, what they're thinking, the history of the building they're sitting in, maybe a rundown on every molecule of oxygen that enters their lungs. The fact is, you could write a fucking encyclopedia about any given thing, and every single volume would be infinite. Call it *Clayton's Encyclopedia of Everyday Objects*. One of my future projects, write one of those encyclopedias about, say, this teacup and then write one about the table it's sitting on, then about this pestilent green carpeting: hmmm, wasn't that rug factory built in 1968? Write all these encyclopedias then cross-reference them to one another: "See page 10,948 of *Table* for more information," or "Ibid., Huehote, p. 675,924," so, yeah, write all those encyclopedias, link them all together and then the next thing you know, you've got . . . the Empire! Yes! It all made perfect sense! Even sitting at a miserable little restaurant in Huehote while the waiters did their best to ignore me, dare I say, out of existence, I could see that I definitely would have to put that on my list of things to do, the main problem being the enormous amount of time required to follow even one single object through the full range of its quintillions of connections. Even so, I was too charged up to sit still. I felt incredibly benevolent, so I threw down a few big Chinese notes and one of the Khan's ninety-sevens, not even asking my loyal subjects to bring me a bill. Good-bye, sons and daughters! Keep the change! Who at this moment can say that I am not indeed a True King?

I rode that one around for the next few days. Huehote felt like Tokyo, that old Edo that I'd tried to settle and gotten so far off track. By the time the buzz wore off I'd even visited the tomb of Wang Zhaojun, a Han concubine who had to take the big sleep beyond the Great Wall to buy the Han a few more years of peace. In return she got a big mound of earth with people selling souvenirs at the top and fake Mongolian yurts at the bottom for Taiwanese to snap their photos in. Lu Xiao Yu would have died laughing.

I rented a bike, hammering the guy down to seventy jiao a day, the Chinese price, just on general principle. Huehote had two cities, the modern one and the old one. In the modern one Good Communist architecture marched around in a lockstep of big featureless blocks duplicated again and again, monolithic Morse code saying "there is no escape." The Old City held me: low and squat, square mud buildings interspersed with public latrines and monasteries. The smell of urine reared up in any place that promised a grain of isolation, but you could look down one of those muddy little passageways and see the fifteenth century. Market carts lined the smoky wide street, and cave-like stores sold sweets or unidentifiable pieces of hardware. My favorite part: funeral trappings sold right next to fireworks, like they knew everybody should go out with a bang.

At night I wrote letters on that great stationery that said INNER MONGOLIAN HOTEL with its strange script, sent people pages from an illustrated geography text written in Mongolian. It was full of maps and strange cutaways of geologic phenomena, all explained with that barbaric and incomprehensible writing that I liked so much. "Figure that one out, buster. It's the secret of life." Another big entertainment: watching the poor people out on the main square at night, where they sang along with video monitors. They couldn't afford a hotel karaoke bar and their slick drinks, instead paid a few jiao to one of the dozen impromptu television setups scattered around between food sellers. Factory workers and People's Liberation Army conscripts singing out their lonely hearts in the cool evening in front of TV-beautiful youths who mooned longingly in some Hong Kong skyscraper or other part of the luxurious south Down There Somewhere in the unreachable distance. So ludicrous and moving at the same time, there in the field of pavement under the smoky stars.

I checked out a few monasteries, then it was time to go. Located the bus heading north over the Da Qing mountains, a dozen rough faces turning at once as I stepped on. Right-angled seats made of metal tubing with planks on them. These buses are always the same, just a question of how many years ago the shocks should have been replaced and how far away from your feet the puddle of vomit is. In this case, about eighteen inches. We advanced at the speed of continental drift, even so, everything lighting up into a deafening rattle and every piece of trim jouncing crazily: the smooth part! The real bumps hurled me six inches into the air, a splendid vantage point to watch the little mud villages roll past from, and also the small cities of the plateau that lay north of the velvety green bones of the Da Qing range.

After nine hours of this I realized that the bus wasn't going exactly where I thought I wanted to go. It seemed like if I went the wrong way enough times I would eventually get there; kind of like going from A to B by circling the globe instead of in a direct shot. It's a curved universe: even light doesn't travel in a straight line. An old hippie told me that. The driver let me off at a crossroads. Someone had thrown a sort of inn together there: I got a bare concrete room with a charcoal brazier and a rusty metal bed frame. A suspiciously corroded bucket had been thrown in for good measure. Great: how nice to be back in the Middle Ages. Through the window I could see a large pig.

The inn had the two prerequisites of its type: the bad restaurant, the filthy bathroom. I expected them. I almost looked forward to them. Bad restaurants are like a kind of parasite that lodges itself in the intestinal track of trips like that. They're always made of concrete, and in the winter you eat with your coat on, spitting out your foggy breath between a succession of greasy noodles and rancid meat. The green vegetables have black spots on the leaves and the bamboo chopsticks have a sodden, slippery texture. A curtain of plastic strips always hangs in the doorway to discourage flies, but some sort of superrace of bluebottles always manages to blast through and take over. This one was a classic. The tables were a simple wood, polished a dull brown by centuries of tea, chicken bones, spilled rice, dirty elbows. You could probably carve your name in congealed grease without ever getting down to the wood. They'd painted the walls some sort of Pea Green or Sea Green, a shade too miserable to be included even in the deluxe pack of Crayola crayons. I'd need a really large set to color in this picture: Minimalist floor "color me Concrete!" and of course the essential bare fluorescent light fixture, so that the whole room seemed skewered like an animal on the white tube. Hmmm . . . is that "Incessant Blue" or "Void Gray"? The seats were all stools, and I chose a place against the wall so I'd have something to slouch against. Across from me, some young guy in a shabby black suit kept spitting on the floor and smearing it into the filthy tile with the sole of his shoe, a sanitary measure that didn't impress me. I checked out the fixed-price lunch: some kind of greasy mutton shreds with noodles, followed by mutton soup.

A middle-aged woman in a white apron brought me a spotty glass that she cleaned by filling with tea. This is the life! I thought. And afterward I can go relieve myself in a concrete trench. Some kind of tub of old stale water to wash my hands. Welcome to high adventure. Something else, though. With all of the smallness and the tawdriness, it gave me a feeling of safety. No one knew me or anything about me. It was far away. Far away's a funny thing: it has a habit of sneaking up on you and becoming the center again. But for the moment, this was staying far away, and I liked that.

I heard a bus pull up outside, so I rushed out to see if it was going in my direction. No, it was headed back to Huehote. I reclaimed my table as the passengers filed in for their lunch, workers dressed in solid blue or gray clothing ornamented by dust. One man had a suit jacket on, its wide lapels hung over from a century beyond style. They all stared at me as they came in and again after they'd sat down, surprised to see a foreigner at this crossroads. I thought of the bus back to Huehote, and the train that went from there to Beijing, and whenceforth to the network of memory and information that led back to Hong Kong. From Hong Kong it didn't lead anywhere: my parents in their Florida retirement, Andy at his desk. Holt in the air someplace.

And where was I now? Looking for something that likely didn't exist at a place that might not exist, cruising on the strength of something that was at best exaggerated, and likely on the downside to be a complete fiction. It was coming on again, the dizzy feeling of being nothing and nowhere, a meaningless bag of bones in some anonymous barren plain far away from everyone I knew and whatever structures that could possibly have meaning. My friendships meant nothing, my sculptures meant nothing; all of it just momentary shelters against the terrible randomness. I kept trying to stitch it together again, the little stars of memory and possibility and distance, but my ideas were shattering right in front of me, falling to pieces and leaving me at some horrible crossroads in Inner Mongolia, stranded, dying slowly, nothing in the future and a past long since out of reach.

It was coming on way too strong for me now, way too strong. I wished I could Blind Auggie it, say, "Oh dead black man I'm with you now!" or name it "The Emptiness" and look at it, find some way to put some distance between me and it, but instead all I could think of was Silvia saying, "You just defend yourself that way, by turning it into something. But what if it doesn't change?" Hong Kong, me trying to tell her what it was like while we ate dim sum and drank a thousand cups of tea. She always ate with that gorgeous South American accent: I don't know, something about the way she handled the chopsticks, the Silvia way, holding them wrong but still making them work. She did everything with her own accent. And I told her, You're far away. The world's falling all around you in little bits—Shanghai's over here, Geneva's over there. Hong Kong's broken off from Kowloon and they're going in opposite directions. Chicago...who even knows where Chicago is? Your old girlfriend in Berlin is writing you her last postcard— No, she wrote it a few years ago. Your parents are getting closer and closer to death, or maybe they're already dead and you remember all the time you didn't spend with them. And it gets bigger and bigger and then, pop! You realize it's your old friend The Emptiness, and as soon as you recognize that, it changes, it turns into something else, some sort of reference point and you say, Hey, yeah, I've met you before, *Ni hao*, big guy, how's your health? and then"—stretching back with my hands behind my head—"and then you're surfin'."

She'd blown out a puff of air. "You just defend yourself that way, by changing it into something else. What happens if it doesn't change?"

That supremely scornful look, as if he wanted to tell her to drop dead, then he'd gotten cool and said with the confidence of a general, "I can always make it change."

She'd smiled at his answer to her challenge. She liked the fact that she couldn't shake him. That was his power, that he could make it work. He'd done that in Tokyo, where Holt had corroborated his story of wild success, and in Hong Kong, too, differently. He had a hard way of pursuing his vision, disciplined and impossibly focused on garbage and the commonplace. She'd tried to get him to make beautiful things again, like the ones that had made him so successful. She had urged him and taunted him, insinuating that he couldn't do it anymore, but he'd explained to her over and over again that he could still make them if he wanted to but he was looking for something bigger than that. Finally she realized that he really didn't have it anymore, that he had lost it along the way somewhere and that this metaphysical cowboy constituted a mocking remnant of what he'd once been. The last time she'd brought it up it had been more to ridicule him than anything else. "It's really too bad you can't make those beautiful sculptures anymore. Then you wouldn't have always these problems with money."

She'd noticed the barest flinch, almost a waver in the atmosphere rather than something physical, then he pushed his chair back from the table. This time, he'd decided to skip the first part of the argument. "Silvia"—getting up—"it's easy to choose."

And so had ended the first year of their little *amor*. In some way, she respected him more for it. He'd fought her to even; not many men could do that. She'd kept wondering whether she should call him and get together, but she'd clung to her siege, filling in the space with other men who entertained her. Then he'd wavered, animating her telephone in the middle of the night from someplace in China. His outpouring of stupid intellectual grief bobbing in a spume of static. He'd said something about a place he was trying to reach, not telling her everything and what he told her not having very much sense. He seemed to be ashamed of what he was doing. She'd never heard him like this, and she didn't like it. He sounded weak and sad. She thought of how he'd walked out of the restaurant on her. Fine, Clayton. Yes, I'm still working for Jeffrey. And you are where? Oh, of course it is a secret. Everything must be secret, I remember now. Everything must be invisible with you. That's what I like about you, Clayton, you stay close to your ideas. What? It is very difficult to hear you, perhaps I'll be in China this month but only in Shanghai: no, I don't have time to come and meet you. Yes, I have to go now. I have an appointment very early tomorrow.

Hanging up the telephone, she realized that the balance had been tipped decisively in her favor. She'd lain back, but after less than a minute the panic had come, the horrible panic of wanting to call him back, to pluck him out of whatever miserable place he had put himself and take care of him. Maybe he would call back and she could tell him, I'll meet you in Beijing, Clayton. This week if you want. We can go to the water garden of the Summer Palace and you can tell me again about your resonance of absent things. She could picture their favorite roast duck restaurant and the acrobats of the Chinese Opera flying around like sparks, and at the same time she could see it all rushing away from her at an unbearable speed, tortured by the impossibility of distance as the phone persisted in not ringing, not ringing, with a deafening sound not ringing all night. By morning she either had to go crazy or slough it off as a minor episode in the war of the sexes. What right did he have to ask for her support now? It was his own fault he had lost his talent. And it had been he who had walked away.

She sipped at her Scotch, thanking some unknown joint-venture partner somewhere for insuring that the bar here at the Zhao Zhun Hotel, "the finest hotel in Inner Mongolia," had real Scotch. It fit this exciting time in her life, one she could enjoy completely alone. No chance of running into anyone she knew, no false smiles to give out, no explanations. It would be days before Andy arrived in Huehote, if he even attempted to come. He probably felt sour that she had taken the robe from him, but it had been hers, actually, and what complications would have resulted if she had tried to explain that to him! The sight of him sleeping came back to her, and the way he had felt so bad about hurting the money changer. She would call him on the phone and explain everything. Maybe they could meet up in London. She would buy him a ticket. Then there would be time to explain everything, to apologize and even find him a robe as good as the one she had taken back from him. It was simply a temporary difficulty, all this bad feeling. It came from the circumstances.

The tapestry would solve everything, and soon. Even now it felt so close that thinking of it sped her heart up. According to the note, the monk would just give it to her. If she needed money, she had the dollars she'd brought to buy Mr. Tran's stones. And if something else, she would do something else, period. Fine. She would be a rich woman in a few months. How would she use all that money?

Considering that challenge entertained her much more than trying to solve the purchasing problem. Hong Kong had become tiring. She would keep an apartment there so that she could continue doing business with Mr. Tran, just for interest, but maybe she would branch out to Europe. It was sure that she could sell the gems there as well as in Hong Kong. She'd get an apartment in Rome or Paris, and she would keep one in Buenos Aires, too, just to be able to go back and eat a decent *churrasco* once in a while. She could see it already, the barbecues with her friends there and so many bottles of good red wine with a splash of soda. She would amaze people with her places and her languages, have interesting lovers and crack them open like peanuts. She would be free, like Holt. People would say to one another, "I think she's in Europe" or "She sent me a letter from Cambodia last month. I don't know where she is now." And that part, the part of not being there, was the most attractive part of all. Nowhere. Existing as a rumor, and maybe, if she kept that rumor always in her head, it would be almost like not existing at all. *Free.* She could understand Clayton now. She smiled. There had been many things he had known better than anyone.

Ah, but Buenos Aires... She must get an apartment there. Nothing could replace the wrought iron and the cool faces behind a coffee cup, all looking into the distance with that permanent wanting. Chachy would be there, and the rest of them, a dozen good friends who knew the difference between the sweet tangos of Gardel and the smoky gutter tangos of Goyeneche, and many other things that these Chinese and Americans ignored so completely. That had been the problem with Clayton: he didn't understand tango. In tango one always lost in the end because it was a corrupt world, and if someone stronger or richer didn't cheat you, then death itself would steal away your lover, now or later. Clayton hadn't understood that, that one always lost. Yes, that was the problem with him. He wasn't very good at drinking his bitterness and setting his face to the future again. What a pity he hadn't grown up in Argentina. He would have learned it well there.

"Miss, you want, don't want other drink?"

"Don't want, thank you."

This bar bored her. A few Taiwanese businessmen kept looking at her from the table by the door. Another group of businessmen pledged loud eternal friendship and cooperation among empty bottles and cries of *Gan bei!* PRC Chinese: she could tell by the cut of the suits. Boring. One always hoped something momentous would happen in a bar, it kept people hanging on all night, long after they'd become too tired to enjoy it. It had the same feeling of when the telephone rings in a hotel room, that mysterious few seconds when perhaps some destiny could be ringing you up. Just for a moment, that possibility . . .

"With me it would be my creditors."

"Clayton, you know your creditors don't find you in hotel rooms."

"Mine do. They find me anywhere they want."

The moment was rotting away beneath her feet. She had too much time to think here, and really, it was bothersome that she had not heard from Andreas and that she could not locate him. Certainly a message would be waiting for her in Hong Kong.

That had been unfortunate, to see that sadness on Jeffrey's face. Perhaps she really had gone too far. If she had only known that things would turn out so well, that she would get the robe back, she wouldn't have had to do it. Clayton was to blame. She had only taken the Paracas manta to get the money to pay for the things that he had stolen. Clayton! Now she would have to pay for it all, because Jeffrey and Andy would talk, and Jeffrey would soon know about the robe and the Yüan brocade and what she had done so many years ago. And then in Buenos Aires Jeffrey would let his poisonous knowledge drip so casually into his conversations, always with the correct philosophical twist, of course, that Silvia was a traitor, that Silvia is *militar*, that Silvia had made an innocent person die. Then there would be no grilled meat with the old group, no sitting again at their favorite bars, only their badly hidden faces of disgust when she said hello. She had known that it would cost her a lot to betray Holt, and the mystifying part of it, the wrenching inexplicable part was that she had done it anyway.

Fine. She would feel bad about it later. She would feel bad about everything later. Now she would be in the moment, the way that Clayton had always told her. Look at those three Americans, how they announce themselves with their accent. Of course it didn't require much time before they invited her to their table. Two plump, crude business types, the third, younger, a little handsome, wearing a black turtleneck and blue jeans. Mineral consultants from Colorado working on a coal mining project. They traded the usual identities like clerks making change, and she explained that she had come to Inner Mongolia for textiles business. She left it vague. She didn't really want company. They got her through the moment and after a while she went back upstairs. Her bus would be leaving at six the next morning.

She lay in bed and tried to imagine the tapestry. Clayton had painted it as deep blue, with Mongolian and Latin writing on it, golden thread demarcating the limits of the Mongol lands and beyond it some unknown regions. He'd said something about clouds, too, and human figures done in great detail. "...Down to the eyelashes. I'm telling you, they're alive!" Like the Song dynasty *kesi* from the Shanghai Museum, where one could practically hear the figures' voices. Little else of Clayton's description remained, only something about the Uighur lands and Xi Xia. He'd only described it to her once. She could see herself looking at it now, at last beholding in the dim light of the monastery the glittering outlines of the Empire and its subjects. Terra Mongolis. The undulating rows of weft threads as they buried a warp thread, then submerged themselves again under the next one. The soft shine of silk, standing out from the dingy plaster of the wall. Nearby an angry-looking statue of an *arhat* holding his sword and halberd. The monks would be stalking the grounds, heavy and stolid in their brown robes, their shaved heads glistening as if waxed, old men, young boys somehow at once serious and childish spinning the prayer wheels. Cords of incense smoke would waver in the darkness, denying gravity and everything gravity implied. The monk Rartha would stand beside her, and he would give it to her, as Clayton had asked him to, and she would fold it up and be gone, taking back something of Clayton himself to the world, holding under her arm his strange dream made real, and he would be looking down on her and thinking: Okay, Silvia. We had a lot of problems. But you finally understand what I meant, don't you? You finally know that I could imagine something into existence. That even if I'm broke and exhausted, sitting at some miserable crossroads in Inner Mongolia with a bad case of diarrhea I can still grab a piece of pulp fiction and prove that it's real, and along with that prove that all the other things are real too.

I kept telling myself that, anyway. The lunch crowd at Crossroads Hell were hoisting out their worn yuan and heading for the door, setting off a ferocious "Go back/No back" struggle that got my blood screaming for about fifteen minutes. Finally some handy intestinal microbes put in their opinion, little Confucian advisors sending me running toward the trench at the last minute. Ah, Lord Clayton, the True King follows the Will of Heaven, watches the old bus/livestock transport roar off over the grasslands, the tortured sound of its gear changes scraping and cracking against the horizon. That settled that. From here I was headed to someplace that started with an *H*, and after that, who knew? Just have to shrug sometimes, hurl yourself into the universe and hope you don't get body slammed.

I pulled a photocopy of Whitcomb's text out of my shoulder bag. I'd spilled tea on it back in Beijing, so it had gotten wavy and tan on some of the pages, a not very official-looking document. I took out a map of Inner Mongolia and looked at the same characters for the thousandth time, checking out the characters in my dictionary to get the sounds. Okay. This place, that place. I'd already labeled most of the place-names I thought might be anywhere close, but none of them seemed to jibe with Whitcomb's asinine spelling. Now I was working on the little settlements far to the west or east, places I knew were impossible. The five or six other people left in the place were all staring at me. I caught the eye of an old man at the next table, something not very difficult, since he'd been staring at me like a zoo animal the whole time. He looked like he'd been a trooper in the Third World War, the one where the Mongols retake the world: ancient black Mao suit held together with stains and patches. A little billed cap covered his graying hair, held up by two ears that stuck out toward the horizons. His skin had been burned red underneath the deep tan, and every gust of wind that had ever blown across that face was still there. His guttural Mongol accent and bad grammar told me Chinese was his second language. He waited a second before taking the cigarette out of my hand, then struck a match behind a wall of long yellowed fingernails that looked like they were carved out of horn.

I took a few silent few puffs, then started running down all the conceivable pronunciations of Whitcomb's miserable transliterations with him. Hoo Len. Huh Lin. Ho Loon. Couldn't be sure he even understood what I wanted from him, or if he would reply. I told him near Ulamqab and he repeated Ulamqab, and then by himself he said it, the words that I knew were right, Helan Qi, yes, not far from Ulamqab, and my world suddenly jumped open again. Have, not have temple at Helan Qi?

Not have. My home not far Helan Qi. Not have temple.

I felt the collapse starting again inside me, then he went on: Temple not at Helan Qi. Half day walk from Helan Qi.

He suddenly had the most beautiful face I'd ever seen. I wanted to hug him, appoint him my honorary grandfather. I didn't want to ask about the tapestry for fear I might sound some alarm bells, so I didn't say anything else. The other five people in the restaurant had been tuning in to every syllable, and now it touched off a major discussion about the monastery at Helan Qi. A young girl said it was more than one thousand years old, but a fellow who had on a dirty brown sport jacket and a year or two of school to elevate him to the role of local Sage insisted no, it was Ming dynasty, or Qing. Say, that only leaves a spread of about five hundred years! The usual interrogation began, like every other one of its type, starting with "Where are you from?" and finally getting around to "How much money do you make?" The Sage grilled me, brilliantly producing all those hard-to-know words like *money* and *work* and *train* from his little storehouse of English: very impressive. The girl and another man weighed in once in a while with their own nosy questions: "Why don't you have a wife?" Or "Why did you leave Beijing?" I kept an eye on the old man, who took it all in without saying anything. It went on like this a half hour, then everyone drifted back to their own things except the Sage, who seated himself at my table in a proprietary way, like he might start charging people admission to talk to me.

I went over to the old man's table and asked him if he was returning home. I thought he might be able to tell me something helpful. He said no, he was going in the other direction, to Erenhot. Hmm: Erenhot. I'd seen it on the map, up by the border with Outer Mongolia. Probably a four-day round-trip.

Was I going to Helan Qi? I told him I was.

He fixed his cataracted eyes on mine: Why?

I want to go to the temple.

Why? he asked. It is not a famous temple. It is very far.

Ah yes: a man unafraid of the obvious. I thought for a second of being cagey and careful with him, tell him I was a student or some other semiplausible door-to-door story, but he'd already called bull-shit so frankly and neutrally and without prejudice that I thought he could handle what I'd tell him. I leaned close to him, trying to escape the intrusive ears of the Sage. He didn't lean back, so his black eyes loomed nearer and nearer to mine. I said: I'm going to tell you the truth, even though it will sound very strange. I am trying to draw a map of an Invisible World. I have been trying to draw this map for many years and I think that I will find something at this temple that will help me draw it. And then I can go back to my home in peace.

He looked at me without expression, then he slowly reached up and rubbed a little scab near his cheekbone. There's no such thing as a little bit pregnant, right? So I went on.

You do what work? I asked him.

I have sheep. I have few goats.

You have places you bring the sheep to eat, yes?

Have.

And at one time you bring them to one place, and another time you bring them to a different place. That's so, isn't it?

It's so.

And do you remember them all?

I remember.

You remember even the places you went to long ago, with your father and your mother? You can close your eyes and remember them?

A faint quickening of intensity in his cloudy gaze. The lines around his sockets deepened and moved like the surface of a calm ocean: can remember.

You have visited Huehote, yes?

Have visited, also Beijing, many years past. I still remember. Also Baotou, and Dongsheng.

Have you ever visited America?

His hard face erupted into a smile, and one single deep laugh escaped from his chest, followed by a tiny cough.

But you can think of America?

He was still smiling. Can.

You can think of Hong Kong?

It seemed like something ticked over inside his brain, the evidence that his thoughts had gone outward one order of magnitude, and now his attention started to sharpen. He tilted his head down as he answered: Can.

I couldn't tell if I was making any headway but at least I was amusing the guy. I didn't imagine he got a lot of foreigners coming around asking him about his memories. I asked him if he could think of England and Japan and Guangzhou, and every time he said yes, except for Australia, when he said, "Where's that?" I wasn't sure how much farther I could go with him, so I just played it. I said, Do you want to know how to draw a map of the Invisible World?

He reached under his cap and scratched his gray hair. Tell me.

You close your eyes and think of all those places that you have been to, the ones you went to this week, also the places you went to many years past.

He closed his eyes as I spoke, something I hadn't expected. He looked almost like a child waiting for a surprise. Very easy, he said.

Now also think of the places you want to go, and the places you imagine, even if it is heaven, or the Islands of the Immortals, or Sheng Du, the garden of Kublai. You can't leave those places out. Everyone thinks that those places are all apart, but they aren't, they are on the same map. It's the Invisible World. It's the real world. It's the Empire.

The Empire.

You have to keep all of them together at the same time.

He opened his eyes, favoring me with a chimplike grin. He pointed to his head: already all together.

I tried to imagine his grassy watering places and his long-ago Beijing, all the marriages and rainstorms and deaths mixed in with the sameness of sheep and magazine vistas of Hong Kong. I could tell he had a map, and he seemed to have settled the Empire to some degree, but I couldn't tell how extensive it might be.

The waitress came and refilled the teapot from a grimy thermos. The Sage had gotten tired of trying to listen in on our conversation and gone outside into the sunshine, so I could talk a little more freely now. I took my cup from my own table and brought it over. I poured for him, and he tapped twice on the table to say thank you. He offered me a cigarette, its saffron color signaling that he smoked the absolute cheapest brand available. I lit up the harsh tube and took it into my lungs. He was sitting back on his stool appraising me, his eyes barely half open, and a milky black at that. A fly walked across his jacket cuff, but he ignored it. You look for what at temple?

I'm looking for a cloth from the Yüan dynasty. A Yüan king made it. It's a map of the Mongol lands.

A map of cloth. He inhaled again and a slight cough pulled his eyes away for a second. You said you want draw map. You not say find map.

I wasn't sure how much I could explain to him about unifying the Empire, I was on slippery ground here myself. I said: maybe there is no cloth.

He put a dab of saliva on his fingertip and pasted down a gap in the seam of his cigarette.

I read about it in a book. A storybook that isn't true.

I was worried about losing him now, so I added quickly, Some of the book is true. Like Helan Qi. But if I had stayed in Hong Kong I would never know that Helan Qi is real. The cloth is the same. It might be real, but I have to make it real. That's how I draw my map.

A pebble of ash tumbled from his cigarette onto his jacket and he rubbed it into the surface, then kept looking at his coat as if he were trying to read some message in the greasy threads. He must have been thinking behind that nicotine mask, Check out, like, just *check out* the white guy's madness! I was really riding on my status as foreigner now, some state of grace hopefully still in sway this far away, because by now I could feel the borders of ridiculousness brushing up against the back of my knees. Even I wasn't too sure what I was talking about. Why was I telling him this? Did I think if I bared my silly little soul enough times all the gates would magically open? I'd been doing that for the last fifteen years, and it hadn't worked yet, except briefly, in Tokyo, and I'd torpedoed that one myself. I shrugged and backed up behind my cordon of smoke. Few things could shame me, but I suddenly felt embarrassed in front of this old peasant whose simple world I'd tried to inflate to the grandiose and absurd level of my own. I would have gone away and hid but I was too mortified to admit defeat by getting up from the table. He seemed to have lost interest in me, was puffing away and looking out the open doorway. I looked out there, too, trying to fake the same self-containment that he had, but I could feel it coming on again, sucking at me from behind like a big wave drawing up to a monster crest.

The old man went into a long run of coughing like some kind of dissertation about the evils of tobacco. When he could finally get his face back up from the table his eyes were wet from the effort. I realized that he was going to die soon, Erenhot or no Erenhot, wind or no wind, and that I had taken up fifteen minutes of his precious precious time. I'd never felt so ashamed.

He wiped his mouth with the back of his hand and looked directly at me, a vista that terrified me. I have other American friend. Soldier. After Japanese.

I tried to fit it together in my head, the strange vast time that he was putting out on the table. The Japanese had cleared out more than fifty years ago, and there hadn't been any American soldiers around since Liberation. In my peripheral vision I could see the long ash of his cigarette smoldering close to his big nails.

He like grasslands. He like ride horses. I spotted a smile that didn't quite make it to the surface. He very badly ride horses.

He leaned back, then reached into his pocket and took out a grimy handkerchief. I could see the dark cracks of dirt between the whorls of his hardened fingers. Slowly he unfolded the grayish cloth. Inside it was a plastic bag, all wrinkled and nicked, with several rolled-up Chinese bills and a few coins. I saw the white gleam of old silver among the copper and bronze. He picked it out of the little pile of change in his palm, keeping his eyes on it as he handed it to me: a Standing Liberty quarter, dated 1934, that beautiful Greek goddess in her worn but flowing robes bringing back to me in one overwhelming flood everything about the United States of America I'd ever felt or tried not to feel, the resonance of home filling my chest and throat. I turned it over to the soaring eagle, its feathers flattened by decades of fingerprints, then back to Liberty again, gorgeous and serene and trusting in God the way I never could. I looked up at the old shepherd, who was watching me.

He said he come back to ride horses.

He turned back to the open doorway again, then, leaving between two short sentences one of the deepest and most expressive empty spots I'd ever seen, he said: I take you to temple of Helan Qi. Today.

It took a few seconds for me to get it, that he meant now, and not after his trip to Erenhot, and it stunned me, the coin and the offer handed over at once. The whole time I thought I'd been coasting on silly foreign glamour I was actually hanging on to the coattails of some GI who'd been here with General Stilwell long before my stupid birth, and that in my jeans and smelly T-shirt I was the best thing that antique soldier could do to get back to his long-remembered Inner Mongolia, and that the man in front of me, this soon-to-exit pastor who'd never heard of Australia, had on his map of the Invisible World locales and personages as distant and outlandish as any of my own, that they lived with him in his world, and he in theirs. I realized that he was settling the Empire as we spoke.

I looked again at the piece of silver in my hand. Even as I closed in everything still lay far apart, somewhere between the out-of-circulation home contained in that coin and this crossroads restaurant located at the farthest extent of my own bizarre mania. I tried to imagine the soldier who'd given him this keepsake, and it made me think of Andy, who was still in his far office instead of where he should have been, which was checking into the Inner Mongolia Hotel, hanging ten on the big question mark. He'd want Jeff there to translate, even though he'd be a pain in the ass. Jeff would want to stay at the Zhao Zhun, because it's central and new, but Andy would insist on the Inner Mongolia, the one with the cavernous lobby and the worn green carpet, knowing I'd stayed there and that I was still flitting around the deserted handicraft counters and cocktail lounge.

He imagined that in the summer it thronged with tourists, but now the lobby gave off a feeling of abandonment. They'd spent the last two days in tourist offices and at the university, walking around the icy streets looking for taxis and trying to figure out where to go next. He kept cursing himself for losing the letter, and for not being able to remember the place-name it had contained. They'd paid a woman at the desk two dollars to read aloud scores of place-names from the map, but Andy hadn't recognized a single one of them. For another two dollars she had let them scan the guest register for Silvia's name.

Next Holt had struck up a relationship with the concierge at the Zhao Zhun, who, as a special favor to his foreign friend, charged them only ten dollars to reveal that Silvia had stayed there the previous night, checking out at five-thirty that morning. As her ongoing destination she had listed Shanghai. Andy felt his stomach twist as Holt translated. His bleak addendum didn't help. "So she's a day ahead. And she knows where she's going." The merchant's next word surprised Andy: "Bitch!"

They resigned themselves to touring the sights of Huehote in the bitter cold, buying themselves several layers of underclothes, like the locals, and finding, after a half day of brutally cold searching, where they could buy the thick shearling hats of the Inner Mongolian regiments of the PLA. For the cold days since Shanghai Andy had been surviving with a windbreaker and a cashmere sweater he'd bought in a Friendship Store: now he bought himself a long heavy trench coat lined with sheepskin, its white tendrils poking out the middle and sleeves. He found thick fur mittens, and gloves to wear inside of them. Holt had taken his down coat with its hood, the light and practical traveler.

In the restaurant of the Inner Mongolia Hotel they saw another Westerner sitting in front of a pot of boiling water. He looked at them as they came in, and the hostess broke off her conversation with the other staff long enough to seat them at the next table over. Even in a land where every floor doubled as a crowded ashtray, the man stunk of cigars. Holt seemed to decide out of habit to ignore him, but he addressed them after listening to them talk for a few minutes.

"Excuse me." He had an English accent. "Would either of you fellows happen to know what the weather forecast is for tomorrow?"

Holt waited for a moment before he spoke to him in a voice supremely devoid of friendliness. "I'm sorry, I don't."

"They might know at the front desk," Andy put in.

The man seemed to have finished several beers already. His hot pot flame had burnt out, and no more steam escaped from the little pan of water. "It's been this miserable twenty below here for the last week. I must go to Dongsheng tomorrow, and I'm hoping that it will warm up just a bit for the trip."

"I sympathize with you," Holt said.

"I daresay you'll sympathize with me more in a few days."

Andy couldn't resist asking, turning full toward him to signify the beginning of a conversation. "And what are you doing here in the dead of winter?"

"I'm buying cashmere, or rather, trying to. You see I'm in the cashmere business."

"What part?" Holt asked, interested at last.

"I'm a broker. I buy the raw material for various firms in Scotland and England."

"You don't say. Do you produce any piece goods?"

The man seemed to withdraw a little at Holt's pointed question. "No piece goods. I work strictly with mills."

"Tops?"

"No, greasy." The man cleared his throat, suddenly defensive. "You seem to know quite a bit about the cashmere business."

"I do silk and leather for clients in South America and the States."

"Do you then?"

"I have one client in Italy. Nobody in England, though."

Andy listened quietly as they discussed the business climate in China, trading stories about disastrous business ventures they had undertaken and the long chain of payoffs and delays that always threatened profits. "By the way," the man said, "I recommend the Mongolian hot pot. It's not so bad here, if you like that sort of thing. Stay away from the Western dishes. I think the bloke who cooks them is still doing his bit for the Cold War. Of course, I suppose once in a while a man might hunger for a steaming hot dish of chicken foot tetrazini."

Holt went on talking to him about business. He asked him about the Zhao Zhun Hotel, and the man agreed instantly as to the higher quality of the lodgings. "I stay here because it's familiar, that's all. It has a certain grim charm, don't you think? There's actually quite a bit of hustle and bustle in the summertime. At this time of year it's like the Ming Tombs, although"—he grew thoughtful—"I don't think the Ming would be serving Mongolian hot pot, would they?"

Holt lightened a little at the joke, explaining to Andy that the Ming had overthrown the Mongols.

The man came to Inner Mongolia every few months. Between the scarcity of cashmere fiber and the Japanese buying up every spare kilo of hair for their joint-venture factories, he had to come and hold hands with his suppliers every few months to insure that he got his raw material. "May I ask what brings you two gentlemen to Huehote at this wonderful season?"

Holt met Andy's questioning eyes. "We're here for a little business also. I am, at least. I'm exploring the possibilities of doing some production using a tussah silk/wool blend yarn. It's more than fifty percent silk, so it doesn't need quota. You know what getting quota can be like."

He rolled his eyes. "I know."

The man finished his beer. Andy could see him considering

whether to buy another one, but he asked for the bill instead by waving an imaginary pen across an imaginary piece of paper. After he had it he reached into the pocket of his jacket and took out a small leather case of business cards, turning each one upside down and handing it to them with a little bow, Chinese style. "Protocol is everything here, you know. Fabian Ritchie. Call me if you ever get to Edinburgh."

Andy felt at a loss, then he remembered. "Hold on a second." He took out one of his business cards and handed it to the man.

The man looked at it and his head moved back subtly, as if there had been a small explosion on the face of the pasteboard rectangle. "'Invisible World.'" He hooked his eyes into Andy's. "And what does your company do, Mr. Mann?"

"My company?" Andy could sense Holt looking at him, imploring him to produce the kind of bland story that he had. He had never thought about what his company might do because he'd only shown the cards to Holt and Silvia. "I guess you could say my company finds things." He glanced over to Holt as he finished. "Even if they don't exist."

"Ah," the other man answered. "I see you're a friend of Clayton Smith's."

The three stared at one another. Andy said, "You know Clayton?"

"Of course I know Clayton!" He sat down again. "I think I'll have another beer after all."

"I'm buying."

"I'm accepting! So where is Clayton these days? He owes me a round."

Andy looked over at Holt, then he answered. "I'm afraid I have some bad news for you. Clayton got kind of depressed, well, very depressed..."

Fabian Ritchie finished for him. "Did himself in, didn't he?" The cashmere merchant nodded his head slowly, dropping his eyes to the table to give himself privacy, then letting his gaze wander around the room to end up absently fixed on the nubby rocks of a miniature landscape. He sighed, turning back to Andy. "You can give me the gory details later."

The waitress appeared. Holt spoke to her in Chinese, and she noted his words on her pad and went away. The Scotsman's fingers scaled his beard and lodged on top of his lips. He rested his elbow on the white tablecloth, addressing Andy. "You're his friend, are you?"

"We both are. How do you know him?"

He had met Clayton nearly...he puzzled it out for a moment...nearly three and a half years ago. Clayton had been looking for some sort of antique tapestry at a monastery somewhere in the Autonomous Region, but he hadn't specified where.

Holt broke in. "Did he find it?"

Fabian Ritchie looked at him without any particular friendliness. Two long seconds passed before he answered. "Now that is an intriguing question." He had a chopstick in his hands and he tapped it on his beer bottle several times. "The two of you have come after the tapestry, is that it?"

Andy remembered too well how he had told Silvia everything and where it had gotten him. There could be consequences; surely they were committing some kind of transgression. Something about the man made him trustworthy though. He'd seemed to immediately understand everything about Clayton and his suicide, without needing any of the particulars of time and method. "We have come after the tapestry. I grew up with Clayton. He had me come all the way from America so he could give it to me." He told him about the fax, and the plane ticket, and the business cards and money in Hong Kong. "I met this cabdriver and he helped me out. Great guy. I wish I could have understood what the hell he was saying." He told him about kicking in the door.

"He also trashed some money changers."

"Oh, that. Yeah, that was kind of weird. Anyway..." Andy had again that feeling of being a foreigner in his own life, unable to completely believe that the story issuing from his mouth involved him, or that he was sitting with the textile smuggler and the cashmere merchant in the Inner Mongolian Hotel in the dead of winter. He shook his head to clear it. "Wow!" then he told them about the note and how Wilda had helped him find the Chinese Opera. "Then I went backstage to meet this Lu Xiao Yu..." The box with the imperial costume and the note, and then the awkward part about Silvia. Andy appreciated Holt's silence as he said, "And well, it's a long story, but the robe and the note kind of got stolen from me." He drifted into a backwater of introspection, then hoisted himself out again. "Anyway, we called up our friend Chang, in Hong Kong, and he sent us the part of the book that Clayton was going on. Although really... at this point we're kind of up in the air. We've tried to match the book to a map, but it could go in a few different directions." He shrugged.

Fabian Ritchie's tobacco view rested on Andy for a minute. "Let's review this for just a moment. You live in the States. Have you ever been to China before?

"I've never been anywhere before."

"Right. So Clayton gives you a pack of business cards with your name on them and bombards you with plane tickets and packages until here you are." He leaned back, giving a single loud laugh. "It's fantastic." He shook his head sadly, but at the same time he seemed happy. "What a shame he's dead, eh? A bloody shame." He raised his glass, spilling a little over the edge as he made the loud announcement to the forty or so curious diners who looked at them quizzically. "The king is dead!" He sat down again. "I happen to be a citizen of Clayton's private country, as a matter of fact." He pulled out a strange bank note with Mongolian writing on it in a denomination of seventeen. "Take a look at this."

Andy examined it. "Seventeen? Where'd it come from?"

"Clayton gave it to me. He must have had them made. Why don't you hold on to it? I've got a couple more of them." He turned to Holt. "So where do you fit in? Are you the translator?"

Andy interceded. "Jeffrey's an old friend of Clayton's, too. They knew each other in Tokyo a long time ago."

The cashmere broker examined Holt. "Tokyo. You don't say. Then... was Clayton the great artistic success there that he claims he was?"

"Clayton was very successful, yes. I was there."

The gray beard disappeared behind the man's hand again, as did the tightly closed lips. He took his wallet out and found another of Clayton's bills, this one a three. "Why don't you take one of these."

His voice had softened. "I'm sure he would have wanted you to have it."

Holt thanked him quietly, examining the bill. Clayton had printed it up beautifully, the perfect agglomeration of bank note elements: curlicues and faint scrollwork in the background, a well-known portrait of Kublai Khan in the center. Mongolian letters hung vertically along the borders like barbaric streamers. On the reverse side a large walled garden stretched across the center of the bill, taken, from the looks of it, from a nineteenth-century European book. Holt recognized it immediately because he'd seen the image before: Xanadu. He took out his wallet and put the bill in carefully, next to his passport, so that it wouldn't get bent up. "Thank you," he told the Scotsman.

Fabian Ritchie acknowledged him and went on. He was talking about Clayton. "When I knew him, he was already in trouble. I could see that from his conduct when I met him. It didn't bother me. I've been in that kind of trouble myself and I knew it was simply his turn. Maybe next time it will be my turn, or yours. One has to keep it in perspective. We talked about different things. He told me he was searching for his tapestry. He had read about it in an adventure novel of the twenties, I believe. We had quite a cordial evening and I left the next day. Oh, why don't you go organize your dinner before they take it all away?"

The waiters had begun to clear away the buffet of vegetables, meat, and sauces that they would cook in the pot of boiling water on the table. When the two returned he had ignited a small dark cigar that was blueing the atmosphere around their table. "You two don't mind?"

"Well . . . ," Andy answered.

"It's sort of every man for himself in China, isn't it?" Ritchie smiled and continued on. "As I was saying, I didn't hear from Clayton for several months, and then I got a marvelous letter from him. He was back in Hong Kong, and he seemed in excellent spirits."

Holt broke in. "What did he say about the tapestry?"

"You really know how to spoil a good story, don't you? Very well. We'll cut to the chase, as you say in your Hollywood." He paused. "They do say that—?"

"Yeah, yeah, they say that!"

"Well he found it."

"He told you that?"

"He found it! He couldn't have put it more clearly. He found it and it surpassed all his expectations. He said it was the most astounding thing he'd ever seen."

Neither of them could say anything. Suddenly the possibility that the tapestry really existed renewed in both of them the figment of something so gorgeous and powerful that merely being in its presence would irrevocably transform their lives. The ephemeral details of it began to swirl in their heads, mixing quickly with transactions and dim millions, with half-imagined departures and elegant affairs and finally, bringing it all to a halt, the recognition that Silvia was getting farther and farther ahead of them.

Andy leaned toward Fabian and spoke. "Where? Where did he find it? Did he say where?"

"No," came the reply, "not a whisper."

They settled into a disappointed silence for a few minutes, and Fabian Ritchie bought them beers to cheer them up. The advancing hours bounced their conversation from the restaurant to the bar, then from the bar to the vast empty lobby with its drowsy receptionist. They talked about Clayton and about the Mongols. They wandered into the martial arts and the imperial monuments of Beijing. Andy talked about the situation with his father, a subject both men sympathized with. Holt told about how his father had greeted his departure with near indifference, and then he'd realized after his death that he'd taken it as a rejection of his choice to be a carpenter instead of an academic. Each of them wound out the events of their life as the events of their companions' lives called it up. Fabian told about how he had worked his way into the cashmere business after starting as a bobbin changer in a clothing mill. It made Andy remember sorting copper pipe fittings on the floor of the dusty warehouse, and as he told about his Clean Rite fiasco, Holt laughed and narrated his own first business venture, an attempt to start an English language school in Tokyo. Clayton had been one of the teachers, but he'd attended even more sporadically than his students. Their stories sprang around the shadows of the darkened lobby until two in the morning, when the clerk refused to get them more beers and shut himself in his office to sleep.

"Gentlemen," Fabian announced with a light slap on his thighs, "every night has an infinite number of ends, and I think I've reached my particular one. I believe I'll step outside for a breath of fresh air before turning in. You're welcome to join me."

"It's thirty below out there!"

"I said *fresh*, didn't I?"

They ambled over to the big entryway and pushed the glass doors open. The cold felt to Andy like a metal hand gripping his spine.

"Bracing, isn't it?"

Standing in the frozen white light of the carport, even the humming city noises seemed to have solidified and fallen to the earth. Only the sweet aura of coal smoke implied any human endeavor in the frigid night. The cold entered with every breath, frosting his nostrils, then chilling his lungs like menthol. It had a purity that drove everything else out of his mind. He stood there thoughtlessly, looking at the mist that billowed out of his mouth and hung drowsily in the still air. Suddenly, for no reason whatsoever, two words came shining forward in his mind.

"Helan Qi!"

"What?"

"Helan Qi!"

Helan Qi turned out to be one of those places that's exactly how you imagine it when your imagination is just a bunch of ideas with only a few shifty images to attach to them. The basic mud brick village, which I could construct out of the dozen I'd seen along the route, but with all the unforeseeable touches that actual existence lends things. The bloody sheepskin hanging from a post, the little fake yurt made out of concrete blocks... Yes, the state of Material World always retains the advantage of surprise. The houses were typical Mongolian—"rhapsody in mud brick!"—ranch houses with all the windows on one side, facing southeast to collect the sun. They each had stone or mud brick walls extending out in front to form a corral that they could put the creatures inside at night.

Mo Mo's sister came out to meet us in a printed cotton dress. She had that square flat face and strong rectangular body, the human equivalent of the mud bricks that stacked themselves into a village around us. It surprised her to see Mo Mo back already, doubtless the meddling of that shabby-looking excuse for a foreigner he was dragging along beside him. She questioned Mo Mo in Mongolian, a throaty bitten-off language that in this particular interchange needed no explanation. She didn't buy Mo Mo's excuses: I translated her face and her trailing-off words to mean, "Send the guy off to Erenhot and he comes right back with some . . ." She took another look at me, examining the outfit that would look unimpressive even on a Mongolian peasant, and she pursed her lips. I held my arms out, said in English with a big smile, "Here I am, baby! Signed, sealed, delivered: I'm yours!" then said in Chinese, "Your brother is very kind to help me. His benevolence is a great gift. But he never told me that he had such a beautiful sister." I turned to him: "Mo Mo, did you not trust me? Miss, I'm very honored to meet you. I'm called Clayton."

She looked at Mo Mo, who let a smile come out on his leathery face, then she laughed at me and waved me away with her hand, muttering something, then beckoning us into the house. She took out a block of pressed black tea leaves and broke some off to make a fresh thermos, offered it along with the cigarettes that always spelled Welcome in China.

She had a cheerful little two-room house, furnished with the discount-store accouterments that look sleek and modern to poor Chinese workers. A green vinyl couch and a linoleum table took up one room, along with a cabinet that held a few books and some souvenir plates. A television set and cassette player rounded out the essential possessions roster, all set off by a plastic bust of a Western woman and various cartoon characters in living styrene holding up dust on a knickknack shelf. Next to them pictures: her son in a PLA uniform, a man and woman in a sepia city years ago, probably an earlier incarnation of her and her husband. Blue tinsel arced down from the ceiling. Maybe a century before it would have been something woven out of wool or horsehair, but now it had degraded to glitter. In the other room the typical Mongolian sleeping platform made of plaster-covered bricks took up most of the space. A large wool carpet covered it, with a stove built underneath the whole thing to provide winter heat. A neatly folded pile of bedding was stacked up in the corner. The little kitchen took up a tiny space in back of this: a brick stove with a hole to put the wok in, and next to that a worn little chest for knives and dishes.

We talked in their halting Chinese about who I was and where I was going, though I didn't get into the Invisible World stuff with her. I didn't want to try and go for a second helping of incredible good luck. I let her put two spoonfuls of sugar in my tea as I listened to the comfortingly incomprehensible exchange of woolly syllables between them. For the first time, I was beginning to feel peaceful. Even listening to a language I didn't understand, I had a strong sense of being in the right place, something that had been eluding me for many years. I'd kept going here and going there, always finding out when I arrived that the Right place was still a little bit farther off, or in a different direction. I couldn't escape the idea that each place I went, no matter how important a site, was really the center of a whole constellation of secret beautiful places that only the locals knew about: a minute and precious temple, or a hidden waterfall, too small to attract anyone. It could even be the sight of the town goddess, graceful and simply dressed, carrying a bundle through some hamlet where the world would never find her, a part of the mysterious geography that always holds out that promise of love and salvation. I always wanted to find those places, could sense their presence all around me in a maddening infinitude that never let me rest. I'd finally reached the right place, drinking tea and eating cold rolls of steamed white dough and taking in with Mo Mo the soothing infusion of smoke that was killing him and would kill me, too, if I gave it time. I had reached the first of a series of right places.

Mo Mo had left his horse with her, and he borrowed another one on my behalf. He topped the thin gray with a little wooden saddle covered with a shred of carpet and a few brass studs polished to a gleam by innumerable pairs of pants. I decided to share the bounty of the Empire with her, and she squinted at the bills, then at me. Mo Mo said something to her in Mongolian like, "Don't worry, he's insane," and then she smiled and thanked me, holding the colored paper in her fist. We set out for his house, where we would spend the night, taking a path out of the village that grew fainter as we went. The land here gave itself over completely to grass, no trees, barely even a shrub to interrupt the floating green carpet that rode the hills out to the horizon, bulging and falling away again. The sun was ripping down out of an Oz blue sky, lighting up white white Kansas clouds and warming my skin through the thin cloth of my jersey. Just the feeling of voluptuous space, green and blue forms lying over each other the way two sleepers lie over each other in bed, the kind of space you could walk into forever. The most prominent sound was of the crickets; I could see them sailing out into the breeze and landing again fifteen feet away to try out a new spot, while all around us the tips of the grasses vibrated to the moving air. From the ridges of a hill we saw a flock of sheep and cashmere goats scattered across the ground like flecks of sea foam.

We rode slowly. Mo Mo told me in his limited Chinese and sign language that before he had ridden very fast, but that a few years ago he had fallen off his horse, and now he went very carefully. He pointed to his nose; old man. He told me I rode well. Okay, of course it was a lie, especially coming from a man who'd been riding since infancy, but I decided to take it in the spirit it was meant and feel like Master of the Steppes for a half minute, like old arrogant Whitcomb himself. Occasionally Mo Mo would stop to dig up some mushrooms that had burst out of the soil and put them in his plastic burlap bag for dinner. We crested another hill, and when I looked back toward the village of Helan Qi I saw a little shrine of stones with branches sticking out of it. This was an *aobao*, Mo Mo said, and he made me understand that it served as a meeting place in the featureless knolls of the grasslands. He pointed and I followed his finger to another smaller one on a hill off to the side of us. In front of us lay the next basin, cradling a small stream that formed a Turkish-blue oxbow of reflected sky.

We rode down into the flock of sheep, and I could smell their wool and manure fragrance. The soft crunching sound of breaking grass stalks formed a background for the bleating of the animals and the occasional bark of the dog. The flock scattered as we approached it,

STUART   COHEN

and a shepherd walked toward us, giving one solitary wave of the hand. Mo Mo dismounted with an involuntary little complaint, and I did the same. He tied the horse's bridle to his leg to hobble him, then tied my horse to his. The three of us sat down cross-legged in the space left by the sheep.

The other shepherd wore the same peasant uniform as Mo Mo, down to the billed cap and the yellow cigarettes that he offered us. He carried a wooden stick with a little leather whip at one end and a shovel-shaped piece of metal at the other for digging mushrooms. He put them in a burlap bag that also held a plastic rain tarp and his cigarettes, and probably some small bit of food. His face hadn't absorbed as much wind and sun as Mo Mo's. He asked Mo Mo about my age, where I had come from, why I was here. Mo Mo translated these into his halting Chinese and I answered them, then asking how many children he had, boy or girl, where they were; the simple things that express basic friendliness. I don't know what Mo Mo told him was my reason for being there. It must have satisfied his curiosity; they slipped into pure Mongolian, and I guessed from the appearance of the word *yuan* and their glances toward the flock that they were discussing the price of livestock. I took out a pack of Double Happiness I'd brought up from Hong Kong and offered a round. Mo Mo told me to let him see the packet, and he looked oddly at it and the white cigarette, then lit it. After a while the man got up and shouted "Hu! Hu!" at his sheep and walked away.

We stayed low, letting the hills form a high curtain against the afternoon sky, concealing behind themselves all the rest of the land with whatever it held. We followed the basin around, passing a little cluster of mud brick houses that could have been from the last millennium, then on along the little stream. The basin opened up into another basin, this one scraped by a plow and crossed by a primitive-looking electric line. A girl went riding across the short grass on a bicycle, giving Mo Mo a greeting and staring at me as she passed.

The afternoon was already in decline when we reached the solitary house and corral that belonged to Mo Mo. The saddle was definitely sending me a message by now, waking up hot spots on my inner thighs and my tailbone. A long pyramid of what looked like brown dirt had been piled up outside the corral, and a teenage boy was troweling a wet brown paste over it, his hands and arms covered with the stuff. As we approached and tied up the horses I realized that it was an enormous pile of manure that was being cured and dried for fuel. A little farther away I could see where the finished product had been cut into tiles and stacked, odorless and ready for winter. The boy was elbow deep in shit and he couldn't have cared less, merely stood up and gave me an unsmiling wave with his trowel and said something to Mo Mo that I couldn't understand. It turns out the kid had learned Chinese in Helan Qi, hoped to go study in Huehote, maybe open a restaurant there. Mo Mo's wife came out, tiny and energetic in her blue Mao suit. She didn't look as old as Mo Mo, and her clothes hadn't been subjected to as extensive a staining and patching process as her husband's. Her hair had plenty of black left in it to go with her quizzical eyes. Mo Mo said a few words, and then she turned loose a shy smile and said some words of welcome in Mongolian. They had a short conversation, then Mo Mo stretched out his dirty hand toward the door.

This house had a similar layout to the one at Helan Qi, except for being smaller and meaner. The furnishings were all of worn wood, and no television or cassette players lounged around waiting to bring in the big electric world. Tea arrived, and I was offered a jar of caramel-colored sugar to put in it. The wife got to work kneading dough to make noodles. The boy, whose relationship to Mo Mo I never did find out, had taken the horse to bring in the sheep; I could hear them sending their calls out into the deepening sky. Mo Mo sat and watched me as we sipped the hot water; speaking Chinese seemed like an effort that had lost its charm. We'd said everything anyway.

Something kept pulling at me and I went outside, wading into that marvelous space that resounded outward from the tiny house, like some magnificent chord. I had to walk. I headed away toward a low hill in the northwest, long exhilarated strides that took me farther and farther into the open country. The sky and the humid green swells seemed to be dancing, and I felt like I could go on forever into the quiet peace and never come back. I was wearing the universe now, like a new suit of clothes; the mountains, the heavens, the far-off seas. By the time I'd mounted the hill the bellies of the eastern clouds had gone blue, little strips of evening moving into that trailing end of afternoon. From the summit I looked down into the next basin and a tall hill on the other side cutting a horizon out of the air. I knew that over it somewhere I would find the monastery and whatever it held. I had finally reached the heart of Inner Mongolia, if it has a heart, and I realized you can spend your life making the trip, and that once you get there it's beautiful and green, that the next ridge reveals another ridge, that the grasslands extend far to the north, to Outer Mongolia and beyond, full of everything that is already here: more farms and more horses, more emptiness, more lives, and more people dreaming about an America they'll never see. Always that sense of something still farther away, that was my Inner Mongolia.

A trembling sound started up and a herd of horses without bridles or anything else came running toward me from underneath the hill, prehistoric and heart stopping. They came galloping, and I didn't have a boulder to stand on or a tree to hide behind so I just stood there as they came on, seeing somewhere in back a horseman driving them, silhouetted in the dim light. I stood my ground and they came rushing all around me, thundering and frothing, eyeing me as they passed and filling the air with the ghosts of motion. I heard the man shouting at them, and then they had all gone past, leaving me in silence again that the crickets little by little filled in with their songs. I sat back down. In front of me the rags of lilac clouds lay across the yellow-gray sky, uncollected.

Over the long hill-disturbed plain that spread out from the clay village, Andy could see the *aobao* pushing its empty branches toward the sky. It looked like a stone wedding cake, its three gray tiers crowning the small hill so that it could be seen from all around. Holt translated what the man had told them, that the *aobao* was a shrine and a meeting place, a small man-made exclamation point amid the trackless grass. The grass now had turned to straw, crumpled and close to the earth in its few windblown patches among the snow.

The tiny drab room hung tight around the cots covered with dusty saddle blankets and cheap synthetic mantles. Their host, the village schoolteacher, had moved his grandparents into the kitchen to accommodate them, and since the village had not even a teahouse he assembled each meal for them from an assortment of mutton, noodles, cabbage, and root vegetables, usually ordered into a greasy broth. When they sat in the main room the family made shy conversation and other villagers dropped by to stare at the foreigners. The rest of the time they had spent huddled in the prisonlike little room waiting for the monks to come and get them. It was too cold to travel the full day required to reach the monastery.

Silvia's passage through the village was evident in the inquisitions of the villagers, who were intrigued by the visitation of not only one but three outlanders in the middle of winter. "You know the pretty lady?" they asked. Holt had given his weary confirmation, discouraged by their news. Four days ago, the day before their own arrival, she had paid one of the villagers an entire month's salary to take her to the monastery, and then the cold had set in, and they hadn't seen her.

The two of them had discussed the implications, all of them inconclusive, realizing that whatever the outcome of Silvia's adventure, they had no choice but to finish their own. Andy had accepted it with a certain fatalistic tranquillity that Holt, after a few hours of irritable musings, gradually fell into.

They waited. Holt taught Andy how to play Chinese chess with a tiny paper chess set the family had produced, then slaughtered him in a series of games, each time overcoming a larger handicap. After that Hold had suffered the more serious upset of finding out the missing part of Silvia's story, about her father and the mistake she had made. This had sent him into a melancholy that had lasted nearly two days, hemmed in and preserved as it was by the chill little room. The urgency they'd felt had turned sour, and they had to get out of each other's way: Andy had taken a walk to the distant *aobao*, reaching it after twenty cold minutes through the shallow snow. Little prayer cloths fluttered from the branches. A small pool of ice had locked itself into the altar. Looking out, he could see the white swells rolling out to the horizon like a thunderclap. The wind persisted.

When Holt tired of beating Andy at Chinese chess he spent his time trying to learn a few words of Mongolian, carefully questioning the members of the family to see if the verbs declined and if they had tenses. He had filled several pages of his notebook with the strange Mongolian script, cataloging the sounds in English, along with a small list of vocabulary: *food, friend, go, give, cloth.* He procured the numbers and the pronouns, and practiced rough sentences on the family. Only the younger people spoke Chinese, and most of them badly at that. Andy stretched his muscles, read in the guidebook about other Chinese places he would never visit. The days fell wearily over and past them, eventless except for the waxing of the light in the morning and its waning in the afternoon. They held nothing to distract the two men from the subjects that they turned over incessantly in their minds.

"Something I don't get. I mean about you and Silvia. You knew how she was: about being a shark and all. Why did you keep her in your company?"

"I did know how she was, didn't I?" Holt put his mittened hands fully around the hot jar of tea, then held it close to his stomach. A blast of wind raised the pitch of the constant moan outside. "I did know. I knew her father was in the military. I saw her savage one boyfriend after another. I had every reason to look into the future and see that exactly this would happen. "

He let the silence intercede again, not actually silence, but the uneasy sound of the wind forever trying to get around the house. Andy didn't mind the long pauses and digressions that cushioned everything. They had so much time that Holt knew an immediate reply wasn't necessary. The weather noises, the muffled clinking of a metal pot in the next room, all of it seemed inseparable and necessary.

Holt continued as he stared into his jar of tea. "You'll laugh when I tell you." The grandmother's high irritable voice swirled suddenly to a crescendo, made a few staccato additions, then faded into a low grumble. Holt peered through the doorway. "The baby got too close to the stove." He scrutinized the twisted black leaves that hung in the bottom of his jar. "You know why I kept her with me? Because she reminded me of a friend of mine." Holt gave a short dry laugh. "Alejandro. He was Argentine. He was the one who got me really looking at textiles."

Holt sipped the tea, his unshaven beard and cheap down coat reminding Andy of a bum crouching behind a cup of coffee. "He wasn't a serious collector. Or perhaps I should say that he was the most serious kind of collector. It wasn't a status thing, like Mr. Liu, or some of my other clients. He drove a cab for a living, so by the time he paid his travel expenses he never had much to spare. He had a good eye, though. He knew the styles. He couldn't afford the important pieces, but occasionally he'd turn up some little fragment of a master-piece, a little gem, like that woven gold *jin* Clayton gave you, and then he'd buy it. That's how I made my first connections in antique textiles. He introduced me. Believe it or not, one of my reasons for getting into business in South America was to have an excuse to go back to Buenos Aires and visit him and his family."

"What happened to him?"

The tea steam turned Holt's glasses into two translucent glazed discs. Andy could see the blurry azure of his corneas behind them. "He disappeared."

"He disappeared?"

"During the Galtieri dictatorship. Alejandro would go down and protest, circulate petitions, that sort of thing. Even after people began to know that it was dangerous. One day he went out in his cab . . . They never found him or the cab."

"Did you go to the police?"

Holt's voice had a lifeless quality to it. "They wrote it up as auto theft."

The wind had settled to a swishing sound in the eaves outside their window.

"I'm sorry to hear that."

"Oh, that was a long time ago. It's only peripherally related to what's happening now. But when I met Silvia in Hong Kong, she had the accent, she knew the music. . . . You understand. Looking back on it, I think having her work for me gave everything a sense of cohesion, as if I was somehow keeping Alejandro close by. It's stupid, isn't it?"

Andy remembered the file in the corner of his bedroom full of letters he'd never been able to throw away. "No. It's not stupid." He sat motionless for a while, then he lay down on the bed. He wondered if Silvia could really have falsified everything, both to Holt and to himself. It seemed impossible. He put his forearm across the top of his head and stared up at the gray wooden branches that made up the ceiling. Grass and mud had been wedged into the gaps between them. Dusty spiderwebs bound them together and to the wall. "Maybe she'll change."

Holt left him plenty of time to give him a reason why, then dropped his last word in. "Maybe."

The next day the weather improved. At eleven o'clock two men appeared swathed in thick brown robes, the rough wool as hoary and animal-like as their ponies in the bright sun. The two of them seemed stocky and tough, their cheeks red and ruddy and their noses chapped from being wiped on the back of their hands. Andy estimated their age as about twenty, with an out-of-place taciturnity that intimidated him a little. Their shaved heads seemed to glimmer faintly within the shallow darkness of their hoods. They had left the monastery before dawn so that one of them could now produce a single letter from beneath his robes and hand it to the schoolteacher along with a few coins. They came into the house for tea, watching the two foreigners without particular friendliness as the teacher explained about them. Their host translated their guttural reply into Chinese. "They say you are welcome at their temple." Holt had already arranged for horses, and they took a few minutes to tie their belongings onto the short animals. They set out toward the barren mountains ahead of them.

After the extreme cold of the previous few days, Andy had never felt so comfortable. The wind had calmed and he felt like he was bobbing up and down in a peaceful fluid landscape. A trampled path led away from the village. He looked back to see it a few times, the few mud brick buildings looking almost familiar and civilized, but gradually the town fell behind a large hill, and he glimpsed it one last time from a rise before everything around them became a rolling surface of shallow snow and brown dead grass.

Away from the village the monks' shyness gradually dispersed, and they made a few attempts to converse with the foreigners. Holt managed an interchange about everyone's respective age and marital status, then his Mongolian vocabulary came up empty and the four of them went on in an amiable silence. At midafternoon the two guides brought out a crumbly, hardened gravel that Holt identified as dried whey. They mixed it with salted milk tea that they poured from a large thermos, then offered the bowls to Andy and Holt. Andy sipped at the warm musty drink as he surveyed the sparse landscape around them. An occasional cluster of tiny buildings gathered around a corral, and in a far-off ravine a few small trees congregated, but most of the plain had been scoured clean by the wind. Despite the wintry void around him, a delicious sense of luxury came over him. All he had to do now was to soar along over these steppes and listen to the sound of hooves hitting the earth, as if every beat of them was pounding into place the ephemeral survey markers of his new domain.

He had the whole afternoon to picture Silvia a hundred ways, to replay bits of conversation and expressions. He could see Silvia as he'd seen her the first time, in Hong Kong, her face marked with grief, then in Shanghai on the Nanjing Lu, wearing her shearling coat and that perfume of foreign glamour. Sometimes the anger came up, but it drained away quickly into the emptiness of the landscape. At moments it was hard to believe he had been to all those places; they seemed mere excuses for him to ride this horse and smell the steely aroma of the winter earth. Clayton visited, most of his images coming from more than a decade in the past: wearing the white dishwasher's apron of Burger Underworld, or speaking Chinese in the Liberty Grill. There seemed now to be so many things that Clayton was trying to explain to him, but instead of words Andy felt only his intention to explain, expressed in the grainy sky and hills all around him.

The fading light of late afternoon escorted them into the foothills, where the path climbed the course of a frozen streambed. The valley narrowed abruptly into a canyon with the remains of a tumbled stone building guarding its entrance. Rust stains in the corner implied some furnishing that had left in orange-brown a last vestige of domestic moment. A file of strange writing had been carved into a boulder next to the ruin.

"Tibetan," Holt explained. "'Om mani padme hum.'"

"You know Tibetan?" Andy asked.

"No. That one's a standard. 'The jewel is in the lotus.' Let's go. I think we're getting close."

They discarded the little phrase and went on. The canyon narrowed to the width of a living room, sometimes loosing narrower fissures that created little grottos off to the sides. Andy spotted a seated Buddha carved into the cliff wall, painted red and blue, then beyond it a line of little wedge-shaped objects strung on a line between two trees. He dismounted. They were bones, each one inscribed with a little prayer in Tibetan or Mongolian letters, clicking and clattering their supplications with the gusts of wind. He looked ahead at the monks. They were watching him, their faces ancient and indistinct within the twilight of their wrappings. Holt said nothing. Andy looked at the sky, heard the creak of the saddle's girth as he hoisted himself into the stirrup. The horse began moving even before he had fully settled, eager to get on before the winter night closed its grasp on them completely.

Evening had come pouring down from the top of the canyon when the trail opened into a valley, and in the scarce light Andy glimpsed something against the hillside above him. He thought at first that he had seen badly because of the light and the distance. That had to be it, because Holt, a distant hundred yards ahead of him, would certainly have turned and shouted, or stopped. With the passing seconds, though, the eerie sight became clearer even as it faded into the accelerating darkness, and for the first time since his childhood Andy felt the long-forgotten chill of passing through a graveyard at night.

He was entering a city of ghosts. The outbuildings scattered down toward them in jumbles of rock and tilting walls, while farther up the empty-eyed skeletons of hundreds of apartments climbed higher and out of sight around the hill. Their rotting masonry had collapsed over their foundations, holding occasional patches of plaster or the horizontal beam of a windowsill, but without roofs or doors, nothing to hold in the meager charcoal light that fell from the darkening shell above them. He searched for the two monks, the shapes of their bodies nondescript among the forms of boulders and hills around them. He dug his heels into the sides of his horse to catch up with Holt.

"Cultural Revolution," Holt said quietly when he came abreast of him. "This must have all been destroyed in the sixties."

"By who?"

"Red guards. Mao really, at the heart of it."

"Why? Why would he do something so vicious? And *stupid*?"

"Power. Control. I can tell you the political background, but essentially . . ." The sound of the horses' hooves formed a backdrop to his thoughts for a moment. "Because he was ruthless. Eventually the only things left to destroy were the treasures."

"Like Silvia's father."

Holt received the words in silence, then said, "He's one of a long list." He picked up the loose end of his reins and slapped the flanks of his mount, as if to ride away from his memories of the dictator Galtieri and of Andreas.

Only the hindmost of their guides remained visible now, and Andy urged his pony to go faster. They followed him up into the black and gray collage of wrecked walls and empty doorways, their horses' footfalls ringing against the stone pathway. He made out a strange dome with a spike poking toward the sky, and he pointed it out to Holt, who identified it as a tomb.

"The plaster's new on that one."

Holt didn't answer. Above and ahead of them, they spotted the soft yellow light of a lantern, and as they rose, more intact buildings appeared, little huts and one-story apartments whose new whitewash glowed among the stony surroundings. The temperature had dropped considerably, and Andy's fingers and toes had begun to hurt, but the anticipation of reaching the monastery, in whatever form it might be in, pushed the cold into the background. He flexed his shoulders and arms to keep the shivering at bay, but what was shaking him now was the proximity of Clayton's final reckoning, and of Silvia, who almost certainly awaited them.

They sighted a high white building looming above them, intact and gigantic among the shambles they had just passed through. Three rows of the small trapezoidal windows perforated the commanding white wall, and Andy could recognize the style from pictures he had seen of Tibet. Some of the windows had faint candles in them, and as their path circled around the back of the building he began to see buckets and piles of bricks, wheelbarrows, discarded cans.

Several monks had already assembled in the courtyard to greet them with stares. Like their guides, they seemed inflated into barrels of brown cloth from the many layers of underwear and woolen hides beneath their robes, nearly comic except for their hooded and indecipherable faces. One took the reins of their horses from them as the two foreigners dismounted, fanning his fingers toward his mouth to indicate that he would give the horses something to eat and then leading them away. Holt and Andy stood uneasily with their bundles in the courtyard as the monks looked at them. They seemed neither pleased nor distressed by the appearance of the two strangers.

An older monk spoke to them in syllables that sounded rough and blurry. Holt answered him in Chinese and then haltingly tried his Mongolian. The monk gave a nearly imperceptible smile and motioned for them to follow him.

"What did he say?"

"I don't know. Some sort of welcome."

"So what did you tell him?"

"I ordered you a steak," Holt answered over his shoulder, "Is Thousand Island dressing okay?" Slowing down so that Andy drew up to him, Holt smiled. "I told him we wanted to speak with Rartha. It's possible that he actually understood me."

The man led them up a flight of stairs and through a thin gateway building that opened into a bigger courtyard, this one occupied by a huge bronze prayer wheel and another of the strange *stupas* whose ivory surface reflected the dim lamplight coming from the windows. Several of their hosts trailed behind them, and as they entered the biggest of the buildings they began to hear a faint low droning whose timbre washed through the stone passages like the sound of the ocean in a cave. Down corridor after corridor, the monk led them at last to a dark wooden door that he opened for them.

A small wooden table and two rough stools constituted the cell's furnishings, along with two dusty-looking gray mattresses that lay folded in the corner. The half-melted remains of a candle sat on a clay dish on the table, and the monk pried it loose and thrust it into his own lantern flame to light it. He backed toward the door, smiling and indicating with his palms that they wait there.

Andy went to the window. Outside the few lights of the monastery scattered down the valley, giving way to the vast India ink steppes that he knew went booming out to the limits of his imagination. He had almost settled it now, the way that Clayton had urged him to from the beginning. Without Silvia and the note, he had almost settled it, even though he still didn't know what that meant. When he turned back to the room Holt was warming his hands over the candle flame. "So we're here," Andy said.

"We are most definitely here."

Andy had the urge to say something profound or deeply meaningful, but nothing came to mind, and he limited himself to simply looking at his breath glimmering against the dark background.

Holt looked at his watch, contributing the non sequitur: "Six-nineteen."

The older monk came back with a large bowl of steaming soup made of cabbage and potatoes. He poured them bowls of salted milk tea, then excused himself with a soft grunt and backed out of the room. The two men ate without comment, taking in the primal warmth of the food like a blessing. The hot meal dispersed the chill that had overtaken them, and they pulled off their stocking caps and loosened their coats.

The door of their room swung open and Rartha came in. Even with his flowing habit and shaved skull, he lacked the gravity Andy had expected. His wrinkled, smiling face reminded Andy of the little anthropomorphic illustration on the outside of peanut cans.

"Hello," he said in English. "How are you?"

"You speak English?" Andy asked.

He kept the grin on his face, carefully piecing together his reply: "I speak little English." He said something to Holt in Chinese and Holt answered him, then they conversed for a minute. Andy watched the expression of surprise make its way across Holt's features, then Holt laughed.

"What's he saying?"

Holt turned to him, chuckling. "This is Rartha. He said he's a friend of Clayton's. He's been a very great distance. He's been to New Jersey." At the sound of the words *New Jersey* the man nodded his head, smiling.

"New Jersey? What was he doing there?"

They exchanged a few more sentences and Holt explained. "He says the Chinese government sent him." Rartha continued his explanation and Holt raised his eyebrows. "It was some sort of cultural exchange."

"Does he know about Clayton?"

Holt said a few more things to him and the man nodded in a way that made his answer obvious even to Andy. He said something in Mongolian that neither of them understood, then went on in Chinese to Holt. His cheerful expression turned serious as he spoke.

"Silvia told him about Clayton. He's very sad for us."

Holt acknowledged the condolences by telling about their long friendship with Clayton and how they had come here at his request.

The old man brought in a small bench from outside and sat at the table with them. Holt translated for Andy. He'd been at the monastery a very long time. His parents had brought him to be a monk when he was a small boy. And where did they come from? America? From very far. A great honor to receive old friends of Clayton's. The food is very bad. He hoped they could eat just a little bit.

He refilled Andy's bowl with the milk tea, then used Andy's chopsticks to collect a gooey white mass from one of the saucers and put it into the tea. He motioned for Andy to drink it and Andy reluctantly put it to his lips, then smiled. It was butter.

Andy urged Holt to bring up the subject of Silvia again and the old man answered. The foreign woman had arrived four days ago. Also a friend of Clayton.

"Is she here now?"

Holt translated, and the monk answered Andy directly. "Yes."

"Well, what's she doing?"

The monk looked to Holt for the Chinese, then smiled slightly as he responded. Holt grinned as he related the answer. "He says 'Pretending to study Buddhism.'"

"Did she take the map?"

Holt raised his eyebrows. "I think that's getting a bit ahead of ourselves, isn't it?"

"Just ask him."

Holt posed the question, eliciting from Rartha a thoughtful silence. He answered them with a short phrase. "He says she was looking for something." The monk added something in a guarded way. "He says she didn't have something she needed."

The conversation dropped as they considered his answer, then Andy remembered Clayton's last note.

He went to his shoulder bag and began to root through the familiar textures of his belongings. The plastic box with the cards in them had drifted to the bottom of the bag, sunken there amid lint and grains of sand. He slipped off the rubber band and pulled the lid off the little stack of cards. Once more the alkaline smell of the cheap fresh ink ushered out of the tiny compartment. Clayton's moment was arriving, having migrated year after year across the world, it was fluttering in now on the wings of this little white business card. He took one out and gave it to Rartha, presenting it upside down, with the Chinese side facing the monk, with a bow, as he knew was the correct way.

The monk held it close to the candle flame, moving it farther from his eyes to bring it into focus. He looked at the blue characters and then up at Andy. He read it aloud. Andy recognized the same words he had heard the cabdriver say in Shanghai, that Lu Xiao Yu and Wilda had pronounced in Beijing, and in that fraction of a second all the cities came together in the two syllables tolled out in the monastery near Helan Qi. *Qian Xing.* Invisible World.

Rartha fell silent, turning his eyes down to the candle and then up to Andy. Andy had the queer sense that the table, with its steaming bowls of milk tea and its brilliant candle, was not a meal but an altar, and that he was taking part in a vast and profound ceremony. He looked at Holt, but the experience had become so intensely personal that he couldn't communicate it and didn't want to try. The monk bowed to Andy and said a few words of Chinese. Standing up, he motioned for them to follow him.

They filed out into the cold and moved through the courtyard past the first hall. Another courtyard came behind it, and behind that small space a large hall, much larger than the first one and now, in the early evening, dark except for a soft yellow light that made its way through the cracks in the unlocked door. They climbed a small flight of stone steps, and as they approached, Andy heard a sound from inside, somewhere between a moan and a low rumble. Rartha tapped twice on the door, and as it opened the sound of the chanting spilled out to them along with the lurid emanations of hundreds of burning candles. The chanting monks sat cross-legged on the floor surrounded by sacred texts unbound from yellow wrappings, before them the image, draped in silken cloths, of a placid seated Buddha. Saffron-colored silk hung in banners from the ceiling, intermixed with red streamers embroidered with glittering thread. Mongolian letters, Tibetan letters, and around and about a repetition of swastikas. A huge brass urn sprouted burning sticks of incense like a smoldering head of hair, and the intoxicating smell of it hung thick and blue in the atmosphere. Beside them a man pounded slowly on a drum on the face of which Andy could see a rampant dragon, snarling among the clouds. It felt like he was inside the fabric of the Emperor's robe, between the four mountains that defined the corners of the universe. As they paused there Andy thought he almost understood the mantra, that it had something to do with a limitless and benevolent unfolding, and then Rartha was leading them around behind the altar to another room, this one lined with statues of fearsome demon warriors that brandished their weapons in the vivifying candlelight, then through that room to another doorway, at which the monk paused and said something that Andy knew instinctively was "It is here." He reached up to the wall for a small lantern that hung there and gave it to Andy to hold while he unhitched a padlock and slowly drew the huge wooden bolt that transited the door.

First it was dark, and then the shimmering came back to them.

Far away, in the indistinct limits of the room, a strange shimmering, uneven, interrupted by fissures and faint borderlines. It drew them forward, and as they approached it grew huge and imposing, taking form with every step closer that they moved and seeming to tremble softly in the lamplight. Andy could make out the texture of monumental stones. It was a wall, a magnificent wall of gold extending across the entire room, reaching nearly to the distant ceiling. There seemed in the musty lamplight to be a sort of map on it, but it was so faintly done that it faded in and out of sight, at one glance existing and at the next receding back into the surface again. Andy walked closer until it covered his entire vision, then closer until it became the world. He heard Holt's hard leather paces drifting away from him along the length of the burnished surface until they disappeared, then he heard them approaching again. They ended at his side, and in a low whispering voice the words entered his ear. "It's made of paper."

Holt moved back to survey its entirety. He thought of the countless pack loads of pulp and paint somehow procured and hauled into these mountains, of the construction of the giant armature and the careful layering of strips and sheets. The immaculate etching and texturing showed a level of meticulousness that he hadn't thought Clayton still possessed. He remembered his condescending attitude these last years and it shamed him, and then that disappeared, and he began to see it. He saw the *Gateway to the Ancient Garden* and this final enclosing wall, and between them, resonating through time and events, the ephemeral entirety of Clayton's sculpture. Constructed of letters and textiles, of conversations he'd engendered and tickets bought and sent, it constituted the fantastic and incontrovertible proof that the ultimate map of the Invisible World was everything that could be seen or heard or touched, the unruly chart of a dominion that expanded infinitely beyond the grasp of the senses and whose unity far surpassed the petty considerations of business or material empire. That was Clayton's map of the Invisible World. And true to his word, he had given him half of it.

Andy, too, stood in front of it a long time, staring at the fabulous golden thread that had risen to the surface to show itself, and then would dive once more into the fabric. He didn't want to walk away because he knew that with this boundary he had reached the end of the last journey he would take with Clayton, one he'd waited for his whole life and that could never be repeated. Clayton had brought him here to provide him this glimpse, and it would have to last him forever: his first step toward the door would be the first step of the long path home, starting with his transit of the room and the ride back to Helan Qi, and from there to the airplanes and oceans of the disappearing past. Maybe a person had to go all the way to Inner Mongolia before he understood the substance of a friendship and the invisible bonds, so easy to depreciate or deny, that still had the power to move a person across the earth or renew a life. Clayton had never given up on him, could never consider his Empire settled without finding some way to make Andy its citizen and its king.

Maybe it had been pathetic for Clayton to keep thinking of someone so completely lost from him as his best friend, as pointless and grandiose as building a masterpiece where no one would ever see it. He'd lived his whole life that way though, never bothering to separate the sacred from the futile, knowing they were the same thing and letting them be separated the only way they could, by the eye and heart of their witness, like a priceless tattered scrap of woven gold.

An eddy of indecipherable prayer rose from the other room and subsided again. Holt's voice came from behind him. "You know what this is, don't you."

Andy didn't turn around. "It's the final part of his Tokyo thing—the wall of the *Ancient Garden*."

"Are you disappointed?"

"No. Are you?"

Holt looked silently at the giant sculpture, considering all it had cost him. "No."

"So, I guess it's basically over."

"I wouldn't say that." Holt's voice became slightly more neutral. "There's still Silvia."

Andy's disappointment with the Uruguayan woman now felt remote and insubstantial. "I don't particularly care about Silvia anymore."

"She has your *chi fu*. I'm getting it back for you."

Andy looked at the textile expert, his tousled hair and dirty clothes hard to reconcile with the pompous and elegant man he'd encountered in Hong Kong. Andy knew it had gone far beyond the robe. He shrugged, and Holt turned to seek out Rartha at the door. They exchanged a few words and Holt came back to him. "She'll be right here," he said. "I'm sure she'll be glad to see us."

Striding into the dim space of the room, wearing a fur hat and the shearling coat that had lent her its worldly cachet in Shanghai, Silvia seemed as if she had just crossed the neighborhood for dinner. She took off her hat and shook her hair out, smiling, craning her face up to Andy to give him a kiss. "*Amor!* They told me that you had arrived!"

Andy looked down at her features. Unadorned by makeup, incoherent shadows moved below the surface of her skin, surrounding eyes that sought him out from some recess of fear or affection; he wasn't sure which. A frailness of voice and gesture undermined her breezy approach; she distributed her kisses as if expecting them to push her away. How glad she was to see them, she said. Five days of waiting at this monastery was not like sitting on the beach at Punta del Este—

"Don't bother, Silvia," Holt said.

She flinched, and then she smiled and took a breath, as if to speak. The faintly gleaming presence of the wall took her over, though, drawing her gaze to its wide burnished expanse like a panoramic overlook drawing her to its edge. It had a strange familiarity, as if she'd seen a picture of it once, or it fit a description given to her long ago.

Jeffrey spoke, sounding almost friendly. "Quite a construction, isn't it?"

"It is, Jeffrey! The monks are so able at making their holy things!" She glanced toward the doorway, but Rartha had gone. It felt awkward, this happiness at seeing them. Jeffrey, there in his fluffy jacket, unshaven and discomposed for the first time since she had met him. Andy, too, even though he so carefully guarded himself as he watched her. That was a problem with making enemies: some part of them always stayed friends.

She took another breath and made a little grimace, as if they might commiserate with her discomfort. "You know, I do not understand why I always end up as the adversary of the people I love, but it always finishes that way. Even when I don't want it. Perhaps it is my . . . *destino.*" Turning: "That means *destiny* in English, Andy."

"I understood."

"You see, I know the English word is *destiny,* but mine can only be *destino.* It has more of the feeling of . . . like tango, you know?"

"Which tango, Silvita?" Holt intruded. "Let me guess: '*Rouge*'?"

"That is an excellent one! Do you know the version by Goyeneche? It begins, '*Éste ilusión celeste de cielo, paraíso pintado con verdín. . .*'" turning to Andy. "That means 'This blue illusion of sky, a paradise painted with—'"

Holt stepped on her translation. "Oh, I know it, Silvia. I know it. And thank you for your explanation of your personal feelings about the word *destino.* Perhaps someday you could explain your feelings about the word *deception.*" He felt a satisfaction as he saw his irony take away her smile. "But not now. Right now what we'd like is Clayton's robe."

"Very funny, Jeffrey." A trace of annoyance came across her face, then she looked down at the floor then up at them again. "I am trying to apologize, you know."

"Oh, I'm sorry, Silvia. Let's hear it."

"Thank you. I thought I would come here alone and then later I will find the way to correct everything, and in place of that I have just made this . . . *fracaso!*"

"This is quite the *fracaso,* isn't it? And I'll bet it's all someone else's fault. Why don't you start by giving Andy his robe and then you can tell us all about it."

She walked over to Andy. It was sad to see him look at her in such a neutral way, a man who had looked at her before with such adoration. "I am just sorry, Andy, that is all. I am just very sorry about everything. When I explain—"

The loud slow clapping of Holt's hands bounded across the chilly space of the room, slapping down her soft words. "*Bravo, Silvia!*" With his false smile: "*Que verso extraordinario!*"

"If you will let me speak!" She turned down the corners of her mouth, then started again, to Andy, who finally began to soften the expression in his eyes a bit. "The point of this is—"

"No, Silvia," Holt broke in. "The point is we want Clayton's—"

"It never belonged to Clayton!" She exploded across the room toward Holt, her arms pressed tightly against her sides. Lifting her chin, her face suddenly haughty and cool, her tone crisp with anger. "You want to know about Clayton's robe? Let me tell you about that robe, Jeffrey. First, it never belonged to Clayton. He stole it from me."

"Don't be ridiculous."

"And not only the robe, Jeffrey. Also the *jin*, the riding jacket. He stole all of them, all of the marvelous things that he gave to his friends so generously. Andy, where do you think he got the money for your airplane tickets? And the rest of it?"

Andy remembered the pile of Hong Kong dollars spread across his bed, and later, the note that had accompanied the robe:

It's not completely mine, technically.

He cleared his throat. "You know, Jeffrey—"

Holt put his hand up. "No, Andy, it's bullshit."

"Do not be so sure it is bullshit, Jeffrey. Why do you think there were no good pieces in Shanghai? Why? Did you think it was an accident?"

"I knew something was—"

"Oh! Now you knew something! How interesting, because last week at Mr. Gao's you seemed very surprised when I told you that Mr. Gao has another buyer. The truth is Clayton was buying your textiles from beneath you for more than a year. You were too obsessed with your business deal to pay attention."

Holt sounded less certain. "That's impossible."

Silvia bore in on him. "Is it? Why are you so sure, Jeffrey? Was Clayton always so clean with you? What about in Tokyo, Jeffrey? Was he so clean?"

Her insinuation hit the merchant so forcefully that he seemed to visibly curl inward. She went on, "That's why you sat and watched him struggle year after year, no? Laughing at him! I have not forgotten what you said: 'Clayton has constructed another garbage tower! Isn't that amusing! He has no money and he keeps trying to sell garbage!'"

"I didn't—"

"'Oh, and now he is going to Inner Mongolia! Ha ha! What stupidity comes next?' You enjoyed watching him fail, Jeffrey. Because you were his friend and he paid you back by sleeping with your woman! And what has it been with the women since then, eh? Not very much? How good that you still have your weavings."

Andy stood aghast at the spectacle of Silvia tearing her life apart. Whatever truth she had been trying to conceal or make known had now been rendered irrelevant by her wincing and incomprehensible attack on her friend and employer. The man who had helped her make a new life in the Orient now reeled silently before her accusations, and Andy realized that she didn't want to succeed, that by some terrible accident of character or self-hatred she wanted to destroy everything that was important to her or ever would be, and that she would always realize it too late. Even now, having humiliated her mentor into wounded silence, she went on accusing him with the cold and minute authority of an interrogation: did he think that Clayton hadn't known how he felt? Did he think he could conceal it? Clayton himself had told her—

Andy intoned softly, "I think you've said enough, Silvia."

She answered him with a haughty, almost comic air. "I'm speaking, Andy." To the gray-looking Holt again: "You want the robe? Fine. We can make an arrangement. It is not important now." She crossed her arms tightly against her chest and paced about in a small circle, then blew a cloud of vapor into the still air as if it were cigarette smoke and she were a master spy. She started up again briskly, nervously, addressing both of them and some unseen interrogant. "Okay, we have finished that matter. We all made mistakes. It's certain. But we have something much more important to resolve, *muchachos*. What is important is the tapestry, and I think we can all share it, yes? Because I don't think you can sell it without provenance, and I don't think you want a witness suddenly appearing at the auction to dispute it, or fulfilling her patriotic duty to the people of China. Unless you plan to kill me, of course." She smiled at Andy. "I suppose that is always an option."

Andy looked at her, knowing without further evidence why she had left him in Beijing and come to Inner Mongolia. The practical Silvia of Shanghai and Beijing had trapped herself in a reality every bit as ephemeral and disconnected as Clayton's own, except that instead of Clayton's gorgeous daydreams hers had fallen to a dictatorship of the spirit that had made it ugly and corrupt. Her lies and her appetite for power had transformed themselves into a vision, and like every deeply held vision, they had become the world.

Having entered the Forbidden City that was Silvia, though, he found it difficult to leave. People made mistakes: everyone did. They could make them for the best of reasons. Maybe it didn't have to mean that they were guilty. He spoke softly to her. "If you mean Clayton's map . . . "

"Yes, the map! The Mongol one. Clayton told me everything."

Holt's laugh sliced into the room's heavy atmosphere. "No, Silvia, I'm afraid Clayton didn't tell you quite everything."

Holt's sudden humor stopped her for a moment, and Andy put his hand on her shoulder. She turned to him and looked at him expectantly. "Silvia—"

"No, Andy. Let me explain it to her." The merchant approached her. "You're right; he did promise it to all of us. But I never heard him say that it was a Mongol map. Did he ever say that to you, Andy?"

Silvia answered as if commencing negotiations. "He said it to me, Jeffrey. He said it very clearly, and he described it. He said that it is blue, that it has Mongolian words, and . . . and that the Great Wall is embroidered in gold. I am sure Rartha—"

"Silvia!" Holt cut her off. "Relax. We already have the map."

She looked relieved. "*Perfecto!*" She grinned. "May I see it?"

"It's right behind you."

She turned around, finding only the luminescent cipher of the wall before her. She ran her eyes along its glowing dimensions, and back again, then opened her mouth as if she were going to speak. She turned to Andy. "This is not it, this . . . thing? You are making a joke?"

"It's not a joke."

She managed an impoverished smile, then she picked up the kerosene lamp to better examine the wall, looking first for the door to a compartment, then stepping closer to it and brushing its pebbly texture with her fingertips. Pushing at the yielding surface.

"It's paper!" Her voice emerged in a bewildered protest. "But he said that it was blue! And that it had the Great Wall ... in gold!" Her eyes widened and she moved back and looked again at the height and length of the barrier that had been embroidered so majestically across her delusions of fortune and escape. Her voice fell to a broken undertone. "It's only a joke," she said slowly. "All of this ... and it is only a joke!"

The dimensions of Clayton's joke began to define themselves as she stood before their brilliant punch line: the Great Wall couched in gold, the human figures, embroidered in such detail that one could hear their voices, voices now ridiculing her in Jeffrey Holt's biting timbre: "Then I suppose we would all be laughing, wouldn't we? But I don't hear ..." She remembered their amiable chats poured out of teapots and his translations of the signs and wonders of China. Looming like a Greenland bigger than South America, she recalled the drowsy mornings together and the comforting late-night declarations that had made her feel for once not so very dirty. She'd ridiculed him for not making something beautiful, never realizing that Clayton could have made this wall anywhere, in Hong Kong or in Tokyo, could have chosen money and adulation but instead had chosen his emptiness, just as he'd always told her. He was real, he had loved her, and she had ruined him as casually as she ruined everything: for spite, and to prove that she could win.

She sank down against the wall and pressed her hand across her face, unable to contain the warm wetness that soaked the hollows of her eyes and coursed out alongside her delicate nostrils. A deep gasp lurched out of her. Her voice emerged high and constricted by grief. "I stole the textiles, Jeffrey. I bought them and sold them to Mr. Liu."

"I suspected that. From Mr. Gao?

"Yes."

"Who else?"

"From Mrs. Chen—"

"And Mr. Zhou?"

"Yes!"

Holt looked at his protégée crumpled at the foot of the hollow structure for which she had discarded everything. "There's more, though, isn't there."

She took her hand from her face and looked up at him, her features glossy. "That's all, Jeffrey. I'm sorry. Clayton never stole your textiles.

He wanted to stop me, but he didn't know how without . . . exposing me. And . . . he didn't want to do that."

"You mean to say that's all?"

She thought a moment. "Yes."

"That's the whole truth?"

She didn't seem to understand his insistence. "It is."

Holt pressed on, his voice firming into that of an inquisitor. "You're telling me that's all of it, even the ugly parts? Even the parts that you think I don't know?"

"That's all of it, Jeffrey."

Andy knew where Holt was going and he tried to interrupt. "Silvia—"

"Forget it, Andy. It's just another game. Let's have the *chi fu* now, Silvia. It belongs to Andy."

"But I told you—!"

Holt's voice cut in, official and cold. "You told me, you told me. You told me a lot of things. Just give us the *chi fu*."

She looked confused, then seemed to remember something. "I can't do that!"

"What do you mean you can't?"

Silvia's voice had a whining, astonished quality as she stood and approached Andy, still absently holding the kerosene lamp. "I can't give it to you, Andy. I have to give it to Mr. Liu. He gave me the money to buy the robe. It belongs to him. I told you that Clayton stole it from me."

Holt clapped his hand to his head, proclaiming dramatically: "Clayton again! My God! I never realized how diabolical Clayton really was! Now I understand what Andreas was talking about!"

Andy didn't understand the look of shock that possessed Silvia's shining face at the mention of the name Andreas. The dumb bewilderment endured there a moment, and she seemed to hang on the edge of an even deeper earnestness. Then, to his horror, it began to change, almost reflexively, into a surprise so obviously feigned that it embarrassed him. He wished that he could stop her, but he watched wordlessly as she put on a grotesque imitation of innocence. "Who is Andreas?"

Holt answered her with a facade of polite surprise. "Oh, that's right: you don't know Andreas. I'm sorry. Andreas is the man who clued me in to what Clayton was really like. It's all so clear now. I should have warned you. You see, Clayton wasn't satisfied with a few bits of silk. They weren't enough." He moved menacingly close to Silvia. "He wanted that Paracas weaving."

He ambled off a few steps again, then turned with an airy flourish of his hands. "Not to say that he wasn't operating in a spirit of benevolence. After all, each of the major religions cautions us from becoming too attached to material objects." Stopping to include the monastery with his gaze. "*Particularly* Buddhism. But I'm digressing here. We were talking about how clever Clayton was. You see, he knew that I was traveling through Lima with certain, well, some call it contraband, although personally I've always found that definition somewhat shallow. But there I was. So Clayton, diabolical Clayton, arranged with his friend Andreas that I have an informal little visit with the *aduana* in Lima." The merchant produced a piece of paper from his pocket and began to unfold it as he approached her. "Now here's the part that amazed me: look at this. Not only did Clayton learn Spanish to do all this, but he even learned to forge your handwriting to absolute perfection! In fact, when I saw this"—he held the gray facsimile message a few inches from her stupefied features, then laughed at his own foolishness—"I thought it was yours!"

"You don't understand!"

"No, wait! Because here's the best part: are you ready? He did all this when he was already dead! And *that* is truly amazing."

"Shut up!"

"No, I think it's fabulous. If Clayton had only been this clever when he was still alive we'd all probably be sitting in his penthouse at the Sofitel Shanghai right now eating roast duck! He should have died years ago!"

"Shut up! You don't understand! I had news that there were people in Lima who knew about you, and they knew about the Paracas piece. So I arranged it with Andreas—"

"That's a lie!"

"—to protect you."

"You're lying!"

"I can get it for you. I can get it back for you!"

"Stop lying to me!" Holt shouted. "I'm sick of your lies! You can't get it back! Andreas is a monster, and so are you! You're a monster! You wanted Clayton's map? There it is. Take it! Go ahead! Take it! I'm giving you my share!"

She managed a choked little smile. "Really, Jeffrey, I do not think I am a monster. I have made—"

"Oh, I understand. You're not a monster. You're only a liar. You only betray your friends. You're only a murderer. Or, as they would say in Uruguay, *asesino.*"

Silvia cringed. Andy could sense her trying to back away until the wall blocked any farther retreat. "Really, Jeffrey. You are embarrassing me in front of Andy. Calling me a . . . a monster. Calling me *asesino*—"

"I think that's the most appropriate term, don't you? I know all about your father. And your little friend."

She made a silent little gasp, and then the words seemed torn out of her chest. "Who told you that? Who told you that!" She looked at Andy and shook her head back and forth, then her face disintegrated into a painful wound. "It was an accident!"

Holt moved closer, now almost face-to-face. "I'm sure *everyone* will agree with you, Silvia."

Andy saw her body go rigid, and she said in a low threatening voice: "You *can't!*"

"I'm sure Chachy—"

Her frustration and rage exploded in a short piercing shriek that ripped apart the quiet of the room, and with that surrender of her last veil of artifice Andy saw her body twist convulsively. The lamp came from nowhere, a vehicle of enameled metal and flame that appeared suddenly on the far side of Holt's head and crashed there with a soft hollow ring and the low clacking of its hot glass chimney breaking unostentatiously into several large pieces against Holt's forehead. She'd swung it from the hip, like a tennis racket, and Holt went down to one knee without offering a return, his glasses hanging crookedly from one ear. "It was an accident!" she screamed at him. "It was an accident!"

Andy moved when he saw her hand moving back for another

swing. He leapt between them and grabbed Silvia's wrists, immobilizing them while she kicked feebly at him a few times, grunting inarticulately, then at last she looked up at him with her eyes full of tears. "It was an accident!" she cried, her voice collapsing. "I told you that." She stopped moving, and he took away the still-burning lamp and placed it on the floor.

"Are you done now?" he said.

She averted her gaze and went limp. He let her go, bending down to where Holt had sunk to one knee. "Let me take a look, Jeffrey."

The merchant was grimacing, his head ducked down toward the floor. "I can't see out of this eye."

"Look up at me." He pulled Holt's hand away. "Don't rub. There might be glass in it." Blood had covered his eye from a gash the lamp had opened beneath his brow. He examined it for several seconds. "Can you see any light?"

He gingerly opened his eyes. "I can. It's red, but I can see."

"I don't think it's your eye. I think it's only blood. Cover your good eye. Okay. Blink."

He blinked. "It's still red."

"I know." Andy searched through his pockets for a tissue and held it over the cut. "Okay, blink again, and tell me what you see."

Holt gingerly raised his gaze from the floor and opened his eyes. "Fire." He shut and opened them again. "Fire! It's on fire!"

The gilt was burning a deep violet blue, gorgeous against the golden plane. It seemed at first more like a strange consuming light rather than mere fire, pouring out of a hole opened several feet above the floor. The strange veneer of flame spilled astonishingly fast up the surface of the wall, leaving in its wake a tissue of crumbly orange cinder. Nearby sat the kerosene lamp, its glow now overwhelmed by the bigger blaze it had started.

"Silvia!"

He turned to the door and he saw the flutter of leather as she disappeared from view. He let her go, quickly pulling off his coat and holding it on the flames. Uselessly: the wall was being consumed from within, and the burning gap above his head had expanded to the width of a man and begun to move steadily across the top. In the firelight he could see yellow flickers exploring the black wooden beams of the ceiling. "Get Rartha!" he shouted.

The wall was beginning to speak now, muttering in a deep timpani roar as the hollow structure drafted in the room's musty oxygen. Andy stepped back and looked at the stiff gold paper made so precisely into cut stone that it even had chisel marks. He took a deep breath and with a shout he drove his fist through the metallic surface. Only paper, as delicate as the memories that could be written and held on it. He grabbed the powdery edge with both hands and ripped off a long golden bolt, revealing Clayton's pencil marks on the wooden slats underneath. He halted a few seconds, as if he might interpret one last coded message, then the crowd of monks surged in. He could hear their excited cries behind him and see them shedding their thick woolen robes and beating at the flames. Holt's voice came from behind him. "There's no water in this building!"

The monks began to peel away the paper also, flaying the burning mass like a tribe of ants. In a half minute the bottom of the wall had been stripped bare, leaving only wooden slats and the flaming golden covering above it, like some strange medieval siege instrument that had unsuccessfully assaulted a city.

"We've got to pull it down!" he yelled to Holt. Andy located one of the main braces and kicked at it until it snapped in two, then moved to the next one. The monks were pulling and kicking also and the wall began to shudder and lean, lowering its hollow head toward its assailants. At last some deep and critical part of the foundation cracked, and with a sharp report the wall's last proud bit of stature came sagging to the ground. The collapsed heap of wood and paper blazed with renewed ferocity, like an immense New Year's dragon that suddenly lurched forward through the smoke.

Holt's voice came from behind him. "Outside! We're pulling it outside." A door had opened up at the far end of the hall and the others had already seized hold and begun to haul it away. The framework slid quickly across the floor, leaving pieces of its strange skin and bones crackling and flickering in its wake. Andy felt steps beneath him, and then the night cold. What was left of gold and wood and paper lodged briefly in the doorway and then with a last giant tug burst suddenly through, charging like a frantic burning animal out into the courtyard.

The others rushed back in to finish, but Andy couldn't leave what remained of the wall. Every sheet of it that turned to blue fire separated him further from the boundless Inner Mongolia that Clayton had installed in his imagination, leaving him instead with this other Inner Mongolia, with its monastery and its winter night, its horses plodding over snow and the sound of their snuffling breath. The friendship that had started nearly three decades ago had culminated in a fabulous illusion, and then the illusion itself had turned to smoke. He stood for a half hour next to the warmth it gave up with its last flitting bit of life, watching the vivid orange sparks escape upward into the dark sky. It was settled.

By the time Holt came out the wall had been reduced to a few scattered particles of light on the ground, and the cold had started creeping into his toes and under his coat.

"I had a bit of explaining to do," Holt said. Someone had bound a large piece of gauze over his eye.

"About the fire?"

"And about Silvia. And this." He touched the bandage.

"Looks like a little overkill there."

"I don't have a mirror."

"You look great. Like a pirate." He pushed his shoe into the ashes. "Where's Silvia?"

"I believe she's in her room. I don't imagine they're going to convoke much of an inquisition tonight. Besides a few charred spots here and there, there's no damage."

"That's a miracle."

"It is."

Neither spoke for a while, then Andy said, "You know, he must have been protecting her."

"What do you mean?"

"That's why he wanted me to keep everything secret. He thought he could straighten everything out without exposing her."

"A rather misguided loyalty, I'd say."

Andy let Holt's lingering bitterness pass by him. They stood there a few minutes longer. Holt began again. "For what it's worth, there is a certain circularity here. For me, at any rate. I told you I lost a piece on the way to Clayton's funeral. It was a Paracas manta, which is the most mysterious kind of textile there is, because they've never found the people who made them. Paracas weavings just exist, all by themselves. Now I've replaced it with a textile for which we have undisputed provenance, but that only exists in our minds. Figure that one out."

"We'll run it by Chang. I'm sure he's got some kind of Confucian saying that applies."

They waited until the ground had become black and sparkless. Orion was standing on the mountains of the horizon. Holt had begun to shiver. "Am I the only one getting hypothermia here? At this point, I'm ready to have room service send up a nightcap and call it even." Andy didn't reply, but Holt wouldn't leave him standing out by himself. "We'll figure out the rest of it tomorrow, Andy, when we talk to Silvia. It's been a long day."

Andy loosed a heavy sigh, then looked up at his companion. "You're right. Maybe tomorrow she'll finally be ready to tell the truth."

The next morning they realized that Silvia was gone.

She had evidently left during the fire, procuring once more the advantage of a head start in her race to her own obscure finish line. She left nothing in her room but an empty bag of crackers and few tissues smeared with makeup. Andy could imagine the sensation she would create, the pretty white woman appearing at the lost little houses in the dead of winter and paying someone a fortune to take her to Huehote, but it left him strangely neutral. He and Holt had no desire to catch up with her. They had no indisputable rights to the robe, and they finally gave up hope of ever extracting from her the whole truth. The weather stayed warm and they decided to leave right away.

Rartha seemed to harbor no ill will for the strange drama that had been played out at his monastery. He applied fresh ointment to Holt's cut and changed the bandage across his eye. The monk passed off the fire with a single comment and then talked about Clayton. He told them that Clayton had first appeared some three years ago, when the monastery had begun the difficult process of re-creating what had been destroyed two decades before. He had stayed to help for a while, then proposed building an altar. The monks had been skeptical, but he'd built a model, and when they saw it they had let him proceed. Over the course of the last year he had constructed the wall, finishing it some four months ago and asking them to leave it unadorned until Spring Festival or until a visitor came with a card that said Invisible World. Rartha laughed at the idea of a valuable tapestry being at the monastery. That had all been stolen long ago. Still, he said, he was glad that they had come. "When you want to study Buddhism," he said with a mild grin, "you can return."

They spend the whole ride down speculating on what had really happened; something they'll never know with any great precision. Jeffrey supposes he might be able to puzzle it out later, assuming, of course, that Mr. Liu or his textile suppliers will be willing to talk. He can't help wondering just how much innocence his old friend C. Smith managed to hold on to. Andy doesn't worry: a guy interested in personal gain doesn't steal a bunch of textiles just to give them back again, he says. And then build his own personal Great Wall out of paper.

Jeff considers it and gives up on the trivia. I suppose, he says, the biggest part of life you simply can't run the numbers on.

Me, I'm supposing Inner Mongolia. Up a little higher I'm seeing Outer Mongolia with its Altai range, and way off to the west those unruly Uighurs. A rivulet of gold flows eastward, fortifying a border long since overwhelmed. In the margins of the world the subjects of the Empire pose in turbans, robes, and trousers, drawn by countless filaments of silk in countless colors, embroidered on a sky dyed bluer than indigo, bluer than sulphate of iron can ever make it. In its center two horsemen ride down past bones inscribed with prayers and ruined walls, speculating on the emptiness that drives a person to suicide. In the final analysis, if there is such a thing, when you've got nothing left but a concept, you wake up one day and figure that out, and then you've got nothing. Even the Great Wall itself couldn't keep the barbarians out forever.

Is that true? Andy asks him.

Certainly. It was breached by the both the Jin Tartars and the Khitan, not to mention the Mongols and the Manchus.

Yeah, well . . . Andy's looking out at the world's most extravagant failed engineering project as they roll down the Western Hills toward Beijing. It's still the Great Wall.

Blind Seer that he is, he doesn't see Silvia getting back to Shanghai with nothing left but a badly completed contract with Mr. Liu and a circle of friends that despise her, or that eight weeks later she'll weigh in from Karachi, Pakistan, in a long letter scribed out with explanations and apologies. Yes, she had made some mistakes, but with everything so complicated . . . it did not mean that she didn't care for him. I see that one getting circular-filed, along with the next three and a fourth, two years later from Calcutta, where she'll have gotten a position with an import-export company. How is the invincible spirit man from the United States? Why doesn't he answer her letters? She hoped that he wasn't still angry about those misunderstandings . . .

No, *querida*, just letting you sort out your innocence on your own, something I should have done myself. Jeffrey just beginning to think about the long swim to shore after his business *Titanic*, he puts it aside and rides back to the Kong with Andyman, even unfolds his hide-a-bed couch for the first time in eight years and treats his guest to a night of springs and bars across his back. Andy's packing up the next morning, slipping the woven gold brocade in among all those athletic insignias and petrochemical fibers. Jeffrey takes the *jin* back out again, spreads it out on the bed for a last look. He drifts his voice around that disinterest that he's perfected over the years. He says, "You realize that this piece constitutes a violation of the UNESCO convention. You don't have proof that it was legally exported from the source country."

Andy stops and looks at the piece. "Yeah."

"We had my friend waving us through when we left Shanghai. That won't be the case when you get to U.S. Customs. It could get sticky."

Andyman thinking himself not so very dumb anymore; a shred of suspicion narrowing his eyes a bit. "You don't think I should take it?"

"I didn't say that." He walks over to Andy's nylon bag with that stupid Bears logo, upends it with a quick motion and turns it inside out, checking the seams and the extra layers of vinyl fabric. He gives Andy that little smuggler grin, the one that's barely even there. "Why don't you let me make a few alterations?"

And of course the big powwow with Chang at the Blue Heaven, Andy washing his chopsticks in tea: the old China hand now. The two adventurers take turns laying out the whole bizarre tale from the plumbing office to Silvia's getaway. That gets them from pickled garlic cloves all the way to the final soup, and they settle at last into a noodle-stuffed silence. "So, Louis," Andy starts in, trading smug looks with Jeff, "Silvia's got the robe, the wall went up in smoke—"

"As did my business venture—"

"As did Jeffrey's business venture. I've got some money and a little scrap of cloth"—he leans forward and says in a lower voice— "that Jeffrey was kind enough to sew into my bag." Leaning back again: "And tomorrow this will all be a memory. Does, uh, Big *M* have anything to contribute to this?"

A half-minute of his chin-stroking, space-staring routine. It's looking like for once the proper Confucian epigram might just escape him. "Yes. Perhaps." He sips from his teacup, then realizes it's empty, clears his throat. "As far as Silvia, and her . . . untrustworthiness, I believe he would say: 'When regicide is committed in a state of ten thousand chariots, it is certain to be by a vassal with a thousand chariots, and when it is committed in a state of one thousand chariots, it is certain to be by a vassal with a hundred chariots. A share of a thousand in ten thousand or a hundred in a thousand is by no means insignificant, yet if profit is put before rightness, there is no satisfaction short of total usurpation.'"

Blank stares. Andy takes a bite out of a spring roll. Chang tries to recover. "I realize that perhaps something more expansive is in order." The boys start creaking their chairs and checking their watches. "I'll go over the Mencius tonight . . . I could send you a postcard."

Chang, I say, Chang! Get your head out of the dumplings! It's about settling the Empire! The real Empire! and then he rallies, pulls together the moment with his raised hand. "No. Silvia is not important. Nor Mr. Liu. Mencius would say: 'There are cases of a ruthless man gaining possession of a state, but it has never happened that such a man gained possession of the Empire.'" He holds his teacup out to Andy for refilling, his ministerial duties correctly discharged at last. He taps twice on the tabletop and then Counselor Chang cracks a smile. "Put that one in your pipe and smoke it, Mr. Holt!"

Gan bei gan bei! I'll drink a last mai tai to that one, see Andy off on his flight back to Meiguo with Holt the eternal departure man actually giving him a tiny embrace at the gate, an embrace that will be multiplied into his marriage a year later to a woman he still hasn't met. Tiresias, you clear your passport, impressed by those new Chinese stamps in it, and then you start wondering if they can spot that gold *jin* with the X-ray machine. So far, so good; you pick up a box of chocolates for Mom at the duty free and take your seat.

And on this long flight back you just keep thinking about that big golden wall erected forever in your imagination, and about Silvia and Jeff and with a foggy complicated sadness, about me, now permanently at large, Clayton C. Smith. More and more, though, as the hours to your destination wear away, you can't stop remembering that little bit of contraband sewn into the lining of your bag by your new-found friend. Gee, buddy, thanks: in Shanghai you tell me I'm a bad liar and now you send me home with The Goods burning a hole in my carry-on. You're wondering if those drug dogs can sniff out this sort of thing. You go into the bathroom to practice quietly what you'll say and the tone you'll use, none of which sound right even though San Francisco is at this very moment being divvied up into porthole-shaped pieces below you. You land exhausted and nervous, step up to the officer and present your documents, your stomach getting tight and trembly, speculating about what kind of clemency you can still buy with a full confession, because, after all, officer, this isn't really my life, I mean, it's not really my domain, this smuggling thing and I say, *Andyman!* We're fugitives!

And you think about your wild card, you straighten your back, smile at the Customs man and look him in the eye. He asks you this, he asks you that, and you answer him and take back your passport. You go walking toward the green light; No time, no order, no limits.

Nothing to Declare.

ABOUT THE AUTHOR

STUART ARCHER COHEN has traveled extensively through the Americas, from Tierra del Fuego to the Arctic, as well as China. His trading company, Invisible World, imports and retails wool, silk, alpaca and cashmere clothing from South America and Asia. Cohen's other novels include *17 Stone Angels, The Army of the Republic* and *This Is How It Really Sounds* (April 2015). He lives in Juneau, Alaska, with his wife and two sons.

STUARTARCHERCOHEN.COM

CPSIA information can be obtained at www.ICGtesting.com
Printed in the USA
LVOW11s0422300814

401482LV00002B/2/P

9 781940 423043